Steve Lunn's new novel is a page-turner with a very serious message – none more so: how corrupt and potentially murderous individuals within all society's centres of power, from local government, big business, the police, and even academe, are taking control of land and indeed of all our lives. It's a work of fiction but it's firmly rooted in reality and is all too horribly plausible.

Colin Tudge, author of The Great Re-Think www.colintudge.com

I loved The Price of Dormice! It's an amusing and fast-paced thriller with a cast of memorable characters and lots of references to Oxford. But it's also a commentary on the huge forces behind large-scale development, and how difficult it is to protect the environment.

Prof. Riki Therivel of Oxford Brookes University, strategic environmental assessment specialist

In pitting the hapless, heroic Mick Jarvis and friends against the forces of contemporary corruption, Steve Lunn gives us what we desperately need: hope. Seriously researched and seriously funny, this joyous thriller puts a wry smile on the face of the Oxford novel.

Cathy Galvin, poet, journalist, founder of the Word Factory

A powerful new voice in the world of crime fiction. With a cast of involuntary, hapless heroes, Lunn takes on the force of greed that is wrecking our country and our countryside.

Linda Proud, award-winning novelist, co-founder of Godstow Press

Pacy, entertaining, clever, and very funny, The Price of Dormice is, at face value, a pacy, romantic, thriller - but the topical politics and social relevance cloak a steely message within the levity.

Charles Pither, chair, STARC (Stop the Arc)

What a fantastic book – I had a lot to do today but did none of it, I just HAD TO keep reading... The Price of Dormice is brilliant. The intricately plotted threads all come together in the end, and what an ending! Absolutely delightful.

Stephen Lunn (no relation), international bestselling author of the US-based trilogy Theodore Bobnoggin and The Backyard Chronicles

THE
PRICE OF
DORMICE

STEVE LUNN

The Book Guild Ltd

First published in Great Britain in 2024 by
The Book Guild Ltd
Unit E2 Airfield Business Park,
Harrison Road, Market Harborough,
Leicestershire. LE16 7UL
Tel: 0116 2792299
www.bookguild.co.uk
Email: info@bookguild.co.uk
X: @bookguild

Typeset in 11pt Adobe Garamond Pro

Printed on FSC accredited paper
Printed and bound in Great Britain by 4edge Limited

ISBN 978 1835740 552

British Library Cataloguing in Publication Data.
A catalogue record for this book is available from the British Library.

To Catherine and Richard, without whom many small beings would never have been.

A little piece of Legoland
will set you back three hundred grand
but lizards lost and vanished vole
will halve the value of your soul.

Anonymous graffiti found by Catherine Robinson
on the Frenchay Road Bridge over the Oxford Canal in 1999

CHAPTER 1

May Day, a public holiday, celebrated in differing degrees and ways across the British Isles and elsewhere. Celebrated with ribbons and bells and great fervour in Oxford, where students and young townies drink all night, sing, fight and jump off bridges. Unbearable.

I live in Wolvercote on the north-western edge of the city and work in the centre. People think Oxford is all dreaming spires and scholarly dons strolling through quiet cloisters. It's not. It's always been noisy and busy, but around nine o'clock this Mayday morning I picked up a first hint that, behind the dignified facades, it's more like the Klondike Gold Rush. Not that there's any gold around.

It was a Monday. I'd come back from a morning jog and given dog Friday her breakfast. I wanted a grapefruit and went over to the shop to get one. Coming out of the shop, I saw a bus had stopped halfway round the corner, apparently waiting for three badly parked vans to move themselves. The bus was blocking the main road.

I looked both ways at the pedestrian crossing, as you do. To my right, the bus, stuck. To my left, a car coming down the hill from the railway bridge. Coming much too fast. A dark green

Bentley, on the wrong side of the road. It fish-tailed towards me and mounted the kerb like it was trying to run me down. If I hadn't jumped back, I'd be dead.

It purred past, the driver's window open. He stared at me, saying something unintelligible. I gave him the quizzical eyebrow. He was still mouthing off over his shoulder when he slammed into the back of the bus.

Ha, I thought, in the sudden silence. Then steam hissed, and children cried inside the car, and a woman's voice, quite calm, was saying, 'What are you doing? Are you mad?'

The shopkeeper looked out, decided it was none of his business, went back in. There was no-one else about. It was down to me. I ran over. Nothing to see through tinted windows. I pulled on the driver's door. 'You alright? Need any help?'

The driver pushed the door wide. 'Bastard!' he said.

'Yeah,' I said, sympathising. 'Stupid place to park a bus.'

'You bastard,' he said, hauling himself out and upright.

'Conrad, don't be ridiculous, he's only trying to help,' the woman said, still inside the car.

I backed away. The man she'd called Conrad was a balding redhead, taller than me, older. Overweight and out of shape, but not the sort to pick a fight with. I'd never seen him before.

The bus driver approached, arms spread. Conrad ignored him and advanced on me. I kept going round the back of the car and put its width between us. The woman got out. I'd never seen her before either. She was real class. Black hair, black dress, black boots. Black eye, too, which Ray-Bans and make-up didn't do much to hide. Was she one of these battered wives you read about? She was younger than the man, full of life, animated, until she looked at him and her face just emptied. I backed away from her, too.

She opened the rear door. 'Alasdair?' she said. 'Alasdair! Are you all right? Can you hear me? All of you, turn off those blasted machines! Take out the earbuds. *Get out of the car!* Alasdair can you hear me? Are you okay?'

'S'pose.'

'Bella? Charlotte?'

'Yes, Momma.'

'Good. Now get out, quick. It might explode.' She turned to me, her hand out. 'Card?'

'Eh?' Was she after a bank card? Birthday card?

'Business card.'

'Oh. Yes.' I fumbled one out of my wallet.

'Give me two,' she said.

I did.

'Here's his details,' she said, passing one to Conrad. 'Mick Jarvis. He's a witness.' The other card disappeared, like magic. How did she know people called me Mick?

'A witness?' Conrad said.

'To the accident.'

'Why?'

'Don't be a buffoon. Call the police, now. And your insurance.'

'I already called the police,' the bus driver said. Again Conrad ignored him and advanced on me. Why was he so angry? I backed up until I reached the wall by the post box. He followed, a pace behind. The road was snarling up with impatient drivers trying to turn round, so the police might be a while getting through. A small crowd had gathered around us. *Someone's bound to help*, I thought.

Conrad grabbed me by the shirt-front, slammed me against the wall, got right in my face. 'Stay away from my wife,' he said, half whisper, half growl.

I tried to meet his eyes and hold my ground. I should have said, I don't know your wife from Adam. I should have said, stay away from me, if you don't want your features rearranged. I should have said something, for fuck's sake. But I didn't. I'm not one for conversation before breakfast at the best of times, which this wasn't. All that came to mind was the Om chant, like Kanhai had us doing in Summertown Stars when we were kids, before we kicked off at football.

3

'Om' came out, loud and long.

'Shut the fuck up!' he said.

'Om.'

'You go near my wife again,' he said, 'I'll kill you.'

Typical hyperbole of the entitled, I thought. *Probably went to Eton.* 'Om.'

He hit me with a right that left me seeing stars. 'I mean it,' he said.

I spat something out. Possibly part of a tooth. Tried to catch a breath. He hit me with a left that put the lights out.

***

I could see again. Two uniformed officers were manoeuvring Conrad into the back of a squad car and telling him he didn't have to say anything, but that anything he did say, etc.

'I'll certainly say something to the Chief Constable,' he said. 'She's a friend of mine, you know.'

'I'm sure she is, sir,' the female officer said. 'I'll be sure to mention that in my report. Will you and the children be okay, madam?' she said to the man's wife. 'I can get someone…'

'No, we're fine,' the woman said.

'And you, sir?'

I nodded. My head hurt.

'We'll be taking a statement in due course. Name, address, contact number?'

I told her.

The street returned to a weird kind of normal when they'd driven off, taking angry Conrad with them. I sat on the ground, back to the wall, exploring my head for bumps and bleedings. Three pale children stood on the pavement in front of me: a tubby red-haired boy of twelve or thirteen and two small mousy girls, twins, presumably Alasdair, Bella and Charlotte. All three looked shaken and embarrassed. The woman knelt, put her arms round the girls. The boy backed away when she reached for him.

She looked at me, smiled, shrugged. 'Let's get you back to your flat,' she said, glancing across the street, 'and cleaned up. Can you stand? Walk?'

I rolled onto my knees, pulled on the wall to get upright, held tight for a few seconds while the world settled.

'Over there?' she said, pointing the right way. She knew I had a flat, and roughly where it was. How did she know? For a wobbly moment I wondered whether she was stalking me, then remembered she had my card, and she'd heard me give the plod my address.

I was less woozy by the time we'd climbed the steps up to my landing. I let us in, put the kettle on. Dog Friday said ya-ya-yoo to everyone, meaning *hello, where's my breakfast?* 'You've already had it,' I told her. The boy's eyes lit up when he saw my laptop, with its swirling mandala screensaver. 'I coded that,' I said, feeling a touch of pride. I asked if he knew *Player Unknown's Battlegrounds*. He shook his head. I launched it. 'Have a go,' I said. 'It's good.' I pointed the twins at some picture books that I kept for my nieces, then turned to their mum. She pointed to a chair by the kitchen table. I sat in front of a steaming bowl of water, milky white and fragrant with Dettol.

'Shirt off,' she said. She sponged me down, applied Savlon and Arnica.

'Are you a nurse?' I said.

She laughed. 'Just a mum. I'm Kimberly, by the way. That's Alasdair. The twins are Bella and Charlotte. Charlotte's the quiet one. You've hit the spot with them.'

'I didn't hit the spot with their dad. If it was their dad that decked me?'

'It was.' She sagged, suddenly small. 'I'd just told him I wanted out, as we came over the bridge.'

'Out?'

'Wanted a divorce. And he said, "Where would you go? Who'd have you? And your brats?" And I said, "There's a very nice young man in this village, actually. I see him every day. In fact, there he is." Because there you were. I'm sorry.'

'Crumbs.' I didn't know whether to feel shocked, flattered or terrified.

'I knew he wouldn't believe me if I said I'd never actually met you, so I didn't.'

I could see how her husband got the wrong end of the stick. 'You see me every day?'

'On the school run, with the kids. You're usually at the bus stop.'

'I am.' Nice to be noticed. I was between girlfriends, as usual, and she was a beautiful woman. But with three children and a homicidal husband? 'Is he really friends with the Chief Constable?'

'Don't know. He's buddies with a big shot lawyer who pulls strings for him. He'll get off.'

The doorbell rang. Her taxi, which I didn't know she'd ordered. The kids didn't want to go. I promised Alasdair I'd save his game in case he came back. I told the twins to take the book they were reading. Shirley Hughes's *Dogger*, one of my favourites.

'Before you go,' I said to Kimberly, 'can I just say…'

'Probably better not,' she said, from the door.

I raised a hand in farewell, realised there was a grapefruit in it. I wasn't desperate for a grapefruit any more. I was desperate for something, though. To get even with angry Conrad, maybe. Or to see more of his wife.

***

I opened my eyes. I didn't know where I was, what day it was. White ceiling, white walls, flickering strip light. Smells of cabbage, disinfectant, vomit. A grey box on my left, beeping in time with an orange flashing light. My left hand draped with canula, tapes, tubing. Beyond the beeping box, another bed and another less-than-fully-conscious man. My head hurt. I closed my eyes.

6

I opened my eyes again. A man sat by the bed, reading a Reacher paperback. Jaws clenched, shoulders twitching, obviously living the action. Big nose, awful moustache.

'Who are you?' I said. Or tried to. Probably sounded more like I was choking.

He looked up, put the book down, thrust a warrant card in my face. 'Detective Constable Clappison,' he said. Home counties accent with an exotic twang. 'Thames Valley Police. What's your name?'

'Mick Jarvis.'

He made a note in a beige notebook. 'Date of birth?'

'30.11.89.'

'Address?'

'3 Wytham Court, Godstow Road, Wolvercote, Oxford OX2 8NZ.'

'Next of kin?'

'Sandra Jane Cleary. My mother. Bankfoot Cottage, High Street, Finstock.' My voice was working better now, and I was getting irritated. 'What's going on? What time is it? In fact, what day is it? Why am I here?'

'Are you ready to answer a few questions?'

'I just did. Please answer mine.'

'Nine p.m. Tuesday 2nd May. You've no idea what happened?'

'No.'

'Your neighbour Mrs Swainston, flat 5, found you on the floor outside your flat, just after seven this evening. What's the last thing you remember?'

It was hazy; I had to work up to it. 'Tuesday. Yes. I'd been in the office all day. I had a call from your lot after lunch, asking me to make a statement about what happened in Wolvercote yesterday. Then later they said it wasn't necessary. So I came straight home. Got there around six. Collected Friday from Mrs Swainston.'

'Friday?'

'My dog. Fed her. Put something in the oven. Took her for a walk.'

I stalled. Memories were flooding back.

'You got back…?'

'Before seven,' I said. 'Something pinned on my door. A note. Not there earlier.'

'See anyone?'

'No.'

'What did the note say?'

'Don't know.' It said *LAST WARNING*, but I wasn't sure I wanted to share that.

'Let me know if you remember. Did you remove it?'

'No.'

'It's likely whoever left the note removed it, after inflicting this damage on you,' he said, indicating my head, which throbbed. 'Any idea who or why?'

'No,' I said. It could only be angry Conrad. Or someone working for him. He'd promised to kill me if I went near his wife, and I'd promptly let her lead me to my flat and tend my wounds. No point complaining to the police about him, with his friends in high places. But he was a bully. My grandad's number one rule for bullies was: never succumb to a bully's threats – it only encourages them. 'Just ignore them,' he'd say, 'or take the piss, they hate that.'

'I'm going home,' I said.

'Are you sure that's wise, sir?'

'Yes,' I said. 'Tell the nurse, could you? Hang on while they sort me out and you can give me a lift.'

CHAPTER 2

DETECTIVE INSPECTOR JONES

DI Jones sat in his cubicle in the corner of the Specialist Pro-
Active Team office, on Level 3 of the Operations Building. He was
very bored. He was making notes for the round of staff appraisals
that was due to start on Wednesday May 10th. Tomorrow, blast it.
He was pleased to be disturbed by a buzz from his Secretarial and
Administrative Support Operative, Rita. 'The Chief wants you,'
she said. 'She's with the Commissioner.'

Jones had not yet met the new Police and Crime Commissioner,
biggest of the Thames Valley bigwigs. Wondering what was up,
he popped into the gents and peered in the mirror. Should have
shaved more carefully. His hair needed cutting, and some of
that black dye his wife insisted on. An incipient zit on his nose
reddened when he scratched it.

'Bugger,' he said, frowning. Things long forgotten sometimes
crawled out of the woodwork, but not often. He'd detected no
hints of impending trouble, no signal above background noise. He
sluiced his face in cold water, mopped it with a paper towel, tried
to dry the splashes on his trousers. Combed his hair, tightened his
tie. Crossed the compound from Operations to HQ Admin block,

took the lift to the top floor, gave his name to the Commissioner's secretary.

The Commissioner, Martin Carter, had only been in office for a week. Like his predecessor, Carter was an ex-councillor with history in the upper echelons of the military and the arms trade, and owned a property company. Conservative, of course. The last Commissioner had looked like a rumpled rustic, but had been an okay guy. This one looked more Hooray Henry, but Jones wasn't going to jump to judgement.

'The Chief's expecting you,' the secretary said. She poked her head round an unmarked door.

'Yes?' A man's voice, a light tenor.

'DI Jones is here, sir,' she said.

'I asked him to pop over,' a woman said. 'Send him in.' Jones recognised the voice of the Chief Constable, Vanessa Harvey-Wollstonecraft, his boss's boss's boss. He stepped through, saw the new Commissioner behind a large, clutter-free desk, leaning back and, Jones thought, trying hard not to look like the speccy new kid in a tough playground. The Chief Constable was sharp as a tack and not much bigger. She stood before the window, her back to a panorama of flat Otmoor, Brill Hill, the hazy scarp of the Chilterns. Jones's home was over there somewhere. 'Ma'am. Sir,' he said.

'Jones, thanks for popping up,' the Chief said. 'I don't think you've met Sir Martin?' She turned to Carter. 'Jones will know what's going on, if anyone does.'

Oh ye of misplaced faith, Jones thought. If only she knew how baffled he was by the crimes of the modern world. And how, with each passing day that took him closer to thirty years' service, he cared that little bit less. He stood to attention and looked from the Chief Constable to the Commissioner.

'Stand easy, Jones,' the Commissioner said.

Head's still in the army, Jones thought. 'Sir,' he said, shuffling his feet apart and putting his hands behind his back.

'Sir Martin needs to know what's going on, Jones,' she said, 'if anything.'

'In what context, ma'am?' His gut told him there was tension between his superiors. His best interests would lie with her, the career police officer, rather than him, the politician.

'Someone told me they were pulling a dead shark shuffle,' the Commissioner said.

'They being the university. Or one of the colleges,' she said, with an edge of impatience. 'What does it mean?'

She turned away from the Commissioner, met Jones's eye. Did she want him to keep whatever he knew between the two of them? Immaterial, since he didn't know anything anyway. 'What was said, exactly?' Jones asked.

'He said, "A word to the wise. They're going to pull a dead shark shuffle." Then he said to hurry up with the port and I passed it to him and that was it.'

'Dead shark shuffle? Sounds like a dance. Soft shoe shuffle. Where did he say it, sir?'

'High table, at St Mark's.'

'When?'

'Last Saturday.'

'Who said it?'

'Didn't catch the name,' he said. 'Professor something. Beard, glasses. Seemed to think it was a bit fishy, and that we should be on it.'

Beard and glasses. Professor. Didn't catch the name. This guy wouldn't last two minutes in any squad room Jones had worked in. 'He didn't hint at the nature of the fishiness?' Jones said.

'No.'

'How many at high table?'

'Around thirty,' the Commissioner said.

'Was he a guest or a member of the college?'

'Not sure.'

'How many professors with beards and glasses were amongst the thirty? Roughly.'

'Not sure. Twenty-odd?'

The Chief Constable cleared her throat. 'All males, I take it?' she said.

Jones caught mischief in her eye and almost laughed.

'Yes, all males,' the Commissioner said. He looked annoyed.

Jones was busy, his team was busy, and this sounded like a waste of time. 'I can look into it,' he said. 'Put feelers out, take soundings.' If in doubt, reach for the clichés.

'Discreetly, Jones, please,' the Commissioner said.

'Certainly, sir.'

Jones suspected Sir Martin was covering his back, telling Jones too little to do anything with, but enough to be able to say he'd passed it on, if anything blew up down the track. Jones didn't want to rock the boat though; he'd find out, if he needed to. 'Is that all for now?' he said. 'Shall I feed back to you directly, sir, if anything comes up?'

'No, liaise with Vanessa. She can pass anything significant on to me.'

He was treating the Chief Constable like a messenger. Brave man. 'Right, sir. Thank you,' Jones said, backing through the door. 'Ma'am, I'll be in touch.'

Back in his office, he put his feet up and stared at the ceiling. Despite the clichés about feelers and soundings, he'd better look as if he was doing something. Or get someone to look as if etc. The Chief would expect it. He needed someone who was loyal, intelligent, discreet and resourceful. DC Clappison would have to do. Jones called him.

'Do a bit of digging for me, will you?' he said. 'Find out what a dead shark shuffle is, if anything. Don't mention it to anyone. It might turn out to be sensitive. I take it you're busy?'

'Yes sir.'

'Anything I need to know about?'

'No sir.'

'By Friday then.'

'Yes sir.'

CHAPTER 3

I'd seen nothing of Kimberly or Conrad in the week since my hospital visit. Then on Wednesday morning there she was, slowing by the bus stop in a climate crime on wheels: a big black Audi Q7, with the twins in the back and an odd registration, KSS 69. She lowered the passenger-side window, launched a paper dart through it, smiled, waved and drove on. I picked up the dart and unfolded a sheet of white paper with a big red X, tacky, like it was written in blood. Or lipstick.

Beyond cryptic, I thought, looking after her. I refolded the dart, not sure whether to keep it, and looked down at the Goodwood Green wing of an immaculate Bentley. It stopped under my nose. Conrad climbed out, looking ready to kill. My bus drew up behind. He headed towards me, round the front of his car. The bus doors hissed open. I hopped in and scanned my pass. The bus driver clearly saw trouble and didn't want it, and hissed the doors shut just as Conrad reached them. He rattled them. The bus driver honked his horn and edged forwards, threatening the back of the Bentley. Conrad thumped the door, hard, twice. The driver shook his head, unsmiling, gestured for Conrad to move his car, edged closer.

Conrad mouthed something in my direction, thumped the bus's windscreen hard with the heel of his hand, made his grudging way round to get into his car, and roared off, waving a V-sign from his window.

He seemed to resort to violence and confrontation whenever he was angry, which seemed to be all the time. Was he an underworld criminal? A mafia boss? A complete nutter? He was certainly a bully, and I certainly wasn't going to give in to his threats. Quite the reverse. And I wasn't sure what she was up to, but Kimberly seemed nice. Was she really divorcing him? Was I a pawn in a matrimonial chess game, my role to make Conrad jealous? Could she and her kids be in danger? Perhaps I was her get-out-of-jail card, held in reserve. Not sure I wanted that.

She'd made me feel warm and cared for when she tended my bruises, and I seemed to be involved with the two of them, like it or not. My grandad's number two rule with bullies was: know your enemy. I should be finding out what was going on with them, for my own safety if nothing else. But where to start? I needed to talk it over with someone. The only person I could think of was my old schoolmate Kanhai Jamal. I sent him a text: *aldermans pint 630.*

***

After work I bussed and walked to the Alderman's Arms in squalling rain. It was empty. Last time I was there I'd talked to a new barmaid about her DPhil on the phenomenology of dying. She was off duty, worse luck.

I took two pints of Pedigree to a table near the fire, thumbed through emails and found one from an insurance company, wanting a witness statement about the Bentley hitting the bus. I opened the attachment and thought, *Is that serendipity or what?* Because, there on the form, it said: *Driver: Conrad Sefton-Shaw, Springfield House, Berkeley Close, Boars Hill OX1 5HX.*

I knew I was going to use that information. Kanhai could help figure out how.

He arrived at half six, shook rain off his cycle helmet, sat down, raised a glass. 'Evening, comrade,' he said. I stared at the fire, not sure where to start. He'd never been keen on anything controversial, especially since joining the civilian staff at the Thames Valley Police HQ in Kidlington.

'What is it?' he said. 'Lovesick again?'

'No.'

'So not another waitress.'

'What's wrong with waitresses?' I sometimes regretted sharing so much with him. He looked at his watch, as if he was due home soon. 'How are Bethan and the babe?' I said.

'Bethan's fine, thanks. The babe's nearly two. Talks nineteen to the dozen. Runs faster than me.'

'When's she coming over to walk Friday?'

'Soon. So what is it?'

'I told you I got done over by a bloke in a Bentley, May morning?' I said.

'Yeah, he warned you to keep clear of his wife. A warning you're heeding, I hope.'

'What do you think?'

'I think you should forget all about it,' Kanhai said. 'That's what I'd do.'

'But you can't go round thumping people and threatening to kill them. And I think his wife and kids are in more danger than I am.'

'In what way is that your business?'

'Well…'

'There you are then. Let it be.'

'I found out who they are. Conrad and Kimberly Sefton-Shaw. Live in Boars Hill.'

'I know that name. Something to do with the council?'

'Dunno. When the plods took him away, he said he knew your boss. Doesn't give him licence to beat up innocent passers-by.'

Kanhai shrugged. As usual he looked composed, neutral.

'I was thinking I'd go over and have a look,' I said. 'You could come along. Not to do anything, except kind of watch my back.'

'Look at their house? Why?'

I didn't know why, except I couldn't just take Conrad's assaults lying down, and had to start somewhere. Something was telling me to start there.

'You sure about this?' he said.

'Yes.' I wasn't, but what the hell, might as well act like I was. 'Tomorrow evening?'

***

The next morning I took Friday for a long walk before breakfast, wondering what my grandad would have made of what was happening. I couldn't hear his voice. He had died a year ago that day. He'd approved of Friday, unlike my mum, who couldn't stop asking what the dog was going to do when I was at work. The answer was that my neighbour, Mrs Swainston, loved to have her for the company.

In fact, it was Mrs Swainston who decided I needed a dog, and a border collie was her choice, not mine. She had a niece who was training to be a vet in Pontypridd and hated having to euthanise perfectly good animals for no good reason. Mrs Swainston told her niece I was looking for a border collie, and her niece rang me one Friday morning to say she had a neglected three-year-old female in the pound at Merthyr Tydfil, with broken teeth, bad skin, black ooze coming out of her ears, and jumping at shadows. But with a bit of TLC, she said, she'd make a fine dog, and if I wanted to meet her informally, no obligation, I should get over there pronto.

I did. I took the poor thing for a walk in the park, and by the time we were back at the pound, you'd have needed dynamite to separate us. I called her Friday. In a few weeks she was sorted and settled.

I'd had her nearly ten years now and she was my favourite being in the whole universe. That morning, I left her with Mrs Swainston as usual, caught the bus into town and snuck into work, late again. Denise, who fields all the non-techie stuff in the office, gave me a smile. Everyone else kindly ignored me. I hunkered down and watched my workstation boot up, thinking how lucky I was, how much I loved C++. The buzz of clean code. Elegant design. Untangling complexity into simple strands: data flows, objects, events. It worked and I was good at it.

A message popped up, from Dougie Mack on the sales team: *11.30 meeting and lunch. James Alleyn, of Murdoch Alleyn & Co. Lawyers. Want to re-vamp their online presence and push into social media.*

Why was that so irritating? Was it that word: 'lawyers'?

***

Alleyn was in his forties, very tall with a stomach like a sack of cement that's been left out in the rain. Dark hair, red face, prickly frown. I sensed immediately that he'd never understand anything that took more than four words to express, because by then he'd have stopped listening. I disliked and distrusted him from the off. His colleague was in her late twenties and fragrant, in a lavender-scented, lavender-coloured trouser suit. She took notes but said nothing throughout, wasn't even introduced.

At midday we walked to Harry's Hash House in the Castle Quarter. Alleyn led us in. We were shown straight to a table, attracting disgruntled stares from a group at the bar. The menus came in embossed leather folders. Mine was sticky.

Alleyn was talking premiership football, despite knowing nothing about it. Dougie listened with the rapt attention of a salesman on the brink of closing a sale. I zoned out and started people-watching. The crowd round the bar, still waiting for a table, remonstrated with the barman, who shrugged and polished glasses.

A noisy group arrived: two young women and two middle-aged men in suits. The smaller man looked jaundiced, seemed to be itching all over. The other, on the porky side, looked a lot like angry Conrad. He was doing all the talking, the women all the laughing. His voice did it: he *was* Conrad. If he recognised me, he showed no sign. I kept my head down. They were led to a corner table twenty feet past us. I slid lower in my seat, raised my menu. Conrad called 'Wotcha, James' as they passed. Alleyn jumped up and went across to slap shoulders.

From the other direction, a waitress caught my eye, emerging backwards through swinging louvre doors, carrying a tray high, one-handed. Straight dark hair pulled back in a bun, white apron, black dress. I knew her from somewhere.

Alleyn came back, sat down, gave me an odd look.

The waitress came towards us, pale blue eyes alight, a dancer's lissom tread threading a tangle of chairs. I couldn't take my eyes off her. Was it me she was looking for?

No. She walked past, to Conrad's table, where he gave her a hard time over some problem with his drink. I realised Dougie had asked a question. They were all looking at me. I looked at Dougie: no help there, he just looked amused. Alleyn bristled scorn. I'd no idea what they'd been talking about, and was pleased to see a waiter arriving with our food. He looked nervous, like a man on his first day in the job, and announced the dishes in a dense eastern European accent.

Alleyn looked at the plate placed in front of him and said, 'That's not what I ordered.'

The waiter blinked.

'This is beef fajitas, as I think you might have said. I ordered enchiladas rancheras.'

I realised this was a wind-up, Alleyn's idea of fun. Not very kind, though – another bully. The third rule of bullies is: pick your moment. It would be easy to duck it right now, but I was fed up with ducking things. My grandad used to say, 'If you let people shit on people, they'll just go on shitting on people, and tomorrow they'll be shitting on you.' If I was going to work with this guy, I had to establish some parameters up front. This was the moment.

I cleared my throat, forced a smile, leaned across towards the waiter. 'Don't worry,' I said. 'My friend must have forgotten. He did order beef fajitas, I remember distinctly. But do you want to change your order, James?'

Alleyn gave me a look to curdle yoghurt, then just shook his head and looked away. So bullies picked their moments too. But it felt okay.

Dougie gave me the shadow of a wink. We'd all ordered variations on the spicy house specials and he led off into tasteless ribaldry about farts to come and rings of fire. I was glad to hear a ping on my phone, an excuse to step away: *ok for tonight from yours at 6.*

I sent a thumbs up to Kanhai. This was getting real.

Leaving the restaurant, I held the street door open for the others, taking a chance to look back. And there she was, the balletic blue-eyed waitress, a still point in the bustle, like an island in a waterfall. Was she looking back at me? I smiled and raised a hand, just in case, then went out, heart beating.

***

My phone rang at five to six. I thought it was Kanhai cancelling, but it was my mum. She lives in west Oxon, with my stepfather and an intensive backyard farming operation.

'Someone called,' she said, 'asking about you.'

'Who? Asking what?'

'Asking things you might ask,' she said, 'if you were interested in someone you'd met in a romantic way, but didn't know them that well.'

My mum tended to bypass facts and move straight to fanciful interpretation.

'So asking what?'

'Like, about relationships. Past and present. Offspring. What you do for fun. What you do for lunch when you're at work, if you're veggie…'

'This was a woman?'

'Yes, didn't I say?'

'Did you know the answers?'

'I guessed some.'

My mum and discretion run on parallel lines; they never meet. Could it be the phenomenological barmaid at the Alderman's? I'd given her my Tibetan Book of Dying. Surely not the waitress in Harry's. Who else?

'Should I be worried?' I said. 'Do I know her?'

'She said so, yes. Then she said not to tell you she'd called.'

'But you are telling me.'

'Well, you're my son, aren't you? What would she expect? And I didn't promise. She said her name but I forgot to write it down, sorry. Anna something. Annaliese, was it?'

'I don't know any Annalieses. You sure?'

'Sounded Cornish.'

'Her accent?'

'No, her surname. Tre-something. Trevelyan. Trescothick. That sort of thing. Said she'd be in touch, so I'll find out.'

The doorbell rang. Kanhai. 'Got to go,' I said. 'Let me know if you hear more.'

I didn't know what to make of my mum's call, but I had other concerns. Know your enemy and know yourself – ancient Chinese wisdom. A trip to Boars Hill might help with both.

I was glad of Kanhai's company, even though he was only coming because he didn't trust me not to do something stupid. We cycled out through Wytham, round the wooded hill. I loved the free feel of it, like when we were kids and the world was fresh. Through Farmoor, Cumnor, flying down the fast, winding road to Wootton, a quiet mile up through woods, a long freewheel down Berkeley Road. There, on the left, across from the old Open University building, was a sign that said:

BERKELEY CLOSE
PRIVATE ROAD
NO PARKING

We stopped at the corner, leaned on our bikes, men in Lycra having a breather. There were just two houses in Berkeley Close. Big ones.

'Thirty years old, thereabouts,' Kanhai said. 'Look at the styles: log cabin kitsch and nouveau mansionette. And the gardens: bushes, small trees, nothing more than thirty feet. Except that Scots pine, over in the back corner.'

'Which is Springfield House?' I wondered how Kanhai extracted so much from a glance.

'The furthest one,' he said. 'The mansionette. Backing onto the heath, as they call it. 'They' being OCT, Oxford Conservation Trust. That copse behind is theirs too – Ishmael's Wood. Great for bluebells. And owls.'

'Owls? How do you know?'

He turned his bike upside down on the verge. 'My dad volunteers for them. Controls invasive aliens. Puts up nest boxes, roost boxes for bats.' He pumped unnecessary air into a tyre.

I stepped down the Close, a bit nervous. To the right, the first house, wood-clad, had a poker-work sign: The Bothy. Further down, the yellow-brick walls of Springfield House were half-hidden by dense bushes. Down the hill on the main road, a stile gave access to the heath. 'Good place to walk the dog,' I said.

'While I get this tyre off and on again,' Kanhai said, 'why don't you have a nosey? Get it out of your system, whatever you need to do. Back in fifteen?'

I climbed the stile, tried a casual saunter across the heath. Kanhai was out of sight. This was exciting; what Kanhai's police

21

colleagues would call covert observation, if they were doing it. Stalking, if someone else was. Both houses had alarm systems and spiky hedges and a barbed-wire fence a yard from the hedge against grazing animals. The Springfield House windows looked dark and mean. A treehouse on stilts reached halfway up the pine, and a blancmange-pink Wendy house nestled in azaleas. Both were professionally built in quality timber; each would make a family home in some places. It was all of a piece with Conrad's attitude to the world. It had been worth coming; I knew my enemy a little better and had the stirrings of an idea of how to respond to his threats.

CHAPTER 4

DETECTIVE INSPECTOR JONES

Friday morning. Jones was two days into the staff appraisals. He'd finish them this afternoon. An hour ago he'd come out of his own appraisal with the DCI without much to smile about, and he was staring at an HR app that showed what his lump sum and monthly pension would be if he jacked in the job now – much less than if he waited until the end of March next year, when his thirty were up. His knew his policing instincts were still sound, but his motivation had melted away. He was exhausted.

His wife wanted a place by the sea, Porthcawl or on the Gower, away from the bustle and strife of Oxfordshire. He'd like that too. Olwen already had work with galleries in Bristol and Cardiff, and her art would flourish. But house prices kept going up and the dream was always just beyond reach.

There was a tentative tap on his office door. 'Enter,' he said. The door opened. A nose appeared, followed by a moustache. 'Yes, Clappison?'

'Dead shark shuffle, sir,' DC Clappison said. 'You asked for something by today.'

'I did. What have you got?'

Clappison was the only cop Jones knew with a PhD. He was socially inept, but if anyone could get results from a research project, it was him. In this case Jones's expectations were low.

'I Googled it for a start, sir.' Clappison fingered his moustache. 'I could show you.'

Perhaps he'd found something. 'Go on,' Jones said, closing the pension app and making room at the keyboard.

Clappison typed, clicked, scrolled and read aloud. 'Shark playing cards, German. Ten euros a pack. Grateful Dead 'Loser' playing cards, USA, fourteen dollars. More junk like that.'

'Google,' Jones said, 'used to be useful, back in the day. Now it's just sell, sell, sell.'

'Then this work of art,' Clappison said. 'A dead shark in a tank.' Clappison clicked on an image and blew it up. 'By Damien Hirst. Fourteen-foot tiger shark, in a tank of formaldehyde. Called *The Physical Impossibility of Death in the Mind of Someone Living*.'

Jones peered at it. The poor thing made him feel uncomfortable, as if it were an omen. Trapped, pickled and made the vehicle of facile pretension; no wonder it looked miserable. 'That's art?'

'Sort of,' Clappison said. 'He once said he wanted to get into a position where he could make really bad art and get away with it. This may be an example.'

'I hope my wife sticks to painting. Bloody thing must stink.'

'Apparently it did, sir.'

'So you've got a dead shark,' Jones said. 'Where's the shuffle?'

Clappison clicked and typed again. 'Here,' he said. '*Twenty-First Century Art: A Sceptic's Guide*. Page 94: "Dead Shark Shuffle". Doesn't mention Damien Hirst, presumably to avoid libel. A financial manoeuvre...'

'Promising,' Jones said.

'Just so, sir.' Clappison read on: '"...developed in the art world. A wealthy patron and an artist enter into a clandestine collaboration. The patron lends the artist a lot of money. The artist uses it to buy one of his own works, from himself, for an enormous and highly publicised price, through an anonymous consortium of which he is the sole member. He uses the proceeds of the sale to repay the patron's loan. The artist can now sell his work for millions rather than hundreds. The patron's collection of the artist's work is worth millions too." Almost everyone is happy and it's probably not illegal.'

Everyone's at it, he thought, *even bloody artists*. 'It does sound fishy,' he said. 'But how is this relevant to Oxford?'

'I don't know, sir.'

'At least you found something. Well done. Make a summary of that, can you? Pad it out a bit, include a couple of photos. Make it look good. I'll forward it to the Chief Constable. Keep an eye out for an Oxford angle, but be discreet. And keep me in the loop.'

CHAPTER 5

Early on Saturday afternoon I arrived on Boars Hill with my dog Friday and a frisbee, carrying binoculars and looking like a plausible birder if you didn't look too closely. Friday sniffed and I ambled across the heath, light-hearted with the adventure of spying and disguise. I paused to follow birds across the sky with my binoculars, contriving to include the grounds of Springfield House in the sweep. No sign of anyone there, though that didn't mean there wasn't.

In Ishmael's Wood I settled with my back to a beech, breathing a sweet and sour mix of honeysuckle and wild garlic, method-acting the birder role, studying the house through a gap in the undergrowth. Treecreepers, woodpecker (great spotted), various tits, warblers, finches. No owls. Still no sign of life at the house. Friday lay in freckled sunshine, opening an eye whenever my hand strayed near the frisbee.

After two hours I decided no-one was home. I stretched, bagged my binoculars, headed back towards the road on a line to pass the corner of the Springfield House garden. Friday was pleased to see the frisbee come into play, happily plucking it from the air and retrieving it to hand until I "accidentally" threw it into the garden.

No Saturday afternoon walkers were in sight. By the fence, I told Friday, 'Lie down. Stay.' I crossed the barbed wire, peered through a gap in the hedge. Dust got up my nose and I struggled not to sneeze. The frisbee poked out of rough grass on the far side of what looked like a tiny brook. I eased through the hedge and out onto the grass, tiptoed across, jumped over the brook, then paused by the frisbee. The house still looked deserted: dark windows, no movement, no sound of talk or music. No ground-floor windows were open, but one to the right of the French doors reflected the light differently, as if at a slightly different angle. Perhaps left on the latch for ventilation. Worth a closer look.

I bent to pick up the frisbee and heard a click and a rustle. A big brown dog burst from bushes at the side of the house. Very big. A mastiff. Pounding towards me.

I leapt across the brook and backed to the hedge. The dog followed, jaws a foot from me. I could go no further. The dog gave out a low grumble and the smell of raw meat, jaws dripping, red-rimmed eyes squinting through fleshy black folds.

I made what I hoped were calming noises. Friday warbled from behind the hedge, sensing something. I told her, 'Shush. Stay.' I locked eyes with the mastiff. It might have been safer to look away, feign a lack of interest, but I couldn't: its fangs were inches from my balls.

It was an impasse. With a dog like Friday, I'd just throw the frisbee and it'd be away and after it, but this beast wasn't like Friday at all. I was trying to think of another diversionary tactic aside from staying quiet and hoping it got bored and went away, which didn't seem likely, when I became aware we were not alone. There was a strange noise, a kind of snort, from the bushes, then quiet again, but a different sort of quiet. Someone was watching from the corner of the house. I couldn't see angry Conrad lurking like that, nor Kimberly. So who was it? I don't usually have a problem with silences but this one felt uncomfortable. I had to break it. 'Call your dog off please,' I said, with scarcely a tremor.

I broke my gaze from the dog, looked across, tried to see who was there.

'I just popped over the fence to get my frisbee,' I said, raising it in evidence.

The dog shuffled closer.

'Didn't think anyone was in,' I said, returning the frisbee to its protective position between dog's snout and my groin.

Whoever was there was staying unnervingly quiet. I'd run out of things to say and went quiet too. I could make out a still form through the leaves. I waited, counting every moment without bloodshed a small victory.

'What's it worth?' A boy's voice, breaking, squeaky. Its owner stepped through the bushes. The boy Alasdair. He stopped, stared at me, freckled nose held high, eyes screwed as if short-sighted. He had a red baseball cap, back-to-front, a tight Manchester United shirt, drooping tracksuit pants. A heavy-duty dog's leash was wrapped round one hand and he was scratching his bottom with the other.

I could smell adolescent sweat across ten yards. 'Did you say "what's it worth?"?'

He nodded. Perhaps he really was short-sighted and didn't recognise me. I looked down at the mastiff and back at the boy, annoyance displacing fear.

'Are your parents here?' I asked.

He shook his head.

'What do you want?'

'Twenty.'

'Pence?' I reached into my pocket. The mastiff growled.

'Pounds.'

There was a complacent smirk on his face. I didn't like it. I looked at the dog's wet jowls. *All's fair*, I thought. 'He's going to have me if I move,' I said. 'I'll need to check I've got the cash. Call him off. Then we'll see.'

The boy frowned, gave a small nod and called, 'Lovelump!'

'Lovelump?' I said, looking at the dog, suppressing a smile. 'Really?'

The dog's mournful eyes looked into mine. The boy shrugged. 'Lovelump! Come!' The dog turned, trotted across to him and sat docile while the boy clipped the leash to its collar.

I breathed deep, letting out a sigh and a 'Phew' that morphed into a quiet undulating whistle. There was a rattle and a rustle as Friday scooched under the fence and through the hedge and there she was, at my side: head low, ears forward, hackles raised, tail stiff.

Lovelump tucked his tail between his legs and got behind the boy. The boy's smirk disappeared. His eyes flicked right and left but found nothing helpful. He tried to get behind Lovelump.

I whispered 'Whisht' and Friday streaked across the brook, straight for the mastiff, which turned and ran, dragging the boy through the bushes and round the corner.

I could hear the boy squeaking and his dog snarling. Friday stuck her nose round the corner. 'Let's head back home,' she said. We squeezed through the hedge and jogged back to the car. Driving away, I reflected that this spying and revenge business held interesting possibilities. I was having more fun than I'd had in years.

***

Friday and I were back on Boars Hill the next day. We sat in the car from two o'clock, covertly observing the Close. Spies are probably trained to still the mind, relax, pay attention. Dogs do it naturally, for a while. But we saw nothing and by half seven we'd both had enough. We crossed to the stile for a stretch and a last look round. Down the hill, a woman was walking towards us. She looked familiar, from way back. There used to be two of them, I thought. Mother and daughter. Always in long dresses, always purposeful, a daily sight in North Oxford when I was young. My mother knew them, or was at school with someone who knew them. She called them "the Walkers". Both slim and upright with hair that flopped forward, repeatedly swept back with identical unconscious gestures, one grey, one mousey blonde. Proud noses, soft chins. I'd not seen them for ages.

There was only one today. Must be the daughter, looking like her mother did twenty years ago. As I watched, she half stumbled, lost her easy rhythm, leaned forward to thump each knee in turn with a clenched fist – left fist to right knee, right to left, like tying a reef knot with limbs. Then back upright and gliding on, eyes intent on something across the heath. In my mind they were always in the city, on Woodstock Road. What was she doing up here?

We returned to the car. Friday jumped in the back, I sat on the tailgate, trying to watch without staring, trying to look unthreatening. She walked past the car on the road, keeping a distance, not making eye contact. Walked on up the hill, crossed, turned downhill. At the entrance to the Close she turned in, walked a few steps towards the Sefton-Shaw house, stopped and studied it. She walked back out of the Close, left down the hill, then crossed and repeated the process, again stopping to stare at Springfield House with no attempt at concealment. Out to the road, down, across, back up again, like some sort of obsessive.

I was curious. I stood, stepped back a yard, smiled, cleared my throat, raised a hand. She began to turn away.

'Hello,' I said. 'Please excuse my impertinence. I remember you walking on the Woodstock Road with your mum.'

She stopped and turned towards me with raised brow.

'You're no doubt going about your lawful business and all that,' I said. 'But it looks to me like you're paying particular attention to Springfield House.'

'Why shouldn't I?'

'No reason. But I wondered why. Because I am too.'

'Why?'

I looked at her. Her bright eyes looked back steadily enough, but not completely connecting, as if looking through a window or as if haunted, her attention somewhere beyond the present. I felt sincerity behind her distance and awkwardness. I took a deep breath and tried to explain about the crash, angry husband, assault, death threat. 'Now I'm casing the joint,' I said, 'to see if some appropriate way of getting even might present itself.'

'Like what?'

A good question. I wasn't sure. 'I'm tempted to give him a good thumping, like he gave me. But I don't want to be unkind. So I could repay his unkindness with something so genuinely kind he'll not trust it. Or something that takes the piss, makes him look ridiculous. He'd hate that.'

'Wouldn't stop him wanting to kill you, though. The reverse, in fact.'

'Yeah, good point.'

She frowned. 'Trust you, can I?'

Another good question. Why should she? She could trust me to mean well; not necessarily to deliver well, though I always tried. 'Yes,' I said, wearing my most open smile and crossing my fingers.

We perched side by side on the tailgate. Friday stuck her head between us, said hello and nuzzled her. She tousled Friday's mane and studied my face. I'd once heard someone say you can judge a man by his dog. If that's what she was doing, Friday's good nature weighed in my favour.

'Okay,' she said. 'Pro tem. Different for me.' She held out a hand. 'Mycroft. Gail. Good to meet you.'

We shook hands like neither of us knew how to do it.

'Jarvis. Michael. Known as Mick. Good to meet you too.'

'Where to start...' she said.

'At the very beginning?' She did look slightly like Julie Andrews.

'Well, all right.' She swept back the hair that fell across her face. 'Always lived in Park Town. Know it?'

I nodded.

'Don't really remember Father. But they always walked five miles, every day, he and Mother, until he died. After, Mother carried on, taking me with her.'

'I think my mother used to know yours,' I said. 'Can't remember how. Was she at Wychwood?'

'She taught there sometimes. Mandarin, Russian, Modern Dance.'

'Crumbs. Right. So you walked with her every day? On top of school?'

'Yes, every day. But no school. Home-educated. Governess for reading and writing and so forth. But Mother thought walks more important. Said most education comes from the world. From intelligently supported engagement with it, to be precise. So, every day, up Banbury Road, across Five Mile Drive, back down Woodstock Road. Or vice versa. With a loop round St Giles.'

'The traditional five-mile circuit,' I said.

'Yes. Took us three or four hours, talking all the time, stopping to look at things, meeting friends. Went on most of my life. Then… seven years ago – I was forty-something, Mother sixty-eight – coming down Woodstock Road, by that little school, The Griffin, pre-prep. There's a tiny cut-through, one-way, Roberts Lane. "No Entry" signs all over, where it comes out onto Woodstock Road.'

'I know it.'

'Only used by parents on the school run, driving through from the other end. Walking past, you look up Roberts Lane to see if anyone's coming out. You don't expect anyone to come screeching across Woodstock Road and into the wrong end. But he did, Conrad Sefton-Shaw. Hit both of us. Up over the bonnet of his ghastly great tank of a vehicle, one of those with rings. German.'

'Audi?

'That'd be it. Anyway… Mother never wanted a fuss. Just got up, a bit wobbly. Dusted herself off. "Damned fool, why didn't you look?" from the man. "What's your address? I'll send the bill for the damage." "You're the damned fool," from Mother. "See the No Entry sign? It's been there fifteen years." "Oh," from the man. "Don't apologise, please," from Mother. "We know you don't give a shit."'

I couldn't help laughing.

'Cold as ice, she was. And off we went, limping down the road, knees hurting, ribs hurting. At home, Dettol bath, linament, arnica, strapping. Later, doctor. Cracked ribs, ruptured ligaments, don't know what. Mother never walked further than the end of the garden after that. Took to her bed. Slow decline. Died a few months ago, Easter Sunday.'

'So sorry. Good Lord. How awful for you both.' I didn't know what to say but felt I had to say something. 'Was he prosecuted?'

'No. Mother never wanted a fuss.'

'What about you? Are your legs okay?'

'Knees go funny sometimes, need popping back into line. Can be sore. But I'm ticking on. And back to doing the walk again now.'

'How did you know he lived up here?'

'Came for a guided walk in the wood over there last year. An OCT thing, happens every autumn. Waiting for the guide just there, by the stile, and saw him drive by and turn into the Close. Later, came back and checked, made sure. Come back quite often now, to walk and think and remember Mother. And make wishes.'

She was haunted by the ghost of her mother, whose death had left her isolated and precarious.

'Make wishes?' I said.

'Oh, these superstitions. From Mother of course. Like seeing a magpie. If the first magpie you see is on its own, just one, that's bad luck, unless you say, "Good morning, Mr Magpie sir, how's your lady wife?", and keep your fingers crossed until you see a four-legged animal. That neutralises the bad luck. If the first thing you see is two magpies together, you can still say good morning, but it's good luck. And you can make a wish.'

33

'Okay.' I'd inherited a similar practice but without the wish.

'And if a load of hay goes past, you cross your fingers and keep them crossed until you see a four-legged animal. You can make a wish then, too.'

'Yes, I know. I do.'

'Or, if you travel down a new road or path, one that you haven't been on ever before in your life, you can wish on that. You see? So out here you often get to make a wish, with all the birds and farmers and new paths to explore.'

I was genuinely curious about this sort of thing. 'When you make a wish,' I said, 'who do you wish to?'

'Well.' She hesitated. Was there a hint of embarrassment? 'It's the Fairy Queen that makes wishes come true, isn't it? So you make them to her.'

I looked at her, in her late forties or fifties, talking seriously about fairies. Although to be fair, who did I wish to? 'What do you wish for? If you're allowed to tell.'

'In general, for him to get his comeuppance somehow. Suffer from someone's random carelessness, like Mother did. Or lose someone dear to him, like I did. Not very Christian, I know.'

'Okay,' I said, 'I get it. I can see you bear a real grudge. But I'm still not sure what you're doing here, prowling around in the dusk.' I didn't want to be lumbered with someone unhinged, but perhaps I'd become slightly unhinged too. We might both have slipped the bounds of normal behaviour, normal being to accept outrageous boorishness without making a fuss. Meeting a fellow traveller felt good to me. Perhaps to her too. Perhaps we'd be good for each other.

'What am I doing here?' she said. 'Research. Pondering. How to get closure, move on. Those lovely modern words. And realising closure might only come through retribution. But is that possible? Or should I accept that closure will never come, and just get on with life?'

'Yes, I see.'

34

'But now I'm wondering whether a wish has been answered, in the shape of you. Problem shared, problem halved sort of thing.'

CHAPTER 6

The following Wednesday was one of those pure mid-May days that would make anyone glad to be alive. I decided on an evening visit to Boars Hill, for more covert observation. I collected my chalk pastel sketching kit, a broad-brimmed straw hat, a paint-spattered blue smock, and a false moustache, made of real hair – not necessarily human but quite nicely soft – which I'd used for a school play years ago and never had the heart to throw out.

I got out of the car, pulled the hat low over my eyes, stuck on the moustache and set off to do art. Birds were singing, bees were buzzing and I was enjoying myself. Friday ranged ahead while we walked across the heath to Ishmael's Wood, then cut back towards Springfield House. I settled with my back to a fencepost by the thickest bit of their hedge, confident that any passers-by on the heath would take me for an artist rather than an eavesdropper.

The sun was sinking towards the wood. Ultramarine overhead, grading down to shining duck-egg blue, and a bright golden haze on the horizon. Deep violet shadows at the wood's edge, trunks streaked with silver and gold where the sun caught them, a cathedral of luminous blue spaces under the fresh green canopy. Honeysuckle in the hedge and an occasional waft of wood-smoke on soft air. I chose mid-blue pastel paper with a hint of violet. I closed my eyes, breathed in deep, exhaled slowly.

My practice in drawing landscape *en plein air*, as they say, meaning outdoors, came from a sculptor named Godfrey. The aim was looseness and freedom. I'd do three sketches of the same subject, allowing up to twenty minutes each: small, medium, then large. I'd look carefully at what was in front of me for five minutes, then sketch with my eyes closed, picking chalks at random out of a box, from which all the greens had been discarded. Closed eyes and the elimination of green were my personal extensions to the Godfrey method.

On this occasion I was well on with the third sketch when I was disturbed.

'Ow!' A juvenile shriek.

'Come back here, you little bugger!' An adult male, shouting.

Running feet, sniffs. Someone crashed into the thicket behind me. Friday sat up, ears pricked. I gathered my kit together in case a swift exit was needed.

'Where are you, you little bugger?' The adult male again, no doubt angry Conrad.

'Oh Alasdair, don't be silly. You'll only make it worse. Come out now, darling.' That must be Kimberly.

More rustling and small squeaks from nearby, then a girl's voice, betraying her big brother's hiding place. 'He's in here, Momma.'

'We know you did it, you little bugger.' The father again. 'Bella and Charlotte saw you. And you had dirty hands. And your Momma found the matches under your bed, with those horrible magazines.'

'I did not. They're lying,' Alasdair squeaked from the tangle of shrubs and brambles. He must have realised immediately that opening his mouth was a bad move. The thicket bulged. He pushed through head-first, then stood, trailing twigs and blinking, in the gap between hedge and barbed-wire stock fence. I hadn't expected a close encounter with these people; my preparations were meant for the eyes of passers-by on the main footpath, while I listened in to the Sefton-Shaws from a discreet distance. I crossed my fingers, hoping my artist persona would survive closer scrutiny.

Alasdair goggled, clearly surprised to find anyone there, let alone a straw-hatted artist with an interested dog. His eyes wore a momentary frown, flickering from one to the other, like he half-recognised us.

Friday sat up straight, pricked her ears and sniffed, looking the boy in the eye. I looked back at him too, pondering. He was an extortionist, for whom I should have no sympathy. But whatever the rights and wrongs, I'd never weigh in on the side of adult power. I glanced around, calculating his best chance. The road was hopeless, as was the open heath. It had to be the wood.

'Quick. Here,' I whispered, holding strands of wire apart while he squeezed through. 'That way.' I pointed to the wood a hundred yards away. 'Just get there. Run. And hide.'

He stared at me, clearly needing time for his brain to catch up with events.

'Run,' I whispered. 'Hide in the woods. In an hour they'll have forgotten they're mad with you. They'll be worried instead. Go on!' I pushed him in the right direction. 'Run!'

He made a better fist of running than I'd expected, but pursuit could not be far behind. I'd better get in character and create a diversion. I tucked myself against a fencepost, took up a cerulean blue and added random daubs to my third sketch, humming a hum about rabbits running and farmers getting guns.

Twigs cracked, thorns rasped against cloth and a ginger-bristled balding crown appeared, then an angry, pasty face. Barrel chest and belly broached the hedge. Crazy man Conrad straightened up and stood high, wide and wheezing. I kept still. He hadn't seen me. Across the heath, the boy gained the shelter of the wood.

Conrad squinted the other way, towards the stile by the road, the obvious direction to look. He started to climb the fence. I coughed, deliberately. Can a cough sound French? I tried. He pulled up short, straddling the barbed wire. 'What?' he said. Squeaked. 'What the fuck are you doing here?'

He couldn't possibly recognise me, could he? I was out of context. In disguise. He'd really only seen me once. And I couldn't suppress a smile of delight, because I'd always wanted to be asked that question. I pulled the brim of my hat further down over my eyes and summoned my best French accent. 'Everybody 'as to be somewhere,' I said. 'I sink your Spike Milligan said zat.'

He made a small humphing noise and closed his mouth, then opened it again to speak.

'I am artiste,' I said, before he could launch himself. 'I make ze design, ze drawing, of ze scene, 'ere.' I indicated the heath and wood and setting sun, and held my sketch up for his inspection. 'If you 'ave interest, you may telephone or email. 'Ere eez *mon carte*. Mon studio eez en Morlaix, Finisterre.'

I fished for a business card that I thought I had in my back pocket. Whose was it? Rainbow House Chinese Takeaway, Eynsham. *Mieux que rien.* I'd have prepared better if I'd known it was going to come to this. I held it out to Sefton-Shaw, who ignored it and hoisted his trailing leg over the wire. He seemed to focus on me properly for the first time. 'Did you see the little bugger?' he asked.

He must have swallowed the disguise.

'I comprehend not, what eez "ze leetle boogger"?'

'A boy. A boy!' he explained, loudly.

'Ah oui, a boy, a boogger, yes. For why you search him?'

'Because he set fire to the girls' Wendy house! The wife had to put it out. Singed her eyebrows. Not that it's anything to do with you. Did you see him, for the love of fuck?'

'Ah oui, I sink it eez so. I see ze boogger.' I smiled, pleased with the fluency of our communication, and my success in frustrating his hot pursuit of the boy.

'Yes? So where is he? Where did he go?'

'Ah oui. Ze boogger. 'E runs. Down zere.' I gestured towards the road. 'La bas. By ze *clôture*. Ze fence. To *le coin*. Ze angle. Ze corner. Zen 'e runs to ze… what eez eet… portal?… door?'

'What?' Sefton-Shaw squeezed out the word through clenched molars. 'Where?'

'Ze 'ole in ze *clôture*. In ze fence. By ze road.' I waved my arm with conscious imprecision. 'Ze portal? Ze gate?'

'Stile. It's called a stile. Which way did he go when he got on the road?'

'Ah monsieur, *je suis desolé*, I know not. I pay not ze attention. When he runs, I return to *le dessin*. Ze design. Ze drawing.' I held out the drawing again. 'If you 'ave interest, you may telephone or email.' I pressed the business card into his hand. ''Ere eez *mon carte*. Mon studio eez en Morlaix, Finisterre.'

Sefton-Shaw put the card in his pocket, paying it no attention. Looking at me again, he shook his head and turned, then stretched leg after leg back over the fence, only slightly snagging his crotch. He de-snagged himself with a hiss and forced his frame back through the brambles, disappearing into the tangle without a word. Not a man for polite leave-taking.

I wasn't sure whether he was agitated because he really cared about his son, or whether it was wounded pride because his son had defied and eluded him. I listened as he grunted through the undergrowth, then heard him speaking. 'He's gone. Run off.' *Orff.*

'Oh, poor boy.' Kimberly.

'Don't go all bleeding-heart fucking socialist on me, you. Some fucking frog artist out there saw him run across to the road but didn't see which way he went. He said. Weird fucker, actually.'

'Never mind him. Where's Alasdair?'

'Well, how the fuck do I know?' he said. 'Look. I'll take the Audi. I'll find the little bugger. Toast, he is. Fucking toast.'

'Don't do anything awful to him, please. Just bring him home.'

'You shut the fuck up. And stay here. And phone me if he

comes back, straight away. And don't mollycoddle the fucker. Lock him in his room. I could murder the little bastard actually.'

I heard footsteps and a door slamming.

'He's not a bastard. Worse bloody luck.' Kimberly again, quieter, presumably addressing Conrad's disappearing back. I felt sorry for her. He showed her no respect. If you don't respect someone, how can you love and honour them? And if you don't love and honour your partner, what does marriage mean? Possession and control on one side, subjugation and dehumanisation on the other? His anger with me arose from perceived threats to his ownership of a beautiful human being. A shiver crept up my spine.

Time to go home. I knelt to pack my kit. Something amplified that creepy sensation. What was it? Someone watching me? I straightened up, swung my bag up over my shoulder and looked slowly round towards the wood, across the heath. No-one there. No-one on the path back to the road. But behind me, staring through a gap in the hedge, were two small girls. The twins. One sucked her thumb, staring unblinking at my feet. One looked me in the eye, bracing herself.

'Hello,' she said.

'Hello.' My phoney French accent had vanished. The big black Freeloader roared out of the Close and down the hill, thumping out 'Another One Bites the Dust'.

'We don't like the Daddy,' the girl said.

I turned back to her. 'Don't you?'

'We asked Momma for a new one.'

'Oh?'

'Are you the new one?'

I gulped. 'No,' I said. 'No, sorry.'

'Oh,' she said, studying me. 'You gave us a nice book.'

'I did. Dogger.'

'When the Daddy smashed the car, Momma said you might be.'

'Eh?'

'We see you at a bus stop.'

'Do you?'

'Yes. Momma says you catch a bus. I never catched a bus.'

'You should. It's fun.'

'Give me your moustache.'

I pulled off the false moustache and handed it to her.

'Thank you,' she said. 'Bye.'

'Bye,' I said. She had better manners than her father.

She took her sister's hand. They disappeared through the hedge.

I shook myself, wondering where all that came from.

Halfway to the stile I paused and looked back across the heath. The fugitive was lost in the wood's deep shadow. He'd hidden himself well so far. I threw a telepathic 'Good luck – you're going to need it' to him over my shoulder, and to the two girls in the garden, and their Momma. And another to Conrad: I'd a feeling he was going to need it just as much as his poor little bugger of a son.

You reap what you sow, I thought. *One man gathers what another man spills and all that.* But what an interesting evening it had been.

À bientôt, Sefton-Shaws.

CHAPTER 7

DETECTIVE INSPECTOR JONES

Jones woke his phone. 11.23, Friday 19th May. Four minutes since he last looked. He was hungry. The canteen didn't start lunches until quarter to twelve. Even then it wouldn't do to be first in line. He'd heard sniggers from uniforms in the car park when he couldn't reach to tie a shoelace. He didn't like it.

He skimmed through his notes for the end-of-week staff meeting. They'd do. He buzzed his secretary. Rita's head appeared round the door. He held out a sheet for her to type up and circulate.

'Your wife called, sir,' she said. 'Didn't want to disturb, just said to have a look at your email.'

His first thought was a worry about their girls. They seemed to be doing well at school – and so they should, after what he had to do to keep them there. Fees for boarders added up to forty-five thousand per child per year. No wonder they were broke. And wouldn't his old ma have given him grief? She'd hated private education, but what could you do? They'd certainly suffer in a local state school, rubbing shoulders with kids he'd crossed or whose parents he'd put away.

He opened the message. From an estate agent, initiated by Jones's wife Olwen: 'Check out this 4-bedroom detached house for sale in Landimore, Gower, Swansea, SA3'. They knew Landimore – a fabulous location. It was on the quieter side of the Gower, near Llanmadoc, where Olwen's oldest friend lived. They'd passed some merry evenings with her and her husband in their local, the Britannia.

He read through the details. Three reception rooms, orangery, balcony... garage, workshop, greenhouse... an acre of garden, a small woodland, views across salt marsh and estuary to the Carmarthenshire coast. No wonder she'd picked it out: their dream. But even if you added up the value of their current house, all their savings and the maximum lump sum from his pension, they'd still be well short.

He checked the time again. 12.10. He could go for lunch without looking overly desperate. He stood and pulled his jacket on. His phone showed an alert: a Signal message from Alleyn: *19th 2pm be there.*

What did he want now? There was always something, these days. Jones's mind leapt back ten years. Fresh up from Cardiff, he'd been coping nervously with his first Saturday night duty. The front desk called him down to look at a guy that Traffic had left in the holding tank, clocked at eighty miles per hour in a thirty limit, fifty micrograms over on the breathalyser. The desk sergeant wanted to order a blood test but the guy was asking for the duty CID officer.

Jones had found a big, well-dressed, well-spoken gentleman, not far off his own age. The guy explained how he'd been having a beer after a round of golf – did Jones play himself, by the way? – when he'd had a call from the hospital, where his wife was in very premature labour. He'd just jumped in the car and raced off without thinking. He apologised, wouldn't dream of doing anything like that in normal circumstances. Jones knew how it felt; six years earlier, something similar had happened with his own wife and their second daughter. Jones had rung the desk and arranged for a squad car to run the man straight up to the maternity unit.

Two days later a gift had arrived, a thirty-year-old Aberfeldy, with a note saying, 'Help me wet the baby's head!', and an application form for the Hinksey Heath Golf Club, with the name James Alleyn inked in as sponsor. He didn't want to appear ungracious. He'd hung on to the whisky and sent in an application to the golf club.

A mistake. A first small step onto a slippery slope. Now Alleyn's contributions paid the school fees and more, and Alleyn thought he could demand a crash meet at any time. It was bloody inconvenient sometimes though, like today. He'd have to ask Grant to run this afternoon's meeting for a start. Grant would love that, and the team would no doubt think he'd done it better than Jones ever did.

***

At two thirty Jones took another large G&T to his table by a window overlooking the green of the eighteenth hole. He was waiting for James Alleyn in the bar of Hinksey Heath Golf Club, The 19th Hole. Alleyn was half an hour late. Jones cringed at each gust of laughter from the only other occupants, a group in the corner who looked like they'd stepped out of an Orvis catalogue and had overdone the liquid aspect of lunch. He thought about asking Traffic to run some breathalyser checks at the exit, but thought better of it; the bastards would jump at the chance of testing him too.

He sipped his G&T, gazing mesmerised at a swirl of starlings over the trees lining the eighteenth. Lucky things. Free, not a care…

A slap on the back jolted him forward, his teeth clanking on the rim of his glass, drink spluttering and spilling down his chest. Alleyn towered over him, unapologetic. Jones said nothing and forced himself to stay calm.

'Clubs?' Alleyn said.

Jones nodded at the door.

'Come on then!' Alleyn strode off, as if it was Jones that was late, and led the way to the first tee. 'Ball,' he said. Jones handed him a ball marked with a yellow spot. Alleyn added it to the red-spotted ball already in his hand and tossed them in the air. Jones's ball came to rest a yard away; Alleyn's rolled twice as far.

Alleyn teed off. Jones followed, playing badly. He sank a nine-inch putt for a treble bogey at the fifth and marked his card. Twelve strokes behind. He should be somewhere else.

'It's no fun beating you if you're not trying,' Alleyn said. 'Let's turn here, make it just the nine.'

Jones agreed. They crossed to the fifteenth.

Alleyn leaned on his driver at the tee and looked round. There was no-one in sight. 'A word,' he said. 'Strictly need-to-know. Not a dicky-bird to anyone.'

'Okay.' Jones shrugged. Did he have a choice?

Alleyn looked round again. 'Something significant is being put together,' he said, 'to do with some development land. Ballator will be bidding. Okay?'

'Where is it?'

'The land? Between Water Eaton and Kingsbridge. Glebe Farm, it's called.'

Jones knew it. Olwen went sketching by there, on a nature reserve. 'Isn't that green belt?' he said. 'What's the development?'

'Green belt means nothing, legally,' Alleyn said, 'though that doesn't stop people bleating about it. There'll be a science park, enterprise zone, techno-incubator hub, retail park... you know, part of the Growth Arc.'

'Oh.' Jones felt deflated. His wife wasn't going to like that at all. 'Expecting opposition?'

'Only lightweight,' Alleyn said. 'But make sure you're the one that's dealing with it. We want to know who they are and where they live.'

'Well…'

'Bastards think they can get away with anything. We don't want any of this lying-down-in-front-of-bulldozers bullshit. It can really delay things.'

'It's not illegal, you know, peaceful protest. In most cases. Not yet, anyway. Obviously we'd keep an eye, intervene if they did start breaking…'

'These bastards can create a lot of trouble without breaking the law. We don't want to be dealing with them. That's your job.'

Not really, but he wasn't going to argue nuts and bolts before he had the full picture. He stared at the starlings, now swirling over Chilswell Farm. *There's skating on thin ice,* he thought, *and we've done a lot of that. Why do I feel as if he's going to ask me to walk on water? In concrete boots.*

'Here's the deal, on top of the usual retainer,' Alleyn said. 'Fifty K now, to come on board, and the same when the land deal goes through, nice and quietly. Which will be in a couple of months. How about that?'

Jones had a queasy feeling. It was a lot of money. Not as much as he needed to close the gap on the house on the Gower. And it wouldn't be money for nothing. Agreeing to anything with Alleyn was always the thin end of a wedge, and he hardly dared think about what Olwen would say, if she ever found out, which God forbid. 'A hundred altogether,' he said. 'Why?'

'There's big money in this one deal,' Alleyn said, 'but more important, it's setting a precedent that's worth billions, down the track. That's why it must be done under the radar, without bad publicity. You'll just be doing your job, in a way that helps make that happen.'

'Make it two hundred,' Jones said, 'if it's that important.'

'You're trying it on,' Alleyn said.

Jones just looked at him.

'All right, I'll find out. No promises.'

'What if I say no?'

'I thought you'd be pleased. You're saying to stop the retainer too?'

Jones shook his head. That wasn't possible.

'Frankly, you're not in a position to pick and choose,' Alleyn said, looking round again. 'We know how important family is to you. Your daughters' education. Your plans to retire to sunny Wales. You'd not want to jeopardise your pension with a misconduct case. You'd not want anything to happen to the lovely Olwen. Or to the girls.'

Jones felt a chill. He didn't like this one bit. He looked across the flat flood plain of the Thames, to the spires and tower blocks of the city. How had he got himself into this? Everything he'd done, he'd done for his wife and daughters. Now they were at risk too. He squared up to Alleyn. 'Are you threatening my family?'

Alleyn just turned his back, placed his ball on the tee, settled his feet and rehearsed his swing. Jones ducked and stepped back.

Alleyn drove hard down the fairway. The ball bounced twice and rolled up onto the green. Alleyn strode after it.

CHAPTER 8

On Friday lunchtime, I took a cheese salad baguette down to Bonn Square, hoping to catch the busking Venezuelans. But there was a three-piece band on the corner playing 'Nearer My God To Thee' and the square was full of people with banners, protesting about over-development and climate change. I had to be back at work otherwise I might have joined them. But probably not.

I perched on a free bit of step by the memorial, munching away and feeding crumbs to pushy pigeons. A small girl, four or five years old, was feeding them too. And I looked and thought it couldn't be, surely. But it was. Because her mother was calling her back and the mother was Kimberly, and the girl had turned in my direction and she was one of the twins. The other was sitting beside her mother a few yards away.

The girl ignored her mother and looked me in the eye. 'I keep it in a box,' she said quietly.

'What?'

'The moustache. I stroke it. It tickles.'

'Bella, come here,' came from her mother, who was giving me a look that said something. *Go away. Leave her alone.* Or, *help me out here. Get her an ice-cream. Get me a coffee.* Or something.

'It does tickle, you're right,' I said. 'And fancy meeting you here,' I said to Kimberly. 'You're not here for the climate protest, then?'

'Not really. Conrad had some of his cronies round. The girls are off school and he doesn't like them playing, making a noise. Doesn't want me around either, poking my nose in, as he calls it. So we came for new shoes. Look.'

'Yes, very nice,' I said. One had black patent leather, the other tan suede. Pale crepe soles.

'But I'd heard about the demo and we did join 'til they got hungry. I'm all for it.'

'But you drive that massive Audi,' I said, realising I was being presumptuous, but not caring. 'How does that square with…'

'You don't think that's my choice, do you?'

'Dunno.' I'd assumed it was.

'Well, it's not. We should talk about that some time. But listen. You're a kind person, actually, aren't you? You could do me a favour.'

'Yes?'

'Keep an eye on these two for a minute while I pop to the loo. I'm desperate. This is Bella, this is Charlotte. You can tell them a story. Girls, listen. This gentleman's called Mick. He gave you the Dogger book. He's going to tell you a story. Okay? Won't be long. Be good.'

She dumped her bags and picnic blanket by me and hurried away. I was flattered that she trusted me with her children, but it really was not the sort of thing I was used to. I wasn't sure what to do. The girls sat either side of me, looking expectant.

'Hello Bella. Hello Charlotte,' I said.

'Hello,' Bella said.

I cleared my throat.

'Story,' said Bella.

'Okay,' I said. 'How do stories start?'

'Once upon a time,' from Bella.

'Yes. What next?'

'There was a beautiful princess.' Bella again.

'Good. What do we know about her? Apart from that she's beautiful.'

'She was good and kind,' Bella said.

'And she was married to a cruel, horrible man,' from Charlotte.

'What did he do that was cruel and horrible?'

'He was a prince. And he kept the princess locked in her room,' from Bella.

'In a dark dungeon under the palace,' from Charlotte.

'That is cruel and horrible, you're right. So...'

'One day a young woodcutter drove past on his cart. He heard her singing.' Bella.

'The princess was singing in the dungeon? And the woodcutter heard her.'

'Yes. In the dungeon under the palace.' Charlotte.

'What was she singing?'

'A song. And there was a fairy who made a spell and he fell in love.' Bella.

'Who fell in love?'

'The woodcutter.'

'With the fairy?'

'No, silly.'

'With the singing princess?'

'Yes.'

'He fell in love because of the spell?'

'Yes. But he would have anyway. And he fighted the prince and he killed him,' said Bella.

'With a big knife,' from Charlotte. 'And he rescued the princess.'

This wasn't so difficult. I'd begun to enjoy myself. But I saw their mother coming back. She'd made me feel like this before: relieved but also disappointed. We waited while she settled back on the blanket. 'Did you have a story?' she said.

'We made a story,' Bella said. 'I'll tell it again. Once upon a time there was a beautiful princess. She was good and kind and she was married to a cruel, horrible man who was a prince. He kept the princess locked in a dark dungeon under the palace. One day a young woodcutter drove past on his cart. He heard her singing in the dungeon.'

'She was singing a song,' Charlotte said.

'Yes,' Bella said. 'And a fairy made a spell and the woodcutter fell in love with the princess and he fighted the prince and he killed him with a knife and he rescued the princess. That's where we were.'

'It is,' I said. 'Well remembered.'

'And,' Bella said, 'the woodcutter married the princess and looked after her and her two little girls and they all lived happily ever after.'

'The princess had two little girls? What a lovely story!' from their mother. 'Thank you. Do you come here often?'

'Do I come here often?' I said, thinking what an odd encounter this was. 'Now and then, I suppose. Often on a Friday, I guess.'

'Thought so. Good.'

'What? Why?' Someone had asked my mum some odd questions, like what did I do for lunch? Surely that couldn't have been Kimberly?

'We'll look out for you. Say goodbye, girls.'

'Goodbye.'

The square seemed empty when they'd gone, though it was still full of people. I realised I hadn't thought about Conrad and his threats once, despite meeting his wife and defying his dictum. I noticed two women amongst the protestors, sharing an enigmatic banner:

STOP THE EXPRESSWAY
SAVE THE DORMICE
LEARN TO CHANGE OR LEARN TO SWIM

At one end, a cherubic blonde. At the other, the dark-haired waitress from Harry's. I went back to work but couldn't concentrate. I knocked off early, promising to catch up over the weekend.

***

The next morning, back from a jog with Friday, I could smell gas before I even reached the flat door. I opened it just an inch, sniffed, shut it, went back outside, Googled 'gas leak' and called the number. They told me they'd have someone there in five, and to clear the block.

Everyone was in this early on a Saturday morning. Some weren't all that pleased to be woken and urged onto the street. I was still urging people out when two vans arrived. We all handed over keys. Three gas men and a gas woman went in wearing hazmat suits. Five minutes later, the woman came out and called me over.

'We found the leak in the hall cupboard, by the meter,' she said. 'The damage looks like sabotage. And we found this card in your letterbox.'

The card was in a plastic bag. She held it out for me. It said: 'BANG YOUR DEAD'.

'We've notified the police,' she said. 'They'll be over soon. You need to be careful. This could have destroyed the whole block.'

Bloody Conrad again, I thought. *Can't punctuate and doesn't care who he kills and maims*. He must have found out I was with Kimberly in Bonn Square yesterday. I couldn't see him doing it himself – watching until I went out, picking the locks, taking a bolt-cutter to the gas-pipe, getting out again without being spotted. He must have people he can send out on that sort of mission.

Gail arrived to pick me up just before eleven. The police still hadn't shown and when I phoned no-one knew what I was talking about, so I left it. Gail and I were going up to Boars Hill, to implement a plan she'd come up with that seemed like a natural escalation of my "take the piss out of Conrad" project. After this morning's excitement I was even more determined to go through with it. I was worried that the plan might be compromised by Wednesday's artistic exchanges with the Sefton-Shaws, but not worried enough to mention it to Gail. Not yet, anyway. Or to change the plan. I liked it too much.

In line with the plan, I'd shaved, combed, gelled and parted my hair, and put on a suit and tie and proper shoes, and dug out a gold-edged Bible bound in soft leather that had once belonged to my great-grandmother.

Gail wore black patent shoes, a calf-length navy skirt and buttoned-up matching top, and a string of what looked like real pearls. She was carrying a stack of folded A5 leaflets with a picture of panicked sheep and a handsome bearded and robed man on the front, under a prominent banner heading: THE WATCHTOWER.

The Witnesses were coming to call.

We parked in the empty Foxcombe Hall car park, in the shade of a copper beech. Nothing was happening in Berkeley Close. Gail wound her pearls into an iridescent tangle. She seemed to have stage fright.

'A quick rehearsal?' I said, a bit nervy too.

'Idiotic,' she said. 'Should never rehearse in real life. Didn't you know that?'

'No.' I was only trying to help. 'Why not?'

'Get it right in rehearsal, you'll be over-confident and get it wrong when you do it for real. Get it wrong in rehearsal, you'll be even more nervous than you are already and completely cock it up.'

There was a perverse logic to that. I tried a different tack. 'Let's hit the roof of the car with rolled-up newspapers for a few minutes instead.'

'If we must.'

We shared out yesterday's Guardian, and got stuck in. There were no passers-by to notice, fortunately. I explained that the boss at work had enrolled the entire staff on a positive thinking "Close Your Sale!" course that nearly bankrupted us. The only bit that wasn't completely counter-productive was hitting the car with a rolled-up newspaper, to get in the right mood for a challenging meeting.

Gail loosened up immediately. I was still on edge after the gas incident, and wasn't hitting the car with full attention. I was also conscious that there were things I should have told her and hadn't, like how my French artist persona had tried to sell dodgy drawings to Conrad to distract him from his escaping son, and all that.

Three men came out of the house. Alleyn, the lawyer I'd lunched with at Harry's; Conrad's itchy companion that same day; and Conrad himself. So these three were on more than saying-hi-in-a-restaurant terms; they were lunchtime-drinks-at-home buddies. I wondered what Sefton-Shaw did, apart from threatening innocent bystanders, boozing with cronies and being unkind to waitresses, wives and children. Something to do with the city council, Kanhai had thought.

'They had visitors. Recognise anyone?' Gail said.

'That tall dark one. James Alleyn, a lawyer, and a sales prospect for my employers, Hypermedia. I was doing tech support for our sales guy and we took him for lunch. Sefton-Shaw was at another table with the other guy, the seedy one. Aways scratching. And two – what can I say? – rather expensive-looking young ladies.'

'Conrad won't recognise you?'

'He might, I suppose. But I've only met him two or three times. Once when he crashed into the bus. Once at the bus stop. He had someone else do the hammer stuff at my flat. Then Harry's, where he didn't see me. Then the other night, when I was observing the house disguised as an artist.'

'That's four or five, not two or three.'

'Okay. But he's always preoccupied with something, you know? So he doesn't actually look at what's in front of him. I'm in a different disguise now. You're going to do most of the talking, aren't you? And what if he does recognise me? What's the worst that can happen?'

'Hope we don't find out,' she said. She looked less than delighted. She straightened her pearls and her shoulders. 'So. The Bothy first. For authenticity. Not rehearsal.'

She rang The Bothy's doorbell. I knocked on the knocker.

We waited.

The curtains twitched.

The sound of a key. The door opened.

A sharp face peered out. Sharp eyes looked us up and down.

'Good afternoon,' Gail said, smiling, stepping forward.

The door slammed shut. A key turned.

'How rude,' Gail said. 'But at least it suggests that we look the part.'

We walked on to Springfield House. Gail pressed the buzzer and fronted up. The opening bars of Glenn Miller's 'In The Mood' rang out.

We waited.

It went quiet. We heard footsteps and the door creaked open.

Dark eyes, long black hair, wide smile. Black T-shirt with a stylised sky-blue tree on the front. *Yggdrasil.* Faded cut-off denims, tanned legs. Embroidered orange and blue mandalas on black espadrilles. A scent that made me close my eyes and breathe in.

And in.

I opened my eyes.

Kimberly was gazing into them.

'Hello,' she said quietly. 'I'm so glad you came.'

It was almost as if we were expected. Or I was.

She looked at Gail and said, 'My husband's in his office. I know he'd be pleased to chat. Straight in front of you at the top of the stairs.'

She made a shooing motion.

Gail blinked and looked at me. She was in disguise and had only met Conrad once, years ago. It would be perfect if she could spy out the territory up there and steer him away from coming down and finding me with Kimberly. But I didn't want to pressure her. I shrugged. She went up.

Kimberly waited until Gail was out of sight. 'Come,' she said, then turned and walked away.

Gail and I had lost the initiative immediately. Might as well go with the flow. I followed Kimberly along a corridor into a sitting room at the back of the house. Parquet floor, sofa, fireplace, logs, TV, well-stocked drinks cabinet.

She closed the door behind us, turned a key in the lock, left the key there. To stop anyone coming in, rather than to stop me getting out, I guessed.

She seemed to be studying my face, working something out. 'How've you been? I always give you a wave at the bus stop. Makes my day, on the average morning. But I'm never sure you've seen me.'

I didn't get why someone like her would find me interesting. At best I'm Mr Average looks-wise, and tend to the boring, by all accounts, conversation-wise. I didn't know what she wanted.

'Conrad thinks you're stalking him, with your bird watching and frisbee throwing. And he's even more angry, after that French artist bit. Took him in, until he clocked the business card. So watch out. And now you're a God-botherer. Well. I know better, don't I?'

'Do you?' I asked, on shaky ground.

'How did you track me down?'

'An insurance form, from that bus crash. It had your address. Why did you think it was you I was tracking down?'

'Because you were. But why did you have to turn up with that woman? She's not your big sister. Or aunt. Or mum. Not really a Jehovah's, is she?'

I shook my head.

'Anyway,' she said, softening and smiling. 'You're here now. That's what matters. And there's something you might be able to help me with. Would you mind?'

I tried to focus on the here and now, and ignore the man upstairs who might well kill me if he found me here. 'Of course not,' I said. Sometimes, good manners are all you have. So when she lay down on the rug in front of the fireplace, and reached into the hearth to point up the chimney, and explained that the thingy that kept the chimney closed off in summer, to keep the draught out, was stuck, and her useless husband hadn't even tried to unstick it, I felt obliged to do what I could.

I knelt on the rug. Lay on my side. Tried to see what she was reaching for.

'It's just here,' she said, guiding my hand, which for some reason was trembling. Shaking, actually. She was very close. Our shoulders touched. Our hips touched. It occurred to me that I was lying next to a very real, fully feminine grown-up woman. *Get a grip*, I thought. And I got a grip, on a rounded metal loop projecting from behind the cowl.

'That's it,' she said. 'You should be able to just pull it towards you.'

I hooked the fingers of my left hand through the loop and found her fingers there too. Our faces were two inches apart. I could feel her breath on my lips. Good manners rarely took me into situations like this.

'Come on,' she said. 'I'm sure we can do it. Both together.'

I pulled warily. Nothing budged. I glanced round the room. No-one was going to burst in on us; the door was locked, curtains were drawn over the French doors. What was going on upstairs, with Gail and Conrad? I could rely on Gail to play her part, I was sure.

I braced myself with a hand on Kimberly's shoulder, said, 'Okay... one, two, three... now!' and gave a sharp pull. It came all the way to the end of its travel in a rush. I rolled across her, unbalanced. My arm slipped round her shoulders, seeking support. The thing up the chimney hardly seemed to have been stuck at all.

'Oops, sorry,' I said.

'Don't apologise,' she murmured, her arm over my waist. 'Just hold still a minute.' Our eyes met. I tried to untangle myself, not very hard.

The door shook.

Oh no. Conrad? No more violence, please.

The door rattled.

Stopped.

Rattled again.

I was up on my knees, on my feet, looking down at her, feeling all sorts of things.

A child shrieked, 'Momma! Momma!' from the hall.

I breathed out.

'Yes Bella, what is it?'

'Momma! Alasdair's taken Charlotte prisoner. He says he's going to execute her.'

'Oh my God.' She rolled on to her back, raised her arms. 'Haul me up. Better see what this is all about.'

I grasped her hands. Pulled her up. Let go.

She unlocked the door and opened it to the teary face of one of the twins. 'Don't worry, Bella,' she said, clasping the girl to her. 'Let's go and sort it out.' She pushed the girl towards the door but Bella resisted, staring past her, staring at me.

'Momma,' she said, 'this is the nice man who gave me a moustache.'

'What?'

'When Alasdair set fire to our Wendy house.'

Kimberly looked at me, amused. 'A nice man, is he?'

'Yes. Much nicer than the Daddy. Can we...'

'That'll do. We need to see to your sister.'

'But is this the new...'

'Hush now,' Kimberly said, forcing her through the door. 'Hush. Come on.'

Halfway through the door she turned back to me.

'Come again. When himself's at work and they're at school. Bring your Bible, if you want.'

She winked and was gone.

I felt like the snow in one of those snowstorm shakers.

Back in the hall, Gail was coming downstairs with a puzzled frown, carrying the sort of short whip that jockeys use.

I called the police again when I got home, to see if they'd been trying to track me down about the gas leak. They had no record of the report.

CHAPTER 9

I felt like I'd poked a hornets' nest with a stick and it was only a matter of time before they came back at us, but the next week was blessedly quiet.

Early the following Saturday morning I walked by the river with Friday in a sparkling dawn and pondered some imponderables. Like, the police had no record of the gas leak: was that bureaucratic inefficiency, or did Conrad have a helping hand in the cop shop?

Was Kimberly really interested in me, or was it just my imagination? I'd be delighted if anyone fancied me, over the moon if it was the waitress from Harry's. But Kimberly? Beyond unlikely. And how had she known so much about my attempts at covert observation? Seemed like I hadn't achieved covertness at all. Was I playing out of my league in that sense too?

I'd also like to know what had gone on upstairs between Gail and Conrad, though perhaps that was a stone better left unturned.

I biked down the canal to Summertown, shopped at the Co-Op, went into a quiet nine a.m. coffee shop across the street. I sat in the window with a flat white, reflecting on the range of human varieties passing a dull corner of a dull city in a dull country. Then I saw Gail, cutting like a clipper through wallowing tugs, on course to pass close by my window.

I leapt up, banged on the glass, waved, to dark looks from baristas, a raised brow from the other customer, startlement from Gail. I beckoned and ordered her a cappuccino.

'I'm glad I saw you,' I said as she sat down. 'The other day I was so busy telling you about me that I didn't even ask you what went on with Conrad upstairs. But I can't stop thinking about it now.'

'Never mind that,' she said, brandishing the Oxford Times, index finger stabbing a photograph. 'Look! Was going to call about this.'

The headline said, GLEBE FARM PROJECT APPROVED. She pushed it under my nose, her finger tapping a photograph of Conrad Sefton-Shaw outside County Hall. He looked angry, as usual. But my eye was drawn to another picture attached to the same story: four people by a five-barred gate. On the right of the group, a twenty-something woman, long dark hair, face stern in half-profile: the waitress, from Harry's Hash House. The caption said, 'Protest leaders, from left: Glebe Farm tenants Tom and Linda Simpson; Andrea Turner, Small Mammals Officer at the Wildlife Trust; Naomi Goodman of Affordable Oxford.'

Naomi Goodman. I knew where I'd seen her before. At a community meeting, in Cutteslowe Pavilion, years ago. She'd spoken, raising pledges to underwrite a bid for the old university depot, just off the ring road. I'd signed up, quite taken with the co-housing idea, and with the dark young woman promoting it.

The bid had come to nothing – some big builder got it. I'd not seen her since, until I half-recognised her, out of context, in the restaurant. And here she was, back in context, seriously protesting a planning decision.

'I know her. Sort of.'

'Who's that?' Gail said, reading where I was pointing. 'Naomi Goodman. Don't know about her. But look. Conrad Sefton-Shaw. Director for Sustainable Development, Oxford City Council.'

'Sustainable my arse.'

'Well, yes. But it's him. Very strange man, actually.' She frowned, shook her head. 'And if you read the article…'

I skimmed it.

'What do you think of this vision of his?' Gail said. 'Oxfordshire will be full of busy-ness, wherever there used to be fields and woods.'

'I don't like it, obviously. Who in their right mind would? But there's nothing you can do about it.'

'These people think there is. Naomi thinks there is.'

She was right. That was interesting. Should I be doing something about it too?

'So shall we go?' Gail said.

'To the protest?'

'Yes. It's at the entrance to this place, Glebe Farm,' Gail said. 'Ten thirty this morning.'

'Today? Will Naomi be there?'

'Suppose so, she's one of the organisers. Does it matter?'

'Half nine now. Can't be more than a mile away. We could walk it and be there by ten.'

'I've got my bike,' Gail said, nodding to the bike rack outside the bank.

'Me too. Let's go.'

***

It was more like two miles on the roads, then off the A44 road through an open gateway, along a rough track between hedges and across a hundred yards of meadow that was already halfway to being a building site, large mounds of gravel either side of the track.

We laid our bikes behind a mound in a tangle of nettles and knapweed and walked across to a closed five-barred gate. A sign on it said:

GLEBE FARM ONLY
No Public Access
For Dunmore Copse Reserve please
use Stratton Brake – Nether Eaton bridleway.

A well-kept hedge ran left and right from the gate, which was latched but not locked. 'We're early,' I said. 'Unless it's somewhere else.'

'Look,' Gail said, pointing back the way we'd come. Two big white Police vans had turned off the main road – riot control vans, with protective mesh shields. Walking down the track in front of them were twenty-odd assorted people. The first van sounded its horn and pushed up right behind the people, who were refusing to get out of its way. Both vans pulled off the track, onto the meadow, and roared past the walkers in low gear.

'And look,' I said, pointing up the track the other side of the gate. An oldish couple were approaching on foot. The farmers. I knew the man from around the village; he did things with horses on the common. And I knew her by sight.

Gail and I seemed to be at the focal point of all approaching parties. I didn't like it. 'Not keen on this,' I said. 'Let's get out of the way.'

I set off along the hedge, away from the gate. Gail followed. She looked puzzled, but I didn't mind. I wanted to watch a while, not start off in the middle of something I knew nothing about. I stopped when we reached a point where the hedge gave way to post-and-rail fencing. We leaned on the fence. My eyes caught a skylark in the field beyond, rising vertically for two feet, then flying low and flat for thirty yards before spiralling up and singing like a star. Further across the field, a handful of square-winged birds wheeled and zoomed. Lapwings. Long parallels of ancient ridge and furrow met close to infinity on the far side, where something like a curlew stalked through long reedy grass. This was a nice place.

Gail nudged my arm. 'Back there,' she said.

The couple who I took to be the farmers were now in front of the gate, flanked by people with placards. The police vans were parked side by side, about fifty yards back. A semi-circle of police in visored helmets, carrying large transparent shields, outnumbered the crowd, which they seemed to be penning against the gate. More officers were busy closer to the van: one with a camera and telephoto lens trained on the protestors; two in uniform and one in plain clothes, standing watching. The only female officer present was setting out what looked like refreshments on a long white folding table.

Between the semi-circle of police and the crowd by the gate, another man with a camera and a woman with a microphone, presumably local press, were talking to two women protestors. One was Naomi. They kept looking down the track as though expecting another arrival.

My grandad had survived a spell in the army by keeping his head down.

'I don't want to be in any police photos. Or press, come to that,' I said. 'Wouldn't go down well at work. Especially as that's where I was supposed to be about an hour ago.'

'On Saturday?' Gail said. 'Oh. Hadn't thought of that. What do you want to do?'

'Drift back to the bikes and just keep an eye on things?'

We crossed the meadow in a wide arc, towards where the bikes were stashed, a hundred yards behind the police vans. As we approached, a big black SUV roared off the main road and bounced along the track, raising clouds of grey dust. Registration KSS 69. It came to a histrionic halt by the vans. A big balding man got out. Angry Conrad.

'Look,' I said. 'Here he is.'

He marched up, shouldered the press people aside, and began a shouting match with Naomi and her friend. The press camera person was shooting away, delighted. The police photographer seemed to be looking at a hedge.

'I can't do it,' I said. 'Just isn't my thing. And if I left now I'd be in work by twelve.'

'Before you go,' Gail said, pulling out the newspaper she'd brandished in the café. 'Just think. Your friend Naomi…'

'I wish.'

'Well, yes. And her friends. Look.' She pointed at the text. 'Andrea Turner, Small Mammals Officer at the Wildlife Trust. Their Dunmore Copse reserve is over there somewhere. That's her, with Naomi now. And there's the Simpsons, the Glebe Farm tenants, being evicted.'

'Yes, I know him, the farmer,' I said, 'from the village.' I studied the demonstrators. They all looked pissed off with angry Conrad.

'You can tell, can't you? They really don't like him.' She was looking at me in expectation. Or exasperation.

'Good spot,' I said.

She nodded, clearly expecting more.

'Are you saying…?' I was trying to sense what was in her mind. 'You're saying there might be…'

'A confluence of interest. Yes. Between them and us. Conrad Sefton-Shaw practically killed my mother. Wants to kill you. Treats people like peasants. The city's Director for Sustainable Development, who only sustains the green belt by building over it, according to these people. And has a terrible record on affordable housing. And now he's throwing those two off their farm. Where they've been for…'

'Nearly two hundred years, it said. Their family.'

'They're very upset.'

'They are, aren't they? Food for thought.'

The crowd seemed to be chanting 'Stop the Orc. Stop the Orc.' Engaging with these protestors could offer ways for me and Gail to get back at Conrad, certainly. But there was another possible confluence of interest, I thought. It could also lead to my crossing paths with Naomi again, when she wasn't being a waitress. Who knew where that might lead?

'We're all pissed off with him.'

'Yes,' Gail said. 'That's what we have in common.'

'So perhaps we could work together. Let's invite them to a pissed-off party,' I said, pulling out my phone, opening my diary, 'How about…'

She frowned. 'What's that? Never been to one.'

'No?'

'What happens?'

'Like bring and share. But opinions and ideas, rather than food and drink.'

'Oh. Are you going to ask them now?'

'No, they're busy. But it shouldn't be a problem. I'll contact Naomi through Affordable Oxford. She'll be in touch with the others. I'll send an invitation. RSVP and all that. In a pub. Early evening, a Monday so it'll be quiet. In Jericho.'

CHAPTER 10

DETECTIVE INSPECTOR JONES

Jones paused in the open doorway to the Chief Constable's office, trying to breathe normally. The Chief looked up from the newspaper that lay open on her desk. 'Are we on top of these demonstrations?'

She always looks so cool and collected, Jones thought. It was a hot morning, and like an idiot he'd tried to run up the first flight of stairs. He'd taken the lift from there, but was suffering.

'Yes ma'am,' he said. He wanted his jacket off for coolness, but kept it on to cover sweaty armpits, and took a handkerchief to his liquid forehead. 'There were twenty-two protestors at Glebe Farm the other day. Though two of them were ours. Most melted away when the uniforms moved in.' He realised the handkerchief was one of his wife's paint rags, crusted with pigment. He pushed it into a pocket, hoping he didn't look like a pointilliste landscape. 'The local media made it look bigger, but the nationals didn't pick it up. In fact, is that the story there?' He could read the headline, upside down, from his position just inside the door.

'Take a seat,' she said. 'Tell me about these people.'

She was interested in a very modest demonstration. It was surprising, but made things easier, in that he could use police resources to answer Alleyn's questions without worrying. But it was odd that the Chief Constable and Alleyn wanted the same information. He didn't know why, and something told him he should. 'The four in that picture, they're the main movers,' he said. 'They were really getting in the face of Sefton-Shaw. Actually, do you know him?' He thought it was worth fishing. Sefton-Shaw was director level in the council and might well have contacts, influence even, in the upper echelons of the Force. 'If you don't mind me asking.'

'I meet all the senior council officers, it's part of the job. Well, you've kept it fairly low-profile so far. Best it stays that way.'

'Understood, ma'am.' She hadn't taken the bait, but her oblique deflection of his question was suggestive. She did know Sefton-Shaw, directly or through someone senior like the Commissioner, or the council's chief exec. She didn't want to tell him an outright lie, but also didn't want him digging around there. And she didn't just want the same information as Alleyn: she wanted the same outcome, everything kept quiet. Curious.

'Just run me through who they are, these main movers.'

'Thomas and Linda Simpson, the farm tenants,' he said, pointing. 'No record. Naomi Goodman, waitress. No record, but known associates have gone down for drugs and firearms offences. And Andrea Turner, Wildlife Trust officer. No convictions, but an arrest record as long as your arm. Interfering with hunts, assault, obstruction, violent assembly, round here and across the UK.' He had done a bit of unofficial digging and decided he may as well share it. 'I had an informal word with a contact at the trust, one of Ms Turner's colleagues. She says Turner's brilliant at her job and it's not their business what she does outside work. I'd a feeling she'd like to be protesting too, actually.'

'Who's she, then?'

'Well, just a contact, you know?' He wanted to bite back the words. The contact was a long-standing student in his wife's contemporary painting group. He'd bumped into her when he dropped Olwen off for the class last Thursday, realised she would know Turner, and broken a golden rule of keeping work and family completely separate.

'I see,' she said, looking down at her notes. They were both aware, he thought, that there was less than complete openness on both sides. 'Are you monitoring movements and communications?'

It felt like she was asking questions she'd been told to ask, surprisingly detailed questions. 'That would be routine, ma'am, yes,' he said. And it was almost true, certainly within his discretion, given Goodman's associates and Turner's arrest record. 'But we only pick up open comms channels. With apps like…'

'Yes, WhatsApp and Signal. Encrypted. But with those, I think you can still pick up that there is a message, from X to Y, even if you don't know what's in it?'

'Not without the co-operation of the app provider, ma'am. And only in exceptional circumstances.'

'You might put together a request for such co-operation, just in case.'

'Yes, ma'am,' he said. Why was she pushing so hard on this? It was just a run of the mill demo, small, peaceful. The brass had never paid attention to such things in the past. Good to have her backing, though. 'So you would authorise it?'

'Of course. And thank you for the paper on dead sharks. Wild goose? Red herring?'

'Yes, ma'am,' he said, 'in my opinion.' Partly because that's what she seemed to want to hear, but also because he couldn't see a way of pursuing it without talking to whoever had slipped the phrase into the Commissioner's ear. His phone vibrated in his pocket. 'Will that be all for now?'

***

He took the lift down, checked his phone. A Signal message from Alleyn: *Call me.*

It was almost as if Alleyn had known he'd been with the Chief. But how could he? Jones checked his watch. Quarter to four. He'd planned to pop into the canteen for tea and Welsh-cakes on the way back to the SPAT room, but decided to make the call first.

'Jones.' Alleyn sounded busy. 'Two things.'

'Fire away.' *He's getting into a habit of issuing orders,* Jones thought. *He could take that too far.*

'Send me everything you have on those tossers at Glebe Farm on Saturday.'

'The protestors? Okay. There's not much.'

'Send it. And you know Conrad Sefton-Shaw? Planning?'

'I know of him.' And was just talking to the Chief Constable about him.

'He was in the photo with them, in the paper.'

'I saw it.'

'He thinks they're being stalked, him and his wife. Spied on. By a middle-aged woman and some punk his wife has been flirting with. Find out what's going on, if anything. Let me know as soon as.'

Alleyn rang off. Jones wasn't happy. Alleyn was treating him like some sort of private detective. The Chief was pointing him at all sorts of stuff that Alleyn was also interested in. And all of it was nothing to do with what he was supposed to be doing, which was writing reports: one for the Commissioner, on progress against serious and organised crime targets; one for Finance, explaining variances between spending and budgetary allocations. He looked round, realised he'd come to a halt in the middle of the car park and some uniforms going off shift were staring at him, laughing. He headed for the canteen, thinking that when coincidences start shoaling, something's up.

CHAPTER 11

Naomi had no idea who I was, but seemed happy enough to hear from me, and to round up Andrea and the farmers for a pissed-off party at the Globe on Monday 5th June. We gathered at seven in the back room. Naomi seemed professional, the farmers Tom and Linda uncomfortable. Andrea was last to arrive, petite, blonde, something of My Little Pony about her. She tossed her head and led the others to a table as far from the dart board as possible. I got a round in.

Gail introduced the two of us to the group. She said I'd recognised Naomi from a meeting about the old university depot on the ring road. Naomi tipped her head back and looked at me, perhaps seeing through my duplicitous pursuit of confluence. I concentrated on my pint. None of us had done this before, there was no normal way to proceed. It didn't feel much like a party.

Naomi said something. I missed it, being close to her and all a-flutter. 'Say that again, please,' I said.

'I said I don't understand how they get away with it. I think there must be something really dodgy going on.'

Silence.

They were all looking at me. In expectation? I don't think of myself as a leader, but sometimes end up in that role, willy nilly.

Never works. But a man's got to do… I put my pint down and grasped the nettle. 'You're pissed off. We all are. Shall we go round the table, share reasons why? Then think about what's behind it and what we can do?'

I sensed a following wind. 'Has anyone been to a pissed-off party before?' No-one had. 'It's like bring and share. Only not food. We bring reasons for being pissed off about something or someone. See if there's common ground and whether it makes sense to work together.'

'Nice. But I've never heard of them. Do you have them often?' Naomi said.

'Well, no. We only invented them last week. This is actually the world premiere. Andrea, you want to go first? What are you really upset about? We know it's the nature reserve, the woodland, but can you tell us a bit about why it's important and what they're going to do?'

'Certainly,' Andrea said. She looked dreamy on the surface, underlain by a hint of steel and an air of entitlement, as if Daddy owned an estate in Wiltshire. Which, as I later learned, he did. 'It's an absolute bugger, what they're doing. It's green belt, for Christ's sake. Or was, before they redefined it. It has some of the best ridge and furrow systems in the three counties, hedgerows over a thousand years old. But the big thing for us is our reserve, Dunmore Copse. A small wood, very old.' She opened what looked like a hand-made notebook and thumbed a page, not really looking at it. 'Twelve acres. Coppiced from before Domesday until the eighteen-nineties, then neglected for a hundred years. When the trust got involved, it was a mess. Too many mature standards, lots of sycamore, really dense canopy. We've been working on it, mostly with volunteers, for twenty-odd years. It's coming on, it's much better than it was.'

'Better how?' Gail asked.

Andrea leaned forward, like it was hush-hush. 'We aren't broadcasting it, but we get nightingales every year. We've had turtle doves breeding. They're practically extinct in Britain. And… a dormouse population has become established. That's really unusual in an isolated pocket of woodland between large conurbations. It's so good.'

I saw smiles around the table. 'How many dormice would there be?' I said, 'in whatever you'd call it – the colony?'

'There are two colonies on site, three or four animals in each. The new link road will cut straight through both territories. Then a park and ride on one side, a retail park on the other, and there goes the reserve. Zapperooni. So I'm angry. Not just because of the work people have done, the thinking and research. Not just because they all promised – all the councils, the university, St Mark's – over and over, that there was no chance of development. Until they decided to build four hundred thousand houses in Oxfordshire, on top of existing targets. Like six new Oxfords. Or two Bristols.'

Frowns all round, apart from a titter from Naomi.

'How can that be?' Gail said, speaking for the rest of us. It seemed disproportionate.

'Dunno. But it can. Because some committee says it's necessary to meet targets set by some other committee. All the committees being made up of construction company directors, of course. How England works, isn't it.'

'Is it?' Gail said. 'How depressing.'

'But I'm angry most of all because of these poor beautiful little animals. They found their way here, found somewhere to suit how they live. There's not many places left that do, but this did. It was so good. And now they're going to bulldoze it. Destroy their home. Kill them.'

Andrea wasn't the only one with tears in her eyes.

'No wonder you're angry,' I said. 'Do you know where they came from? How they knew the way? Presumably they walked.'

'Correcterooni. Probably from the Chilterns, around Christmas Common.'

'That must be twenty-five miles,' I said, 'across roads, rivers, railways, miles of arable land. How do they do it?'

'We think they travel alongside major roads and railways. They can ignore fumes and noise and machinery hurtling past, as long as they don't have people wandering about. It's like linear coppice to them. Not disturbed by farmers, or by people generally. But saplings are cut back every few years, just like coppicing.'

'What does that mean, coppicing?' Gail said.

'You let them grow. Five, ten, twelve years for hazel and ash, fifty for oak, depending on what you want the wood for. Then you cut each stem off, low to the ground, leaving what's called a stool. Each stool sends up five, ten, twenty new shoots. You let them grow in turn, for another ten years or whatever. And so on. And you do it in strips, so you have a succession of ages across the wood. Used to be standard practice everywhere. Now it's really only on our reserves and places like that, which are managed for wildlife. Makes for very specific assemblages of flora and fauna.'

'Fauna like dormice,' Gail said.

'Precisamenti. Really important for their over-wintering hibernation sites. I'd do anything for them. They're such harmless cuddly little things.'

'Wow. Is this what you do? Your job?' I asked.

'Part of it,' Andrea said. I caught a glance flashing from her to Naomi. Saying something. *See? Told you so?* Something like that.

'Wow,' I said. 'Thank you.' I looked round. Gail was beaming at Andrea, radiating empathy. Linda looked thoughtfully at Andrea, as if a penny was dropping. Tom glared, probably wondering, I thought, why we're all so worked up about a few fuckin' mice.

I looked to Tom and Linda. 'What about you guys?'

Linda straightened up, took the lead. 'Simple really. My family's farmed the Glebe since 1840. Never had a problem renewing the lease. I grew up there, like my dad, and his dad, and… Tom's from Cutteslowe, was helping on the farm before he left school. Fourteen, weren't you, when my dad first set you on?'

75

Tom grunted.

'And never left. We've been married forty-two years. The farm's our whole life. There's thirty years left on the lease, which would have been fine – see us out, and our son's not interested, so okay. Thought we'd retire in a couple of years, with a good bit of lease to sell, give us something to retire on. There's lots would have been interested. But there's something in the lease that they can terminate at twelve months' notice, if they need the land for something else.'

'So they say,' Tom said.

'Yes, so they say. Our solicitor wants to fight it but he would, wouldn't he? Four hundred pounds an hour! Can't afford it. So we're out on 31st March next year.'

'Don't know what we're going to do,' Tom said.

'We've always put every penny back into the business,' Linda said. 'We'll have a farm sale, clear a few thousand, but what's that? We'll have nowhere to live. In our sixties, both of us. Farming's all we know. Who's going to give us a job?'

No-one had a suggestion.

Gail next. She explained her family's walking habit and the reckless driving that put a stop to it.

'How bloody awful,' Naomi said. 'He practically killed your mother, injured you, didn't even apologise?' She looked at me. 'You know, I think I'm beginning to see what you're getting at. He's a menace on the streets, and a disaster in his job.'

I gave her an appreciative nod.

Naomi said she'd been on the protest partly to support Andrea. 'And partly because I've a long history with the city planners, especially Sefton-bloody-Shaw. And with the university. I've lost count of the uni sites we've put in bids for.'

'Who's we?' Gail said.

'Affordable Oxford. We often bid in partnership with housing associations or co-housing groups. Charities. Even Nemeton Homes, the builders, they're interested in visions like ours.

Permanent affordability. Rethinking how housing and workplaces are configured. Like mixed-use courtyards, shared resource organisations. Things that facilitate, enable, empower community, rather than make it next to impossible. But we're amateurs, we all do other things for a living. Each time you put in a bid it swallows all your spare time for months. And all your emotional energy. So it's not really any consolation that your bid's ranked second or third. If you don't come first, it's wasted time. And we've never come first on anything to do with the uni, despite putting in some bloody brilliant bids. So I think it's fishy. And I smell a rat: Mr Sefton-Shaw.'

'Okay, thank you.' Her passion sent shivers through me. I looked away.

'Another thing,' she said. 'I used to work in planning for the city. Sefton-Shaw's empire. Started as a junior, after uni. I wasn't bad. Good appraisals, increment each year, promotions. Then my boss, an okay guy, had to give me a message from the top. I needed to think about how I conducted myself in a professional role. Basically they didn't like what I was doing at Affordable Oxford. I'd done it seven years, always declared an interest, couldn't see any reason to change that. Neither could he.'

'Can't fire you if you follow the rules,' Gail said.

'There's always a way. They had a consultation on departmental structures and job specs. Everyone gets consulted, everyone gets ignored, you know. All the jobs get new titles, everyone has to re-apply for their job. And one post is lost, which turns out to be mine. I pick up some redundancy and get a job waiting on tables in Harry's, in the Castle. Where I frequently serve modest little luncheons to Sefton-Shaw and his hangers-on. Sometimes he acts like we never met. Sometimes he treats me like dirt.'

'Well, thank you,' I said.

'And,' Naomi said, with a hard eye, 'it makes me wonder whose side you're on. Because you weren't on the demo. And you were in Harry's one lunchtime, with one of Sefton-Shaw's developer buddies.'

'Was I?' I was shocked. 'Don't think so. Only been there once. With our sales guy, and some prospects. A guy called Alleyn, from a law firm.'

'Spell,' she said, waking her phone. I did. She keyed a search. Everyone waited. I began to wish the floor would swallow me up.

'Here he is. Ballator Developments. Directors. Second row down. James Alleyn, BSc, LLB, LLD. Appointed Non-Executive Director 1st October 2011.' She held her phone out. 'Look.'

I looked. It was our client. 'God, you're right,' I said, aware that I sounded so condescending. 'I thought he was just a lawyer.'

She took back her phone, scrolled down. 'And listen,' she said. 'Here. "Dr Alleyn's expertise lies in planning law… Planning frameworks at national, regional, and local level… Land acquisition and zoning strategies." Blah blah. Deputy Chairman and Senior Independent Director since 18th August 2014. Also, senior partner of Oxford law firm Murdoch Alleyn & Co. Chair of Oxfordshire Growth Board. Member of the Local Enterprise Partnership. And listen to this!' She snorted. '"In his spare time, James is a scratch golfer, and a leading light of Kennington's amateur operatic society, where he has sung Calaf in Turandot, and Wagner's Siegfried, inter alia." God's grinding molars.'

She looked at me. In fact, all eyes were on me. My story felt small, but I had to tell it: Conrad's belief I was after his wife, death threats, assaults, my attempts at espionage and seeking revenge for violence by taking the piss, like the Jehovah's Witnesses bit. It all seemed a bit tawdry and personal, miles away from the principled positions some of them were coming from. And I knew my story was incomplete, because it wasn't the right time to mention the possibly flirtatious interactions with Kimberly, which I didn't believe in anyway. Nor that my covert observations had been rumbled from the outset.

'We went to the demo,' I said. 'Me and Gail. But I don't think it's my kind of thing. Some people need to stand up and be counted, despite knowing it makes no difference. That's great, but it's not for me. I'd rather lie down in the undergrowth and sneak up on the bastards and shoot them down. Sort of.'

'Some do both,' Andrea said.

'Yes, good on you. But that Conrad... selfish, greedy, ruthless. In his personal life he's a thug. Professionally, he earns more than the Prime Minister and all he does is turn Green Belt into tarmac. My stunts were just getting after his personal life, because I didn't know about the rest. Be better if I could really hit him where it hurts: in the pocket.' I hauled myself in, took a few seconds with my mantra. 'So Naomi thinks there's something dodgy going on.'

'I do.'

'We both do,' Andrea said.

'Can you explain?'

'Certainly,' Naomi said. 'Please say if I don't make sense, and chip in if I'm missing something. And before I start, to be clear: we are not against genuinely and permanently affordable housing in the places where people need it. Not at all. We're totally for it.' She took her left thumb in her right hand. 'So, point one. Zoning and planning. The university can do what it wants, like re-zoning green belt to 'reserved'. Which means reserved for development, not reserved for nature like you might think.'

'But,' Andrea said, 'they often don't bother now with the reserved stage. It's straight from ancient meadow to mega-development. And to make sure nobody makes a fuss about great crested newts or creeping marsh-wort or whatever, they send in the heavy machinery first and turn it into a muddy waste, then call it inaccessible worthless scrub. Makes the planning process much easier. Even though inaccessible scrub is the most valuable habitat of all.'

'Yes. So, planning,' Naomi said. 'Outline planning applications always succeed if they're from the uni. People often think that outline planning for two hundred houses means you can build up to two hundred. But it's the minimum, not maximum.'

I took a sip of beer, relaxing for the first time that evening. These two were good.

Naomi continued. 'Detailed planning applications from the uni, or on land bought or leased from the uni, always succeed. We don't know one case where they didn't, usually first time round, sometimes on appeal. Often no-one notices what they're doing until it's half built. Like the graduate flats at Castle Mill. Or Roger Dudman Way, as they're calling it. Sometimes there's a fierce battle, like Oxford North, as they're calling it. It was the Northern Gateway, but that became a toxic brand. Like Windscale.'

'Windscale?' Linda said.

'A nuclear re-processing plant in Cumbria,' Naomi said. 'Renamed Sellafield after a series of accidents. Probably called something else again now. Want to build a new motorway? Call it an expressway, you get ninety percent fewer objections. Still too many objections? Announce that you've dropped the plan, then build it anyway, bit by bit. The Oxford-Cambridge Corridor became the OxCam Expressway and Growth Arc. What is it now?'

'They just call it the Growth Arc,' Andrea said. 'There's only the one. Just don't tell any northerners.'

'Lovely. Keep giving things different names and the average punter thinks they're different things, or just gives up in confusion. Opposition makes no difference at all. No matter how stupid the idea is, they always get their way. Always. That stinks.'

'What about the builders?' Tom said. 'Especially...'

'Ballator, yes. Point two,' Naomi added an index finger to the thumb, 'they always know exactly how to pitch their bid. If Nemeton bid thirty million, Ballator bid thirty point one. Against a bidder with an ethical stance, like Affordable Oxford, they know exactly how to green-wash their bid to negate our distinctiveness. That stinks too.'

'Anybody'd think,' Andrea said, 'that someone with access to other bidders' thinking was passing everything on to Ballator.'

'Surely not. That would be unethical.' Naomi added a middle finger to index and thumb. 'Point three: who's it all for? Well, everyone ends up happy. Except for the little people, who get shafted, but who cares? The city council's always happy. They get development, which means targets hit, revenue, infra-structure kickbacks. Section 106. Community infrastructure levy.'

'Bribery. Institutionalised cronyism,' Andrea said.

'The county council is the same.'

'Yes,' I said. 'Did you know, the county's vision is to turn Oxford into another Reading? He actually said that, their big cheese, in a restaurant in Witney. My mum was at the next table.'

'Another Reading?' Gail said. 'Has he ever been there?'

'Seems unlikely,' I said.

'The university's always happy,' Naomi said, 'turning property assets into mountains of money.'

'Though their property assets aren't unlimited, are they?' I said. Something tickled the back of my mind. The old colleges had owned their land for seven or eight hundred years. Selling it off for development made it seem like they didn't care at all about the long term. Did that really ring true?

'And Ballator Developments are always happy,' Naomi said. 'Appealing to national planning inspectors on the odd occasions that public opposition persuades enough councillors that they don't like their plans. Dodging social housing obligations by playing the viability card. Net profits thirty percent plus.'

'So the only people who aren't happy,' I said, 'is everybody else. We can't afford their house prices and rents, can't match their budget for consultancy and legal fees, haven't the time and willpower to read and respond to eight-hundred-page so-called consultations. Which I tried to do once. That stinks as well.'

'By George, he's got it!' Naomi and Andrea said, in unison.

They were both giggling. I felt teased and wasn't sure how kindly it was meant.

Gail interrupted, slightly tetchy. 'I've got it too.'

Andrea and Naomi were still behaving like naughty kids on the back row at school.

'And us, I reckon,' Linda said, for her and Tom.

Naomi straightened up and composed her face. 'Wheels turn so smoothly for fat cats,' she said. 'Someone somewhere is pulling strings and oiling wheels and making sure the gravy train rolls on. Without let or bloody hindrance.'

'I can see how the council and the uni might get cosy,' Gail said, 'scratch each other's backs. And why developers are queueing up to join in. But why Ballator? Is it Alleyn? Is he the glue?'

We were all staring into space, needing to pause and reflect. It felt like we'd come a long way, become allies, were starting something. Time for more beer.

I went to the bar. Two laughing women were playing darts. I wanted to join them, forget this serious stuff. But then I had one of those shifts in perspective that is irreversible once it's happened. I was looking down on my life as a diligent and hard-working journey across a temporal landscape. A life of conforming to expectations and avoiding confrontation, until Conrad and Kimberly flipped me from comfort to confusion. And now Naomi and Andrea were showing me it was possible to do something positive together, rather than just accept and accommodate wrongs in isolation. We all know the word 'activism'. I now knew what it meant. I came back to the table with fresh resolve and a fresh round of drinks, caught Naomi's eye, returned a smile.

'So is there something here worth pursuing?' I said, feeling more grounded. 'Is it worth looking at how we could work together?'

Affirmative nods from Naomi, Andrea, Gail, Tom. A wince from Linda could have been grudging acquiescence.

'Shall we go round the table,' I said, 'so everyone gets a turn? Share any ideas about what we might do, no matter how daft. We're in a divergent phase, generating ideas, so no criticism please.' Andrea raised a quizzical brow but I pressed on. 'We can winnow it down to sense later. Okay? Good. Who wants to go first? Tom?'

'Well,' Tom said, 'I'd say we've done enough protesting, for a start. It's water off a duck's back, they take no notice. Unless we do it like them French farmers. Get the muck-spreader on their offices. Block the ring road with tractors. Drive five hundred head of cattle through the town centre. They'd take notice of that.'

'Excellent,' I said, loving the idea of French farmer tactics. 'Great stuff. Linda?'

'Well, I don't want no trouble. I don't think we know enough about them. You know where they live, these Sefton-Shaws. I'd like to know what sort of people they are, him and his wife. Whether she's in it too. Who their friends are. That kind of thing.'

'Good thought,' Naomi said. 'And what about Ballator? Don't they have offices in Summertown, not far from that uni services place? We could dig around there, see whether we turn up anything interesting.'

'Good idea,' Andrea said. 'But Alleyn's law place is in Summertown. Ballator are in Botley.'

'Okay, good,' I said. 'Be interesting if they're connecting up outside of work, like uni property services and city planning people. And Alleyn, or anyone else at Ballator. We know that Alleyn and Sefton-Shaw hook up out at Boars Hill, Gail and I saw them. Andrea, you were going to say something?'

'Sounds good to me.'

'Other thoughts?'

'Not really.'

'Okay, thanks.' I'd expected more from Andrea, felt she was holding back. 'Gail?'

'Hmm. No, not really. Sefton-Shaw is a council officer. What about the councillors themselves? Can you go into council meetings and listen? I think so.'

'Yes,' Naomi said. 'Some of them.'

'So,' Gail said, 'they'll be discussing Glebe Farm, Oxford North, new corridor arc expressways... be good to know who's saying what. They'll take minutes. Get copies?'

'Fantastic,' I said. 'Lots of good stuff.' Except it all sounded too easy. I thought a caveat was needed. 'Can I just say... they want to develop Glebe Farm, which would mean bulldozing the dormice. We're trying to stop them, whoever 'they' are. Sefton-Shaw and friends. He won't like it. He might like it even less than he liked me seeing his wife.'

'Which you weren't,' Naomi said.

'True,' I said, 'though he didn't seem to know that. But he tried to kill me. It could be dangerous. And we may not succeed. But at least we'll have had a go. So, now what?'

'What do you mean, now what?' Andrea said.

'Now what do we do, exactly? And who does it?' I said.

I waited. Tom and Linda looked at the table. Andrea and Naomi looked at each other, as if agreeing to give me plenty of rope, thinking I might hang myself. *In for a penny*, I thought.

'A few suggestions, all up for grabs. Andrea, how about you and Gail work on the council?'

Gail nodded agreement. Andrea raised an eyebrow.

'Naomi, could you look at uni services and Ballator? I could help you with that.' My heart skipped as she hesitated. But she nodded, and gave Andrea a small smile. 'And Alleyn, I guess. I'll talk to a mate about how to bug conversations, that kind of thing. And Gail, we could take another look at Springfield House? When we know better what we're doing.'

The spread of workload was uneven, but I didn't want to change it.

'Linda and Tom,' I said, 'you seem busy enough keeping a roof over your heads. If there's anything we can help with, let us know. Especially if it involves cattle in Cornmarket. Shall we meet here again in two weeks, see where we are? Oh, and meanwhile, we'll need to communicate. There's an app called Signal. Anyone got it?'

'I have,' Andrea said. 'Use it all the time for... well. Yes. Use it all the time.'

'Same here,' I said. 'It's good. Free. Secure. So can we all use that if we need to be in touch? If you have any problems setting it up, let me know. Or Andrea. Yes? But it's dead easy.'

***

The others had gone, leaving just me and Naomi.

It was suddenly quiet.

I stared at her reflection in the puddled table.

'Mick?' she said, tentative.

I raised my eyes, met hers, felt a deep-down tingle.

Frightened. Happy?

'Mick?' she said. 'Do you have any weed?'

CHAPTER 12

Friday evening, a few dusty days after the pissed-off party. We'd been flat out all week at work, getting an app ready to hand over for client testing, duly achieved by close of play. I was knackered and needed an evening of relaxed self-indulgence. I was out of the office in a flash and got to the terminus just in time to see my bus disappearing up St Giles.

It was twenty minutes until the next one, giving me a chance to call Kanhai. He answered immediately.

'A quick question,' I said.

'Fire away.'

'If you wanted to do some covert surveillance – electronic – where would you go for kit?'

'That's not a quick question,' he said.

'No?'

'No. One or two issues to explore. Like, who do you want to surveil? If that's a word. Where? Public space, private space – or privileged space, like a doctor's surgery? When? How long for? Why? Do you want something that would stand up in court, or just the information? Sound only, vision only, both? Real time or recorded?' He paused. 'That do for starters?'

'Oh. Thanks. I'll have a think and get back to you.'

'This isn't something to do with Sefton-Shaw, is it?'

'Might be.'

'Well, gang canny,' Kanhai said. 'And talk to me first, before you do anything daft. In fact, before you do anything.'

'Oh ye of little faith.'

'Too right,' he said. 'Ciao.'

Sometimes, I thought, new friends can be more fun than old ones. I'd been in touch with all the pissed-off party people during the week. No-one had done much, but everyone seemed pleased to hear from me. Except Naomi, who'd seemed quite cool, I didn't know why. I really liked her and felt we'd got on well so far, especially the hour after the party. But I didn't want to blow it by rushing things. Again.

***

I put a frozen pasta bake in the oven, jogged the dog, ran a bath, settled in pine-scented suds. Had supper on a tray balanced on my knees, a bottle of Italian red and glass within reach on the loo lid, a new tartan noir propped on the soap rack. I was thinking, *This is as good as it gets*, when the doorbell rang.

I ignored it.

It rang again.

I ignored it again. Had I locked the front door? Not sure. I hoped so.

I waited.

A woman's voice. 'Halloo! Coo-eee!'

Who was that? Not my mum. Not Mrs Swainston from next-door-but-one. Not the Jehovah's or the WI. So who? And why didn't they go away when there was obviously no-one in?

Knocking. A pause. More knocking. Someone trying the front door. The front door opening.

Damn, it wasn't locked.

More hallooing, then the click of the door closing. Someone

talking to Friday, who talked right back, in her "come right in, make yourself at home" voice. So someone Friday knew, or who knew dogs.

I lay still, wishing this wasn't happening. I'd adopted a default strategy: head down, stay quiet, hope they go away. It wasn't working.

Light footsteps, creaking floorboards. Someone was exploring the flat. One person. Her voice sounded vaguely familiar. A bit like Denise, the admin person from the office. She'd been known to drop stuff off, but never without warning. Anyway she wasn't the 'Coo-eee' type, and I'd seen her only three hours ago.

Crisis point couldn't be far off. There were only two-and-a-half rooms and the bathroom, and whoever it was had already been in two of them. Surely they'd realised by now that the flat was empty and the decent thing to do would be just go away.

Christ, a knock on the bathroom door. Did I lock it? I hunkered down under the bubbles, my tray still balanced on knees protruding from the suds. Another knock. I was beginning to feel annoyed. My space was being invaded, my end-of-project chill-out was ruined, and it looked like I was going to be at least slightly embarrassed quite soon. I checked the suds were covering me from the chin down, concentrated on keeping quiet and breathing deep.

The door opened slowly.

Small fingers with clean trimmed nails wrapped round the door's edge.

A blonde fringe.

Laughing eyes, turned-up nose, wide smile, a waft of patchouli. Andrea.

'Aha!' she said

'Oh my,' I said. 'Hello. What a surprise. I mean, what a nice surprise. Lovely to see you.'

'Hello,' she said. 'Can I come in?'

My mouth opened but nothing came out. She came in anyway, hung a huge chequered scarf and woven shoulder bag on the hook behind the door, looked me over. She took in the tray of food, the wine, the book. Smiled a sort of "gotcha" smile. 'Sorry to disturb your meal. But it looks nice. May I join you?'

'Yes, of course.'

She disappeared. I searched my memory. I was sure I hadn't said anything that could be construed as inviting her round, nor given her my address. What was she doing here?

She came back with a plate, fork and glass. I was going to ask whether I'd forgotten an arrangement, but she spoke first. 'Okay if I help myself?'

I nodded.

She poured herself a glass of red, took a scoop of pasta bake. 'Cheers.'

'Cheers,' I said.

'I brought water too,' she said, 'for both of us.' She poured two glasses, passed one to me. Something caught my eye – movement on the back of the door. Something slithered out of her bag, dropped to the floor with a sort of crunchy splat, coiled itself up and lay still.

'It's a fucking snake!' I said, leaping up, dropping the glass, which shattered on the edge of the bath. Water was everywhere, food and wine were everywhere. As I tried to avoid stepping on broken glass, my foot slipped. I sat down heavily, to more overflows, and leapt up again shouting in pain, blood everywhere.

'Bugger,' she said.

***

An hour later, having dried off, bandaged my bum, eaten and drunk a little, we lay on the carpet, backs to the sofa, sharing a spliff. She found the snake's appearance quite funny. 'Hissing Sid,' she said. 'That's his name. Just a grass snake. Harmless. But a stowaway!'

I was still puzzled about her visit. She seemed to find my pursuit of an explanation rather churlish. She had a point. 'But,' she said, 'I suppose it's not a secret. I had coffee with Naomi in the Café Rouge the day after your pissed off party. Which I kind of liked, actually. Cool idea. Might throw one myself. Might even invite you.' She smiled.

I tried to smile back.

'Anyway,' she said. 'We were talking about you. And how we both quite liked you. You must have noticed that.'

'What?' I said. 'No, I hadn't.' Naomi liked me? God, now what had I done? Andrea was bound to tell her about my bloody bottom.

'Well, we did. We had a sort of little bet. But it's a bugger, isn't it? Like something out of Genesis. I might have won, if it wasn't for that blasted snake.'

***

I'd promised to meet Andrea at Dunmore Copse at ten the next morning, to walk round the reserve and look for signs of dormice, so was up early to walk the dog, oil the chain and check my tyres. I left Friday with Mrs Swainston and biked up the canal, crossed a swing bridge, then went up a green lane, under a tumbledown ex-railway bridge, along a cart track, and arrived at the gate into Dunmore Copse at the appointed time.

A few minutes later Andrea appeared, accompanied by Naomi. I was embarrassed and wished I hadn't come. Nothing in their manner indicated whether Andrea had told Naomi about last night. I blundered through her guided tour: where the park and ride would be, ancient hedgerows, link road, ancient lake bed, retail Park, hazelnut shells with tooth-marks, gnawed by this or that small mammal. Andrea and Naomi did all the talking. I followed on, trying to summon intelligent nods and encouraging affirmations. My face ached from wearing a forced grin. I prayed for it to be over.

Which, in time, it was. Andrea invited us to hers for coffee. I agreed, latching on to the idea of thirty minutes solitary cycling down the canal. Naomi declined; she had to meet someone. I didn't know whether that was good, bad or neutral. I didn't care, I was just relieved to be out of the threesome.

Andrea's place in Jericho was in a tall red-brick building. Rented rooms with shared facilities. Six buttons by the front door, *A Turner No Circulars* at the bottom, suggesting she had the basement. I pressed it. The door opened into a threadbare hall. She beckoned me into a shared kitchen with layers of stuff on every surface, smells of stale cooking oil and maturing food waste. She didn't ask what I wanted and made mint tea for two. I followed her down dark steps to her room.

The scents changed, calling to mind an old-fashioned hardware store. It was a tiny room, plastered with posters: animal rights, metal gigs. Like the kitchen, everything was covered in stuff. There was a narrow single bed, a small wardrobe, a rag rug occupying the small patch of open floor, surrounded by rickety piles of cardboard boxes.

I perched at the foot of the bed, clutching my tea. She sat cross-legged at the head. A cooing sound made me look up: two pigeons were on top of the wardrobe. Another was on the floor, pecking grain spilled from a sack in the corner, beside a sleekit brown rat. A black rabbit shuffled from under the bed, settled between my feet, wrinkled a pink nose. I looked round, thinking, *What next?*

Something rustled inside an overturned cardboard box, below a window hung with tattered yellowing net. A hedgehog. And that blasted grass snake raised its jewel of a head over the side of an open glass tank and flickered a forked black tongue.

A cat jumped on to the bed, on to my shoulder. Burmese? Very big. Very interested in my ear. I don't actually like cats. But another one, black, kneaded my thigh, hoisted itself onto my lap, and curled up purring. The scent settled down to zoo.

I realised that Andrea was watching, laughing. Claustrophobia and self-disgust swept through me. I just had to leave.

I drained my mug and stood. 'Thanks for the drink,' I said. 'Sorry last night's meal wasn't a raging success. Thanks for the wound dressing. Nice to meet the animals. Got to go. Places to be, things to do. I'll see you. Through the week or through the window. Bye.'

Those were the only words either of us had spoken since I arrived. I headed for the door, looked back from the top of the steps. What was she thinking? She'd settled into a lotus position on the floor, straight-backed, eyes closed. Probably meditating. She certainly wasn't engaging in small talk around my sudden departure, for which I was grateful.

I unlocked my bike, wondering what Naomi was thinking. I decided to phone straight away to see if I could mend any fences.

A male voice answered.

I hung up.

***

The next morning I loaded dog Friday into the Golf and drove up to Boars Hill for a ten thirty rendezvous with Gail. We walked across the heath towards Ishmael's Wood. She asked about my research into eavesdropping technologies.

'I talked to a mate. The best bet, we think,' I said, bigging it up slightly – the research consisted of a few speculative web searches inspired by Kanhai's questions – 'is a system where you have a mike and low-power transmitter hidden in something that looks absolutely normal around the house. So, like a radio or a table lamp or…'

'Yes, I get it,' Gail said. 'Did you notice, when we were Jehovah's, detector things everywhere. Smoke, carbon dioxide, whatever they are.'

'Not really. It'd be carbon monoxide though, wouldn't it?'

'Would it?'

'I wasn't paying much attention to detectors. If we were going with something like that, we'd need to know the exact make and model.'

'No idea of that.'

'So then you have a transceiver, somewhere in range of the device you've planted, and that basically controls the device and buffers up recordings and...'

'Spare me,' she said. 'How much are we looking at?'

'Well, if we wanted sound only... I found something that could be embedded in a radio or fire alarm or whatever. Battery life five or six weeks. With a transceiver that we'd plant like in the hedge or... The one I was looking at came from America. Two thousand dollars.'

'Hmm. Not cheap. I could split it with you.' Gail gazed reflectively into the wood, noticed a tree-creeper, drew my attention to it. 'That means we have to go back in, decide where we're going to put the bug and get all the details, doesn't it?'

'Yes,' I said.

'Then go back again to install it.'

'Yes. Christ.'

'Are you free tonight? For step one.'

'Yes.' I'd planned a quiet bath with a book, to make up for Friday's *lavatio interrupta*.

'The only way is up, you know,' she said. 'For a tree creeper. When it's creeping.'

'Can we take that as a good sign?'

'If we want to.'

The tree creeper crept to the top of an old birch, then spun down to the base of a neighbouring hawthorn and started up that. We walked slowly back across the heath.

'On another subject,' I said, stopping to look north-east at Oxford's dreaming spires. I told her about my aborted dinner with Andrea and Naomi's apparent coolness. She suggested I steer well clear of Andrea and concentrate on the Sefton-Shaws, an approach I'd already worked out for myself. Except that my plan was to steer as close as possible to Naomi at the same time.

'Don't be stupid,' she said. 'You'd do better if you just stopped trying. Pretend you've got another girlfriend and you're not interested in either of them in that way. Do you see?'

I wasn't used to being told what to do. But she spoke as if she knew, and seemed to care. And my track record wasn't brilliant.

'Okay, I'll try,' I said, almost meaning it.

We veered closer to Springfield House on the way back to the stile. Gail sniffed. 'Woodsmoke,' she said. 'Burnt wood.'

There was a mass of charred wood, the Wendy house, the source of the smoke. Adjacent bushes looked crackled and browned.

Raised voices. A child crying. We steered into the shade by the fence and stopped where we could just see the back of the house through the hedge. Gail sat on the grass and said, 'Picnic,' then handed me an orange and peeled one for herself.

'We TOLD you! We didn't do it,' one of the small girls said, with a note of exasperation. Bella, in charge of talking for the twins.

'It's no use. We know you did.' Conrad Sefton-Shaw.

'We didn't, we didn't, we didn't. It was him again,' Bella said. Her twin sobbed quietly and continuously.

'I didn't do it last time and I didn't do it this time.' The boy, Alasdair.

'Alasdair. Go. Now. To your room. We know who did it.' The father paused, probably waiting for the boy to absent himself. Then he continued, 'Now, Bella, Charlotte. Charlotte, shut up. Now. Both of you. It's time you owned up.'

'But we didn't do it!' they squeaked in rage and exasperation.

'You did.' The father was adamant. 'You didn't mean to but you did. Playing with matches. Well, it's your fault and that's it, you've had it, it's not being rebuilt. Go to your room, both of you. And don't come out until you are truly sorry.'

The mother's voice, Kimberly, interjected mournfully, 'I don't know how many times I've told you not to play with matches.'

'We didn't. It was Alasdair. It was.' It was the girl again, but no longer defiant. Just resigned to being disbelieved.

We felt like eavesdroppers. We picked up our peel and headed towards the gate, catching sight of the boy stepping through the French doors.

'Did you see?' Gail said. 'The boy's face. Ever so slightly pleased with himself. Couldn't quite believe he'd got away with it.'

CHAPTER 13

In the small hours of the following morning, Gail and I waited under overhanging branches at the end of Berkeley Close while our eyes adjusted to the pitchy night. It was two o'clock and cloudy: no moon, no stars, no streetlights, not a glimmer from the houses. 'Must be late enough and dark enough now,' I said, pulling on latex gloves. 'If anyone shows up…'

'I hoot,' Gail said. 'Like an owl. *Tu whit*. If I see you coming, or any disturbance around the house, I'm back to the car and ready to roll.'

'And if I'm not back in an hour?'

'Go home. Come back at nine, with Tom if possible. But come back at nine whatever.'

I felt my way down the Close. My torch, with a red filter taped over the lens, was turned off. The right-hand pocket of my jacket held Kanhai's lock-picks, an old credit card, masking tape, insulating tape, spare gloves. My left pocket held screwdrivers, Stanley knife, tape measure, hammerhead with no handle, and slightly squidgy dog treats in a non-rustling bag. The breast pocket had my iPhone, on silent and in airplane mode.

I eased through the gate. It seemed even darker. There was neither light nor sound from the house.

I moved along the wall, under two small square windows, through the gap between the bushes, round the corner and into the grassed area where we'd met boy and mastiff. Should I be worried about the illegality of what I was doing? Not really. My mum loved walking in the woods. The woods where she lived were owned by a duke, so technically she'd be trespassing. But she felt she wasn't doing anything wrong; indeed, she almost had a duty to do it. What was wrong was some hereditary duke owning half of Oxfordshire. Here, we were trying to stop Conrad doing serious wrong, so we were doing right. *If she could see me now*, I thought, then unthought it. *If Naomi could see me now?* Didn't work. 'Shut up and get on', my grandad said. I checked my pocket for dog treats.

Examined the first window. Closed, locked.

The French doors. Closed, locked. But through them the dog's eyes reflected a glimmer. Lovelump was emitting a low growl, just audible through the glass.

The next window had reflected the light differently. It was latched but in the ventilation position, with a small gap between window and frame.

I put the credit card through the gap, above the latch, moved it slowly down, wiggled it into position and pressed down hard. Nothing. I turned on the torch, peered at the latch. Idiot. I turned off the torch, worked the card through the gap below the latch, pushed up. Still nothing. I wiggled it some more, pressed up harder, felt something move. Harder again. It moved more. Again. The window was open, the dog's growl louder. I threw some treats in his direction. The growl stopped.

I eased the window wide, switched on the dimmed torch for two seconds, looked round the garden. On the grass nearby were a wooden table and chairs. I fetched a chair and threw more treats to the dog, then climbed onto the chair, inched through the window, eased down over a radiator onto a hard floor, threw more treats to the dog and switched the torch on. I was in a snug little sitting room with a fireplace, bookshelves, and magazines on a coffee table. The room I'd been in with Kimberly, on the Witness visit.

I swung the light round to a drinks cabinet. On top, Bombay Sapphire gin, Vermouth, slices of lemon in a small bowl. Inside, whisky, sherries, ports, Warninks. Digital radio by the phone. Lamp on a coffee table by a big, soft sofa. Standard lamp behind it. Paintings on the walls, too dim to see. In the centre of the ceiling, a four-way spot. Just off centre, a pale oblong box. Some sort of detector. Might be just the thing.

I brought a dining chair across from the table and positioned it quietly on the wood-block floor, beneath the oblong box. I gave the dog more treats then climbed carefully onto the chair. The dog sat below, watching intently. I examined the box. Smoke detector, S4S brand, model 9G-ix. I had something similar in the flat. With mine, the mount was fixed to the ceiling and the unit itself would just unclip with a bit of a squeeze. Last time I changed the battery I accidentally touched the test button, and it made a terrible squawk. It would be unfortunate to do that now. But I had to find out whether it was mains- or battery-powered. Battery would be easier.

There was a plastic retaining clip on each of the two longer sides. I fished in my left pocket and brought out a small flat-bladed screwdriver. Operating by feel, I worked the blade in alongside the nearer clip and carefully twisted it. The click as it started to move sounded deafening. I listened, waited. Nothing but a light rumble from the dog. I gave him more treats. I eased the unit off its mount, examined the innards with the torch. It was battery-powered and had a label inside with make and model. The mount was fixed to the ceiling with three cross-headed screws. I pulled out my phone and photographed the mount and the inside of the unit, then eased it back into the mount, helping the clips go quietly back into place with the screwdriver blade. I photographed the outside and gave the dog more treats.

I climbed down, dusted off the dining chair and put it back where it came from. I climbed half out of the window and threw the remaining treats to the dog. I found the chair outside with my feet, lowered myself down, semi-closed the window and put the catch back as close as I could to where it had been. I put the garden chair back where I'd found it. I realised I'd lost the end of the right index finger of the disposable gloves and tried to imagine where it might be, but couldn't. *Stupid to go back looking, so forget it.*

I eased slowly back round the corner of the house, relief building, aware of the need not to blow it at the last minute due to carelessness arising from that relief. I went out into the Close and back to Berkeley Road, where Gail emerged silently from the shadows, looking at her watch.

'Right on time,' she whispered.

'What?'

'An hour. Exactly.'

'Christ, seemed like no time at all. Thank God you're still here.'

'How did it go?'

'Like a dream. Phew. Let's move.'

***

After the night's excitement and an early run with Friday, I trimmed my nails, shined my shoes, put on my best charcoal pinstripe, emailed Denise in the office to say I was taking a day's leave, and left home in good time to meet Naomi in Summertown. I wished I knew what Andrea had told her about our bathroom dining incident.

We were going to see what we could nose out about Sefton-Shaw's lawyer friend, James Alleyn. I drove down, parked in Alexandra Court and walked through South Parade. At half nine, this summery Monday morning already felt tired and dusty, and I felt grumpy and nervous. The gallery was full of god-awful dog portraits. On the corner, the ex-bookshop that had become a café was boarded up again. I hoped it was going back to bookshop.

I turned onto the gum-spattered parade of shops to the west of Banbury Road and looked south. My heart lurched when my eye caught Naomi peering in the stationer's window, dressed like I'd never seen her: low heels, knee-length indigo skirt, cream blouse, designer shoulder bag, hair up in a colourful wrap, a hint of make-up. I tried to quieten the butterflies inside, and to avoid the gabble gathered round a Big Issue seller and his dog.

Naomi seemed absorbed in the window display, or perhaps some small hand-written ads. I approached her with what I hoped would look like a confident smile and said, 'Hello, well done for getting here. You don't half scrub up well, I must say.'

She gave a leap of surprise, perhaps expecting me to arrive from the other direction. If she was pleased to see me, she kept it hidden. I felt I'd put my foot in it but wasn't sure how.

We walked the hundred yards to the Murdoch Alleyn offices in silence and paused at the entrance.

'Ready for this?' I asked.

'As I'll ever be,' she said. 'You're a software whizz. I'm your PA. We want to incorporate your software business and get advice on contracts and intellectual property. If we get that far.'

I pressed a button on the entry phone. It crackled. I said, 'Michael Jarvis and Naomi Goodman for James Alleyn.' The door buzzed. We went in and up a flight of stairs. Halfway up I was hit by apprehension. Naomi's summary of our strategy was all we had. Was it sufficiently well thought through? If it went wrong there could be all manner of consequences, losing my job not least.

The door at the top of the stairs opened automatically. We stepped into a reception area smelling of pine, fresh coffee and serious business. The receptionist glanced up from her screen. 'Can I help you?' An Aussie twang, rising intonation.

'Yes, I hope so,' I said. 'We were in Summertown for another meeting. We thought it might be worth popping in to see if we could speak to Mr Alleyn.'

'He's out?' she replied, her expression suggesting that coming in off the street and asking to see someone was odd to the point of eccentricity. 'Did you have an appointment?'

'Well no, not really. Just dropped in on the off-chance.'

'Would you like to make an appointment?'

'That's a good plan,' I said. I realised that I was being inane, behaving as if I'd no idea how business meetings were arranged. But having started, I had to go on. I called up the diary on my phone. 'And perhaps I could leave a message?'

Naomi interrupted, 'Is he at Ballator?'

'Well...' The receptionist hesitated.

'The Botley office?'

The receptionist gave a hint of a nod.

'Okay, that's fine, we'll catch him there. It's on our way back to base. Thanks. Bye,' Naomi said briskly, heading for the door. I trailed behind.

Outside we headed south, into the sun.

'Are you always as inept as that?' she asked.

'Well, er...'

'Because that was pathetic. Makes me wonder how you ever achieve anything.'

'Oh lordy.' I took a deep breath before continuing. 'Well, to be honest...'

She laughed. Sort of. 'Oh, don't bother with that honesty stuff,' she said. 'Much easier if we just lie to each other. You tell me what you think I want to hear, and I'll do the same for you. People might even think we're communicating.'

'Naomi, this is hard enough without the sarcasm, thank you. And apologies for the cliché. Ironically – or coincidentally might be better – I was thinking about clichés when I was out with Friday. Wondering whether you might be someone I could talk to about them. But...'

'Yes?' She invited me to get to the point.

'Never mind,' I said. 'I was pathetic in there, you're right. I'm not always like that. Not very often in fact. I was nervous. And sometimes when I'm nervous it brings out the best in me. And sometimes the opposite, like today.'

'Why were you nervous?'

'Well. This is embarrassing.' I took a breath, for courage. 'But faint heart and all that. Because of you.'

'What? My fault now? What is this?'

'Not your fault, no. If anyone's at fault it's me. But you know... or maybe you don't. How I feel about you.' I looked at her, unable to gauge her reactions. I decided that having started to lay my cards on the table, I had no choice but to press on. 'I really like you. And I really want...' This was so hard, and her expression was turning from neutral to something more negative. 'God, I've been trying so hard not to blow it.'

'What?' she said. 'Like by fucking my best friend? Is that how you usually go about your wooing? Because I can tell you, it doesn't work.'

I hadn't done that. She must mean the bathroom thing. 'What did she tell you?' I said. There was a lot to explain. It felt like there wasn't much time to explain it. 'I knew at the time it was stupid, but I... well...'

'You just couldn't help yourself? Well, neither can I.'

She slapped me hard, right hand then left, both cheeks. I backed away, unbalanced, tears welling. A small crowd formed around us, passers-by, street people, the Big Issue dog. I backed up against the bookie's window, aware that the punters inside had clustered behind me to watch the action outside, aware of garlicky smells from the delicatessen next door, the beeps of a reversing lorry. I knew I had to decide, right then, what I wanted, how much I wanted it, whether I could follow through. I looked her in the eyes, calmed my breathing. She looked back at me, waiting, with a neutral expression again, anger spent. For now.

'Must be half eleven,' I said, trying a small smile. 'Coffee?'

She inclined her head in agreement, linked her right arm in my left, returned the first half-millimetre of smile. I felt I'd scraped through some sort of test. She got me moving with a little pull. A collective 'Ah', scattered applause. The crowd dispersed. We walked towards the coffee shop at the far end of the parade, steps in rhyme.

'How could you have fallen for me?' she said over her espresso. 'You hardly know me. Or is it just lust?'

I looked up from my flat white, wondering how, despite the best of intentions, I could find myself in situations like this. Thinking how predictable it was, and how depressing. 'Just lust, yes, that must be it.'

'Like it was with Andrea?'

'I was telling you how it was with Andrea and you started hitting me. Can I just say that nothing actually happened, beyond my wounded bottom? And I don't know what she intended, but I intended nothing. It was a stupid mistake not to pull the plug before it even started. Literally.' I couldn't help laughing. I wasn't sure she got the joke.

'How do I know you won't be saying the same thing to some other woman next week? About me?'

'I don't know. I can only tell you the truth. My truth. For what it's worth. It's up to you whether you hear it, what you do with it.' Was there any point, though? She was reading the coffee grounds at the bottom of her cup. What were they telling her?

She looked up, gave a soft, fleeting smile. And I remembered what the point was.

'We could call it a day,' she said. 'Or go over to Botley, see if we can spot him?'

***

We drove to Botley, found a space near the Co-Op where we could see Ballator's car park. I did a quick recce. All the directors' spaces were occupied. 'Could be a board meeting,' I said. 'Alleyn has a reserved space, at the far end, on the right. Porsche Carrera. Metallic gold.'

Now we'd tracked him down I wasn't sure what to do. 'We can't just front up and go in there,' I said. 'He'll be in meetings. And we've no pretext, like we had at his own office.'

'Yes,' Naomi said. 'Thin as it was… Get us a couple of rolls. From the Crusty Croissant.'

I looked vaguely into the shopping centre. Did I want a roll?

'Bakery. Up there,' she said, pointing, 'and we'll keep an eye while we have lunch. We can play twenty questions while we wait for something to happen.'

I fetched filled rolls and water.

'We used to play twenty questions on long journeys when I was a kid. Animal, vegetable, mineral, all that?'

'No,' she said. 'This is different. It's a sort of getting-to-know-you game. I get to ask twenty questions. About you. Anything I like. You don't have to answer straight away. But you do have to answer some time. And honestly. Then you ask me your twenty. And you can't just ask the same. You have to ask questions that matter, to you. But I think you'll be surprised. It's easy enough to think of the first few. But twenty? Can be hard. And I think the less you already know about someone, the harder it is, for some reason. You'd expect the opposite, wouldn't you?'

'Yes,' I said, feeling apprehensive. I often did, doing something new.

'Okay, I'll start,' she said. 'And remember, you don't have to answer now. Usually it's better if you don't answer straight away.'

'Can I write them down?'

'No. You won't need to. You'll remember them.'

'Will I?' I found this hard to believe and was already reaching for my notebook.

'You will if they're good questions. By the way, why were you thinking about discussing clichés with me?'

'Is that the first question?'

'No. Well, it wasn't. But you can count it as that if you want. Okay. So question two. How do you feel about children?'

'Oh my,' I said.

'Next. How does it feel to be a man?' She paused, apparently pleased by my perplexity. There was mischief in her eyes; she was teasing me, almost laughing at me. 'Four,' she said, 'how do you think you would feel different if you were a woman?'

'Oh Christ. I see what you mean.'

'How do you feel about transgender people? Have you ever seen that possibility in yourself? Or been close to someone who has? And how did that make you feel? That's all question five.' She sat up, said, 'Look. That's him. Going to get in his car, when he's done chatting up the token female on the Ballator board. We'll follow him.'

Alleyn finished his conversation with a crisp woman in a business suit and thumbed his key. The tailgate opened and he slung a bag in. The woman went back inside.

I started the Golf and manoeuvred out of the parking space. Alleyn drove out of the car park then turned left onto Westminster Way. I slipped in behind, followed past Seacourt Tower to the ring road and down past Redbridge. Alleyn put his foot down coming off the Heyford Hill roundabout onto the Reading road. I got stuck behind an overtaking lorry. When we were past the lorry, the Porsche was out of sight.

'Give up?' I said.

'Carry on for five minutes,' Naomi said. 'Just in case.'

***

I turned off the Reading road at the Dorchester roundabout and turned into a parking lot in front of a row of businesses. I pulled up alongside two Harleys, a BM and a Triumph outside a café. We'd lost him.

'Coffee?' I asked.

'No thanks.'

'Okay,' I said. I restarted the engine. 'I'll drop you home.'

'You don't have to,' she said.

'What are you going to do, then? Get a bus? It'd take hours.'

She looked out of the window at the bikes we had parked next to.

'At least let me run you back into town.'

She put a hand on my arm. 'Don't look now,' she said. 'Or don't look as if you're looking. But in the café – isn't that him? At the counter.'

I looked. 'It is. What's he doing in there? Not his kind of place, surely. Where's his car?'

'Look,' she said. 'They're exchanging something. Some kind of deal. And he's going. Through the back.'

We looked at each other in puzzlement.

'There'll be parking at the back. Staff and deliveries,' she said.

'Of course, yes.' *An odd place for a lawyer to be hanging out*, I thought. *And doing deals*. It didn't seem to hang together.

'And look, over there.' Naomi pointed to the Dorchester Road. The gold Porsche took the roundabout at speed, headed back towards Oxford. 'No use trying to follow him. He drives insanely fast.'

'True. I will take you home. But I'll just pop in here first, see what I can see.'

Naomi studied the nearest bike, a black Triumph Thunderbird with leather trim. I went into the café and said 'Hi' with as much gusto as I could muster.

Three grizzled middle-aged men were draped over barstools in Hell's Angels kit, like extras in a road movie. Another man sat at a table, smoking a yellow cigarette – very cool, thin, tanned, with short grey hair, an immaculate grey suit and a collarless white shirt buttoned to the neck.

A nervous-looking youth dried mugs behind the cash register.

I picked the youth as the softest option. I leaned with my elbows on the counter, presenting as much of my back to the bikers as I could. 'That guy who was just in here, not Mr Alleyn, was it? James Alleyn?'

The youth looked at me with a touch of panic, then past me. I became aware of two presences. Bikers, one on either side. Quite heavily built guys. Someone tapped my shoulder.

I turned and found a bigger biker right in my face.

Grey-suit watched from his table with a faint smile.

'What the fuck,' said the big guy, 'does it have to do with you?'

He had a faded Glasgow accent and a slight speech impediment, possibly related to a bruised swelling on his left cheek. It made him hard to understand. He smelled of stale laundry, fried onions, aftershave.

'Please check he's not official,' said Grey-suit in a voice like a 1930s' BBC announcer, plummy, with just a hint of an accent. Eastern European?

'Are ye filth?' the big Scot asked. 'Polis?' He sprayed spittle on my forehead.

'No. Police? No. Not at all.' I was beginning to feel nervous.

'Please search,' Grey-suit said, blowing a cloud of smoke at the ceiling.

The two flankers took an arm each and pushed me over a table, face-down.

One bent my arms behind me, up towards my shoulders. It felt like something was about to break. I tried not to scream.

The other emptied my pockets, spread the contents on the counter. He opened my wallet, shook out bank cards, business cards, my driving licence, notes.

The Scottish guy picked through them. 'Not polis,' he said.

'Please tell me your name,' Grey-suit said. 'And occupation.'

'Michael Jarvis. IT consultant.' My voice was shaking.

'Check,' Grey-suit said, indicating the cards.

The big Scot shuffled the cards, nodded.

'Yes,' I said. 'Not polis. Yes. That's me.'

The Scottish guy signalled to the two holding me. They let go.

I straightened up, my back to the counter, and breathed easier. I noticed that Grey-suit, still at his table, was pointing a small handgun at me – rectangular cross-section, dull grey metal, bright coppery bits. He was smiling. He stood and walked slowly over, training the gun on the middle of my forehead. He was taller than he'd looked. What was this? I seemed to have stepped into the middle of a gangster movie. He stood inches from me and held the gun to my left temple.

'Really? Nothing to do with the police? So please tell,' he said, pushing the barrel harder and harder as I gave way to its weight, 'why you asked about Mr Alleyn.'

A click – the safety catch coming off? With minimal head movement I glanced round at the four faces. Each watched me with steady contempt and looked capable of extreme violence, murder even. My best protection would be the inconvenience of disposing of my body. But I was selfishly thinking only of myself. What about Naomi? What would they do to her?

'Well?' Grey-suit nudged my head with the gun barrel and whispered, 'Tell us what you want. Who sent you?' He paused. 'Not saying? I will count to zero. Then bang. Ten. Nine…'

My brain had frozen. I could answer the questions honestly but not succinctly. And I couldn't decide where to start.

'… Two. One. Zero.' He pulled the trigger. A sharp click. An empty chamber? No. From the corner of my eye, I could see a blue-yellow flame. A cigarette lighter, not a gun.

Grey-suit turned away.

I felt the tension melt.

A heavy fist hammered my right ear. I crumpled to the floor, head ringing.

Grey-suit frowned at the big Scot, shaking his head. A bell sounded. The door opened. Naomi walked in.

'Put it away, you bully,' she said to Grey-suit. 'Mick, time to go.' She helped me to my feet, walked me to the door, pushed me through and went back in. I turned in the doorway. She walked slowly to the counter, ignoring the stares. She leaned over and spoke to the youth in a stage whisper. 'Got any speed?' she said. 'Dexies? Mollies?'

No-one spoke.

The youth looked at the bikers.

The bikers looked at Grey-suit.

Grey-suit looked at Naomi.

She returned his look. 'Just asking,' she said.

He inclined his head in acknowledgement.

She shrugged and walked out, shepherded me to the car. I looked at the door. I knew I should know what to do with it. I knew I was swaying but couldn't stop.

'I'll drive,' she said, helping me into the passenger seat.

***

She stopped in a residents' parking space on a crowded little street between Cowley Road and Iffley Road. We both started to speak, then stopped. Both made "after you" gestures.

'That's where I stay,' she said. 'The blue door. Over there. Number 35.'

I nodded. 'Looks nice,' I said. 'Drink?'

'Not for me,' she said. 'And you shouldn't, you're concussed.'

I felt the need to make sense of the day, to reach some sort of interim closure on all sorts of issues. Especially the state of relations between us.

'Please. I really need to talk,' I said. 'I feel terrible.'

'Not surprised. You look terrible.'

We sat in silence.

I looked at her and waited.

She looked out of the car window and waited.

A robin was singing in a holly tree.

'Oh God then, all right,' she said. 'I'll fetch a parking permit. And I need to wash and change. You wait here.'

She got out and slammed the door.

My head throbbed. And my right ear. My day had a watermark running right through it, of impotence, frustration, personal failure. Was this what life with Naomi would be like? Or was it just teething troubles that would pass as our relationship developed?

She came back in jeans and T-shirt, hair damp from a shower, scented of summer meadows, like the adverts. We linked arms, walked to the nearest pub on Cowley Road, poked heads through the door. It was crowded and stuffy, with machines whirring and pinging, a huge TV, football and tacky music.

'Bloody awful,' she said.

We walked on, to the 'Live and Let Live'. The guest ales were from Camden. She ordered two pints of Hell's Lager. I paid. We went to the quietest corner.

'So what do you really need to talk about?' she said.

'Well, us really, most of all. First, I need to thank you for rescuing me. Twice in one day. And to apologise for not being on form. But, I suppose, I'd like to know that you like me at least a bit. At least, don't think I'm a total tosser.'

I hated the way that had come out so needy. But I couldn't unsay it.

She twitched her nose. One of those unconscious gestures that made my heart do somersaults.

'Oh Mick,' she said. At least she was half-smiling. Sort of. Wistfully. 'I do like you. Quite a bit. And of course I think you're a tosser. All men are. Some of the time, anyway.'

She was studying me. I tried to ignore the scrutiny, concentrated on the wet ring that my glass had left on the polished tabletop.

'I think,' she said, 'that we should finish the twenty questions game first. Before... well, before anything else. Then see where we are. And I'm still asking. Okay?'

I nodded, but held up a hand and said, 'I've a quick question for you first if that's okay? Just for information. Andrea – did you meet her over the Glebe Farm thing? Or did you know her before?'

'Why do you ask?'

'Just wondered. Because one time you were giggling together like schoolgirls. And your, er…'

'Our bet? She made that up, actually,' she said. 'We went through school together. Like, forever. Windmill Road Infants, Juniors. Then Cheney. Okay?'

I nodded again.

'So this is question five,' she said. 'No, six. Who are your true friends? And seven. How did they become friends?'

I slumped back in my chair, cradling a pint on my chest. I noticed I was blinking very frequently and tried to stop, but found that made it worse. 'Okay,' I said.

'Eight. What do you watch, like, on TV?'

'That's easy,' I said, sitting up. 'Nothing. Can't bear just sitting watching a screen. Waste of time. Should be banned. Or at least be illegal for under-eighteens.'

'I see,' said Naomi. 'And there I was thinking you were some sort of easy-going liberal. So. Next, what's your view of capitalism?'

'I'll answer that one now too. The roots of both capitalism and socialism lie deep in human nature. We're animals, but human nature is very plastic. How we've evolved, which makes us different from all other animals, is…'

Naomi was looking towards the door. A noisy trio of twenty-something blokes had come in, all tattoos and steroidal muscle and gratuitously exotic haircuts. The tallest, broadest and most pretentiously coiffed was looking our way.

He waved at Naomi. She raised a hand. He came over, not sparing me a glance.

'Hi babe,' he said. 'Not washing your hair tonight?'

'I already did,' she said, raising a damp end in evidence.

I could see they knew each other well and that some sort of battle of wills was going on. I felt very tired and beyond caring.

I rose. 'It's been lovely,' I said. 'Thanks for everything. Be seeing you.'

The hunk stood his ground. I manoeuvred round him and headed for the street. I looked back from the door. They were both watching me. I flapped a hand and left.

Approaching the car, I heard hurrying footsteps behind me. I turned and saw Naomi catching up. I waited and linked arms with her. She steered us slowly to her door. We stopped on the doorstep, de-linked arms. She turned to face me.

'That's not what you think,' she said.

'How do you know what I think? And why does it matter?'

'He's an old friend from school. A chef, at Harry's. Got me the job there, when I was chucked out of planning. Saved my life.'

I shrugged, hands in hip pockets.

She stood, arms folded, eye to eye. We were the same height, give or take.

'I'm not coming in,' I said.

'I'm not asking you in.'

A woman's voice, a block away, shouted, 'You don't know what that means! You don't know what that means!'

'No, you're not,' I said. Shrugged. 'Okay. Bye then.'

'Just one thing,' she said. 'It's a bit embarrassing.'

Now what? Life was full of surprises. 'Yes,' I said. 'What is it?'

'How are you off for dosh? Because I have to pay the rent tomorrow. And I'm broke. I was wondering if you could lend me a few quid, 'til I get paid. On the 25th.' She stopped, frowned. 'Say, five hundred?'

CHAPTER 14

DETECTIVE INSPECTOR JONES

'Daffy! You're not listening!'

In his head, Jones had been walking the downs at Rhossili; he knew every step, every undulation. He loved the place. The digital clock on the oven said he should have left for work two minutes ago. He put down his spoon and turned to his wife. 'Sorry, Ols. Miles away. Tell me again.'

'Jane and I were there yesterday, sketching. There's a "For Sale" sign at the entrance to the farm, and little yellow notices about planning, and great heaps of earth mounded up, and gravel.'

'Where is this again?'

'Dunmore Copse.'

Oh no, Glebe Farm again.

'You know,' she said, 'where we go to sketch. They've got dormice. Jane says it's going to be developed, that whole area. It's dreadful!'

'Oh. Yes. Didn't you know?'

'No, I didn't. Did you? Why didn't you tell me?'

'Thought you knew. There's been enough about it – protests, what-have-you. In the paper, Radio Oxford.'

'I'm going to join the protests,' she said. 'When's the next one?'

He felt the first twinge of a headache. It was bad enough having the Chief Constable and Alleyn on his back without his wife lining up with the protestors. 'I rather think they've been and gone, weeks ago, around the time they got outline planning.'

'They? Who's they?'

'St Mark's College, it'd be. They own the land. But don't worry, there'll be a consultation before they start work. You can make your views known.'

'What the fuck use is a consultation? It just legitimises the autocracy. If you can't say "No" to the lot of it, what is there to consult about?'

'Well, there's...'

'Dogwood or heather in the herbaceous borders? Lamp standards in grey, blue or black?'

'Yes, well...'

'It's a fucking disaster, that's what it is. It's criminal. And they've already started work, that's what I'm telling you.'

'It'll provide loads of jobs...'

'Jobs? In case you hadn't noticed, there's already full employment in Oxford for those capable of getting out of bed. And the Merry Englanders have taken us all out of the EU. You know what that means, don't you? All those nice hard-working Polish people, and Slovaks and Romanians and so on, will go home and there'll be millions of jobs and no-one willing or able to do them.'

Jones didn't know where to start. He often felt like this when conversations with his wife turned political, which was one reason he hadn't mentioned Glebe Farm before. He loved her and hated fighting with her, especially if he was on the wrong side and knew it, as he did now. She had a true moral compass and an acute sense of justice. His professional role tended to weigh him on the side of the establishment, which favoured development and growth over more or less everything, including morality and justice. And now Alleyn was pulling him further and faster beyond the merely unprofessional into the actively criminal. He had to keep that separate from his family. He couldn't even think about it in front of his wife; she could read his mind, for sure.

His phone rang. *Thank God*, he thought. 'Just a mo,' he said, 'better see who this is.'

'Jones? We have a problem.' It was Alleyn. Christ Jesus, how did he do it? His timing was awful.

'Just a minute,' Jones said, putting his hand over the phone. 'Got to take this,' he said to Olwen, 'and got to dash. We'll talk later. Love you.'

'Love you too. Daffy, are you all right? You look a bit peaky.' She put his briefcase in his hand and kissed his cheek. 'Be careful.'

He grabbed his jacket from the hall, got in the car, plugged the phone in for hands-free, pulled out of the drive and headed for Kidlington. 'Sorry about that,' he said to Alleyn. 'Had to get out of the house.' Out of a relatively comfortable frying pan, he thought, into the fires of hell. Could he ring off, turn round and go back to bed? No. 'What's up?' he said.

'You remember I told you about someone stalking the Sefton-Shaws? Did you ever do anything about that, by the way?'

'Er…'

'Thought not. It's Michael Jarvis.' IT consultant. 'He's been shagging Sefton-Shaw's wife. Conrad's put the threats on the guy but they're still meeting up. And it turns out he's a techie at Oxford Hypermedia, who're doing work for us. You're not telling me that's a coincidence.'

'I'm not telling you anything.'

'Though from what I've seen of him… well, he's what you'd call "challenged". Anyway, he turned up at the café yesterday.'

'Café?'

'You know, the bikers' place, near Dorchester. By the roundabout. Not with the woman that was with him when he blagged his way into Conrad's house. Who is Gail Mycroft, from

115

Parktown, Conrad says. But with one of the protestors from the Glebe Farm demo, Naomi Goodman, who Conrad fired from planning. So you know what that means.'

'What does it mean?'

'It means they're all working together in this protest group. He's been spying on the Sefton-Shaws for weeks, since outline planning went through. And he's been spying on me, through this IT project that he's supposed to be doing for us. Him and this woman Mycroft, they don't do protests, don't do anything public. They're like undercover. Spies. So find evidence of illegality. Or create it, whatever. Just get the bastards out of our way.'

CHAPTER 15

I gave my head a gentle shake. It was Wednesday morning. Yesterday I'd plodded through work feeling concussed and blue. The headache and dizziness weren't *as* bad now, but still bad. The blues were still blue. After Monday's nonsense my self-belief was at zero, self-loathing at max. And Naomi? She was important to me, but I had no idea whether I was important to her, except for amusement, rent money and the occasional spliff.

I closed my eyes, waiting for the bus. I felt the pressure of dusty light on my eyelids and opened them again. I saw a black and white cat come from a garden opposite, something in its mouth. Bird? Frog? Mouse? It crossed the road, threaded through the legs of the bus queue. It was carrying something with pale red-brown fur.

It went up a garden path onto a paved area beside the house and dropped its burden, watching the immobile furry lump, occasionally patting it with a paw, encouraging it to move, to try to escape so it could catch it again.

I wondered what Naomi was doing this morning.

It was a vole. Bank or field. Short tail, soft rounded nose, gingery back. It didn't stir. The cat kept patting it. I was aching to intervene, but someone was in the front window. I couldn't go into his garden and interfere with his cat.

There was a sudden sneeze to my right. The cat looked. I didn't, knowing it was the sour woman from the brick cottages who always cut me. Somehow the vole knew the cat's attention was momentarily elsewhere and it scuttled into undergrowth beside the fence. The cat sprang after it but came up with nothing. It sat watching the spot where the vole had vanished until the bus arrived. I hung back, letting others board first. The cat was still listening and watching when the bus set off.

A tractor passed on the other side, towing a wagon loaded with hay. I held my collar and looked for a four-legged animal, so I could make a wish, using magic inherited from my mum. By the primary school, a little blond Labrador sat patiently beside three chatting women. 'I wish that the vole gets away,' I said under my breath, letting go of my collar. Then I put a curse on the cat, using a kind of voodoo inherited from no-one: 'Flat cat flat cat flat cat flat', as quietly as I could. This sort of thing is best kept to oneself. If the wish worked the vole would survive. If the curse worked the cat would be flat before dark. Not that I really believed in it. But you never know.

Perhaps I wasn't being fair to the cat. It was only being true to its own nature. It wasn't the cat's fault that the cat population had been jacked up to a thousand times natural levels. Small mammals, reptiles, amphibians and birds were the losers, but the cat wasn't responsible. So my curse was wrong and should be reversed. Which was why I was chanting 'unflat cat unflat cat unflat cat unflat' as I stepped off the bus in St Giles, into the path of Naomi, who was walking briskly north.

'What are you chanting about now?' she asked, as if I was always chanting about something.

I began to explain about the cat and the vole and the wish and the curse and fairness...

She interrupted. 'You got time for a coffee?'

She linked arms and steered me into Waterstone's, upstairs to the café. I felt a flood of affection, lifted by her warmth. I collected a cappuccino and a flat white from the counter and brought them over.

She was crying.

'Oh Mick,' she said. 'Oh dear.'

I didn't know what to do.

I waited.

'Sometimes,' she said, 'I have no idea who I am.' She dabbed at tears with a paper napkin. 'Do you know what I mean?'

Did I? I wasn't sure. Like most people, I'd experienced existential crises.

'Possibly,' I said. 'Could you…?'

'It's like, what am I? What is it that I am? Why does it have this label Naomi stuck on it? Why is it in this funny-shaped clumsy body? Why does it feel what it feels? Why does it want to scream? What has this *it* here,' prodding her chest, 'got to do with that *it* over there?' She stabbed at my sternum with a scarlet-nailed finger.

'This *it* says "chocolate brownie",' I said, heading for the counter. An involuntary reaction.

She raised her eyes to heaven when I put it in front of her, but didn't say no. 'If you position yourself as oppressed or excluded or dominated, you're just playing into the hands of the oppressor. Aren't you?'

She took a bite.

I sipped my coffee, watched her eyes. The tears had stopped.

'But if you posit a relational identity. What does that mean for…'

She was looking beyond me, beyond the café area. I followed her eyes. Someone stood at the doorway from the stairwell, scanning the room, looking for something or someone. A woman with short turquoise hair. Tall, thin. Denims, multiple piercings.

Naomi shook her head and turned back to me. The woman turned back to the stairs.

I had a strange sensation, as if I was seeing the room from the other side, through a distorting glass curtain.

'Until just then,' I said. 'I had no idea what you were talking about. Then I suddenly got a feeling like you described. As if I was over there, seeing these two strange creatures that were us. You don't think it's catching, do you?'

She put her hand on mine. 'Mick, it's endemic. In women, anyway.'

I was lost again. I checked my watch. It was later than I thought. 'This *it* over here,' I said, 'must be in work by ten. Is that *it* over there going to be okay?'

She stood, sneezed three times. 'Nothing like a good sneeze,' she said, 'for getting grounded. I'm fine. Thank you. See you when… Monday?'

I left her browsing the feminist theory shelves and hurried downstairs, thinking that if she was using me, I didn't mind. I was paying insufficient attention to where my feet were putting themselves. I missed a step on a corner, lost my balance, and was caught by the tall woman with turquoise hair. She righted me as if she did it every day, and carried on up, trailing a strong waft of French tobacco.

I escaped from store to street, feeling out of rhythm with the world again. I couldn't wait to get lost in a data model.

***

The following afternoon I caught the five o'clock bus home. It was hot and humid and crammed with schoolgirls blowing pink bubblegum and sweaty boys with too much attitude and deodorant. Two old ladies in feathery hats and fur-trimmed November coats boarded at St Margarets Road, adding eye-watering mothball camphor to the mix. I got off at the next stop and cut through Frenchay Road, looking for breathable air by the canal.

I walked north, past residential moorings where I'd once seen and often heard water voles plopping. At this time of year it looked a lovely place to live. Someone was approaching under the railway bridge – a small woman struggling with three large dogs.

It was Andrea, looking smart in black with silver buttons. I kept putting one foot in front of the other until the dogs lunged at me. I stepped back into nettles and stood straight, folded my arms, told them they were good dogs. She hauled them back to the towpath.

'Hello. Didn't know you had dogs as well.'

'Oh they're not mine. Liberated.'

'Liberated?'

'Yes.' She looked up and down the canal. 'The hunt kennels. West Oxfordshire. Where that toffee-nosed twat Cameron sheds the blood of the innocents for fun. Responsible for the biggest cock-up in British politics since Togidubnos, so it's good publicity. They take a lot of walking though. And Tag can't stand them.'

'Tag?'

'The hedgehog.'

'They're foxhounds,' I said. 'You've stolen them. Surely that's illegal. Who's the 'we'? And what's that about publicity?'

'Well, it is illegal, strictly speaking. The 'we' is a secret. But just me and a few mates. The publicity helps because most people don't realise that we're ruled by a bunch of bloodthirsty cunts who actually enjoy killing beautiful wild animals. Do you know that they only stop the dogs tearing the fox to pieces so they can cut its tail off and rub its blood on the foreheads of any virgin hunters?'

'I thought they'd stopped all that. Don't they just do drag hunts now? Drag a bag of aniseed across the landscape and chase that?'

She gave me a scornful look. 'Do you believe in fairies too?'

Funny you should mention that, I thought, but kept my mouth shut.

***

I walked on up the canal. I knew Andrea as an officer in the Wildlife Trust, a protestor against development, a protector of dormice, and a woman of spirit. But this hunt saboteur stuff surprised me. I called Naomi.

She answered straight away. 'Hello Mick'. A neutral tone.

'Hello. Sorry to disturb. I just met Andrea. Walking three foxhounds along the canal.'

'Oh yes? She said she was looking after some dogs.'

'Do you know where she got them from?'

'Do you?'

'Yes. From our ex-Prime Minister's hunt stables. She stole them. With her hunt-sabbing mates.' It didn't seem to me to be the kind of low-profile activity that people hoping to bring down a major development scam might be expected to be restricting themselves to. 'Did you know about this?'

'I did. I was thinking that she might have told you about her animal rights stuff. As you seemed to be quite close at one time.'

I didn't know much about either of them, but I knew I trusted the one I was talking to. I had a sense that Naomi could have filled me in on Andrea's eccentricities, but had been reluctant to do so. Probably thought it was down to me to find out for myself. 'She didn't,' I said. 'And the last time we spoke was when we were with her at Dunmore Copse.'

'You went for coffee with her afterwards,' Naomi said.

'Yes. Well, mint tea actually. Must have spent about twenty minutes there. But she spoke not a word.'

'How weird. So you did all the talking? I thought turn-taking was one of your better points. Or didn't you say anything either?'

'Nothing except thanks for the tea and goodbye. By which time she was deep in meditation.' I could hear her laughing and wasn't sure why. 'But this afternoon, I was walking home up the canal, and there she was, being towed down the towpath by three huge dogs. And it makes me wonder, what else is there I don't know?'

Naomi snorted then sniffed. 'How am I supposed to know what you do and don't know? This is getting silly. You should ask her.'

'I'm asking you because I feel she's not been open with me,' I said. 'If there's stuff I should know, please tell me. We're all having to trust each other, and I trust you and I trust Gail, but suddenly I don't know about Andrea at all.'

'And you're feeling like these foxhounds might be the tip of the iceberg? Well… Do you know about the eco-terrorism?'

'Eco-terrorism?' Not a familiar term to me, but its connotations were obvious.

'She was saying, the other night – I was quite surprised, you know? – something like, "it's impossible to over-estimate the power of power". They own the police, the army, the secret services. They own the comms, the businesses, the banks, the prisons. And if anyone gets uppity, there are guns under the table, she said.'

'Christ.'

'She said, if we want to fight them, we have no chance without breaking the law.'

'Yes, I get that.' The law is on the side of power because power makes the law. 'What has she done then, in that line?'

'She mentioned one thing. Do you remember, a year or two ago? There was a rash of SUVs getting vandalised, all over Britain. People finding messages etched on their pride and joy. Like "TAX+", you know?'

'Implying they should be taxed more?'

'Yes, obviously. But apparently that ran out of steam because a lot of the eco-terrorists had SUVs. Or their families did. She's talking about shale gas drilling now.'

'So she's a hunt sab and eco-terrorist.'

'You know about the court cases?'

'No.'

'The most recent was last October, over some aggro at a drag-hunt meet, up near Chippy. Somebody brained a hunt follower with a fence post, fractured his skull. Andrea and her boyfriend were up in court for it.'

'Boyfriend?'

'Well, sort of. Bill. He's hardly a boy. They've been at it on-and-off since she was fourteen, when he was about forty. All a bit seedy. Lives on the cut, when he's around. A bit of a record. Criminal damage. Burglary. Cultivation. Assault. Endangering safety at aerodromes. Fines, suspended sentences, six months in Leyhill.'

'Good God. What you might call a bad influence.'

'Au contraire. He's nowhere near the shiniest shoe in the rack. She's the brains, always into something. Road protest. Hunting. Fracking. American bases. Trident. SUVs. Gas pipelines. You name it. She ropes him in to help. If they get caught, she denies everything, he takes the fall. Seems to take pride in it, like a manly duty. He's been in Bullingdon since December, doing twelve months for that assault. She walked, of course. Charmed them all. Her dad was in the army, did you know? Major General Turner. Royal Engineers, Signals, MoD. Retired now, in Wiltshire. Owns two villages, three farms, and four miles of the upper Avon. So a nice upper-middle girl with big blue eyes and a warm smile for the beak, who thought she'd been corrupted by an idle good-for-nothing tree-hugging new-age waster. Whereas in truth it was quite the reverse.'

***

Monday morning, a few days later, I met Gail for coffee on the way to work.

'Would you like a family?' she asked, apropos of nothing. 'One day, I mean, not now, necessarily. Excuse my asking.'

A bit like one of Naomi's twenty questions. 'Well, of course I would. I suppose. Wouldn't everyone, really?'

She shrugged.

'I've known people,' I said, 'who see themselves as loners, as if that's something romantic. But it's more like, you can't make it with a loving partner so you tell yourself that you prefer independence anyway. You end up believing it. And you've made your own truth and it's all just ashes.' Not like me, of course. I looked out of the café window, trying not to think about it. A young woman with a pushchair looked at the café like it was the promised land, then pushed on to the Co-Op.

'What did someone say in that Annie Proulx story?' Gail said. 'Takes more than one post to make a fence? Something like that.'

'What about you?' I said. 'How do you feel? Things must have changed since your mother… Would you have liked… Or would you still…'

I petered out, realising I was trampling around in delicate areas.

'Well, yes of course, in a way I would have, I suppose. But…'

I looked at her serious face and wanted to touch her cheek or her hand. I tried to fathom where her "but" came from. 'But there's families and families?'

'That's it,' she said. 'I would only want the right sort of family. And wonder if, to make a happy family, you have to have been part of one when you were growing up. Not all black and white, of course. Mine was probably happy when Father was alive. I just can't remember it. I can remember happy times with Mother, but we were more like friends than family, despite the age difference. Very close and self-sufficient, the two of us. Didn't need anyone outside. Until she died. Then you're left not knowing where to start and it's too late anyway.'

I tried to say something gentle. 'Some families seem happy enough, even without biological bonds. My lot, there's this strange network of friends that behave like brothers and sisters, mixed with actual brothers and sisters, and stepsisters, half-brothers, step-parents' step-children from previous relationships, and so on. Hard to disentangle and it doesn't matter.'

'Sounds lovely.' She looked out of the window, wistful.

'It's not down to any individual, but it's not an accident either. Someone said something about happy families all being happy…'

'Yes, in the same way. And unhappy ones each being unhappy in their own way.' She smiled. 'Tolstoy. *Anna Karenina*. Supposed to be one of the best opening lines in literature.' She brightened. 'Know any others? Opening lines?'

'Do you?'

'Well. "It was the best of times, it was the worst of times."'

'Yes. Dickens.'

'"It is a truth universally acknowledged…"'

'Austen.'

'You're good at this. One more? "The past is a foreign country…"'

'Erm…'

'*The Go-Between*,' she said. 'L.P. Hartley.'

'Never read that. We were supposed to at school, but… My favourite is Chris Brookmyre's first novel. Just two words on the first line.'

'And they are…?'

'"Jesus fuck."'

Gail's snort attracted the attention of the whole café.

'About this evening,' I said, trying to get on to what we'd met to discuss. 'Seven at the Globe. Everyone's coming. Just wanted to run through priorities and who should do what.'

***

An hour and two coffees later we came out into fitful sunshine. 'Look,' I said pointing across the street. 'James Alleyn. Sefton-Shaw's mate.' He was head and shoulders above the shoppers coming out of M&S. Must be six foot three or four, I thought. He crossed the busy road as if the traffic wasn't there, put a twenty-pound note into a coffee carton held out by a man begging under a birch tree and strode on through the discreet entrance of the university property services office. The man gaped after him.

Gail went off to browse charity shops. I stared at the door Alleyn had gone through, struck by his unexpected generosity, and by something about the way he carried himself. It wasn't that he looked guilty. He looked like he didn't care, because no-one could touch him.

I walked to work, thinking about how to play tonight's get-together. Some of us would be breaking quite serious laws. Should I try to find ways of sharing the jeopardy, so everyone was in the same boat? Or should we try to limit jeopardy by working on a need-to-know basis? We knew something seriously illegal was going on. Conrad was only out to get me, at the moment, as far as we knew, but things could become dangerous for all of us. They could come at us with bribery or blackmail, intimidation or physical violence. They could frame us, even if we'd done nothing wrong. Or was I over-thinking this?

I ran a little inventory in my head. I trusted Gail completely. Naomi as well, though she had the whole rest of her life that I knew next to nothing about. The others? Andrea had her own agenda. Linda and Tom were obviously broke and desperate, and would surely have an eye for the main chance. What if Sefton-Shaw got at them with promises about the farm or financial inducements? In fact, they could have been turned already and be spying on what we were doing. A horrible thought.

**

Friday and I arrived at the Globe at seven. We were meeting as a group for the first time since the pissed-off party. Linda was busy elsewhere but Tom was early. Friday settled under the table with her head on Andrea's feet.

I still wasn't sure how to approach the session. I'd been taking the lead too much, and thought I'd just try to relax and let things evolve. I was soon deep in conversation with Gail and Naomi about government plans for rationing. Naomi said it was a PR stunt aimed at brain-dead Daily Mail readers. That applied to most government policy, I thought.

Andrea was talking to Tom, with a glint of mischief. Tom was referring to inputs, Andrea calling them cumulative long-term ecosystemic toxins. Tom switched to infestations, Andrea to biodiversity and pollination. I had a sense that she was leading Tom down the garden path towards an embarrassing contradiction. She shared her home with a lot of what Tom would call pests. Letting their conversation run on was unlikely to do much for group cohesion.

I said 'Excuse me' to Gail and Naomi, stood up, cleared my throat, glanced round, sat down. The talking stopped. They were all looking at me, probably thinking I was barmy. But at least they weren't warming up for a fight.

'Okay. It's two weeks since we met,' I said, happy now to busk it. 'First question. Are we all still as pissed off as we were last time?'

Tom said, 'More, if anything.'

Everyone nodded.

'Last time,' I said, 'we had a few ideas. Can we kick off by going round the table again? What you've done, what you've found, what you might do next, that kind of thing. Who wants to start? Andrea? Weren't you going to look at the council, you and Gail?'

Andrea gave a tight smile. 'Well, there's been one or two things going on... relationship issues,' she said, 'and three new dogs to look after. And a friend was due out on probation last week but they stopped that, for bad behaviour. Just the odd spliff, for Christ's sake. So I've been a bit tied up really.'

'I'm sure we all understand,' I said. 'Please don't worry about it.'

'I won't.'

'And,' I said, 'I hope the dogs are okay and your friend gets out soon. Tom, we knew you guys were going to be busy. Any thoughts on muck-spreading or blockades?'

'No,' Tom said. 'But some news. They've started work on our land. Came as a surprise, specially where they're doing it, on our forty-acre by the A44. Supposed to be ours until next April. We'd made hay, were going to put a hundred stirks on for the aftermath. But they've bull-dozed and levelled and got great heaps of hard-core all over. I don't know which way to turn. You ask the blokes on the machines what's going on. They're just contractors, doing what they're told. They say ask the council. You ask the council. Not as easy as it sounds. If you get through the switchboard, you're passed from one department to another and eventually someone says, ask the landowners, which is still St Mark's. And no-one there knows what you're talking about. They say, ask the university estates office. And no-one there knows what you're talking about either. They say find out who the contractors are working for and ask them. And the contractors are working for the council. It's what they call giving you the run-around, isn't it? It'd be bad enough if we had use of the land 'til April, but the way they're going, they'll have us out before then and bankrupt into the bargain.'

'Grim,' said Gail. 'Wish there was something we could do. Can't see it, though. Anybody else?'

A lot of shaken heads, no suggestions.

Gail continued. 'Think your farm's buggered, Tom, to be honest, whatever we do. And the dormice. Sorry.'

I was surprised by her candour, which was verging on brutal. I wanted to prove her wrong, somehow.

'Mick, should I go next, for what it's worth?' Gail said.

I nodded.

'Main things,' she said. 'Conrad Sefton-Shaw. The city's head of planning... and sustainable development. Don't laugh. Married to Kimberly. Cosy relationship with James Alleyn, lawyer and director of Ballator Developments. Mick and I saw Alleyn at the Sefton-Shaws' with someone we think was Donald Cruickshank from university property services. Those three are at the heart of it, whatever it is. Frustrating. We know they're up to something but don't know what. We need to listen in to their conversations. Heard anything at Harry's, Naomi?'

Naomi glanced at Andrea before speaking. She looked anxious.

'Well,' she said. 'They still come in for lunch. You'd think they'd get bored, but the boss treats them like royals and they love that. Sefton-Shaw's there most days, with a couple of... frou-frous, I call them. Attractive young women with posh frocks and no brains. Sometimes with a shifty-looking guy who seems to be his bag-carrier. Alleyn's often there. Cruickshank too, who always picks up the tab when he's there, on a gold uni Visa card. And drinks a lot, even by their standards. Whisky after whisky, at lunchtime. He doesn't look well. Flabby but thin, yellow skin, red eyes. A Scot, by the way...' She looked at me. 'Mick, how he talks reminds me of your biker friend in that café. The big one. Sounded just like Cruickshank. Identical voices.'

'Oh God, don't,' I said, struck by how much we didn't know. It was like swimming way out at sea, with no idea what was between you and the seabed.

'I get a feeling,' Naomi said, 'they're excited about something, but careful not to talk about it when they might be overheard. Sefton-Shaw polices that, no matter how much he's had to drink. So I don't know what they've got cooking, but I think it's coming to the boil.'

'Terrific, thanks,' Gail said. She described what she and I had found at Springfield House: the layout of the house, especially downstairs; potential locations for bugs; the fact that the Sefton-Shaws didn't activate their intruder alarms at night if they were in the house.

'Good work,' said Naomi, looking at me with surprise and half a frown. 'I guess it's best we don't know how you got that information, the risks you've been taking. But well done.'

'Thanks,' I said, pleased with the unprompted emergence of a need-to-know strategy.

'Probably worth mentioning,' Naomi said, 'that Mick and I

tracked Alleyn to the Ballator offices in Botley, saw him come out, tried to follow, lost him. But anybody know that bikers' café, on the Reading road, by a roundabout? We'd pulled in there to decide what to do, and spotted Alleyn inside, with this group of bikers. He left by the back door. Mick went in to ask a few questions. It got a bit rough. No bones broken though. Were there?'

I shook my head.

'But we thought it was a weird connection for a guy like him. Lawyer. Director. Big shot.'

It was embarrassing to recall my ineptitude. I wanted to be walking home over the common with Friday, in the cool evening air. 'So we know more than we did,' I said. 'We know there's something dodgy going on. Something big. We know some of the people involved. But that's about it.'

'What Mick and I think,' Gail said, 'is that we should press on with tapping into their conversations at Springfield House.'

Everyone seemed to agree.

'If we can help, let us know,' Andrea said.

'Thanks,' I said. 'And I know this is becoming a bit of a bore. But the less you know, the less you can tell, so the less dangerous you are to these people, so the safer you are. Probably. Is that okay with everyone?'

'As far as it goes,' Naomi said. 'But what can we be doing while you and Gail are playing spies? Because it's not going to happen overnight, is it, your bugging?'

Andrea and Tom nodded agreement.

'Ideas?' I wanted people to do their own thinking.

'I'll carry on picking up snippets at Harry's,' Naomi said.

'For sure.'

'And,' she said, 'it occurs to me that because I'm the only one that regularly gets close to them, I'll know their voices better than anyone else here. So if you manage to get any recordings of their conversations, I can help in deciphering what's going on, who's saying what.'

'Great. Fantastic.' Two women crossed my line of vision, dressed identically in black leather jackets, black T-shirts, blue denims. Each had a mass of tight curls, one dark, one redhead. One carried two pints, the other a set of darts.

Naomi was smiling, amused to have caught me noticing the dart players. 'Andrea,' she said. 'I'm thinking that organising a midnight manure drop outside the council offices might be just up your street. How about helping Tom set it up?'

Tom smiled and nodded, and Andrea's face lit up. 'Yes,' she said, glancing across at the dartboard. The women were chalking up for Killer, with two older men and much laughter. 'And I know just the person to invite along. From the Oxford Times.'

'Great.' I was pleased all the ideas weren't coming from me but did have one or two more to put into the mix. 'Andrea, you know how things work at the Wildlife Trust. If you're doing stuff with Tom and Linda anyway, could you have a look at what skills they have, from their lives in farming, that could be useful in areas like… I don't know, reserve management? Habitat management? The practical end of what the trust does. And what sorts of skilling up they'd need. Because I'm sure the trust does lots of work with farmers. Imagine how it would be if someone like Tom turned up with a Wildlife Trust hat on.'

I could see a small spark of hope in Tom's eye. And Andrea's.

'Actually,' she said, 'a report on Glebe Farm is on my to-do list at work. Flora and fauna audit, land use history. For historical purposes, so we'll know what we've lost. But which you'd also have to do if you were going to make a management plan for the future. And it'd be great to have your help with that, Tom. And Linda's. And it'd be a practical way of looking at skills and so on. What do you think?'

'Great, yes, thank you,' Tom said, looking happier than I'd ever seen him.

'Okay.' I was feeling pleased too. 'Lots to do. And no pressure of course, we've all got lives, other things to do, so no rush and no worries. I'm thinking it's going to take a few weeks to get somewhere with all this. Shall we aim to meet again as a group in – what? Four weeks? Unless something crops up...'

Nods all round.

'Okay, see you all then. Monday 10th July, here, seven o'clock? And I'll see at least some of you before then.'

I headed briskly for the loos. When I got back they'd all left, except Friday, who was dozing under the table, and Naomi, who was staring into the dregs of a San Miguel. I picked up my bag, put a hand on her shoulder. 'You all right?'

'Not really,' she said. 'Mick?'

'Yes.'

'I'm broke again. And hungry. And do you have any weed?'

'Come on, you. It'll be lovely. We can walk back to mine, through Burgess and over the common. I'll do a transfer. The Standard can deliver some of their finest. And yes, I do.'

CHAPTER 16

DETECTIVE INSPECTOR JONES

Jones looked up. He was in the Chief Constable's office. He shook his head. The Chief Constable was behind her desk, studying him. 'According to him,' she said, 'three of their best hounds have gone missing.'

'Hounds, ma'am? Sorry, just lost track there,' Jones said, bringing her properly into focus. 'Who said that again?' This sort of thing was happening more and more: drifting off in conversations, missing connections that people expected him to make. Was he past his best? Or was it Alleyn's escalating demands challenging his rather tattered sense of duty? He just needed to pull his socks up and keep his nose clean until he could head for the hills; it was just nine months to the end of March and freedom from all the nonsense. The place on the Gower still hadn't sold.

The Chief leaned back, frowning. 'The Commissioner. Martin Carter. He was telling me about the call he'd had from his old mate Cameron?'

They'd even knocked the price down a notch. Might be worth putting in a low offer, just to test the water. 'Cameron who?'

'David.'

They should do it now. A low offer on the Gower place. He'd do it today. Olwen would be pleased. 'With respect, ma'am,' he said, 'why didn't he tell Mr David that we're not a lost dogs service?'

'Not Mr David, Jones. Wake up for God's sake. Mr Cameron. David Cameron. Used to be Prime Minister. Fucked the Lib Dems and thought a referendum on leaving the EU was a good idea. That Mr Cameron.'

'Ah yes,' Jones said. Was this what despair felt like? Wherever he looked there were strings being pulled, wheels within wheels. 'But all the same, with respect, ma'am, why didn't he tell Mr Cameron we're not a lost dogs service?'

'Because they're old mates. They do a lot of business together,' the Chief Constable said. 'And what would you do if an ex-prime minister rang up and asked you for a favour?'

'Yes, I take the point.' He had to make himself engage, make the right noises, but was dog warden duty what thirty years of diligent policing got you? Mostly diligent, anyway. 'You'd hardly tell him to get lost. Where did they go missing from?'

'From the hunt kennels. Heythrop. Near Chippy.'

'Foxhounds, then, these would be?'

'They would.'

'And they escaped? Or…'

'No. Stolen, by hunt saboteurs.'

'How does he know?'

'He'll have security. The Met do it for all ex-PMs, as you no doubt know. They'll have an eye on what's going on round about him. And apparently a little bird – that'll be someone in the protection unit – told Mr Cameron we should have a word with a certain Andrea Turner, aka Adrienne Journeaux. Ask her where she was on the night of 13th June.'

'Andrea Turner. She's one of the Glebe Farm protestors.'

'She is indeed. Could you pull her in for a chat, put a bit of pressure on? Wouldn't do us any harm if we could help him get his dogs back.'

'Yes ma'am.' *Certainly. Of course. Not as if we're busy with anything more important, is it? Lost dogs, Christ.* He'd put Clappison on it. The more you piled on, the more he seemed to like it. Jones remembered feeling like that himself, in the dim and distant.

'But speaking of Glebe Farm,' she said. 'Everything nice and quiet on that front? I've not heard anything for a while.'

He'd been hoping she'd lost interest. Apparently not. 'Everything's fine, ma'am, thank you. All under control.'

'*Je touche au bois,*' she said, tapping her temple. Clearly her faith in him wasn't absolute. He couldn't blame her. 'Surveillance?'

'You authorised intercept applications,' he said. 'To phone networks and email and app service providers. Nothing back yet but we are chasing. Intercepts in place on mail deliveries, tracking devices on vehicles. And I've got an officer on, erm...'

'ICO?'

'ICO?'

'Intermittent covert observation.'

'Oh, ICO. Yes. I'd need a budget code to do more than that.'

'I'll think about that. And I'll tell the Commissioner we're inviting Ms Turner in for a chat about dogs. He can pass that back if he wants. Press her on their protest plans too, can you?'

Alleyn will be pleased, Jones thought.

The Chief checked her notes. 'Anything more on that dead shark thing?'

'Nothing new. No indication of how it might relate to Oxford,' he said. And another Commissioner-driven waste of effort. 'You couldn't tell him we're at a bit of a dead end, without talking to the person who raised it, could you? We can't go quizzing people at random round the college. Might scare the horses, you know what these guys are like. If he could point us in the right direction...'

'I see your point, Detective Inspector. But he is the Commissioner. Don't you have anyone who's been to university, and is civilised enough to make discreet enquiries?'

Clappison again, Jones thought. *Clappison with his doctorate. Definitely from another planet, despite claiming to be from Stoke Poges. He's prone to social gaffes and comes over as a complete tosser so he'd probably fit in nicely. And beggars can't be choosers.*

'I'll see what I can do, ma'am.'

CHAPTER 17

Wednesday morning in the office, I made coffee for Denise while she talked about some horses she'd inherited, then started mapping out a proposal for a book trade consortium who thought they could do a better job for buyers than Amazon, while taking a smaller rake-off from sellers. It's good when you can buy into a client's goals and values.

I was meeting Kanhai later to talk about ways and means of covert surveillance, so tried to sort out my ideas on that whenever I took a break, and got through the day without dwelling too much on Naomi and her push-me-pull-you stuff on Monday night. She seemed to want me closer until I got closer. Then she wanted me further away. I still had that melting feeling when I saw her, but it was becoming exhausting. And expensive.

After work I went to the Alderman's. There was no sign of the phenomenological barmaid. I brought pints, sat across from Kanhai, got straight down to business.

'We know something's going on. We know it involves the uni, a big building firm and a law firm, as well as city planning. We know some of the individuals involved. We know where they meet for lunch two or three times a week. We know they also meet at

Sefton-Shaw's, in Boars Hill. We want to know what they're saying to each other. Face to face and on the phone and by email. And I wouldn't mind having a peek in one or two bank accounts. And what I need to work out is what kit can be borrowed or bought, and what we can do with it.'

'What's your budget?' Kanhai said.

'Budget?' Despite feeling I'd thought it through pretty thoroughly, I realised I'd focused on what and how, but given no thought to how much.

'Budget. Money. How much can you afford to spend?'

'Well, no budget as such. Thought we might be able to borrow some stuff?'

'Borrow,' Kanhai said. 'Who from?'

'Well, from your lot? Possibly?' That was pathetic, and Kanhai was annoyed. Not for the first time. 'You do have this sort of stuff though, don't you?' I knew I was presuming much too much.

'We must do. I don't know where it's kept or who's in charge of it. But I do know I'd have no chance of borrowing it, surreptitiously or otherwise. Okay? And while we're clearing out nonsense, let's get rid of phones too. Not on, intercepting electronic communications. Much more serious offence than listening to people talking in person, though not so different really. But let's start with your wish list, then look at priorities and practicalities. Bugs first. Who and where?'

I listed Alleyn's office at the law firm; Cruickshank's at the university; the Ballator board room; the group's usual table at Harry's Hash House; somewhere at Springfield House.

Kanhai counted on his fingers, shaking his head. 'Five places. One privileged, the lawyer's. Three quite public. One private house. If you could only do one, which would it be?'

'Springfield House. We know they meet there and we've managed to have a look at it. So we've an idea of how it might be done.'

'Tell me.'

I told him about the website that would supply an audio bug embedded in a piece of everyday household equipment, and that we had the data on a smoke detector in Springfield House. 'An S4S, model 9G-ix. In the same room as their landline and answerphone.'

'Where's this website?'

'Somewhere in the States. I can find the URL if…'

'No, don't bother,' Kanhai said. 'I know somewhere in London. So it won't come through customs. Be quicker and cheaper too. Give me the details again.'

I repeated them. 'White. It comes in two parts. The mount screws into the ceiling. The unit itself is battery-powered and clips into the mount. We'd only need the unit, not the mount. Get a quote first, okay? Because the dollar price for that lot is over two K, for the adapted smoke detector and the transceiver to relay what it picks up.'

Kanhai nodded. 'Who's going to install it?'

'I am. With Gail on look-out duty.'

'It's like something out of Le Carré,' he said. 'Or Enid Blyton. So that's it for bugs. For a start anyway. And we're not listening in to phones. So that just leaves emails and bank accounts.' He looked at his watch. 'I need to get home. But what about I come round after work tomorrow, say half eight, and we make a start on that? Have you got the email addresses you want to get into?'

'Not yet.'

'Get them.'

***

Kanhai was back at eight thirty the following evening, explaining why he needed to do it at mine as he came through the door. 'Basically, if the IP address that's doing this is identified I want it to be yours not mine, for obvious reasons. But I've brought something to stop that happening.'

He stuck a memory stick in my laptop. 'I'm loading a procedure to connect to the web through a chain of proxies. You know about TOR? The Onion Router?'

'Yes, sure. Dark web stuff.'

'Not exactly, though dark web people use it, for anonymous access. Makes it hard to trace where requests come from, because they're wrapped in layers of encryption, and passed through multiple proxy servers, each of which only looks at one layer. So unwrapping it is like taking an onion apart, one layer at a time. Slow and difficult. But the problem is, TOR was developed with US government funding. And the NSA has been known—'

'NSA? National Security Agency?'

'Yes. They've been known to engineer back doors into it. Or into software that's bundled with it. So it's like there's a knife out there that can slice the onion quick and easy. So we don't use it, not directly. We use MetaTOR. UK developed. Launches new TOR equivalents at each node. So it's like you're hiding in this onion. For a micro-second. Then that. Then another. There's never enough time for even the sharpest knife to get past the first layer of your onion before you're in a different one. And I'll get signalled automatically if there's any attempt at interception.'

'Did you make this yourself?'

'I wish,' Kanhai said, tapping the side of his nose. 'No. Our friends along the A40.'

Very arch. He must mean Cheltenham. Good enough for me.

He passed me the laptop, talked me through launching MetaTOR.

'Okay?' he said. 'Got that? So now we're connected and they could get the CIA on the case and they'd still not get near. So who's the top priority? Sefton-Shaw?'

I read out Sefton-Shaw's email, c.s.s@oxfordcity.gov.uk.

'A work email. Good. Unlikely to do anything too nefarious there, though he could be that stupid. You can have a look. But almost certain to have sent things to a personal account from here. Let's see.'

Kanhai went quiet and fiddled around for a few minutes. I watched over his shoulder but couldn't keep track of his fingers.

'There we are,' he said, grinning. 'This is almost too easy. They've left the default admin user set-up and not changed the install password. Which is... guess.'

'Administrator?'

'Spot on.' Kanhai was smiling. A few more twiddles. 'Okay. So we're in to his account. Login name is email address. Password... guess. I'll give you a clue. He likes his dog and can count its legs.'

'Er... Lovelump4?'

'Nearly. Count.'

'Oh. Okay. Lovelump1234.'

'Correct. Upper case L. Then all lower. Okay. I'll have a quick look through his contacts.'

I watched a pigeon settle onto a branch of the ash tree across the way.

'Here's a possible, css67@bluehorizon.com,' Kanhai said, twiddling some more. 'Well. Yes. ID is the email address. Password is, believe it or not...'

'Lovelump1234 again?'

'Yep. Dearie me. So there you are. You're into him. It's an active account so it may have what you want. If not let me know. But I don't want to know anything about what you find there. So, you know how to get in?'

'Yes.'

'And when you're in, don't change anything. Except if you read an unread message, mark it back to unread. Okay? And log out properly. And to close down the onions, just run that procedure again. Do it now.'

He watched over my shoulder.

'Seems straightforward,' I said.

'It is. So you should be okay. If anyone detects that someone's been into the account, they won't track it back to you.'

'Cool, thanks.'

'And you want to have a go at bank accounts. Need to know which banks we're looking at. Sort codes and account numbers if poss. Have a crack at it Sunday afto, five-ish?'

***

I was out for a Friday lunchtime drink with some guys from the office. We were supposed to be celebrating shipping a beta of a booking and ordering app for restaurants, but the actual guys producing it were still at their workstations doing last-minute patches and re-tests and probably weren't very happy. Not my project though. I was talking horses with our all-round admin guru, Denise, when my phone pinged. A message from Kanhai: *kit arrived pick up tonite*

'Got to deal with this,' I said, going outside and beyond the circle of vapers round the pub door. Sent an *okay* to Kanhai, and left a message on Gail's voicemail saying the time had come and I'd be with her at eleven p.m.

Back inside, Denise was talking to someone else about horses. She paused to raise an eyebrow in my direction. 'All cool,' I said, smiling. 'Personal.' She winked at me, assuming, as always, an unwarranted familiarity with my private life, given that we only ever talked about work and horses. I went to the bar for coffees.

When the evening came I was more than nervous. I assembled my kit and a quiet bag of dog treats, and dressed in black, topped off by a many-pocketed black waistcoat with tools and gloves and a black balaclava in its pockets. I picked up the package from Kanhai and went on to Gail's in Parktown. I kept telling myself the reconnaissance mission to Springfield House had gone perfectly; there was no reason to think that the installation mission would be any different. Trouble was, I didn't believe it.

I hadn't been to Gail's before. "1854" was over the front door; three generous storeys of Victorian elegance and a basement. The doorbell looked like it had come with the house. I rang it. She let me in. It smelled of museums and lavender soap, and was full of Victorian furnishings and the accretions of five or six tasteful generations.

She led me through a stately hall and corridor to a large room spanning the back of the house: kitchen, dining and snug sitting area, and a conservatory full of scented geraniums and Lloyd Loom chairs. Lots of house for one person.

We sat at a scrubbed oak table, unwrapped the kit, laid out the components: the doctored smoke alarm unit; the transceiver, matt black, the size of a small bar of soap; batteries; phone charger; and an unregistered 'burner' phone, 95% charged, carrying thirty pounds credit.

Gail plugged it in to top up the charge and fitted new batteries to the transceiver. I put batteries in the smoke alarm. She pressed a button on the transceiver and a pinprick of green light flashed twice. I pressed a button on the smoke alarm labelled "TEST". A red light and loud squark said it was working.

'Noisy, Jesus,' I said, taking a breath to slow my heart. 'What do you think? How do you feel?'

'Like it's the interesting bit now,' she said. 'Just calm, really. Every army going into battle believes God is on its side. But in our case, she is. Don't you think?'

'I hope so.' My mind was conjuring a never-ending series of ways this could go wrong. When in doubt, do something. 'Let's do a system test now,' I said. 'We'll do another when it's all in place. Inshallah.'

Gail held the transceiver with the burner phone beside her.

I held the smoke alarm at arm's length, and said quietly, 'One. One. Two. Three. Five. Eight. Thirteen.'

'Twenty-one. Fibonacci.'

'Yes. That'll do.' I put a finger to my lips, watched my second-hand tick half a circuit. The burner phone gave a quiet ping. Gail picked it up, pressed a button, tapped the screen. After a few seconds, my phone signalled an incoming email. I opened the message, clicked on the attachment. My voice came out: 'One. One. Two…'

'Good,' I said. A big tick on my mental to-do list. Perhaps this would work. 'It's fully charged? And you're going to be all in black?'

Gail took off her sky-blue scarf, picked up the burner phone, her own phone and the transceiver. I added my phone and the smoke alarm to my waistcoat pockets and attempted a smile. Gail snorted with laughter, finding something genuinely amusing.

CHAPTER 18

We parked in the Foxcombe Hall car park just after midnight. We could see into Berkeley Close through gaps in the hedge. I turned off the interior lights so they wouldn't come on when the doors were opened. In the part of the house that we could see, there were three lights on: two upstairs, one down. We stayed in the car, waiting, not saying much. I was more than edgy. Gail seemed calm.

Kimberly Sefton-Shaw appeared with a large green wheelie bin. She parked it on the verge at the end of the Close, to the left of a similar one.

'Isn't that usually the man's job?' I said. 'In most couples.'

Gail sniffed. Kimberly walked slowly back to the house.

'My mum found a hedgehog in ours once,' I said, 'when I was a kid.'

'Dead or alive?' Gail asked.

'Yes. Schrödinger's hedgehog.' I laughed, then stopped, realising it wasn't funny. 'Alive. I didn't know they could run so fast.'

'Noisy blighters too,' she said. 'We could empty it for them.'

'When they're all in bed.'

We ran through timings, contingencies. Gail increased her wait time from one and a half to two hours, after which she'd assume my in-house mission was compromised. She'd keep watch from the heath, where she could see the back of the house, and leave the keys in the car and the door open, giving her the best chance of detecting any problem and getting away quickly and quietly.

Both upstairs lights went off. The downstairs light went off. Came on again. Went off.

As far as we could see, the house was in darkness.

We waited another thirty minutes. No more lights showed in the house. At one thirty we got out of the car. I eased open the hatchback. We pulled on latex gloves. Gail carried the red-shrouded torch. We crossed the road and opened the left-hand green bin. She handed me the torch and said, 'You lean it over. I'll get them out.'

She put five smelly bags on the verge.

'No hedgehogs,' I said.

We heard a car down the hill. Headlights were coming towards us. We shrank back into the shadows of the Bothy's hedge and stayed still. The car slowed, then accelerated up the hill, leaving a whiff of diesel.

'Phew,' I said. 'You don't know how nervy you are, do you, until...'

'No. Come on,' said Gail.

We took the bin bags to the car, put them in the back, covered them with a blanket. We stood in the car park in the dark. There was a soft westerly breeze, no moon.

I listened, breathed the air. 'Badgers?' I said, procrastinating.

She could read my mind. 'Never mind badgers,' she said. 'Come on. Courage. *Vive la République*.' She patted her pockets and pulled out a small black object. 'Transceiver first.'

I watched as she pressed a button and the green pinprick lit up again.

'Still seems happy,' she said.

'Good.' I checked I had cable ties. 'I won't quite believe it until we run a test with everything in place, but... good.'

We crossed the stile and followed the line of the Bothy's trimmed border to its junction with the spiky mass of the Springfield House hedge. It had sounded straightforward when we planned it but didn't look so easy now. I probed it with gloved hands, jerked back as an owl hooted, surprisingly loud: a tawny, calling from the wood across the heath, matching our agreed danger signal.

I withdrew my hands. Thorns tore through thin plastic gloves and thin skin. I shook them but couldn't tell whether they were bleeding. I put on new gloves.

'Don't be such a wimp,' Gail said.

'Do you think it's trying to warn us of something?'

'The owl? God, I don't know,' she said.

'It does it much better than you.'

'So it should,' she said. 'It's an owl. But I've brought a special owl-whistle thing this time. Listen.'

She pulled something from a jacket pocket, turned to face the wood and blew a very plausible imitation of the real thing. 'That's better, isn't it?' she said.

The real thing hooted back.

'Cor,' I said. 'So it is. Come on then.'

She held the dim torch. I reached deep into the hedge, secured the transceiver with two black cable ties, reached in again to trim off the tails. I stepped back, another pair of gloves in tatters. I breathed out a tense lungful that I hadn't been aware of holding.

We walked back to the car in silence. I focused on slow breathing. Gail toyed with the owl whistle. I'd seen the delight on her face when she got a reply. I hoped she'd resist the temptation to start a conversation.

I went through my pockets and took out things I wasn't going to need, like cable ties, then made sure I had everything I might need and knew where it was. I pulled on my balaclava and new gloves. We did one last check that we each knew what to do if this or that happened and synchronised watches: two thirty-five. If I wasn't back by four thirty-five, she'd leave me to it.

Gail headed for the heath.

I walked to the Springfield House entrance, staying in shadow, pausing at the gates to look and listen.

I eased down the side of the house – no lights showing, no sound.

As before, I found the third window at the back latched in the ventilation position. I blessed creatures of habit and used my old credit card to lift the latch, talking quietly to Lovelump. I pulled the window open, scattered dog treats on the floor, then climbed up and in using a garden chair. I eased down from window ledge to floor, gave the dog more treats and scratched its ears. Then I stopped, suddenly uneasy. Something was wrong. A sound? A smell?

I took out the shrouded torch, switched it on, checked that the smoke alarm was still in place, and looked carefully round the room. The answering machine display said "2" in steady green. A bottle of The London No. 1 Gin, next to a bottle of Glenfarclas, was on top of the drinks cabinet, both almost full. Another display flashed "00:00" in red. A radio. The sofa... two legs resting on one of its arms, a head resting on the other, black hair hanging. Kimberly. Asleep. In a white bath robe.

Oh God. I looked urgently round the rest of the room. No-one else was here, thank God. I turned off the torch. But now what? My heart thumped loud enough to wake wombats. I stood absolutely still and counted slowly to a hundred. It was easy to see her now my eyes had adjusted and I knew she was there. There were steady green and flashing red highlights in her hair. I resisted an impulse to run, tried to get a mantra going but failed. What it came down to was, I just had to be quiet, quick and efficient. She seemed to be deeply asleep, thank Christ. With luck I'd get the alarms swapped and be out the window before she woke. If not, it would come down to running.

I moved a dining chair into position, setting it down so gently on the polished parquet, one foot at a time. I put my right foot on the chair and gradually transferred my weight to it, hoisted myself up, straightened. The chair creaked. I froze. I checked Kimberly by the light of the machines. I didn't seem to have disturbed her.

I took the small flat-bladed screwdriver from a pocket and gently levered the existing alarm from its bracket, avoiding the click that spooked me last time. I took the new bugged one from another pocket, stashed the old one and offered up the new. It was designed to snap into place on the bracket. I tried to help it in with the screwdriver but couldn't avoid a click as it found its place. It was a tiny click but still too loud. I sensed movement but the soft sound of her breathing remained steady. My heart was thundering again, I was getting hot and bothered when I needed to be cool and calm. I pulled off my balaclava, fanned my face. I checked round the room in the strange green and red light. Though my eyes were adapted to the dark, I still couldn't see her face, but I didn't think she'd moved. I pulled the balaclava back on.

Okay. Got to do it right. Test run.

I stood straight, mouth as close as possible to the alarm, and whispered, 'Testing. Testing. One one two. Okay?'

I took out my phone, texted *testing* to Gail's mobile, and stayed on the chair, waiting, in case the test revealed a problem that I had to do something about – though I couldn't imagine what I might do if it did. I walked through the process in my head. The bug should have picked up my whisper; any noise above background initiated recording. After thirty seconds of silence, or two minutes after beginning to record, it would transmit a packet to the transceiver. The transceiver would store the data in a buffer and send a "data available" message to the burner phone. Gail's burner phone would vibrate, she'd read the message, download a sound file, play it back. If it was audible, she'd use her own phone to send a text to my mobile. I switched on the shrouded torch and looked down at Kimberly, surprised by the quiet beauty of her sleeping face. No make-up. A faint hint of a smile. Tiny dimples.

I turned off the torch and looked away, hating that feeling of voyeurism. She looked so peaceful, so vulnerable.

I took a deep breath and chased a panicky *What the fuck am I doing here?* out of my mind. I reassured myself: it was okay to be spying on ruthless and corrupt conspirators. In fact, it was the right thing to do, despite involving some illegalities. Necessary evils.

I nearly fell off the chair when my phone vibrated, though I should have been expecting it. A text from Gail: *358 ok*. Phew. I breathed out tension. All systems go. Time to leave.

I lowered my left foot to the floor, transferred weight to it and was down. I put the chair carefully back by the dining table, checked nothing was left behind and nothing was out of place. I began to believe I might get away with it.

I gave Lovelump the remaining treats and moved to the window. I grasped the window handle, pushed gently, quietly, on the glass. It hardly made a sound as it opened. I eased myself up onto the window ledge.

Something. A sigh. A rustle.

I stopped moving. Stopped breathing.

A click. Lamplight.

I looked round.

The lamp was on the coffee table, by the sofa.

Beside it, Kimberly was looking at me curiously. As well she might. A man in black, staring through the eyeholes of a black balaclava, crouching in the open window, one foot on the radiator, the other foot on the ledge. Thank God she wasn't screaming the house down. She'd every right to be frightened. What on earth was she thinking? And what was I thinking, to be doing this?

'You came back,' she said, voice low, as if talking to herself. 'How sweet.' Then, a little louder, 'Surely you're not going again already?'

I stared back in frozen panic. Her gown was slipping open. I looked away, embarrassed. She sat up, covered herself, glanced at the gin bottle on the table beside her. 'Christ,' she said, again very quiet. She looked up at me. 'Did you bring your Bible?'

I shook my head. How had she recognised me?

'Never mind,' she said. 'Why were you standing on a chair, whispering?'

I wished I was standing on the moon. How the fuck was I going to talk my way out of this? I said, 'Because I didn't want to disturb you.'

'How thoughtful,' she said. I wasn't surprised to hear scepticism in her voice. 'Well, you did, but never mind. Come here.'

'Where?' I was still on the sill, still poised to make a break for it through the window.

'Here.' She swivelled on the sofa, pointed to the emptier side. Gave me an appraising sort of look. 'You don't look like a gin drinker. There's whisky. Glenfarclas. Why don't you get down. Remove that horrible mask. Come and take a small refreshment.'

'Er...' I said, teetering.

'I think you'll manage a small sensation with me.' She was trying for a Highlands lilt, succeeding. Smiling a dimpled smile.

I liked it. I smiled back, took the balaclava off and smiled again. At her, and at myself for smiling under a mask. I climbed carefully down from the ledge.

'I'm beginning to think,' she said, 'that you might have at least two agendas here. If that's the plural of agenda. Shouldn't be "agendae", should it?'

'I think "agendas" is good.'

'One to do with me – which seems a bit confused, if you don't mind me saying – and one to do with my husband. So-called. Who I've realised, over the last dreadful decade or so, is a worthless piece of shit.'

'Oh.'

A shadow crossed her face. 'And I think that whatever you were doing, whispering on that chair, is more to do with your Conrad agenda than your Kimberly agenda.'

My Kimberly agenda was all up in the air, for sure. 'You're right,' I said, wondering what her agenda was.

'So don't worry,' she said. 'I won't tell. And I won't enquire further.'

Really? Was she reading my mind, telling me what I wanted to hear? 'That's very kind,' I said. 'Thank you.'

'What I'm wondering is, why can't we be friends?'

She stood, moving to the door that led to the hall. 'Don't worry,' she said again. 'He's away. At a conference. Which is probably being held in a brothel.' She turned a key in the lock. 'That's just in case the kids wake up.'

She crossed to the French doors, passing close. I could smell her scent. She tugged a gap in the curtains closed and went back to the sofa, passing close again.

'Friends?' Why was I trembling?

'I can't have friends,' she said. 'He doesn't trust anyone except his cronies. So for me it's just kids and cronies and cronies and kids and then at no notice we jet off for a month on his yacht, as he calls it, which no-one is supposed to know about and which is just a huge plastic phallus, and when we get there I can't bear it because it's just the same, kids and cronies and booze and cocaine and more cronies, and I can't bear it any more. I just can't.'

She looked away, tears starting in her eyes. I took a tentative step forward.

She looked up. 'Yes, come here,' she said, stretching an arm across the back of the sofa. 'I believe you like a whisky. Bring me one. And help yourself.'

Glenfarclas. Single malt. Aged thirty years. Worth a bob or two. I found two tumblers, poured a finger into each, added a splash.

'Do you mind if I ask,' I said, 'how you know I like whisky? I do, but…'

'Remember when Conrad hit that bus? You gave me your card.'

'But it says System Designer on my card, not whisky drinker. And about that day – how did you know people call me Mick?'

'I'd asked in the village. Just to find out. Because I was curious.'

'In the village?'

'There's a man who stands outside the shop, smoking, chatting to people. He could talk for Britain.'

'Malcolm?'

'Don't know his name. Biggish. Local accent.'

'Malcolm. So when you told Conrad you wanted a divorce, and pointed me out to him as a possible replacement…'

'Yes. I'd done a bit of research already. And when I got your card, with your name and address and where you worked, I could do more.'

Was it her who called my mum with all those questions? I wanted to ask about that. But not that much, not at the moment.

She patted the sofa.

I sat, handed her a glass. We clinked.

'Slàinte,' she said.

'Slàinte mhath.'

'Slàinte mhòr.'

We clinked again, drank.

'Wow,' I said. 'Lovely.'

We lay back, shoulders touching. I stretched my legs out and expelled lungfuls of tension. Putting an arm around her shoulders seemed the most natural thing in the world. She closed her eyes, snuggled her head in the crook of my neck. I breathed the perfume of her hair and held her closer as her arms folded around me.

***

Someone was poking my shoulder, saying, 'Wake up.'

Kimberly. Saying, 'Your phone.'

I sat up. I had no clothes on. We both had no clothes on. The sofa stopped vibrating. My phone was in there somewhere. I searched, found something stuffed down the back. Pulled it out. A TV remote.

'So that's where it was,' she said. 'Thanks.'

I dug some more. Found the phone. A message alert from Gail: *your late*.

Who taught her punctuation? I checked my watch. Four forty-five. She was right. She should have left me to my fate ten minutes ago. I messaged back: *with you in five sorry*.

'Gotta go,' I said, pulling my clothes on, looking for my socks. I noticed two things at once: a funny taste in my mouth, and a bottle on the coffee table, half full of yellow gloop. Advocaat. I remembered what we'd been doing. I lay back, wrapped her in my arms again. 'I don't want to go.'

'I rather think you have to,' she said. 'But thanks for dropping in.' She giggled, gave me my arms back, stood. 'You don't have to climb through the window. I'll let you out here.'

She opened the French doors. Lovelump trotted out for a sniff round.

'Just so you know,' she said. 'I am divorcing him. He'll get the papers in a week or so.'

'Okay,' I said, surprised by a sudden clarity.

'And I'd like to see you again,' she said. 'As soon as. Probably best to wait until the divorce has gone a bit further. Won't be long.'

'Okay,' I said again. 'If you say so.' I was thinking, *Why don't we just run away together?* But children. Practicalities. Life.

I joined her at the door. A big hug. I didn't want to let go. She broke it, ushered me out, called Lovelump back in, closed the door. She gave me a last smile through the glass and pulled the curtain. I stood on the grass, feeling so happy. And terrified.

***

I flashed the red torch three times in what I guessed was Gail's general direction. A very realistic owl hooted. I moved carefully

155

round the side of the house, into the Close. I picked up speed as I got further from the house and was running by the time I crossed the road towards the car. I wasn't sure why. Running away from what had just happened? Running into an uncertain future, with an unfamiliar bubble of joy in my heart?

Dawn was still an hour away, but there was enough light to see that Gail was looking furious as she settled in the passenger seat. I slipped in behind the wheel.

'You smell like a brewery,' she said. 'Want me to drive?'

I bit back a refusal, took a breath then saw the sense. We changed seats. Gail drove carefully down the hill.

'Do you want to tell me about it?' she said.

'I'll explain later. All a bit much, actually.'

The lights turned green as she approached the roundabout. We took the first exit onto the ring road. She was silent.

'Oh dear,' I said, realising. 'Oh no. Did you hear all that?'

'All? Don't know.'

Oh fuck.

'Heard enough to know that she sounded like quite a decent person,' she said. 'Surprisingly. And that you're exploiting her. For sex. Just like you did with Andrea.'

'I did not!' I said, shocked by the gulf between my perspective and Gail's. 'That's not how it was in either case. God, I don't know where to start.'

'Don't start,' she said. 'I'm really not interested in your rationalisations. Your actions speak loud enough.'

I didn't start. Tonight was all too fresh and unprocessed in my mind, and I hadn't wanted to talk about it anyway. I didn't like having her sitting there judging me, but if she was going to dismiss whatever I said, what was the point in trying?

'You're right about her, though,' I said, trying to shift the focus. 'A nice person who's completely trapped.'

We turned off the by-pass, approaching Wolvercote roundabout.

'If you go straight to yours,' I said, 'I'll be okay to drive home from there.'

'And what about Naomi?' Gail said. 'What about her? Thought she was the light of your life. Thought that…'

'Gail. Please. I don't want to be rude. But a minute ago you weren't interested in what I had to say. And now you're asking a question I can't answer. I've been awake for twenty-four hours and I'm feeling pretty shaken, to be honest. Can we just leave it for the moment?'

She pulled up outside her house.

Neither of us spoke.

I was tired and confused but had tried to do everything for the best. I couldn't see what more I could do, whether others liked it or not. I got out, went round to the driver's door and opened it.

'Gail,' I said. 'Well done tonight. Thank you. Goodnight. Sleep well.'

'Goodnight,' she said, getting out and going in. No smiles.

***

Sunrise had paled the sky when I reached home. I took the bags of rubbish up to the flat. I showered, changed, made a brew, spread old newspapers on the table. I pulled on rubber gloves and got to work. It was unpleasant, but it felt like light relief.

The first bag contained kitchen waste, bathroom waste, bits of kitchen roll that had been used as handkerchiefs by someone with a cold.

By the end of the second bag I was beginning to despair, but had a better idea of the family's diet. Half the rubbish was pizza packaging, and half the pizzas were a variety called Hawaiian. I opened the curtains and found a sky that was bright grey, if that's possible. I held an empty carton up to the light and read the ingredients list: cheese, tomato, pineapple, ham. What's Hawaiian about that? Pineapple?

At the top of the third bag, a surprising number of used condoms. They smelled disgusting. Then more pizza cartons. Baked bean cans. Corned beef cans. Instant mashed potato cartons. Frozen pea packs. A sliced white loaf gone green. Ketchup bottles. Indian takeaway cartons. San Miguel and Kronenbourg cartons. Chinese takeaway cartons. Polystyrene fish and chip shop cartons. Nesquik. More pizza cartons. A dairy-free triple chocolate ice cream tub. Kellogg's Honey Smacks.

How come they were still alive?

Then there was a whole stratum of cosmetics, many in unopened wrappers, like there'd been a major clear-out. More takeaway cartons. And at the bottom of the third bag, a damp, torn, screwed-up sheet of paper, drizzled with red sweet and sour sauce and what might be melted chocolate, partially obscuring a message written in bright red lipstick.

I uncrumpled it and laid it on the table.

dear soon-to-be-ex hubby
you spent two mill last month
and I never even got a bunch of flowers!!!
wtf???
your soon-to-be-ex wifey

The message was on the summary page of a bank statement dated 1st June.

Bingo, I thought, looking through the sweet and sour at the sums involved. That'll do for now. The bank stuff was just what we needed. The lipsticked message on top sent shivers up my spine. I laid two thicknesses of kitchen roll on the worktop, laid the document on that and took a couple of photos, just in case. I put more kitchen roll on top, the *River Café* cook book on top of that, and left it to flatten and dry.

I repacked the huge smelly mound on the table into new bin bags and took them outside. I was going to put them in my own bin but thought better of it and put them in Mrs Wilkinson's, three doors down. She never had much in hers. I put the two bags

I hadn't yet processed in the hall cupboard that I never used, on top of the vacuum cleaner I never used. I looked at my watch: seven thirty.

I washed and put the kettle on, then sat sipping a mug of tea, finally with a moment to reflect on the night's events. It was mission accomplished, in that a bug was in place and it worked. But Kimberly knew I'd done it. She'd said she wouldn't tell. Would she keep to that? I felt she would, but hadn't a clue, really. I'd felt so easy with her, easier than I'd ever felt with anyone – which could be affecting my judgement.

One thing was sure, though: I wanted to see her again. And another: she wasn't too fond of her husband. Perhaps she really was getting a divorce. And a question knocked on my mind's door. Should I do something to get her and the kids out of that house, that situation, before angry Conrad started hurting them? But how could I? I hardly knew them. And she'd said, 'wait for the divorce to get a bit further'. And what about Naomi?

Did Confucius once say a man in need of a woman is capable of great foolishness? If he didn't, he should have. A hundred and eighty-six thousand butterflies fluttered in my stomach.

***

There was an imperious "where's my breakfast?" nudge from Friday. I blinked, looked around, looked at my phone. I was sleeping in my clothes in an armchair at ten o'clock on a Saturday morning. Then I remembered. I groaned to my feet, emptied dregs and limescale from the kettle and refilled it. I fed the dog and made breakfast, then checked the burner phone for messages from the transceiver – a lot, mostly from the time when I'd been in the house myself. I needed to sort that lot out pronto, get rid.

First, though, I needed grounding. I thought about phoning someone, but there was no-one I could face talking to. Friday was doing her best; I'd take her out soon. Music wouldn't do it. Nor drugs. I reached down the *I Ching* I inherited from my grandad and tossed three old coins six times: yang, moving yang, yang, yang, yang, yin.

Heaven, and the waters of a marsh mounting above it. Removing corruption, breaking through.

Be conscious of the peril involved in cutting off the criminal. Do not have recourse at once to arms. There will be advantage in whatever way forward is taken.

Okay: be careful, keep your powder dry, do something, anything. Sounded good. I turned the page for the moving line in the second place.

Be alert to unexpected threats. Warn others.

Beware of danger in the night. Fear nothing.

It worked for me again, like encouraging words from a benign and ghostly patron. I pulled on shorts and trainers and took Friday for a run.

Home again, showered and dressed, I started going through the sound clips that the bug had picked up. My soul shrivelled as I listened through my encounter with Kimberly. Gail could have heard any or all of it. I scrubbed everything up to the time I left.

One file remained, recorded at 5.12 a.m. It was Kimberly stirring, waking up, making a noise that sounded a lot like "worra worra worra" and chuckling to herself as she left the room. I scrubbed that too, but found myself smiling. That was the noise a Tigger made. Would she know that sort of thing?

Nothing more after that. Not surprising, given the nature of the room: it was more an afternoon or evening than breakfast room.

I felt easier for having tidied up the bug's outputs, though the butterflies swirled on. I decided to have a first look at Conrad Sefton-Shaw's non-work emails. I ran Kanhai's onion procedure, logged in with Lovelump1234 and looked at the inbox. 184 unread messages. I started with the most recent and worked back.

There were a lot of alerts from a dating app called Moonshine. Several from pusskins99@fmail.com, the latest suggesting a rendezvous at "la pad" this afternoon. I clicked on the sender's address, pulled up pages of traffic from and to it, sometimes only minutes between messages. There was great potential for creating all kinds of mischief, but pusskins was probably irrelevant and it would be asking for trouble. I read on. Two messages stood out because they had empty subject lines. Both were sent from qpalzm@moi.com – someone using a standard English qwerty keyboard.

One was dated Tuesday 20th, four days ago.

xfer 6.21 10M to yr ac payroll etc confirm rect
xfer 6.23 45M to hold ac confirm rect
remind imperative all in place 3+yr
one quit one die
not nec same one :)
relay & confirm

The other, sent this morning, was unread.

all go
wrap deal by 7.18 + confirm
begin pest control asap + confirm

In Sent Mail, there were more messages to pusskins99 than anyone else, and messages to Alleyn and Donald Cruickshank, and another Cruickshank, Graham. Then I spotted three responses to qpalzm's earlier message.

On 20th June, the day it was sent:

relay confirmed

On the following day:

xfer 1 rect confirmed

On Friday 23rd:

xfer 2 rect confirmed

Perhaps I wasn't reading this correctly. But if I was, Sefton-Shaw had received an enormous amount of money from a mysterious and ruthless-sounding source, with an unpleasant sense of humour and an old-fashioned, telegraphic style. Perhaps the sender was actually old; they certainly didn't seem digital-savvy. But they were able to splash mountains of cash, and their plan was now in motion. With a deadline of 18th July, assuming they were using US-style dates.

I leaned back in my chair, put my feet on the table and let out a long, slow breath. My grandmother, in her last year or two, had come to believe that everyone was watching her, talking about her; that a blackbird singing at the end of the garden was sending messages about her to men round the corner posing as telephone engineers. Delusions of reference – thinking everything refers to you. Possibly I was suffering such delusions, in suspecting that me and the gang were the pests that qpalzm wanted Sefton-Shaw to control. But as someone said, just because you're paranoid doesn't mean they're not out to get you. And actually, I'd be surprised – disappointed in them, even – if they weren't.

***

Kanhai arrived at the flat at five o'clock the following afternoon, Sunday.

I made coffee. 'Before we start with banking,' I said, 'I've been looking at Sefton-Shaw's emails. Is there any way of tracing the sender? Or even just what continent he's on?'

'Let's have a look,' Kanhai said.

I logged into Sefton-Shaw's account through MetaTOR and passed my laptop over.

Kanhai pecked and rattled a bit, then stuck a USB drive into a slot and copied something over. 'Just somewhere to start digging,' he said, handing the laptop back. 'I'll look later. Okay. You've been rooting through his bins?'

'Yes,' I said, nudging the grubby A4 sheet across the table. 'These guys are professionals at estate management or planning or whatever. And they're crooks. But they're not professional crooks. Except Alleyn. The others seem a bit amateurish, you know?'

Kanhai examined the sheet. 'You found this? Not very professional, you're right. So we've got the bank and the account number and… Oh. Look at the total movements in the month. Two point one million in. Even more out. Closing balance fourteen thousand overdrawn. Gosh. No wonder soon-to-be-ex-wifey blew her lid. Any more pages?' I shook my head. 'Okay. Coupe and Lombardy. Not one of your high street banks. Let's look.'

I woke my laptop, re-ran the onion, handed it to Kanhai.

'So what I'll be trying to do,' he said, 'is… well I won't be going in through the front door, obviously. I'm going to see if I can get into their online back-ups. Or their corporate cloud.'

Apart from occasional mutters and the clicking of the keyboard, Kanhai went quiet. I looked out of the window. A pigeon was sitting on a branch of the ash tree across the street. A squirrel tried to sneak up on it. The pigeon edged away. I found myself thinking of Naomi. I picked up my coffee and sipped. It was cold but better than nothing. It was time I made contact with her. And the others.

'Ha,' said Kanhai.

'What have you got?'

'Spool file from the last statement print run,' he said. 'Marked as deleted but still readable. No encryption. Ran a search for your man's account number and there you go.' He pointed to the inkjet. 'I'll leave a PDF on the desktop too.'

'Thanks,' I said, picking up the first sheets off the printer. I scanned the entries. 'Look, here. Top of the second page. The transfer in – two million odd. Can you trace where it comes from?'

Kanhai shrugged. 'Don't know. But it's possible, isn't it, that the money and the emails come from the same place. And having two points to trace back to… Like a two-bearing fix. Not as good as three. But better than one.'

CHAPTER 19

Detective Inspector Jones

Jones put the phone down on a charming idiot in the offices of Abertawe Ystadau, the agency dealing with the house on the Gower. He'd rung them yesterday morning, Monday, to make an offer, but it was proving harder than expected. All sorts of information was required, including documentary evidence of sources of funds, and each document he sent seemed to generate two more questions. Blasted money laundering regulations. He'd never thought they'd apply to him. Should have seen it coming, though, being a policeman.

And being a policeman, he'd better get back to work. Clappison had been loitering by his door for ten minutes, looking a bit cheesed. Jones beckoned him.

'Two things,' Clappison said, taking the chair in front of the desk. 'Andrea Turner and St Mark's.'

'Start with the missing hounds. What did you get?'

Clappison held up a bandaged left hand. 'I got bitten, by a hedgehog.' He held up his right hand, with dressings on thumb and middle finger. 'And a snake. And by the biggest cat I've ever seen, outside a zoo.'

Jones smothered his laughter. 'You've filled out one of those injured-in-the-course-of forms?'

'BI100A?' Clappison said. 'Yes.'

'What happened?'

'Thought I might learn more if I saw her in context. She's in Jericho, a basement bedsit. Six more upstairs. Shared kitchen and bathroom. Seedy. You can smell cannabis halfway down the street. Most of the houses round about look okay, but this one...'

'You didn't bust them?' Jones hoped not – territory issues with the drug squad, more paperwork, no credits against SPAT targets.

'No. Drugs said they're just users, leave them be. I interviewed her in her room, with her consent. She seemed amused actually, not nervous at all. I was poking around in a heap of boxes when I met the hedgehog. I was trying to get it back in its box when I met the snake. The blasted cat attacked me when she went for Elastoplast.'

'What about dogs?'

'She knew nothing about dogs. I asked about her whereabouts on 13th and 14th June. It's all here,' he said, indicating his notebook. 'Up at seven. Training volunteers, Rushey Field, eight thirty to ten thirty. Breakfast in Skylight café eleven thirty. Meeting, trust HQ, twelve to two p.m. Coppicing work party, Thorncliffe Hollow, two thirty to six. And so on. Everything that's checkable is corroborated by witnesses, leaving a ten-hour window, eleven p.m. to nine a.m., when she was asleep in the bedsit on her own. So she could have done it, but apart from the suggestion from Mr Cameron's security detail, there's no reason to think she did.'

Jones sniffed. If she had taken the dogs, she was just playing Clappison, which wouldn't be hard, God knows. If she hadn't, why was she being set up by Cameron's security? He didn't like either option. 'Any sign dogs had been present?' he asked.

'I couldn't detect any. No hairs that looked like dog hairs. No doggy smell. No dog food, no leads, no collars. No bowls with DOG on the side. If she's had them there, she's moved them on.'

He's taking the piss, Jones thought. *Bowls with DOG on the side.*
There's hope for him yet. 'Is there a garden?'

'Nothing at the front; a scruffy mess at the back.'

'No disturbed earth?'

'No. I did look.'

'Known associates?'

'One in the system,' Clappison said. 'William Dwyer. Lives on
a narrowboat on the canal. The boat's empty, covered in cobwebs.
He's in HMP Bullingdon.'

Jones stood, crossed to the window. 'Write it up,' he said.
'Briefly. "No Further Action".'

'Unless new information turns up,' Clappison said.

'Of course. You asked her about the Glebe Farm protests?'

'Yeah, she just laughed.'

Jones leaned on a cold radiator below the window, folded his
arms and looked down at the round pink bald patch on Clappison's
head. 'You were also going to poke a discreet nose into St Mark's,
see who might have warned the Commissioner about dead sharks.'

'I did. Started at the top. Asked the Master if she could spare
me five minutes.'

Hell, Jones thought. *Discreet?* 'And she could?'

'Yes. She remembered Sir Martin's visit. She'd invited him. I
explained what I was after. She took me to meet one of the fellows,
Professor Udvari, who'd been sitting across from the Commissioner
at high table that night.'

Jones couldn't help being slightly impressed. 'Go on,' he said.

'I recognised Professor Udvari's name immediately.
Mathematical logician. I referenced his work in my doctoral thesis,
and it transpires he's used some of my results in his work.'

He can't half do smug, Jones thought. 'So the dead shark thing?'

'As it happens, he'd overheard the remark. It was made by a
retired Divinity bod, the Reverend Doctor Barkiss. Nutty as a fruit
cake, according to Udvari. Rabid conspiracy theorist, according to
the Master.'

'Good work,' Jones said, almost meaning it. 'So I can pass that up to the Chief Constable and she can tell the Commissioner there's nothing to it.'

'Well, you can, sir, yes. That's the obvious thing to do.'

'And forget about it,' Jones said.

Clappison was studying his fingernails with a sour expression. 'Yes sir,' he said.

'But...?' Jones said.

'Well, sir. It's nothing, really. Just a feeling...'

'A feeling?'

'A hunch.'

'Tell me.'

'Well, I just felt...'

'Yes?'

'... that he was pleased to have been asked.'

'Pleased? Why?' *He's learning to listen to what his back brain tells him*, Jones thought. *We'll make a detective of him yet.*

'I don't know, sir. But imagine if it actually meant something, this dead shark shuffle thing. And if people in the college were involved somehow. And if the Reverend Doctor Barkiss had somehow got wind of it and was telling the Commissioner sort of in public...'

'And if your Professor Udvari was one of those involved, and was worried about what the Commissioner had heard, and was glad of a chance to shut it down...'

'Exactly, sir.'

Jones turned to stare out of the window. Somebody in admin, across the car park, stared back at him. It was far-fetched: a chain of conjectures, each more or less unwarranted. But each felt plausible to him. If Clappison's intuition was right, the dead shark thing was real and they should be on it. Something told him that wasn't what the Commissioner wanted to hear. It would be much easier to take it all at face value. 'Anything else?' he asked.

'I was just leaving when I thought I'd ask about the Glebe

Farm protests, see if they had anything to say. Because it's their property, St Mark's, isn't it?'

'What did they say?

'Nothing, sir. They both just laughed.'

'Like Andrea Turner did.'

'Yes sir. Just so.'

Jones had one of those wobbly feelings in his gut. There was something to this. But did he want to poke it with a stick?

'What do you suggest we do?' he said.

'Well sir. Close it down, but keep an eye on it?'

'Good thinking, constable. Do that.'

Clappison left. Jones returned to the window, thinking hard, but more about exit strategies than dead sharks. He had some of the money that he needed, courtesy of Alleyn. He needed more. He needed to neutralise Alleyn as a threat. And he needed to free his funds from any suspicious origins. Who did he know who knew about money laundering? The big boys did it and the more you had, the easier it was. Alleyn would know people, but taking Alleyn into his confidence on this was not a good idea. He needed more money and a bent accountant who would keep his mouth shut.

CHAPTER 20

Tuesday evening, after work, I was in the shower when the main door buzzer buzzed. If that was Gail and Naomi, they were early. Or I was late. I looked out the window. They were waiting by the main entrance to the flats, pointing at something and laughing.

I buzzed them in, pulled on jeans and a T-shirt and fixed drinks. They sat side by side on the sofa and started on the nibbles. I was too wired to sit still. I explained what I'd been doing. 'We've made some progress with Sefton-Shaw's bank account,' I said. 'And emails. And the bug is working.'

I showed them the summary page from the May bank statement, lipsticked, spattered and getting more fragrant by the hour. 'This was at the bottom of the third bag I looked through from their wheelie bin. There were five,' I explained to Naomi. Gail already knew. Two unexamined bags were still in a cupboard. I'd forgotten them.

'They had relationship problems, for a start. Not surprising and probably not relevant. He has an account with this private bank, Coupe and Lombardy. A huge amount of money is going through it. This gave us enough to find the full statement for that month. And for preceding months, though the recent are most interesting. It's easier to get at data they think they've deleted from their private cloud, apparently, than get into live files to actually steal money, which is near on impossible without the account holder's unwitting help, according to my mate.'

'Who is this mate?' Naomi said.

'An old friend. He needs to keep anything he does with us completely confidential, for good reasons. You might meet him one day, when all this is done and over.'

I handed them some stapled pages. 'This is May. Look at the third page, the highlighted lines. Four hundred thousand to Cruickshank. Five hundred to MA Compliance & Diligence Services, who looked interesting so we dug a bit. Registered address is the Murdoch Alleyn offices in Summertown. Directors James Alleyn and Graham Cruickshank. Not the uni property services Cruickshank, whose first name is Donald. Two hundred to that blasted bikers' café. Also owned by Alleyn and Graham Cruickshank, as it happens. Donald's brother? You remember in the café, Naomi, the Glaswegian with an oral hygiene issue?'

'Unforgettable,' Naomi said.

'Probably him. Then a hundred and ten to a joint account with Kimberly. And a million to Radcon Enterprises. Registered in the Cayman Islands, ownership unknown. But think – Radcon.'

'Radcon?' Gail frowned. 'Ah. Conrad.'

'That's what I thought.'

'Mick,' Gail said. 'You're pacing the floor like a pack of wolves. We're getting dizzy. Can you sit down for a minute?'

'Of course.' I sat in the armchair, dug about in a file, put another A4 sheet in front of them. 'Here's some emails we found.' I went to the window while they read, to the sound system, to put some music on, but decided not to. Then back to the window, feeling my chin, which was getting stubbly. I kept forgetting to shave. Then to the kitchen, to top up the nibbles plates.

Gail and Naomi sighed simultaneously, rose, rounded the coffee table, took me by one shoulder each. 'Sit down!' Naomi said. They pushed me into my chair.

'Sorry.' I couldn't help laughing. 'We think these mean that he's getting ten million pounds in his own account. For paying people off. Like Alleyn, and people in the uni, like Donald Cruickshank – whoever they need to look the other way, ease their path, help them control pests. Do you think that means us?'

'Might be something to do with the development site,' Naomi said. 'Like an infestation. Remember the uni's old print works? They'd only accept unconditional bids, because they knew it was contaminated with chemicals. But no-one knew how bad it was, so bidders had to take on the risk.'

'Who really thinks it's something like that?' Gail said.

No-one spoke.

'Safer to assume it's us,' Gail said.

'Yes,' I said. 'So ten million into Sefton-Shaw's account, and forty-five million into something called a hold account. On hold for whatever deal they're pulling off?'

'What would Glebe Farm be worth now?' Gail said.

'Six hundred and fifty acres, with outline planning?' Naomi said. 'A lot more than forty-five million. At half a million an acre, three hundred mill. Though it's a big site – the per acre might be lower.'

'So forty-five might be like a deposit?' I said. 'An earnest of good faith, if that's how these things work. Anyway, it looks like they're going for it and expect to close the deal by 18th July. Three weeks today.'

Gail pointed. 'This bit,' she said. 'These guys have to stick around for three years. Meaning stay in their jobs, I suppose.'

'Smooth over any upsets,' Naomi said. 'Act normal. Fight flak, put out fires. On pain of death, apparently.'

'But not necessarily their own,' Gail said. 'Do you think that means...'

'Families,' Naomi said. 'Significant others.'

'This is all beginning to hang together,' I said. 'But the obvious question is...'

'These "pests"?' Gail said. 'You think that's us?'

'I do,' I said. 'But that wasn't what I meant.'

'Who's sending the messages?' Naomi said. 'And where's the money coming from?'

'Exactly. And we've been looking at that. Can't identify who it is. We can track the emails back to a network in China, but that means nothing. My mate set this software thing up for me, to hide where I'm coming from when I do this stuff, which could make it look like I'm in China too.'

Something crossed Naomi's face. Perhaps she was wishing I was in China. I struggled to get back on track. 'The money's coming from a bank in the Cayman Islands. Coupe and Lombardy, by strange coincidence. And the account holder... well, we're still trying. But what we've found so far is not inconsistent with the account holder being absolutely anyone from absolutely anywhere on the planet, as my mate says. Means he hasn't a clue.'

'My God, Mick,' Gail said, shivering. 'What've we done? We're like children poking a lion with a stick. I'm sure we're the pests they're going to eliminate.'

'Almost certainly,' said Naomi. 'And Mick, the bikers' café, remember? That grey-suited man who... well, who threatened you. You know? He sounded like he was Polish or something. Could he be Russian?'

'Well, he could, yes. Or Slovakian. Or Ukrainian. Or anything. His English was old-fashioned but perfect. The accent was very faint.'

'Anyway,' Naomi said, 'all this with the bank account and emails, it's amazing. Well done, you and your mate. And what about the bug? Is it working?'

'It is. It's not picked up anything directly relevant yet. We had some stuff from when I installed it,' I said, looking at Gail, willing her to keep her mouth shut. Which she did, thank God. 'I got rid of that. But it made a good test of the system. Then we've got people coming in and out of the room, looking for something, muttering, clattering. We've got people watching TV, mostly alone. Kimberly making calls to shops, and taking calls. Always people asking for Conrad. Messages being played back. All stuff you'd expect. Innocent and irrelevant, mostly.'

'Can we hear it anyway?' asked Gail.

'You can, of course, what we've kept. But that's over three hours. And I'd better warn you, there's some unsavoury bits.'

'Like what?' Naomi asked.

'Well, for example, Conrad seems to go in there after their evening meal, to watch TV and fart. One time, when Kimberly's there too, he does a long loud one. And she says, "Conrad, really, couldn't you do that outside?" And he says, "Shut your fucking hole, you cow, I'll fart where I like."'

'I don't think we want to hear all that,' said Gail.

'No. And there's a bit where two people seem to be... making love?' Again I caught Gail's eye. 'Having sex? A quickie, for sure. Conrad and someone. Not Kimberly. Sounds like a bloke, in fact. But actually, maybe we should listen to that? Gross as it is. See if you can put a name to the other voice.'

'Okay,' Naomi said, warily.

I started the clip.

'That's Cruickshank,' she said immediately. 'Donald. From uni services. Often eats at Harry's. He's creepy. Always itching.'

'Oh, him. He came in with Conrad when I was there for that business lunch thing.'

The clip ended.

'No more than two minutes, from entering the room to leaving it. They must have been well stoked up already when they came in,' Gail said, surprising me. Naomi too, I thought.

'And,' I said, 'Donald Cruickshank's evening was not yet over. An hour later he's back in the room with the boy, Alasdair. The boy's blackmailing him. Apparently Alasdair lurks on a gay dating site, where he spotted Cruickshank's photo with a pseudonym: Billy Whizz.'

'Oh lordy,' Naomi said. 'Whizz is speed. Amphetamine.'

'Sounds right. Though he looks like an all-rounder, actually, drugs-wise. And Alasdair seems to have played him along a bit, into some compromising position, and is now claiming he's witnessed Cruickshank having his bit of fun with Conrad. And wants to raise the premium.'

**

Five days later, the next Sunday, I woke with a headache and a sense of regret I didn't understand. I checked I was alone in the flat, then washed down four ibuprofen with fresh orange. I fed Friday. She wolfed it, nudged my knee, wagged her tail. We set off for a jog.

I soon settled into rhythm, breathing deep and feeling well enough to plan the day. I'd done next to nothing about Sefton-Shaw and company since getting together with Gail and Naomi on Tuesday. I'd been busy, but also it had occurred to me that nothing might be the best thing to do – certainly the safest. The burner phone had come up with the "data available" message a few times: only once, on Thursday, producing anything of substance: Conrad's end of a telephone conversation, probably with Cruickshank of uni services. I'd type up the transcript when I got home, and check Conrad's emails again.

Conrad Sefton-Shaw telephone conversation: 1550-1600 Thursday 29th June
> *[phone rings]*
> *Hello? Oh hi. Yes. Thanks for...*
> *No, I already told you that.*
> *Yes I did. On Tuesday. The new line on the island fund.*
> *It'll be two point four, give or take. Talk to Robert.*
> *Robert Forster. At Simms and Denby.*
> *You do that. But listen.*
> *Yes, well, it's urgent. Listen. I've been talking to the person that*

pulls the strings on this and…

Yes, I do. I do pull the strings. Your strings. And a few others. But…

Yes, of course. Like a cell. Like the resistance or…

Yes, like the CIA. You don't need to know that actually, that someone pulls my strings. The less you know about that, the better it is for you. Believe me.

Yes it is. Has to be. There's one fuck of a lot of money involved here. We've just…

Yes. He's part of it too. So between us…

That's as may be. But anyway, that person has been pretty clear. We've got to shut these bastards down. Now.

Yes. Whatever it takes.

Well, what do you think it might mean? Yes.

No you fucking don't, you're in too deep, we're all in too deep. No way out now.

Yes. Look at it like this. If we don't sort the problem, we become the problem. Okay?

Yes, I know they're amateurs and…

Yes, they don't know what they've stumbled on. Or what we're doing, really. But let me get this right, I'm quoting: They have introduced a random risk element that is unnecessary and unacceptable. End quote. So…

Yes, so it's down to us to deal with it.

Well, that's what we've got to decide. Have a word with the others…

Yes, and your brother if he can make it. We're going to need him and his mates at some point. If only to…

Yes, at ours.

As soon as. I'm free tonight. Or the weekend. Not Friday. Okay?

Okay. And don't tell them what it's about. Just that something's come up and we need to talk.

Okay. Ciao.

[rings off]

You had to read between the lines a bit, but it seemed clear what was being contemplated. I logged in to Sefton-Shaw's email and scanned recent arrivals. One leapt out: at nine thirty this morning, from Alleyn to Cruickshank, cc Conrad, not yet read by him. No subject. Just *Here it is.* and an attachment: Arc01BidFinal.docx.

I thought about Kanhai's warning not to change anything, but then thought, *What the hell?* I downloaded the attachment and deleted the message. They probably wouldn't notice. If they did, they'd think it was a technical glitch. But if any of them had the wit to think it through, they'd realise the account had been hacked, which would surely ratchet up the paranoia a degree or two.

The document was password protected, so I buzzed it over to Kanhai to see if he could get in. I went back to bed, with toast and marmalade, more ibuprofen, and a large mug of tea. I should be more worried, knowing for sure we were the pests, but in a way I was relieved. No more false hopes that we were not in the firing line.

I was half asleep when I heard a ping from the burner phone: *data available.*

I downloaded an audio file, listened to a few minutes. This would need transcribing. I popped earbuds in and got to work.

Conrad Sefton-Shaw meeting with James Alleyn and Donald Cruickshank: 1410-1422 Sunday 2nd July

CSS:... in here. Graham not coming? Bugger. Okay. Sit... [clinking glass, cork] Donald. Jura? Talisker?

DC: Jura, large one. No, large. Better. Thanks.

JA: Likewise.

CSS: Cheers. Okay. State of play. James. Endowments for chairs.

JA: Done.

CSS: Bid ready?

JA: They've got it. Sent this morning.

CSS: Oh really? Have I seen it?

JA: I sent it to Donald and St Mark's, copied to you.

DC: Yes, I noticed that. But not the dot gov dot uk address. The other one. bluehorizon.

CSS: Oh really? Let me check. You're right not using dot gov, James, anyway.

JA: It was to him, copied to you.

[pause]

CSS: Not there.

JA: Well, it was sent. Look. Cc css67@bluehorizon.com. That's you, isn't it? Sent at 09.14 today.

CSS: Hmm. Strange.

DC: You should check your spam. Might have...

CSS: It's here. In Trash. How did it get there?

DC: Maybe you put it there by mistake. I often...

CSS: Listen fuck-face. I was playing golf at nine fourteen. And I've not touched my email since last night.

JA: You can set it so it automatically junks stuff.

CSS: Can I? I haven't.

[pause]

CSS: Those bastards could have hacked my email.

DC: Oh surely not. You don't...

JA: It'll be Jarvis...

CSS: We've got to sort them anyway. That's the main thing we're looking at today. So. Ideas. James?

JA: Sort them?

CSS: Stop them.

JA: That'll be fun.

CSS: Possibly. But how? Effectively. Minimising risk. And not attracting attention. Your friends in the force on side, James?

JA: Of course.

CSS: Okay. Ideas?

JA: Divide and conquer.

CSS: Yes. Buy them off? Or some of them? Do we know enough about them? There's the farmers. Jarvis. The girls, Goodman and Turner. And the old woman, Mycroft. That it?

DC: *The old woman? Pots and kettles. She's younger than you. And better looking.*

CSS: *Not funny, fuck-face. I said, is that it?*

JA: *Yes, that's the lot, as far as we know. So. The farmers. They're going to be stony. And desperate. Wouldn't need to be much. Twenty grand each, and dangle a wee carrot. They'd grab it and run.*

CSS: *Like it. And they're the salt of the earth element. With them out the picture the rest'd look like middle-class nimbies and losers, much less credible. Yes. So…'*

[Interruption while someone [KSS?] brings coffee. They wait until she's gone.]

CSS: *So what about the others?*

JA: *Jarvis looks like he's just in it for the hell of it. Or for the women. Or both.*

CSS: *He's the weird bastard that's been spying on me. He was there when I had a bump with a bus. And I found out he'd been hanging around my wife. I laid the fucker out but he carried on, so I had Graham put the frighteners on him. He's still at it though. Alasdair caught him in the garden, dressed like a birdwatcher, scoping the place. Then there was a weird French artist, which was him again. And then the two of them came here, bold as brass, Jarvis and Mycroft. Pretending to be Jehovah's Witnesses for Christ's sake.*

JA: *Scoping the place. He works for a software place that's doing some work for us. He was with me and their sales guy in Harry's one time.*

CSS: *When that waitress spilled a rum and coke all down me. And that was the girl, Goodman. They set that up, didn't they?*

JA: *Can't see that. But I'd watch him. He's some sort of wizard coder. These techos can do all sorts of shit. If he was scoping this place, he might have planted some sort of bug. Might be listening to us right now.*

CSS: *No, we'd know if someone had got in here. James, where are you going?*

JA: *Just getting something from the car.*

[sound of door]

DC: *Jarvis has a decent job. Might not want to lose it, but he could get another easy. Maybe a bit of a crusader? Doubt we'd buy him off even if all the others had been taken out. But would he respond to… persuasion? From some of our heavier friends and relations? Do you think? Or could he, you know…*

CSS: *Have an accident? I'd like that. Your Graham already had a run-in with him. Jarvis and Goodman turned up at the café, just after James had delivered some goods. By chance, apparently. But they were asking after James. Where's he gone, anyway?*

DC: *Went for something from his car.*

CSS: *Hmm. The girls. Goodman used to be in planning, did you know? One of our juniors. Competent, bit of a rising star. But we had to move her on when she kept fronting up Affordable Oxford bids.*

[JA returns]

CSS: *The bids were good enough to make it hard for you guys, James, as you'll remember, I dare say. Affordable Oxford, and Naomi Goodman.*

JA: *Yes. I'm thinking, divide and conquer, okay…*

CSS: *Can you thank Jones, by the way, for sitting on that gas leak?*

JA: *Eh?*

CSS: *Never mind.*

JA: *… but also take one of them out, pour encourager…*

CSS: *All she's doing now is that waitressing job at Harry's, and a bit of pro bono stuff for Affordable Oxford. Finding it harder without an inside track. Anyway, she's broke. James, sit down and concentrate, will you? What are you doing?*

JA: *… les autres. Won't be a minute. Just a quick scan to be on the safe side.*

CSS: *But anyway. Goodman. If she thought she could see a way to build her hippy dream housing project, she'd surely take it, it's what she's about, altogether. James, just as an example… Are you listening or what? How much cash would you need for something like that site on the ring road? If you were going for a social housing type plan. For*

site and construction and legal and all, and you had no track record.
How much cash would you need, to get a bank on board?

    JA: Ha! Found it! Must be in this thing, whatever it is, fire alarm?
    CSS: Found what?
    [loud crunching noise]
    [recording ends]

I stared out the window, feet up on the coffee table, watching clouds morphing by. Friday dozed on her dog bed. After half an hour I stood and stretched. I knew what I had to do.

First, bring Naomi and Gail up to date. They could brief the others.

I texted, asking for a meet tomorrow evening, or Tuesday.

Second: arrange for the cavalry to come to the rescue. We'd clearly gone beyond our level of competence and needed the professionals.

I phoned Kanhai's mobile. No answer. I left a voicemail: 'Hello. They found it. But we got some good stuff. Need a friendly face down your way to feed it to. Quickish, please.'

CHAPTER 21

DETECTIVE INSPECTOR JONES

Jones sipped his coffee and checked his watch. 11.10. Monday. Lunchtime minus sixty. It had been a quiet day so far. His in-tray held nothing urgent. Long may it continue. He turned back to the papers on his desk, tagged with green, yellow and orange post-its. His worldly wealth, in three stacks: legit, dubious, and downright dodgy. The legit total was inadequate: he'd have to bring all three stacks into play to do the Gower project that his wife had set her heart on. It was frustrating. He had more money than he'd ever expected, but most of it he couldn't use. He blamed Alleyn.

His phone buzzed. Speak of the devil – a message from the man himself: *Call me.*

Talking to Alleyn was the last thing he felt like doing, but there was no ducking it.

'We found a bug yesterday,' Alleyn said. 'At Conrad's, in a smoke detector in the living room. You need to organise a proper sweep of his house. And my offices, and one or two other places. I'll send you a list.'

Alleyn always assumed Jones could do anything, at the drop of a hat. He couldn't, and even if he could, he wouldn't. 'We need people to make a formal complaint,' Jones said. 'I can't just commission that kind of search without justification.'

'Tell me what you need and I'll get it to you. But get it done.'

The man was exasperating. Jones was sick of it. He had to regain some control, had to start behaving like a policeman now and then. 'You know as well as I do what we need,' Jones said. 'We need reasonable suspicion. Probable cause, as they say in the USA. Good reason to believe something serious is going on. Get me details of people and places, and justification for doing a search in each place. Make it hang together and I'll see what I can do.'

Alleyn just grunted: he obviously wasn't pleased, but there were limits. Jones couldn't order sweeps of five or six properties just like that.

Jones changed the subject. 'How's it all going with the land purchase, by the way?'

'On track,' Alleyn said. 'It's Jarvis and co doing the bugging, you just need to prove it. You got anything on them yet?'

'No.'

'You got your cash, didn't you? How hard are you trying? You got trackers on their cars? And pushbikes?'

'I don't think we do bikes,' Jones said.

'What about tails?'

'We can't do much unless they do something,' Jones said. 'I've got someone keeping an eye on Jarvis.'

'Not good enough. We can't wait until he's fucked things up for us, we need to stop him before he starts, put him out of harm's way. If you can't do it, we will. There's a fuck of a lot of money riding on this.'

Alleyn hung up.

'Why don't you go and stick your head up a dead bear's bum?' Jones said to the dead line. There was no telling what Alleyn might do if he started taking the law into his own hands. His phone buzzed again. A text from his wife. *Call me.*

She wouldn't disturb him at work unless it was important, but he was supposed to be working, whatever that meant these days. 'Ols, hi,' he said.

'Daffy, yes. The Oxford-Cambridge Growth Arc. Have you heard of it? Because Jane – you know, that I go sketching with? We were out this morning, in Bernwood Forest, and she said, "What a shame they're going to build a new town here." And I said "What?" and she said she'd heard it from her husband who'd heard it from a friend who works for the county, who said they've had nearly a billion pounds for it already, for infrastructure. Which is roads and stuff, isn't it...'

'Yes, I guess so,' Jones said, suppressing a groan. His wife's moral compass was strong, and never deviated for expedience.

'Yes you've heard about it, or yes it's roads?'

'Both.'

'And have you heard they're going to build a hundred thousand houses here? In Oakley?'

'A hundred thousand? Oakley?' Jones said. 'That's crazy. I'd heard they were planning one point one million between Oxford and Cambridge, but...'

'There's four hundred houses in Oakley at the moment, since they built that ticky tacky Oakwood Rise that you were up in arms about.'

Jones tried to picture it. A hundred thousand would be a big city, almost twice the size of Oxford. It would swallow Horton, Brill, Long Crendon, Worminghall... and the huge patch of quiet and really rather beautiful countryside in between. All the locals would be up in arms, of course, including his wife. But who owned all that land? And how would this development effect its value? Someone would be making a lot of money. He should be joining dots and building a bigger and better picture, but the dots were just a jumble. 'It can't be true,' he said. 'Surely.'

'It is,' Olwen said. 'So why I'm ringing is... Jane's already got her house on the market. I've got three estate agents coming in to look at ours on Saturday. Ten, eleven and twelve o'clock. You'd better be here. Because we'll have to sell anyway, won't we, when we move to the Gower. And I thought we might as well get a shift on before everyone hears about this and there's a stampede to get out.'

'Ten, eleven and twelve on Saturday. Okay, it's in the diary.'

He ended the call and looked at the wall. Their own house was leasehold. He'd an idea the freehold was owned by one of the colleges. He hadn't paid much attention, because it was a long lease. Or it had seemed like a long lease at the time. He'd better check.

He was shaken by the scale of what Olwen had described: far bigger than any previous 'new town' initiatives. There'd be opposition. The protests around Glebe Farm that the Chief was so interested in would be nothing in comparison. There'd be protest camps, tunnels, treehouses, Swampy-style stuff on a massive scale. He could see Olwen supporting protestors with food and drink and shelter, even joining in the protests. And the more he thought about it, the more he felt like joining the protests himself. The shallow crassness of the NIMBY appellation dawned on him. He didn't want a massive new city in his own back yard, true. But he realised he was a NIABY: he didn't think they should put massive new cities in anyone's back yard. In his teens, in the Rhondda, he'd fought against an oak wood being felled, on the road up to the Bwlch, and failed. He remembered feeling bitter anger, watching the machines moving in. He remembered hating the councillor who owned the land, who'd looked on with a smug smile. The teenage Jones had been certain that there was corruption behind it. The thought of stopping such things had turned his thoughts towards joining the force.

That was all a long time ago. Now he was trapped by Alleyn's money, and the man's increasing volatility was making him nervous. He'd be lucky to get out of this with marriage, job and self-respect intact.

CHAPTER 22

It was Tuesday July 4th. Oxford was quiet. The state schools were still working, but the uni students and private schoolkids had gone for the long vacation, and the EFL summer school students were still finding their feet. It was almost a pleasure to walk through town to the office. A message came through from Kanhai as I walked up the stairs: *aldermans tonite re friendly face. can't open doc btw.*

I was due to meet Gail and Naomi this evening. I replied: busy tonite. tomozz 6.30.

I spent the day working on the proposal for Murdoch Alleyn's website and social media project. I roughed out the project scope and requirements sections of a proposal. I was glad I'd engaged with it when Denise came across at three thirty; she had them on the phone, wanting to set up a meeting tomorrow.

'Can't Dougie do it? It's pre-sale.'

'Dougie's out, he says you can field it. It's only with their techies,' she said. A few minutes later she confirmed that I was to be at their Summertown office at eleven a.m., and to ask for Felicity on arrival. Whom I'd already met, apparently – she must be the silent one who came with Alleyn to the first meeting. What fun.

Gail and Naomi were due at mine at eight. I shopped for nibbles in Magdalen Street on the way home and took Friday out for an hour while my potato baked. I opened a bottle of red, put a white in the fridge, and made tasteful arrangements of nibbles on my best plates. All was ready at seven thirty when Gail rang. She'd just heard from Naomi, who couldn't make it. Gail wanted me to go through things with her on the phone, then she'd pass it on to Naomi.

Disappointing. Was Naomi avoiding me? And exasperating. Didn't they realise this was getting serious? And what was I going to do with all these nibbles?

Never mind, though. I sent each of them copies of the transcripts and selected emails, and phoned Gail.

'Sure he said "the old woman"? Bloody cheek. Can't be older than him, can I, surely?'

'Oh dear, did I leave that in?'

'Yes, you did.'

'Well, I'd say younger. By a bit. Really.'

'Probably said "the older woman" and you misheard it. Older compared to Naomi and Andrea. Which wouldn't be half as bad. Please change it.'

'Will do.'

'No doubt now who the pests are,' she said. 'Sounds like they mean to pick us off one by one, but only to use violence if threats and money don't work. For most of us. For which the lord make us truly thankful. Though they might make an exception for one of us. Probably you.'

I agreed. 'I'm feeling well out of my depth. I've talked to a friend who has friends in the police. He might know someone who could do something with what we've found, without looking too closely at how we found it. We're meeting tomorrow evening to talk about it.'

'Meanwhile,' Gail said, 'we all need to look out for ourselves. And each other. And beware of Greeks bearing gifts.'

'Everyone needs to get that, and to understand why. Pass all this to Naomi and Andrea. Andrea can tell Linda and Tom.'

***

I rolled a spliff, filled a tumbler with cold filtered water and stared out at the darkening sky, feeling uneasy, like I was missing something. I'd never been in a situation like this, up against a group of powerful people that I'd made into enemies.

One possibility: get a long way away from it. Denise in the office had sent everyone an email about how many days of leave we each had left and how we couldn't carry more than five forward. I could save five for Christmas, carry five forward, and take twenty now. Twenty days. Four weeks. A long walk in the Highlands. Wild camping, peachy hill lochs, lush lairigs. Live on fish, fungi, foraging and muesli. Drink clean clear water. Walk towards the setting sun, from Tomintoul, west through Cairngorm, through the Monadliaths, cross the Great Glen, into Glen Affric and wild country. Chill for a few days at the end in a B&B on the west coast. Friday would love it. I started pulling out maps.

The phone rang. Naomi.

'Mick. Hi. Just wanted to say sorry I couldn't make it this evening.'

'That's okay.' I didn't ask whether she'd been washing her hair or anything. 'You heard from Gail, then?'

'Yes, thanks for the transcripts and that. Amazing you can just record people talking in their own house. But calling us nimbies. It's so not true, you know. And bloody terrifying, what they were saying.'

'Yes.'

'And it seems to me that of all of us, it's you that has most to worry about. So please be careful.'

'Yes, I will.' Everyone was saying "be careful", but I hadn't a clue what that meant, short of heading for the hills.

'One other thing,' she said. 'My pay came through today. So I wondered, can I treat you to a takeaway? Tomorrow. Your favourite Standard Indian. I'll order, you pick me up there at seven, we'll eat back at yours.'

I could rearrange with Kanhai, so of course I'd do it. Wild horses and all that...

'Thank you,' I said. 'Yes. That'd be lovely.'

***

Early the following morning I took Friday for a walk. The air was cool and fresh. I wasn't in a hurry to get to the office because I had the meeting at the law firm. And I had a date with Naomi in the evening, that she had initiated. I felt good. Was life looking up at last?

I worked at home for a couple of hours to prepare for the meeting: a first draft proposal and a PowerPoint on the schedule, highlighting client inputs and sign-off points. I copied them to Dougie and Denise in the office. I enjoyed the edge of any sales situation, no matter how big the contract. This would be forty to fifty person-weeks of work: bread and butter, but worth having. And the edge was doubled by Alleyn's involvement.

I put on a suit and tie, caught the ten thirty down the Woodstock Road to Summertown, walked through South Parade towards the Murdoch Alleyn offices on Banbury Road. I was ten minutes early. I took my time, browsing shop windows. In a display of vinyl in the Animal Sanctuary shop I spotted U-Roy, with the Revolutionaries, Live at the Lyceum, 1978. A gem. I went in and paid, to collect later.

A text from Kanhai: *tonite no good. tomozz.*

I had to rearrange tonight anyway now I was meeting Naomi, so that was good. I was looking forward to spending some unpressured time with her. Sooner or later we'd start having fun together, I was sure. And she'd been paid. Not very romantic, but I couldn't help wondering whether she was ever going to pay back the loans. I was down a thousand at the moment. The money wasn't that important, but I didn't want to look like I was trying to buy her friendship. Or have her thinking of me as a soft touch.

I stopped outside a gallery with a window full of photorealistic landscapes. I phoned Kanhai, left a voicemail asking why people bothered making paintings like that, and saying I'd be at the Alderman's tomorrow, six thirty. I walked on, towards a blue flashing light at the end of the street – an ambulance.

Murdoch Alleyn's office was just round the corner. I switched my phone to silent and checked my tie in the hairdresser's window. I barely glanced at the travel agent's as my attention was caught by what was going on ahead. A bike was on its side by the road, front wheel spinning. An ambulance, tight against a silver birch, was half blocking street and footpath. Cars squeezed between the ambulance and the bollards on the other kerb. Horns were hooting on the main road. Two paramedics manoeuvred a stretcher from the back of the ambulance, another knelt beside a bulky man in a bicycle helmet who was lying across the pavement, covered by a space blanket, in the gap between the ambulance and the building site boarding where the café used to be.

I looked at the cyclist with sympathy. I'd given up using my own bike on north Oxford roads; they were too dangerous. *There but for the grace of God*, I thought.

I didn't want to be late for the meeting. I hate keeping people waiting. Politeness of kings and all that. I went to squeeze past. The kneeling paramedic stood, blocking my way. The injured cyclist stood too. The space blanket swirled over my head. *Whoa*, I thought, backing off. What is this, street theatre? I could see the Murdoch Alleyn entrance fifty yards away.

I didn't want to get involved in whatever it was and tried to turn. The stretcher was right behind me. The cyclist fell towards me and pushed me onto the paramedic, who held a white pad smelling of dentists over my face. *Oh fuck*, I thought, trying to shout, trying to push my way out. But my balance, control and strength were all gone. Two of them grabbed a shoulder each, another jabbed a hypodermic in my arm.

I felt myself giving way, everything loose and floppy, strobing vision. They forced me down onto the stretcher, threw a blanket over me. Someone jammed the helmet on my head. They were loading me into the back of the ambulance.

My panic faded; the flickering light slowed.

I fell back into a kind of peace.

CHAPTER 23

DENISE IN THE OFFICE

Denise had a mountain of sales and marketing stuff to get out by close of play, and was fed up with being interrupted by phone calls. While she stuffed a pile of envelopes, she rehearsed a response for the next caller. 'Thank you for calling Oxford Hypermedia. We really value your call. Unfortunately we are currently experiencing an unusually high volume of calls. All our operators are busy. Please call back later, or hold and we will deal with your call as soon as possible. You are currently number… NINETY-FOUR… in the queue.' Follow it with an hour of awful music. Lionel Ritchie or The Archers theme tune. Then break the connection.

At eleven thirty, the phone rang again. She was tempted, but behaved herself. 'Oxford Hypermedia, Denise speaking. How can I help you?'

'Oh hello? Reception here at Murdoch Alleyn? We're expecting your Mr Jarvis? He was due here at eleven for a meeting with Felicity? He's not arrived, and we've not heard anything?'

Denise called down judgement on people who made everything sound like a question. 'Me neither?' she said. 'I'll try to track him down? Get back to you soon either way?'

Mick going walkabout was all she needed. She called his

phones. No response. Sent a text: *Where are you? Why no-show for Murdoch meet? You ok? x.*

She emailed Murdoch Alleyn with apologies for the unforeseen circumstances, promising to be in touch to rearrange shortly, then returned to the day's priority. By four thirty she had a stack of envelopes ready and went out to post them.

She breathed easier as she walked back to the office, then remembered Mick. Should she begin to worry? She was relieved to find a text had popped up while she was out: *Grandfather dangerously ill. Have to take leave. Apologies to clients and colleagues. Will call when know more. Jarvis.*

She rang Murdoch Alleyn. 'I've just heard from Mr Jarvis. He was called away to a family emergency. He's just left the hospital now, and sends his apologies.' Embroidering a bit, but what the hell. 'He's asked me to rearrange the meeting. Could I suggest Wednesday 19th? At eleven again?'

'Thank you?' said the Murdoch Alleyn receptionist. 'I'll check with Felicity? And let you know?'

Denise growled an okay and hung up.

She was clearing her desk at five thirty when she thought, *Mick's grandfather died last year.* She didn't know why but she was sure he didn't have another. She had one of those nagging feelings. You get them when you've set a horse at a fence it's been over many times before, but this time there's something slightly out of rhythm about how it's planting its feet, and you know in your bones it's going to go wrong.

She looked up Mick's emergency contact info and dialled a number in the Witney area. No answer. She left a voicemail. 'This is Denise, in the office at Oxford Hypermedia. Trying to track down Michael Jarvis. Please could you give me a call? 01865 263 087. Or my mobile. 07814 421 411. Thank you.'

She wrote 'Mick' on an orange post-it and stuck it to her screen. She stared at it for a moment, felt that out-of-rhythm sensation again. She didn't like it.

CHAPTER 24

KANHAI

Lunchtime, Thames Valley Police canteen. Noisy, edgy, smelling of institutional food and sub-standard cleaning. Kanhai paid and tacked towards a deserted corner, avoiding the frothy group of IT and tech services people that he sometimes ate with. He needed a few quiet minutes to catch up with life. Bethan, his wife, had a dentist's appointment at twelve: no news would be good news. And he wanted to keep an eye on comings and goings, and to give whatever it was at the back of his mind that was making him nervous a chance to come forward and show itself.

He put his tray down, unloaded a cheese pasty, chips and beans, a side of bread and butter and a large mug of tea. He stirred in two heaped sugars, took a swallow of the tea and picked up a voicemail from Mick, confirming tomorrow was okay to meet. Knowing he'd catch up with him tomorrow eased Kanhai's nervousness a notch.

***

That evening, walking home, his phone pinged. A text from Mick. Not another change of plan, he hoped.

Sorry, not well. Another time. MJ.

He felt his shoulders tighten as he read it. He'd left a voicemail this morning, saying he was okay for tomorrow. And a few hours later he was too ill? Mick hadn't been ill for years. And if they needed to change an arrangement, they always suggested a definite alternative. And never fussed with punctuation or sign-off. Would Mick really send a message like that? But Mick was a grown-up, he could look after himself. No need to panic. When Kanhai had a problem he'd sleep on it, give it a chance to go away. Situations often changed overnight, or the subconscious could deliver a solution, or knit up the tangle into something more tractable.

Best talk to him, see what was what. He called three times; it went through to voicemail each time. By the time he got home he was less persuaded by his own reassurances. It might be time to panic after all.

Bethan's tooth had a stay of execution, a deep clean and a promise of root canal work if it didn't shape up. He told her he was popping over to Mick's, would be back within an hour, and promised to pick up a takeaway from the Mayflower on his way back to make up for dashing off as soon as he'd arrived.

First to Mick's flat. His car was in its usual place, engine cold, dead leaves on the roof. The curtains of the flat were open, no lights on. The main entrance to the flats was unlocked. He went up to Mick's, knocked on the door, peered and sniffed through the letterbox. No sign of Friday's wagging tail and warbling hello. No cooking smells.

He approached the door of Mick's next-door-but-one neighbour, Mrs Swainston. He raised a hand to knock but the door opened before he could. Mrs Swainston peered out through misted horn-rimmed glasses.

'Oh, it's you, Kanhai,' she said. 'Come through. Just doing my ironing. Thought it might be Mick.'

Dog Friday uncurled herself from a rug in front of the TV, stretched, put her chin on Kanhai's knees and said 'Ya-ya-yoo.'

'Ya ya to you too,' said Kanhai, scratching her head. 'Have you seen him?'

'Not since this morning,' Mrs Swainston said. 'And then not to speak to. Went off to work quite late, about half ten, looking smart. Not been home yet. I fetched Friday round for a bit of company after my dinner.' By which Kanhai understood early afternoon. 'She can stay as long as she likes. But he usually says if he's going to be late and wants me to have her in.'

***

At least dog Friday was okay. Kanhai stood by Mick's car, staring at nothing. If something had happened to Mick, it didn't involve his car and didn't happen here. A conversation he'd had in the canteen on Tuesday was on his mind – with Detective Sergeant Angus Grant, the longest serving of the plain-clothes police at TVP Kidlington, and Kanhai's only friend amongst that rather chippy crew. Kanhai had been trying to find out, discreetly, whether Grant would be open to an off-the-record meet with Mick.

'He's a good mate of mine. Since school,' he'd said, across a melamine tabletop bearing traces of previous occupants. 'He's involved with protests against the Glebe Farm plans. They don't want more car parks, science parks, business parks, gated communities and retail parks all over what was the green belt, for some reason. Apparently they've turned up some damning stuff on senior people in the council.'

'Have they now?' Grant had said. 'Have you mentioned this to anyone else round here?'

Kanhai hadn't, and Grant had poked him on the breastbone and fixed him with a cold blue stare. 'Don't,' he'd said. 'And especially don't breathe a word that might reach yon fleshy ears.' He gave the tiniest nod in the direction of the till at the end of the servery counter, where Detective Inspector Dafydd Jones had paid for his food and was turning towards them with a laden tray.

'Let's beat it,' Grant had said under his breath as Jones lumbered across with an apparent intention of joining them. Grant had stood and begun gathering crockery and cutlery onto a tray. 'Sorry Daffy,' he'd said, as Jones lowered his tray onto the table. 'It's not your bad breath or your boring conversation that's driving us off. Just places to be, people to see. Busy as bees, we are. Bye.'

They'd dumped their trays in a rack and headed out the door. Grant had slowed as they crossed the car park. 'There's a nasty smell to this,' he'd said. 'Don't know where it's coming from. But there's real money swilling around in these big land deals. And serious players involved, who don't like protests or publicity. And I've a sneaking suspicion that some of them might have... what can I call it? Influence? With our colleagues and superiors. Like Daffy and his mates. So look out.'

***

Kanhai shook himself back to the here and now, in the street, staring at Mick's car. What had the fool got himself into? His gut was telling him that his usual "if in doubt, wait" policy wouldn't cut it. He wanted to do something, now, and didn't know anywhere better to start looking than Springfield House.

He drove over to Boars Hill and parked in the empty Foxcombe Hall grounds. He walked across the heath to Ishmael's Wood then back to the road and up Berkeley Close for a good look at the house and its surrounds. There were no visitors' cars on the drive or street, no comings or goings, no lights going on and off in the house – nothing you'd call suspicious. But somehow the house had an air of busy-ness.

It reminded him of a student visit to GCHQ in Cheltenham, eighteen years ago almost to the day. He'd arrived at ten a.m. as arranged and was told to wait outside. He had waited until midday, sensing energy and tension inside, but seeing only dull walls, until someone came out to apologise. They'd been dealing with an emergency: fifty-six people dead in suicide bombings in London. His heart sank now, as it had then.

CHAPTER 25

Naomi

She hovered in the least busy corner of the Standard Indian on Walton Street, holding a white plastic bag with poppadoms poking out the top. Half the tables were occupied; it was noisy. She broke off an edge of poppadom. He was five minutes late. She was annoyed. She called his mobile, landline, work phone. All went to voicemail.

She broke off another piece of poppadom. She couldn't believe he'd stood her up. She checked her phone again. Nothing. Take-out customers came and went. Diners-in came, were shown to tables. At ten past, she called the numbers again. Same result.

The food was getting cooler, the restaurant fuller. The staff all seemed to be Mick's friends. They were kind and patient, but she knew she was in their way. He'd never been late for her before. And hadn't he been ranting about punctuality? Yes he had. Surely he wouldn't fail to show and not let her know. Unless he simply couldn't. Because he'd been in an accident. Or been arrested. Or had a heart attack. Brain haemorrhage. Memory loss.

At quarter past, she called his numbers again. Same result.

She went out and looked up and down the street. There was no sign of him. Back inside, her quiet corner had filled up. She thanked the sweet man behind the counter and went to wait in the street. Mick had got cold feet but hadn't the courage to tell her. She called Gail.

'Hi. Sorry to disturb. Just wondering if you've any idea where Mick is?'

'Sorry, no,' Gail said. 'I was trying to get him earlier too.'

Naomi plucked up a bit of courage. 'We had a sort of date, you know? Bloody man. I was going to buy him a takeaway from the Standard. Where I am now. Meet here at seven, we'd said. He's not shown up, and here I am, all alone with a load of food, wondering if he's, you know…'

'Dropping a delicate hint that he doesn't fancy you after all?' Gail asked.

'Not really what I meant, no.' *What's wrong with the bloody woman? Tactful, not.* 'I meant something could have come up that he had to do. Or he just forgot?'

'Never known him do that. But not heard anything either. Give him another five. Call me again if he's not arrived.'

She called Mick's mobile again. No answer. This time she left a voicemail. 'Mick, what's going on? Please call.'

Cars and bikes and groups of language school students went to and fro. A man sat cross-legged outside the cinema, a blanket over his shoulders, flat cap out for contributions. A patient dog, not unlike Friday but not Friday, was tucked in beside him, doing the actual begging.

A Harley with a sky-blue teardrop tank pulled up outside the Jericho Tavern. The guy put it on its stand, settled back into the low-slung seat, lodged his helmet on the tank. He was wearing shades. He stared at her while he lit a cigarette, noticed her noticing him, gave her the slightest nod. Was he one of those they met in that café? Hard to say, with the shades. He threw his half-smoked tab in the gutter, pressed the starter and puttered away.

The man with the dog retrieved the smoking butt and returned to his pitch, dragging on the smoke like oxygen on Everest.

Her phone rang.

Mick, she thought. *Thank God.*

But it was Gail, asking if she had heard anything.

'No.'

'Same here,' Gail said. 'Well. Don't waste your takeaway. Bring it here. Are you in a car?'

'No.' Naomi felt herself surrendering control.

'I'll pick you up. Two minutes. Microwave. Glass of something. Have a think. Okay?'

She's only being kind, Naomi thought. *With a rather bamboozling sort of kindness.*

An ancient Volvo drew up opposite. Gail smiled and beckoned. Naomi crossed the street, dropped a coin in the hat, and climbed in.

***

Gail bustled about like she wanted to wrap Naomi in a bundle of care. She opened wine and sorted food into the microwave. Naomi phoned Mick's numbers again. There was no answer.

'Trying his mobile or his landline?'

'Both. And his office, just in case. Sometimes they work very late.'

'Don't bother with the landline,' Gail said. 'He never answers it and doesn't check for messages.'

'I know,' Naomi said. Although she didn't, and was peeved Gail knew more about Mick's phone habits than she did. 'But just in case. Might be someone else in the flat, for example?'

'Yes, like Mrs Swainston,' said Gail. 'She'd not resist picking up a ringing phone.'

Who the fuck's Mrs Swainston? thought Naomi. 'Who the fuck's Mrs Swainston?' she said, letting a dribble of annoyance leak through.

'Oh. Sorry. His neighbour. The one that looks after Friday.'

Gail put hot food on the table, poured wine and water. 'Don't want to intrude,' she said.

'But you're going to anyway,' Naomi said. With a smile, she hoped. 'Carry on.'

'Okay. Thank you. I will. A little bit. Because of Mick. He's…'

Naomi looked at her, thinking, *Where's she going?* Was she going to get a lecture? Or a grilling? 'He's what?' she said. 'On the spectrum?'

'Funny you should say that,' Gail said. 'I asked him once. They told him he was at school. Asperger's. He said it was a category error.'

'A what?'

'He said it's not a disorder, it's a way of being. And every good software person he knew had been told the same thing.'

'He doesn't do normal, does he?'

'But he tries,' Gail said. 'A bit naïve. Vulnerable. Cares a lot. Easily hurt.'

'I don't want to hurt him,' Naomi said. 'But you're right. And I don't think he's what I need. Or I'm what he needs. But what's he doing, standing me up like this? Pisses me off, you know? Makes me feel a bloody fool.'

'It's not deliberate. Something's happened. I'm absolutely sure.' Gail paused, thinking. 'I never really heard about what happened at that café.'

'No. Poor Mick. We'd lost Alleyn and we saw this little café by the turn to Dorchester. I noticed Alleyn in the café. He left through the back. Mick went in to see what he could find out.'

'Good for him.'

'There were some bikers – you could tell from the bikes parked outside. Hogs, they call them, according to Andrea. She said these must be one-percenters, because ninety-nine percent of bikers are upright, law-abiding citizens who wouldn't say boo. But this lot… I actually saw a guy tonight who looked like one of them, sat on his bike outside the Jericho Tavern while I was waiting for Mick. Anyway, Mick asked the guy behind the counter if Alleyn had been in there and they'd pinned him over a table, emptied his pockets, gone through his wallet and were holding a gun to his head in a few seconds. Turned out to be a cigarette lighter that looked like a gun, but still.'

'None of us have known each other very long,' Gail said, 'except you and Andrea. We're still finding out about each other. I'm beginning to wonder… does Mick think he can sail through anything? So walks blithely into situations that are more difficult than he's expecting, then needs rescuing?'

'Could be. But aren't most men like that? Believe they can busk it rather than think things through?'

'Don't know.'

'Anyway, there he was on the floor and I had to go in and more or less pick him up and carry him out.'

Naomi phoned Mick's mobile again. Still no answer. 'I just don't know what we can do, you know? That isn't letting paranoia and pessimism take control. Those biker guys, they're mates of Alleyn. Alleyn's a mate of Sefton-Shaw. What if they've beaten him up or something, you know what I mean? Started on that pest control stuff.'

'Sefton-Shaw threatened to kill him if he ever went near Kimberly. I was never sure if he really meant it. But…'

'Has he been seeing her? Duplicitous bastard.'

'Steady. Far as I know, he's not seen her since we planted the bug. You could call the police,' Gail said, thinking aloud, 'but what would you tell them? Your friend's half an hour late for a date and you're worried about him?' She shook her head. 'Or we could go looking. To that bikers' café. Or Springfield House. But what do we do when we get there? What are we looking for?'

'God knows,' said Naomi. 'How about we go round to his flat and check he's not in bed with flu or something?'

'I'll just lock up,' Gail said, ushering her to the door. 'With you in a tick.'

Naomi waited out front. She rolled a rollie, lit up, studied the house. It was beautiful, one of the most exclusive terraces on the planet. Gail didn't seem to work. Or to be obviously wealthy in a cash-rich or nouveau sort of way. So inherited. And what an odd creature she was. Gauche and motherly and posh and self-effacing and unselfconscious and really quite nosey.

Gail came out, got in the car, leaned across to push the door open. 'Not in here, please,' she said, pointing to the roll-up. 'Ghastly habit.'

Naomi pinched a glowing ember into the gutter and put the nub in her pocket.

It was five minutes to Mick's flat. Naomi's brain went round in circles. No matter how ill he might be, he'd have sent a message. Flakiness was his number one hate. If he said he'd do something he would. Self-righteous but reliable. She agreed with Gail. He'd not forgotten or stood her up or whatever. She didn't expect to find him at his flat. But they had to check.

Gail parked on Godstow Road. Naomi pointed at Mick's car, feeling brief optimism.

'Means nothing,' Gail said. 'He busses to work. Walks or bikes otherwise, if he can. So the car's nearly always here whatever.' She pointed up at Mick's flat: first floor, to the right. Lights on in all except his. She pushed back a bush beside the path, moved a stone hedgehog, raised the slate it was standing on and emerged with Mick's emergency keys, wrapped in cling-film. The main door was open. They went up concrete steps to a landing, knocked on his door. No answer. Gail unlocked and said, 'I'll have a quick check.'

Naomi paused on the threshold, breathed still air. She knew the flat was empty. She went through, looked round the kitchen. There was bread in the bread bin, reasonably fresh. The milk in the fridge was similar. On the worktop was a tea caddy, bread board, bread knife, butter dish, jar of home-made marmalade. In the drying-up rack, a small plate, a large mug, a glass, a knife, a teaspoon. She was struck by how much she cared for him.

Gail re-joined her. 'Nothing,' she said. 'Nothing untoward, anyway. Fresh bedding. Fresh towels. Left the dog with plenty of water. Turned off everything you'd expect to be turned off if he was going out for the day.'

'Yes. No dog though,' Naomi said. 'He had juice, tea, toast and marmalade for breakfast. Washed up after himself, so wasn't in too much of a hurry.' Her phone pinged. A text. From Mick. 'Hellfire,' she said, pressing buttons on her phone, suddenly angry. 'If he's had to work late or something lame like that I'll kill him.'

Hi. Sorry to miss you, went to wrong restaurant. Another time? Mike xxx

She read out the text and looked at Gail in bemusement.

'A bit odd,' Gail said.

'Bloody odd. It's the only restaurant he goes to. And since when did he call himself Mike?'

'They've got him,' Gail said. 'And his phone.'

'Who?'

'Sefton-Shaw,' Gail said. 'Alleyn. Someone working for them.'

'Christ, this is really getting...' The flat's front door creaked open. Naomi jumped. 'What the fuck?' she said, controlling an urge to scream.

Dog Friday scuttled in and stuck her nose in Naomi's groin. An oldish woman came in and looked at them with suspicion.

'Oh,' said Naomi. 'Dear. Who are you? Is Mick with you?'

'Sorry to alarm you,' said the woman, peering around, not looking at all sorry. 'No. Was going to ask you the same question. I heard someone and thought he'd got back.'

'No, just us,' said Naomi. She wasn't sure about this person and didn't want to share their worries with her. 'He rang earlier,' she said. 'He had to go away. On business. I said I'd dog-sit Friday, if he wasn't going to get home. My friend gave me a lift up.' She indicated Gail, who smiled and nodded.

'And you are…?' the woman asked.

'Oh. I'm Naomi. Friend of Mick's. This is Gail. Another friend. And you must be Mrs…' She searched for the name of the neighbour that Gail had mentioned.

'Swainston,' Gail said.

'That's right,' the woman said. 'Beryl Swainston. Friday usually stays with me when he's away.'

Oh dear, Naomi thought, *her nose is out of joint*. 'Mrs Swainston, of course, yes. He was telling me Friday might be with you if she wasn't in the flat. I was about to come round to see.'

'You were?' She looked less than convinced. 'Well. Here she is. And she obviously knows you. So I'll leave you to it.'

'Thank you, Mrs Swainston,' Naomi said, trying to shepherd her through the door.

'Where's he gone then?' Mrs Swainston asked, turning in the doorway. 'He never said anything about going away.'

Oh Christ, she was weaving a tangled web here. 'Something came up at work,' she said. 'He had to go up north, to sort something out. Bradford, was it?'

'Oh yes? Bradford. By train, is it? Because his car's still here. Well. I'll be off then. You'll be staying here, will you?'

'I will,' said Naomi. 'Not Gail.'

'Got everything you need?'

'Yes thanks.'

'All right. You know where I am if anything crops up.'

'Yes thanks.' Naomi hazarded a guess. 'Number three, isn't it?'

'Five,' said Mrs Swainston, with a sour look. 'This is number three. I'll be off then. Leave you to it.'

'Thank you,' said Naomi. 'Good night.' She closed the door, leaned back on it, breathed out. 'Did I completely blow it? Or only slightly?'

'Only slightly,' Gail said. 'Couldn't see what you were up to. But you didn't want her getting stirred up. Police, missing persons, that sort of thing.'

'Exactly.'

'Yes. Well done. Quick thinking.'

'Not really,' Naomi said. 'Winging it. But I was planning to stay, whatever. Got a toothbrush and stuff in my bag. It's good I've met her, really.'

'Yes. And you've got Friday to look after you. That's good.' She looked at her watch. 'Gone ten. Too late to do much now. I'll be off too.'

'Okay. Doesn't seem right, but… What are you doing in the morning?'

'Coming back here. If that's all right.'

'Certainly is.'

'In the car. And we can go out. Have a look. Do something. Don't know what.'

'Yes. Good.'

'Call me the instant he shows up,' Gail said, 'if he does. Or if you hear anything. Any time.'

CHAPTER 26

Extreme street theatre. An accident that wasn't. The dentist smell. Headache. Eyes glued shut. I was outraged, and not just about missing a meeting.

I went to rub my eyes. My hands wouldn't move. Trying hurt. I tore eyelids apart using muscles and ligaments I didn't know were there, like a sheet of stamps tearing itself along its perforations.

Dazzling white walls. Black plastic ties binding my hands to a steel bed frame. And feet. Everything hurt. I didn't notice the noise until it stopped.

'He's awake,' someone said in a Scottish accent.

No windows. One door with a panel or hatch in it. Stained brown lino, ten feet square. Coved ceiling, like an attic. Warm. Quiet. Rank with stale sweat and aftershave. Movement behind me, and a face; the weighty Scottish biker, from the café. Naomi thought he was Donald Cruickshank's brother. He'd been the injured cyclist in the fake accident. Another café biker in pale blue paramedic cargo pants and dirty white T-shirt, pulling up two red plastic chairs. Hypodermic man.

They'd got me. I was a prisoner. Be nice to know what they intended. I remembered reading – Brian Keenan, was it? Or Lee Child? – that it's important for a prisoner to establish a relationship with his captors, but that it's not as simple as just being nice to them. More like finding common ground. Football? Or motorbikes. And maintaining dignity, mutual respect, distance.

'Are you guys bikers?' I said. Croaked. 'Do I know you?'

'Maybe, maybe not,' the man who could be a Cruickshank said. 'You better hope not.' He leaned over, pinched my nostrils, tipped my head back. What now, waterboarding?

A fist. In the solar plexus. It was unexpected and it hurt. I couldn't get my breath. I shivered, cold, sweaty and powerless. *Don't panic. Tighten your gut. Time will heal. Give it time. Breath will come back.*

I opened an eye, drew in a staggered breath and let it out in lumps. I met Cruickshank's eye – if it was Cruickshank – and thought, *Respect my arse.* He enjoyed that.

I didn't say it though. But the man read something in my face. Scorn? Fear? Enough to prompt a heavy backhand into my left temple.

'Eric,' he said. 'The phone.'

'Eric?' The other laughed. Picked up what looked like my iPhone. Of course they'd have my phone. And wallet. And laptop. What could they do with that lot? It couldn't just be robbery, could it? No. Alleyn set it up. Including the meeting at the law office. *Pour encourager les autres*, he'd said. And to get me off the street, temporarily, while the deal went through... or permanently. If they were concerned about concealing identities that was good; it meant they were going to let me live. I felt a wave of hope and had to stop myself smiling.

'Give him another wee dose,' Cruickshank said. 'He's getting frisky.'

Eric held a chloroform-soaked pad over my face and counted slowly to thirty.

My headache clanged. Cruickshank took hold of my hand, did something with my right thumb. A vibration and a quiet ping. My phone unlocking. Oh fuck. Needle in my arm again.

Pitch black darkness. Loud noise. I recognised 'Statesboro Blues' by Taj Mahal, a classic. I was still cable-tied to the bed. I had sore ankles and wrists, and a shooting pain when I moved. I lay still for a long time. The album looped until I lost count, then stopped. The silence heralded nothing, not even panic or terror.

I tried a chakras chant. It made my head hurt.

Tried a simple Om. Made my head hurt more.

Tried slow breathing.

In two three four five, through the nose.

Out two three four five, through the mouth.

***

Bright light. The door opened. I had no idea what time it was or what day. Cruickshank and 'Eric' came in, laughing, smelling of weed and whisky.

'He's some lovely friends,' said Cruickshank. 'Tell him what they've been saying.'

'They were a bit concerned,' Eric said, 'so we reassured them.' Both laughed again. 'Denise – at your office? – texted your mobile. "Where are you? Why the no-show for the meeting." Want to know what you texted back?'

I closed my eyes. They were going to tell me, whether I wanted it or not. Did they have a purpose in mind? Were they just telling me for fun? And what sort of mischief could they start through my contacts list? By getting at Naomi. Gail. Andrea. My mum. I must have missed my rendezvous with Naomi at the Standard. Had they abducted her too?

I lay back in despair, hurting, dizzy, weak. I couldn't move, couldn't think, and was past caring. But some subconscious logic told me I should pay attention. Eric read out their reply to Denise.

For someone that didn't know me, it sounded quite plausible, educated. Perhaps there was more to Eric than met the eye.

Eric thumbed through to find another message. 'There's a text from someone who's down as KJ in your contacts. Who's that?'

Oh fuck. They must not find out about Kanhai. 'That'll be Keith. Keith Jackson,' I said, glad to find my voice working at all, and realising Cruickshank was watching me closely.

'He wanted to know if tomorrow was okay to meet,' Eric said. '"Tomozz", he called it. So you said you were indisposed. Where is it?' He scrolled, read it out.

'Let's see,' I said.

Eric looked at Cruickshank, who shrugged. Held up the phone for me.

'Fuck,' I said, not finding it hard to feign disappointment and defeat, but feeling a glimmer of hope: Eric's reply contradicted the voicemail I'd left for Kanhai, days ago, it felt like, outside the gallery. And Denise in the office might remember my grandad died last year, and we'd had a conversation not long ago about losing that generation – but not, in her case, that generation's horses. They thought they were being clever. But someone would realise that the messages were a bit wonky, and come looking for me.

Wouldn't they?

***

I woke in darkness, more clear-headed, the drugs wearing off.

There were raised voices beyond the door, faint. Thumping feet and a sudden flood of light came from the hatch. There was movement behind it, like a warder checking a prisoner. The main light flickered on, the door opened and the two guys came in. They didn't look happy.

'No fraternisation,' Cruickshank said. I wondered whether this was directed at me or Eric. 'So shut up before you start. And no damaged goods. For now. So a new regime.' He cut the cable ties, examined my wrists and ankles. 'Eric,' he said. 'Get the stuff.'

I tried to sit up but had to lie back, like a gyroscope seeking a horizontal axis. I forced myself up, very slowly, holding on to the bed frame, and tried to stretch. Everything hurt.

Cruickshank leaned on the doorjamb, arms folded, watching me.

Eric came back with two buckets, one three-quarters full of water, one empty. 'Washing. Toilet,' he said and went out again. He came back with a towel and a tray holding a jug of water, glass, half-empty small blue tube of antiseptic cream, and full hypodermic. And a baguette wrapped in cling-film with a handwritten label saying Cheese Salad. How did they know?

Cruickshank nodded at the tray. Eric applied the ointment and washed his hands. He passed me the baguette and water. I felt oddly cared for and deeply grateful. There was a name for this feeling. Something Scandinavian. The water was lovely. And the food.

'No restraints now,' said Cruickshank. 'As long as you behave. When we're coming in, we'll tell you through the hatch. You'll lie on the bed. Don't move. Okay? And you needn't bother trying to get out. Or making a noise.' He pointed to the walls and ceiling. 'Secure. Sound-proofed.'

I sort of believed him. There was a lie in there somewhere, but not anything obvious. Cruickshank nodded at the tray again. Eric squeezed my left arm, where a bicep should have been. I could see a vein standing out on the inside of my elbow. He injected 10cc of clear liquid with a hint of milkiness. I lay back, washed by drowsiness.

They left.

The lights went out.

It was quiet; there was no music.

This time I felt less out of control and rode the slipping-away like a free-wheeling bike. I didn't know what they were giving me.

Not anything I was familiar with. But nice, if you ignored the context. And whatever it was helped me do just that.

I closed my eyes, tried a bit of meditation, and hit the low E of Om straight away. It felt good. *Interesting*, I thought. *Explore further.*

I felt myself fading and went with it.

CHAPTER 27

KANHAI

Kanhai woke feeling jittery, a question hovering: how did they get into Mick's phone, to send fake messages? There were several possible answers. He didn't like any of them.

He left Bethan breakfasting with their daughter and drove to work, arriving at half six, earlier than usual. He was surprised to see lights on the second floor, in his section of Technical Services. Who could that be? He took the stairs quietly, then went quietly through the open door from the stairwell. Two figures were poking around his desk, their backs to him.

He approached silently.

From three feet behind them, he spoke loudly. 'Good morning, gentlemen. Can I help you?'

The younger one jumped a foot in the air, twisted in flight and landed wide-eyed, moustache trembling. There was guilt all over the pock-marked face of Detective Constable Clappison. Kanhai sometimes talked to him in the canteen. He was a recent fast-track post-graduate recruit, with a doctorate in fuzzy logic, which sometimes raised a laugh.

His corpulent companion straightened slowly, a smug smile

on his rubbery face. He had oily hair dyed too black and dandruff-dusted shoulders. Detective Inspector Jones, Grant's boss.

'Good morning, Mr Jamal,' Jones said. His over-respectful tone made Kanhai's skin crawl. It conveyed categorical disrespect, possibly unconscious; otherwise known as institutional racism. 'Yes, perhaps you can. Come this way.'

They kept up a good pace, Clappison in front, Jones behind, Kanhai in between, being marched like a prisoner down the stairs, out across the courtyard, into the ops building, then up two flights, Jones huffing and puffing and slowing up. They went through a door into Jones's territory – the Specialist Pro-Active Team office, deserted at this hour – and into a windowless room labelled "Break-Out Space", upholstered in pink and overdue for refurbishment.

DI Jones pointed Kanhai to a seat and sat opposite. 'Coffee?' he said.

'Machine or home-grown?'

'Oh, home-grown.'

'Okay, thanks. White without, please.'

Jones nodded to Clappison, who shuffled off to make it.

Jones sat back, stretched out his legs, crossed his ankles, stared at Kanhai for what seemed like a long time. If he hadn't known it was a standard tactic, Kanhai would have found it unnerving.

'So,' Jones said, finally breaking the silence. 'You're probably wondering what this is about.'

Kanhai nodded.

'It's probably nothing,' Jones said. 'But there's someone we've become interested in, you might say. He turned up on the periphery of an investigation we're in the middle of, and he seems to be in regular contact with you. Phone calls, texts. Jarvis. Michael Jarvis. Know him?'

Kanhai wasn't totally surprised. He couldn't deny knowing Mick. He didn't think there was anything incriminating in their electronic exchanges. He'd like to know how they knew about

Mick's phone use. Either they had a trace on him, or they'd got hold of his phone. Or someone they knew had his phone.

'Mick? Known him since school,' he said. 'Okay bloke, I always thought. What's he been up to, then?'

'We're not at liberty to share that at the moment.'

Cagey, Kanhai thought. *Probably just fishing. But if that was how he wanted to play it...*

Clappison returned, nodding to Jones and setting down three mugs of coffee.

'So what have you been texting each other about recently?'

'Football, most likely,' Kanhai said. 'Or darts. Bikes. Pubs. Can't remember. But even if I could, you'll understand that I wouldn't be at liberty to share it with you.' He reached for his coffee, gave Jones a shrug and a rueful smile.

'Why not?' Clappison said.

'Because he's an old friend. I'd have to talk to him first.' He took another sip. 'Nice coffee,' he said. 'Much nicer than that muck from the machine.'

Jones looked at him, his face screwed into a scowl.

Kanhai looked back. No-one spoke. He drank more coffee. Finished the coffee. Smiled. 'Well, that was good. Thanks. So, if there's nothing else...?'

Jones shook his head and looked away.

Clappison stood, said 'I'll show you out.'

'I know the way,' Kanhai said, closing the door on them. He'd put money on there being a connection between Mick's conspirators and someone in DI Jones's team.

CHAPTER 28

DENISE IN THE OFFICE

Why all hell should break loose on a Thursday morning just a few days after a hectic month-end, Denise didn't know, but it had. Suppliers and sub-contractors chasing payment, customers chasing deliverables, staff querying bonuses and expenses. It was half eleven before she had time to grab a coffee and think about Mick.

She called his mobile and landline: both went straight to voicemail. She had to try his emergency number again. She called it up on the system, noticed the contact's name was rather strange.

A woman answered immediately. 'Yes?'

'This is Denise at Oxford Hypermedia. Did you get my message? On your answerphone?'

'Unh?'

'Okay, sorry. Can I just check your name please?'

'Yes. It's Sandra. Sandra Cleary.'

'Okay, thanks. And you're Mick's mother. We've spoken before. I'll just correct our emergency contact data. He's put the phone number in properly but he's got contact name, Mrs Trousers, and relationship, Mother Hen.'

'Cheek. He'll regret that,' she said. 'Why are you calling? What's up?'

Denise explained about yesterday's missed meeting. And the text apologising, and saying he had to take leave because his grandfather was dangerously ill.

'That's nonsense,' Sandra said. 'His grandfather died last year, on his dad's side. My father died years ago. So that's weird. But why lie about it? On his way to a meeting, you said. Where?'

'Summertown. Murdoch Alleyn, a law company. He's setting up a project for them.'

'Look. Send me an email. Who he was going to see. All the names and numbers, addresses, you know. Anything else relevant. Save you reading it out and me writing it down. And I'll go over to his flat, see what I can dig up. Probably find him in bed with flu. Or one of his floozies. But thanks. Speak later.'

CHAPTER 29

Naomi

She woke with a jolt. She was in Mick's bed. She shivered. Got out.

She looked round. It felt odd, being in his flat on her own. She couldn't resist a peep in cupboards and bookshelves. Nothing embarrassing, thank God. A surprising number of socks, all in matching pairs. A surprising number of books on philosophy, psychology, art, science, prehistory, natural history. A whole wall of thrillers, spies and detectives. Lots of vinyl LPs, shelved alphabetically by artist. She fed Friday, took her for a walk on the common. At nine she called Mick's mobile: straight to voicemail. She called his office. He wasn't in. They couldn't say more, on the phone, to a stranger.

She met Gail at the door. 'Stranger?' Naomi said, ringing off. 'Don't feel like a stranger.'

'Rather than sit round worrying,' Gail said, 'and biting people's heads off, how about we drive around worrying. Look at the places we know to be implicated, or feel might be implicated. Which isn't a long list.'

Naomi refilled Friday's water and wrote a note for Mrs Swainston saying she'd be back later if Mick had to stay up north.

Murdoch Alleyn in Summertown was nearest. They parked on Banbury Road, outside a salon, and watched for five minutes. It was a busy street, people going to and fro and in and out all the time. Nothing untoward.

They drove to Ballator Developments in Botley. Alleyn's Porsche was in the car park. It was still metallic gold and not very interesting, in itself. They moved on again.

Springfield House on Boars Hill. No vehicles, no lights, no signs of life.

The bikers' café near Dorchester. No-one parked outside, no-one in the café. Gail parked and they walked over, went in. It was the same young guy behind the counter. Naomi sat at a table near the door, listening and watching. Gail asked for coffee at the counter. It appeared within seconds, poured from a vacuum flask.

'Doesn't your friend want one too?' the youth said, indicating Naomi.

Naomi shook her head.

'Shame,' he said. 'I remember her. Told my arse of a boss where to get off. I liked that.'

He's a possible ally, Naomi thought, albeit with limited resources. 'Do you remember the guy I was with?' she said, joining Gail at the counter. 'When we met your nice boss? Called Mick. Average height. Medium hair. Medium everything really.'

'Not really.'

'He's gone missing,' Naomi said. 'You've not seen him since?'

'No.'

'The others that day. Was one your boss?'

'Yeah.'

'What's his name?'

'Cruickshank. Graham Cruickshank.'

'And he's a friend of James Alleyn,' Naomi said. 'Right? The lawyer.'

'S'pose.'

'You suppose,' Gail said.

'You've been told not to say anything about... what?' Naomi said. 'Mr Alleyn?'

'Mmm.'

'If you do see our friend,' Naomi said, 'Mick, can you give me a ring? Or text? Without letting your boss know. Or anyone else. Is that possible?'

'Maybe,' he said.

Naomi put a business card on the counter.

Gail put a twenty on top of it and said, 'Keep the change.'

***

They parked next to Mick's Golf by the flat at midday. Gail went to the corner shop to buy lunch. Naomi felt hopeless and depressed but didn't want to admit it. She suspected Gail felt the same. She put the kettle on, collected some post from the mat – all circulars– and tucked them between pasta and brown rice jars on the dresser with more unopened post. She found a caddy of leaf tea and a large stoneware teapot. She was giving it a stir when a woman walked in. *As if she owned the place*, Naomi thought. She was slim, medium height, stylish, with a loose tangle of hair, pale to dark grey, tamed by a sky-blue silk scarf. She had pale blue eyes that lingered on Naomi's.

'Who might you be?' the woman said. 'You're not Kimberly...'

'No.' *Why the bloody hell does she think I might be Kimberly?* 'No, I'm Naomi. A friend. You're his mum, aren't you?'

'How did you know?'

'Cheekbones,' Naomi said, going round the table and hugging Mick's mother, asking, 'What's going on? Do you know? Where is he?' through sudden wailing sobs.

Gail came in carrying brown paper bags then stopped and stared at the women in each other's arms. The phone rang: his landline.

Naomi held on to Mick's mum. Gail picked up the phone.

220

'Hello... Yes, Mick's flat. He's not here... Wish I knew. Who's asking?... Kanhai?' Gail relayed the name to the others.

'I'll speak to him.' The older woman released Naomi, advanced on Gail and took the phone. 'Kanhai? Kanhai? It's Sandra. His mum... No idea. We can't raise him either. He was going to a meeting in Summertown, yesterday morning. Never got there. I think the idiot's mixed up in something way out of his league... Warned him? You know something about this?... Can't discuss it on the phone?' She looked round at Naomi, eyes raised to heaven. 'Get over yourself! And get over here, pronto... Yes you can. Take a fucking lunch break for once. We'll get you a sandwich... Too right. See you in five.'

Sandra humphed and said, 'Somebody put the kettle on, for God's sake.' She flopped down into what looked to Naomi like Mick's favourite armchair.

Naomi headed for the kitchen.

'And here's a fiver,' Sandra continued, holding it out to Gail. 'Get another sandwich, can you? Please. For Kanhai. I did promise him one.'

Naomi topped up the teapot. 'Tea for four, is it?'

'Yes, dear. Naomi, isn't it, you said? I was going to ask you what you know about whatever it is. But I think we'll wait 'til the others are here. And I'll just try Denise in the office.'

She fished a phone from her bag. 'Denise? Hello. Sandra. Mick's mum... Yes. At his flat. Meeting some of his mates. No sign of him... Yes. About the meeting he was supposed to be going to. You're sure he never arrived?... And it was at Murdoch Alleyn?... Yes, I know it. On Banbury Road. With... Okay. Project manager. So this was a live project?... Right. So more a sales meeting than a progress meeting? Who asked for it? And when?... Just the day before. Okay. Was there a sudden crisis?... No, you wouldn't. Who's the salesperson? Is it Dougie?... Why wasn't he going too?... So. A sales meeting. With no salesman. Fronted by tech support. Arranged at twenty-four hours' notice.

But not because of some crisis… Yes, it does seem odd when I put it like that. Okay, thanks. We'll let you know when we track him down.'

Naomi put a tray of tea things on the table. 'Sounds like that meeting was a set-up,' she said. 'I was talking to him on Tuesday evening. Told him to be careful. He promised he would. That bloody man Alleyn will be behind it. And Sefton-Shaw. Unpleasant bastards.'

Gail came in with a brown paper bag and a thirty-something-year-old man with receding black hair, deep golden skin and, in Naomi's eyes, a welcome air of calm and kindness.

'This is Kanhai,' Gail said. 'Met him outside. Kanhai, you know Sandra. This is Naomi. I'm Gail, by the way.'

'Delighted to meet you,' Kanhai said. He gave a shallow bow to Gail and Naomi then crossed to Sandra and air-kissed.

Naomi picked up her tea, blew on it, put it down. Time to take the bull by the horns. She cleared her throat, took a deep breath. All eyes were on her.

'Mick disappeared, as far as we can make out,' she said, 'between half ten and eleven yesterday morning, en route from here to the Murdoch Alleyn offices in Summertown. He could have been abducted. And if he was, I think we have to assume it's something to do with the Glebe Farm land deal, and the poking around that some of us have been doing. There's lots we don't know. But I suggest that, if we put together what we do know and what we can guess, there's a chance we can find him. And get him back.'

'We can all trust each other,' Gail said, looking round, 'so full disclosure. Everything we know, without wasting time. Because we don't know what the poor lad's going through, but he's most likely not enjoying it.'

Gail went first, Naomi filling in motives and scary moments.

Kanhai described the bugging and hacking. How he was setting up a meeting with a friendly detective, which Mick had

222

wanted as a kind of insurance. And how they'd been trying to meet to talk about it for a few days.

'And two other things,' he said. 'Mick called me yesterday morning and left a voicemail, confirming we'd meet this evening. And criticising some landscape paintings, so he'd have been outside that gallery on South Parade.' He pulled out his phone and checked the time of the call. 'At ten fifty-two. So that means, if he was abducted, it was between ten fifty-two and eleven, because he would have arrived on the dot. From that gallery to their offices is about two hundred yards. And second thing. I had a couple of detectives asking me about him this morning. I caught them going through my desk. They were fairly polite, really, for them, but then I am a colleague. Anyway, the DI sent the other one out to get coffee. He was gone a good while, and I had this feeling… so when I was coming over here, I stopped at home first and gave the car a quick look over. I found a tracking device under the wheel arch. Metal disk. Magnetic.'

He held up thumb and forefinger to show the size of the disk.

'Standard police issue,' he said. 'I took it off and put it on my bike, in the garage. I'll put it back on the car later. And leave it there unless I'm going somewhere I don't want them to know about. I suggest you all check your vehicles. And Mick's, just in case. And anyone else's who you think they might be connecting with Mick. But don't destroy them. Don't do anything that will make them think they've been found. Does everyone understand that? It's important.'

Sandra seemed to soak it all up, but contributed little except to agree that yesterday's meeting was a set-up and Mick walked into a trap. 'And your policemen this morning, Kanhai,' she said, 'asking about Mick. Treating Mick as suspicious in some way, and you, by implication – it could mean that information is passing between whoever kidnapped Mick and the officers in question. Who were…?'

'DI Jones and DC Clappison,' said Kanhai.

'Okay,' said Sandra. 'So those two may be linked with Alleyn. And those others you mentioned, the planner and… What's the link? Are they all Masons? School buddies? All getting backhanders? Or what? Can you find out?'

'Not the sort of thing I can wander round HQ asking questions about,' Kanhai said.

'That's fair enough,' Naomi said, trying to refocus. 'How are we going to find out who's got him, and where?'

'I don't think Sefton-Shaw would dirty his hands with kidnapping,' said Gail. 'Or Alleyn. Or Cruickshank. They'd have heavies for the dirty work, like those bikers. Naomi, you saw Alleyn there.'

'Yes,' Naomi said. 'But if it's them, it doesn't mean that Mick's in Dorchester, you know? Cruickshank lives somewhere in north Oxford; those places have bloody big basements. He could be there. Alleyn's out in the sticks somewhere. Could be there. Or trussed up in Sefton-Shaw's shed. But yes, the bikers'll be the muscle, as far as we know. They're getting a fair slice of the cash that's being spread around; they must be doing something for it. So suspect locus number one is the café, but he could be almost anywhere.'

'Suspect locus number one,' Gail said. 'I like it. So the café. Sefton-Shaw's. Find where Cruickshank and Alleyn live, have a look there.'

'Kanhai,' Naomi said. 'Could you impersonate a police officer?'

'That's illegal.' Kanhai's brows furrowed.

'Or a VAT man. Customs and excise or whatever. Wouldn't they have powers, like to search business premises? And,' Naomi said, 'they've been using his phone to send those messages, pretending to be him, replying to our texts and stuff. Could you get someone to trace where they were sent from?'

Kanhai wasn't enthusiastic. 'It's not easy,' he said, getting up to leave.

It went quiet. Friday stirred from her bed in the corner, came across and put her head on Naomi's knees.

'Friday,' she said, ruffling floppy black ears. 'Cool dog. You can come with me and Gail.' She got up and followed Kanhai to the door. 'Let us know if you get anywhere with the phone use, please. This evening? Thanks.'

She closed the door on him and felt herself drooping. She flopped down on the sofa. She found it hard to hold it all in her head, but could see that they knew much more about Sefton-Shaw than they did about his mates.

Sitting in silence with Sandra was making her nervous. While Gail tidied up lunch and Sandra drank tea and fiddled with her phone, Naomi found home addresses for Donald Cruickshank: St Margarets Road, in north Oxford. And James Alleyn: Sotwell Barns, Brightwell-cum-Sotwell, near Wallingford.

'Cruickshank lives alone,' she told them, 'according to the electoral roll. Alleyn has half a dozen people registered at his address. All different names. Employees? Servants? Some sort of commune?'

Gail flicked at a fly with a tea towel and shrugged.

***

Naomi put Friday in the back of Gail's car, which was tail to tail with Mick's. Where did Kanhai say they put that magnetic thing? She fumbled around beneath Mick's car and found a shiny round magnetic disk, two centimetres across, under the nearside rear wheel arch. Sandra watched. 'We're not using Mick's car,' Naomi said. 'Might as well leave this there.' She felt under Sandra's car and found nothing, then checked Gail's; there was another, in the same place.

'They know about me too, then,' Gail said. She looked thoughtful. 'We could put this with the other, on Mick's?'

'Unless you put it on mine?' suggested Sandra. 'That might confuse them.'

'And put you right in the firing line,' said Naomi. 'No.'

'But confusing them might be an idea.' Sandra took a few paces into Godstow Road. 'Look,' she said. 'Outside the shop.'

'A post office van, at the letter box,' said Naomi. 'And a delivery van. Fruit and veg.'

'Yes. Don't want to play yes-but-no-but,' said Sandra, 'but both of those will end up back at base, be easy to find. And then they'd know that we're onto them. Like Kanhai was saying, best to avoid that. I was looking at the car just along. A smart new Mercedes estate. German plates. My German's not bad,' she said. 'Give it here, I'll go and find out.'

Sandra scuttled across to the shop and emerged moments later chatting animatedly to two large grinning people wearing identical patterned pullovers and olive-green walking trousers. Naomi heard her say, '*Gute Reise, auf Wiedersehen*', and saw her hand slip down to the wheel arch as she rounded the car to come back across the road. They both waved as the couple drove off, then grinned at each other.

'Fab,' said Sandra. 'They're Inspector Morse fanatics, touring famous spots. Just had lunch at the Trout. They're sailing on a Stena ferry from Harwich to the Hook at ten tonight, then driving to the far side of Berlin.'

Mrs Swainston appeared in a smart coat and climbed into Sandra's car. Sandra joined her and waved. Their job was to visit Dorchester Abbey and take afternoon tea at the bikers' café. Mrs Swainston would soon find out that Mick wasn't working in Bradford, Naomi realised, making a mental note to apologise to her later.

***

'Cruickshank first,' Gail said, 'he's just down the road.'

They parked in an empty residents' slot twenty yards from Cruickshank's house, a detached Victorian villa. A dented dark red Saab covered in dead leaves and bird poo sat behind shabby wooden gates.

'He works in the uni offices in Summertown,' Naomi said. 'A ten-minute walk at most.' She looked at her watch. 'Quarter to three. Should be there now. But can he possibly live alone in a house like this? It's huge.'

'There's no-one else on the electoral roll, you said. No signs of life. No harm in a little look around,' Gail said. 'Can you hoot? Like an owl?'

'Yes.' Naomi hooted.

'Good,' said Gail. 'That's the alarm signal. You walk Friday up and down out here, and keep an eye out. Then we'll think about what's next. Right? Let's go,' said Gail, looking both ways.

Naomi followed her across the road, then watched her go through an open pedestrian gate and press the bell by a front door with 'YES' chalked on flaking green paint. Nothing happened. Gail pressed again, knocked and turned back to Naomi, shaking her head.

Gail went round the side of the house, behind the old Saab. Naomi walked Friday thirty yards past the house, crossed the road, walked back, crossed again, repeated. Two cars and a taxi went by without paying undue attention. One cyclist. No pedestrians.

Gail came back through the gate. 'No-one in,' she said. 'Normal untidy house. There's a basement. A coal hole by the front door, not used. Whited-out skylights at ground level at the back. If they're keeping Mick down there there's no sign of it.'

'I'll take Friday for a quick sniff round,' Naomi said. Gail had a habit of ordering people around that could easily become annoying. 'You're on patrol out here.'

Naomi led Friday to the front door. The dog stood looking up at her, not interested. 'Come on then,' she said, going round the side to a half-glazed door at the back, through which she saw a spacious cluttered kitchen. She went down stone steps to a dusty door to the basement, the same faded green as the front door. It was cobwebbed and painted shut, hadn't been opened in years.

Friday still looked puzzled and gave no sign that she'd scented Mick or anything else interesting.

Naomi took her back up the steps and walked her slowly round the garden. In the far corner was a large, rickety wooden shed under a beech tree. Again, cobwebs over the door spoke of disuse. She could see nothing through the windows. A shrill hoot came from the street. Naomi froze. It was the danger signal, right enough. But what sort of danger, and what should she do about it? *Give it thirty seconds*, she decided. *Time for him to let himself in, if that's what's happening, then get out down the side.*

She'd counted to twenty when the kitchen door opened and a man stepped out, cleaning spectacles with a handkerchief. He had greasy greying hair, sunken yellow cheeks, corduroys and a tweedy jacket. He put the glasses on and fumbled in his pockets with one hand while shaking a cigarette from a crumpled pack with the other. Donald Cruickshank, the uni property services boss. He hadn't looked her way yet, being preoccupied with lighting up. She might as well take the initiative. She set off towards him across the lawn. He did an exaggerated double take. Did he recognise her? His eyes goggled and his lips moved, only smoke coming out. *Perhaps he's shy*, she thought. *So I won't be.*

'Hello there,' she boomed, approaching with bold strides, holding out her right hand. 'Peggy Anstruther. This is Rover.'

He looked at her hand. He didn't move his.

She dropped her hand. 'Looking for Anselm Jacobs,' she said. 'Sculptor and monumental mason. Someone said he had a studio in the back garden here. But I can't see it.' She swept her hand in a wide "look, no studio" gesture.

'Ah,' said the man, coughing a cloud of blue-brown smoke. 'You want Polstead. Next road up. Going north.' He waved helpfully in the direction of the street.

Naomi took the hint with gratitude. 'Thank you. Sorry to disturb,' she said with her best smile. 'We've been trespassing, haven't we? Forgive us our trespasses.' She almost curtsied, then walked past him, upright and brisk.

'Just a minute,' he said.

She ignored him and strode down the side of the house, then out and across the street. Gail was waiting with the tailgate up, Friday jumped in and they were away.

'Phew,' Gail said, putting her foot down. 'Well done. But sailing a bit close to the wind. We don't want any more abductions.'

'No,' said Naomi, feeling a shiver cross her shoulders. 'But come on. We've just got to find him. Alleyn's next. Okay? Ring road. Reading Road, at the Sainsbury's junction.' She fired up her phone and entered the post code. 'Follow signs for Wallingford, then Brightwell-cum-Sotwell.'

***

A sign on sandstone gateposts with ornate fluting and pineapple finials read:

SOTWELL BARNS
PRIVATE
KEEP OUT

It had CCTV and an entry-phone system. Tall, black wrought-iron gates with spikes on top were set ten yards back from the road. A brick wall was topped with shards of glass. Through the gate they could see a tree-lined drive fringed with rhododendrons, the edges of a large building visible through branches.

'Some kind of bloody fortress,' Naomi said. 'Let's get out of the traffic, see if there's a way to sneak up behind.'

***

They went back into Wallingford at the height of its afternoon rush and out again on the Shillingford Road, then left down a farm track in abrupt hammering rain. Gail tucked the car behind a heap of gravel on some hard standing behind an unkempt barn.

The rain stopped. They walked along a tall gappy hedge strung with gappy barbed wire. The field boundary was signed as a public footpath but didn't seem much walked. Friday ranged and sniffed. Gail scanned the area ahead through binoculars.

'See anything?' Naomi asked.

'Just a high fence. And a yellow sign saying "Guard Dogs Patrolling". No-one about.'

They came to the fence. Two parallel fences were two metres apart and two metres high – chain-link with razor wire on top and warning signs on every post. A well-trodden path ran right and left outside the perimeter.

'Certainly doesn't want uninvited guests,' Naomi said. 'And look at all this dead stuff. Sprayed with Round-Up, both sides of the fence. Smell it? Horrid. And look. Not a happy dog.' Friday's ears were flattened, her back hunched and her tail between her legs.

Bare earth was in the gap between the first and second fences, covered with paw marks and decaying dog-poo. 'Large paws and large poos,' Naomi said. 'Therefore large dogs. We'll not try to get in there. Just look up and down the fence.'

It ran in a south-east to north-west line. They turned left, to the south-east. After thirty yards the boundary turned ninety degrees to the right and a glass-topped brick wall, similar to the one along the road at the front, took over from the outer chain-link.

Gail put a shushing finger to her lips, pointed to a steel post in the middle of the clear strip between the outer and inner fences, and led the way back along the fence to the point where they'd first joined it.

'Three things pointing in each direction,' she said, 'on that post. Along the fence and along the wall. One would be CCTV.'

'And motion sensor?' Naomi said. 'And I don't know what.'

They walked another seventy yards to the far end of the fence and another post carrying high-tech sensors. There were dense evergreens all along beyond the inner fence, impassable, opaque. Only in one place, a few yards from the far corner, could they see anything through the tangle.

'That looks odd,' Gail said. 'Like a whole bunch of... what are they called? Portakabins?'

She pronounced it with the stress on the second syllable: por-TAK-abins. Naomi was puzzled, not sure whether the pronunciation was a mistake or an obscure joke that she didn't get.

'Yes,' she said. 'Can I borrow your binocs? And climb on your shoulders?' She could see a little more from there. 'Two rows of them,' she said. 'Ten or more in each row, facing each other across a covered walkway. Green roofs. Sedum. Tall trees everywhere. Leylandii. Lower branches lopped up to twenty feet or so.' She scanned to and fro. 'Nobody about,' she said. 'Ghost town. Gives me the willies.'

'Know what you mean,' said Gail. 'Let's go.'

Friday wagged agreement.

'Funny,' said Naomi, as they approached the car. 'Those roofs and trees and all. Seemed like just a messy jumble. But then I was thinking, if you wanted to hide it, from the air...'

'It's what you'd do,' said Gail. 'Yes. Have another look on Google planet or whatever it is.'

Naomi zoomed in on the rear of the Sotwell Barns grounds. 'Look,' she said. 'From above the whole plot looks like lawns and trees, apart from the house.'

CHAPTER 30

Noises. Rattling door. A splash of light from the hatch.

'He's on the bed.' Eric speaking.

The main light came on and the door opened. I didn't think of moving.

'Stay right where you are.' Cruickshank came in a step and stood by the door, arms folded, bringing a definite waft of marijuana. He worked hard at looking tough and vigilant, but I was thinking that this jailer role wasn't his dream gig. He nodded Eric through. Eric shuffled over to the buckets looking sheepish, holding a loo roll. 'Forgot this,' he said. He peered into the buckets and sniffed. 'Good job you didn't need it.'

I wondered about Eric too. Another pressed man. He wasn't stupid, but perhaps inclined to gravitate to the lowest rank in any pecking order.

'Food,' said Cruickshank.

Eric fetched a jug of water and baguette on a tray. Cheese salad again.

'Leave him to eat,' Cruickshank said. 'Smokes?'

Eric nodded.

They went out, locking the door behind them. I ate and drank. They came back, smelling of tobacco and grass.

'You got the hypo?'

'It's ready,' said Eric.

'Go on then, it's time.' Cruickshank stood in the doorway, looking both ways. There was a sound from outside, a door closing, hurried footsteps. Cruickshank turned through the door and pulled it closed behind him.

Eric rubbed my forearm with a cotton wool pad soaked in alcohol then raised a vein. I decided there was no harm in asking. 'What is it?'

'Roofies. Cat. Horse,' Eric said quietly.

Cruickshank opened the door a wedge and spoke to Eric. 'Gotta go. You got wheels?'

'Yeah, the van,' Eric said.

'Okay. Clear up here. See you later.'

Eric did the alcohol rub again, found a vein easily and painlessly, slid the needle in, eased down the plunger, withdrew. He put his bits and pieces on the tray, backed out of the door, locked it and closed the hatch.

I felt the flood of the hit and lay back. Perhaps Eric had been a medic. I knew cat was ketamine, popular with brain-dead gooners. Horse was heroin. I'd not used either. Roofies I wasn't sure, but something negative was at the back of my mind.

The light went out. I forced myself to move, groped for the empty bucket in the dark, wee'd like a horse. I felt my way back to the bed, lay down, meditated into the drug's trance, repeating a simple mantra in my inner voice. *Acceptance. It is what it is. Do what you can.*

Of course I was concerned about Naomi, Gail, Andrea. The farmers. Kanhai. But there was nothing I could do except watch and wait and stay alive. *Be ready but don't be stupid.* I trusted them to use their heads, help each other.

Acceptance made space for a clear spring of joy. Bubbles of pure happiness poppled into absolute peace and warm darkness. The mantra rang on without conscious effort. An inner eye opened, with the sigh of a soul catching fire. In the deep dark was a golden light, pulsing.

CHAPTER 31

NAOMI

They hit the road back to Oxford in gathering dusk, Gail driving. Passing the bikers' café, which was closed, like its neighbours, Naomi said, 'Pull in anyway, just for a quick poke around. And find somewhere less conspicuous to park, can you? Rather than right out front.'

Gail turned left at the roundabout onto the Dorchester Road and drove past the end of the row of businesses and ranks of cars with price-stickered windows. 'Turn in there,' Naomi said, pointing to a concreted alley between the used car lot and a perimeter fence. They found themselves in a large paved area. The backs of the businesses that included the café were on their left. Opposite, to their right, was a long row of workshop units. On both sides, everything seemed to be shut up and in darkness.

'All closed,' Gail said. 'Everyone's gone home.'

'Didn't know all this was here,' Naomi said, looking round. From the back you wouldn't know which was the café. 'If they're keeping him here, I'd assumed it would have to be above the café. But all those places over there, they could have one of those. Look.' She pointed to the units further down on the right. 'Speedy Logistics.

JackBallers Inc. 10cc Bikes – Repairs, Servicing, MOTs. When we saw Alleyn in the café, he came and went through the back door. He didn't park out front, didn't show his face out front at all.'

'Funny name for a motorbike place,' Gail said. '10cc. Wouldn't a thousand be more like it?'

'There was a band. Seventies? Smoochy American soft rock. 'I'm Not In Love'. 'The Things We Do For Love'.'

'Yes?' Gail said.

'Called 10cc. From the size of a syringe used to mainline heroin. And what Mick and I saw looked like a deal going down. So is this about drugs? I wonder.'

'Can't do much with that right now,' Gail said. 'What shall we do?'

'I'll take Friday for a quick stroll. Have you got a good torch?'

Gail reached into a door pocket and held out a small black torch. 'Bright,' she said, switching it on briefly. 'LEDs.'

'Thanks,' Naomi said. 'You take it.' She climbed out and opened the hatch to let Friday jump down. 'You go round the other side. Take the car. Don't park outside the café. But shine the light up on its chimney stack, so I can see which back belongs to it. I'll let Friday have a sniff round the café back door, see if she picks up any scent. Okay? Keep an eye on the front for a few minutes, in case I disturb someone and they come out that way.'

'Okay,' Gail said.

'Back here in ten,' Naomi said, closing the passenger door. Gail drove away slowly. The sun had sunk behind the workshop unit; a dark cloud obscured what was left of its light. Everything was shut. There were no vehicles except an old white-ish Transit van, parked or dumped not far from 10cc Bikes. She shivered as she walked past it, aware of how alone she was, of how empty and isolated this space was, out of working hours.

She let Friday off her lead and said, 'Whisht.'

Friday looked at her, head on one side, one ear cocked, saying, 'What do you mean, whisht?'

Naomi shrugged and said, 'Oh, come on then.' She set off walking briskly, keeping to the centre of the space, keeping an eye on the chimneys to her left.

She wasn't quite halfway to the far end when a chimney stack lit up. As she watched, the light flicked to and fro, from that to the next along. *Okay*, she thought. *Thanks Gail, well done. The café's between those two.* She approached its rear: a flat-roofed brick extension, with two small square windows with frosted reinforced glass either side of a deep recessed porch. A door was set back six or seven feet into the porch – clean white PVC, half glazed, new. The kind that would have a multi-point locking system, not making it easy for breakers and enterers. In the recess, to the left of the door, was a crate of empty bottles. She moved her head from side to side, trying to make out what was behind the frosted glass windows.

No lights. No sound. No sign of life.

Friday stiffened at her side and turned to face outwards, ears pricked, hackles raised. She'd heard something. Naomi heard something too. Footsteps. Gail coming back? She'd been quick. Naomi hadn't heard the car.

She stepped out of the recess and saw him the moment he saw her. A paunchy guy in denims.

He'd been walking towards her, jiggling keys in his hand, then stopped, staring, as if something didn't compute for him.

Might as well grasp the bull by the nettles, she thought. *In for a penny.* 'Excuse me,' she said, setting off towards him with as confident a stride as she could muster, reassured to see Gail's car nosing round the corner by the used car place.

The man looked right and left, clocked the approaching car, then turned and ran towards the parked white van, in a sort of shambling crouch, like he wasn't used to it. *Suspicious behaviour if ever I saw it*, Naomi thought. Friday barked once. Naomi said, 'Whisht' and Friday was after him, snapping at his heels, backing him against the door of the van as he fumbled for keys. She was growling, deep and menacing, making sharp snaps at his legs and arms. He flattened himself against the van, arms raised high. Friday concentrated on his ankles, dancing around futile kicks.

Naomi walked towards him. Gail's car approached. Naomi gestured in Gail's direction, not taking her eyes off the man. Gail read the gesture right and parked nose to nose with the white van, effectively blocking it in. She turned off the engine and got out.

'Have you got one of those things for changing wheels?' Naomi said to Gail. 'In your boot? Wheel brace? Like a big spanner thing. Quick-ish, please.'

Naomi stopped six feet in front of the man. She was as tall as him, maybe an inch taller. He glanced at her but his focus was on Friday, who had taken against him, nips turning to bites.

This guy had seen her and run. He was guilty of something, knew something. She needed him to talk.

Gail put a wheel brace in her hand, a heavy old Volvo original with scratched metallic blue paint, fifteen inches long. She gripped it with both hands, gave it a trial swing. She looked at his face. He didn't meet her eye.

Right, she thought. *If this is one of Alleyn's heavies, he's probably drugged up to the eyes, and barely competent. They all look hard, they think they're real toughies, but they've probably got soft centres. And you're doing it for Mick. So get your retaliation in first, as someone once said. And soften up the outside too, ready for a question or two.*

She raised the wheel brace high to her left and swung it down and across, aiming to hit his upper right arm hard enough to let him know she meant it, hard enough to loosen his tongue and reduce his ability to fight back.

He ducked and raised his arm as she swung, deflecting the blow onto his right temple, just above the ear. He went down like a sack of coal and lay still. Naomi felt sick. It had felt like breaking icing on a cake. Friday backed off and looked up at Naomi, puzzled, her ears bat-winged.

'Impressive,' said Gail. She nudged the fallen man with her shoe. No response.

Oh fuck, Naomi thought. She knelt and put the back of her hand to his nostrils.

'Breathing,' she said.

She raised his arm and put her fingers to the inside of his wrist. 'Pulse,' she said.

'Suggestion,' Gail said, 'put him in the recovery position. Get in the car. Get out of here. Phone for an ambulance as soon as we're on the road. Anonymously.'

***

Naomi was still in shock when Gail dropped her at Mick's flat. She guessed Gail was too.

'I'm not sure what to say,' Gail said. 'Or do. You'll be all right? Speak later. Or tomorrow.'

Naomi just nodded and raised a hand in farewell. She let herself in, fed Friday, made tea, sat down, tried to stop shaking. She drank the tea then took Friday for a quick walk in the dark.

When she came back to the flat, she found a bottle of whisky, poured some into a glass and took a gulp. She spluttered over the sofa. She added water, took another gulp. Better. She sat down again, still trying to stop shaking.

The phone rang. Mick's landline. She picked up. It was Andrea.

'Yes. I'm here. But Mick isn't,' she said. 'In fact, he's not been here since – what? – yesterday morning. He's gone missing.' She hadn't kept Andrea in the loop and felt guilty. But things had happened so fast. She needed company now. Had Andrea eaten? No, she hadn't. 'Why don't you come here? We'll grab a bite and have a catch-up… See you in half an hour,' she said. 'He has wine. I'll open a bottle. Italian red. You bring pizza.'

Naomi called Mick's mum and Kanhai.

Mick's mum Sandra and Mrs Swainston had drunk surprisingly good tea in the café. They were the only customers and had seen nothing of interest.

Kanhai's contact in the cellphone networks was away until Monday, so there had been no progress in tracing the messages from Mick's phone.

She didn't mention her assault on the biker to either of them.

Andrea arrived and gave her a great big hug.

She stopped shaking.

***

Dark.

There was something wrong.

Her phone said 02:17.

She was in Mick's bed. It was her second night here; she was beginning to feel at home. An arm was across her waist. Not Mick's. She rolled onto her back, turned. Andrea.

Of course. Nothing wrong there. But something had disturbed her. A noise.

She listened hard. Two noises. One, a rumble so low she felt it through her bones rather than ears. And another, intermittent, faint, metallic. She sat up. The low rumble was dog Friday. Not dreaming whiffles or welcoming warble, more a deep, restrained growl. What was the other noise?

Moving slowly and quietly so as not to disturb Andrea, she folded back the duvet and swung her feet to the floor.

'I can hear it too,' Andrea whispered behind her, making her heart leap. 'I'm with you.'

They tiptoed to the bedroom door, inched it open and looked round the living room. There were dots of light from appliances and the music system. Friday stood stiff in the middle of the room, ears up, hackles up, pointing to the front door, from which metallic clicks and creaks came. A dim light flickered through a gap at the top, where the door didn't quite fit its frame. Someone was holding a Maglite in their mouth, or using a head torch.

Andrea crept back to the bedroom and returned carrying her

phone. She put her finger to her lips, thumbed a message and held it up for Naomi to see.

picking lock

Naomi nodded. Andrea thumbed some more.

call police?

Naomi shook her head; it might even be the police breaking in.

Andrea continued.

scare off

or let in and capture

How could they scare them off, whoever it was? Why would they be scared of them? Let in and capture sounded even more dodgy though. It was quite likely the lock-picker would be thinking the flat was empty. An element of surprise would be on their side. They would have to make it count. She pointed at "scare off" and mouthed 'How?'

Andrea looked around. Pointed at Friday. Mimed pulling the door open, fast. Pointed at the stereo, mouthing 'Very loud.' Pointed at the light switches, mouthing 'Very bright.' Fetched Naomi's phone from the bedroom, mouthing 'Both recording.' Pointed at Naomi and the stereo remote and the light switches.

Naomi nodded understanding.

Andrea took a wok and a large saucepan from the hob and put them to hand by the door. She held up ten fingers.

Naomi nodded again. She checked her phone was on silent, started recording and put it on the table. She switched the stereo onto CD and upped the volume to max. There was a quiet hiss from the speakers. She waited with her right thumb over the play button and her left hand on the light switches. Andrea counted down.

On zero Naomi pressed play and switched all the lights on.

'It Was A Real Nice Clambake' blared out of the stereo – from some cheesy fifties' musical, so bizarre she couldn't help a bark of laughter.

Andrea pulled open the door, threw out her pans.

Naomi said 'Whisht'. Friday streaked out.

Someone swore, stumbled down the steps and ran out of the communal door. Friday followed, snarling at his heels. The saucepans clattered and rolled and came to rest at the bottom of the stairwell.

Naomi offed the stereo and joined Andrea in the flat's doorway, looking down the empty hall. Bits of lock-picking kit were scattered across the floor. Friday reappeared. From outside came the sound of a motorbike starting, going away. No-one stirred in the other flats.

'Potato, potato,' Andrea said.

Naomi didn't bother asking what she was on about, just hugged her.

***

Naomi woke again at three thirty. They were lying back to back, Andrea breathing softly beside her, warm and comfortable, but it couldn't go on forever. She fetched two cups of tea and put one on Andrea's side. She got back in and cleared her throat.

'Wake up, you. I've been thinking.'

'Unh.'

'There's tea. Over there. Listen.'

'Unh.'

'Listen. Yesterday. After I laid that bloke out. With the wheel spanner thing. By accident.'

'Unh.' Andrea rolled onto her back, stretched, looked at the time, frowned.

'I panicked,' Naomi said. 'I just wanted to get out of there. I wasn't thinking about anything else. But I'm wondering now. Because imagine. If they've got Mick somewhere – I mean, assuming they've not bumped him off, you know? – they might be thinking that if they keep him out of the way for a while, we'll be preoccupied with getting him back. Which we are. So we'll not be interfering with whatever they're trying to do. Which we're not. And we're not going to until we get him back. Because that's the most important thing. So…'

'Mmm,' said Andrea, sitting up and reaching for tea.

'I think they're holding him until their deal is done and dusted. Which they said was…'

'18th July. The big meeting at uni property services, to decide whose bid to accept for Glebe Farm.'

'That's eleven days away. Even if they're being nice to him, he's going to come seriously unglued in that time.'

'Indeedy-doody.'

'So we've got to get him, you know? There's no choice at all.'

'Correcterooni.'

'Assuming they're holding him somewhere. They'll need jailers.'

'The bikers. Like that guy you decked yesterday.'

'To make sure he doesn't get out,' Naomi said, 'and to keep him alive. Food and stuff.'

'Yes. And they need a jail. Somewhere isolated, so no-one can hear if he shouts.'

'Or soundproof,' Naomi said. 'Or noisy. Or where you could make it noisy when people are around. And where the jailers, doing what they have to do…'

'… don't look out of place doing it.'

'Yesterday we saw three places, me and Gail. Cruickshank's, Alleyn's, and the café. And Sefton-Shaw's, too, in the morning. Was that only yesterday? So four. And those buildings out the back of the café, they match that profile best by a mile. You've got the café handy, for feeding jailers and prisoner. All those workshops, busy places in the day, noisy machinery, people to and fro, Radio 2 drivelling away in the background all the time. Deserted at night. The biker guys could work in one of those units. Like 10cc Bikes. They wouldn't look out of place at all.'

Andrea wrapped her arms around Naomi and held her close. They sank beneath the duvet.

'What I'd like to do,' Naomi said, a few minutes later, 'is stay right here, until it all goes away. But what we should do – at least, what I should do – is get out there and have another sniff round. I can take Mick's car. If I go now, I'll be there before half four. Before anyone's about. I'll take Friday.'

'And me,' Andrea said. 'Come on.'

Naomi took the tracking device from Mick's car and showed it to Andrea. 'Police,' she said. She stuck it to a steel panel on a lamppost.

The road was quiet, the eastern sky luminous. There were no cars or bikes out front of the café. She nosed past the used-car place, into the area round the back. The white van was gone. No other vehicles were around.

'That's good,' she said. 'No sign of that bloke's van. We're the first to arrive. We'll let Friday have a sniff.'

She parked just short of the café's back door, let Friday out, gave her a 'whisht' and a shoo gesture. Friday trotted off, looking back to check Naomi was following. She trotted diagonally across the open space, in the rough direction of 10cc Bikes, then stopped and raised her head, looking at the row of closed-up workshops, at a gap between two units. She looked back at Naomi, then back to the gap, ears raised, nose twitching, tail wagging slowly. She set off towards the gap, paused for a little skip and a warble then looked back at Naomi, clearly saying, 'Come on.'

Naomi followed her into the alley between two anonymous workshops. Each building had a side entrance halfway down the alley. Friday had stopped by the one on the right, wagging her tail and looking from the door to Naomi and back again, saying "open this" as clear as day.

Naomi looked at the door: solid wood, handle and Yale lock on the right. It would open outwards, to the left. She tried pulling it. It was locked. But she was thinking, this could be where that guy appeared from, last night. And this could be where they're keeping Mick.

Andrea caught up.

'I think this is it,' Naomi said. 'Friday does too.'

'Let's get somewhere we can watch from. Safely,' Andrea said. 'Before people start arriving. It's gone five already. Shift ho.'

'Watch safely? Easy said.' There was a chain-link fence behind the units. Naomi looked carefully at the bushes beyond it and fixed their configuration in her mind, so she could pick the right gap if she could get herself on the other side of the fence.

They got back in the car. Andrea Google-Earthed while Naomi drove back past the used car place, through the empty car park in front of the shops, the café, more motorbike businesses.

Andrea asked her to stop outside a place selling almost anything for almost nothing. 'I'll go down there,' Andrea said, pointing to a gap between the discount store and a bike sales business, 'and tuck myself away. I'm good at that. I'll watch the front of the café and be able to see most of the space between the back of the café and that unit where you think he is.'

'Keep your phone on vibrate,' Naomi said. 'Text if you see anything. Text every half-hour if you don't. So six o'clock first up, unless... Okay?'

'Yes *bwana*. And you take care. Put the car somewhere out of sight. And look,' Andrea said, pointing to her phone. 'There's a lake there, behind all those units. With a walkway round it. And a sort of scrubby hedge between that and the backs of those workshops. You could take the dog down there, by the lake, see what you can see.'

'Yes *mtumwa*.'

'*Mtumwa*?'

***

Six a.m. Naomi's phone vibrated. It was a text from Andrea: *why are we doing this again?*

She replied: *to be sure M is there no good attacking wrong place.*

Andrea: *ok nothing doing here where are you.*

Naomi: *in bush by lake lotsa boyds can see door and alley.*

Andrea: *ok bwana til half past or event.*

***

Naomi watched birds. A robin fed pickily by rushes. A swan moved over the lake. Her phone vibrated, jolted her. Six twenty. A text from Andrea: *harley arrived out front.*

Fuck, she thought, *I was drifting away. Not good enough. Too busy watching robins and dreaming Irish.*

Another text: *heavy dude into café.*

She texted back to Andrea: *ok ta.*

Friday had lain still for an hour. Now her ears pricked up. Naomi patted her head, told her she was a good dog.

Minutes later, another text: *nothing just half hour check.*

Naomi replied: *ditto.*

She made herself watch the alley. Six jackdaws worked on fast-food discards. House sparrows gathered jackdaw spillings. There came the sound of a door opening, out of sight. Closing.

A text from Andrea: *dude out back of café.*

Someone came round the corner, carrying a tray, crossing the open space towards the alley: the big Scots biker. He approached the door that had excited Friday, balancing the tray on one hand. He extracted keys from a pocket, unlocked the Yale, opened the door, went in and slammed it shut. Naomi felt a tingle of vindication.

She texted Andrea: *gone in.*

Three minutes later he came out, leaving the door hanging open. He walked towards the chain-link fence. Naomi skulked deeper, a gentle hand on Friday's shoulder. He stopped at the fence, eyes on the lake behind her. He lit a roll-up – a spliff, she realised as the scent wafted through. He smoked it down to the roach. He flicked the roach over the fence, looked over his shoulder, then shuffled closer to the fence and unzipped his trousers. He made hard work of releasing his penis, probably because it was quite small for a big man, king prawn size at best. And shape. He pissed on a patch of nettles, dribbled down his trousers. Shake pull dribble. Shake pull dribble. Finally put it away. *Thank God*, thought Naomi. He went back inside, leaving a smell of unhealthy urine.

She'd like to be out and away now. They'd learned a lot. But no, they should see it through.

Ten minutes later he came out again, carrying the tray one-handed. He locked the door, walked towards the back entrance to the café. She heard the door open and shut.

She called Andrea, speaking quietly. 'Just had the spliff 'n' piss show. Bloody awful. But they've definitely got someone in there. And if it's not Mick, who is it?'

There was a noise behind her: a man in combat gear, coming towards her in dark glasses and a beanie, shuffling along the lakeside path, fiddling with his trousers. 'A bloody fisherman here now. Coming right at me. Looks like he's going to… Just a minute. Have to emerge.'

She upped, told Friday 'Whisht' and bustled back towards the car, averting her eyes.

'Ha,' she said, 'that woke him up. You keep an eye, let me know if anything happens.'

'He's coming out,' said Andrea. 'Helmet on. Getting on his bike. He's off. Potato potato.'

'Potato potato?'

'The noise a Harley makes. Apparently they tried to patent it.'

'Let's get out of here,' Naomi said. 'I'll pick you up by the car sales place in two.'

***

She drove back to Mick's flat, deep in thought. They had to enter a new phase in this strange journey. And had to get it right. She parked in Mick's usual place, breathed out a mass of tension. She put the tracking disk back under the wheel arch.

They went in. She fed Friday. It was still not long after seven o'clock, but she felt she'd put in a shift already. 'I'm going to take her for a walk,' she said. 'And try to sort my head out. Can you ring Gail? Bring her up to date. Tell her I'll ring Kanhai and Sandra later, and Denise in the office. Back in half an hour, in time for breakfast. Tea, toast, marmalade. Please. Mick's got lovely home-made.'

'Yes *bwana*,' said Andrea.

Naomi kissed her on the cheek and left.

***

She walked at a good pace across the common. Friday danced ahead, tossing manky old sticks over her shoulder, inviting Naomi to throw them. She didn't.

Her phone rang as she crossed the ditch. Kanhai. He'd been in work extra early, done a trawl through the active tech-ops database, in the guise of checking that a recent software upgrade was functioning as intended. He had got into the log of telephone surveillance intercepts and had found that one had been active on Mick's mobile since 00.01 on 13th June, opened at the request of Detective Inspector Jones – after their first visit to the café. Then it was taken off at 13.00 on Wednesday 5th July – two hours after Mick disappeared.

'Does it tell you the location of the phone when the trace was taken off?' Naomi asked.

'Yes,' said Kanhai. 'It was…'

'Let me guess,' said Naomi. 'Dorchester-on-Thames?'

247

'How did you know that?'

'We think we've found him,' said Naomi. 'That kind of confirms it. Thanks, Kanhai. Good work. Speak later.'

She walked across Port Meadow to Mick's favourite Bronze Age mound. She sat on a log to take stock of what they'd learned.

He was alive.

He was able to eat and drink.

He was being held in the unit three up from 10cc Bikes.

The unit was accessed through a locked side door.

He was left there alone much of the time.

His biker jailer came alone to service the prisoner.

He was held securely inside the unit, because the jailer left the outside door open.

The jailer's visit took about twenty minutes.

The jailer's morning visit was before anyone else turned up for work.

She carried on across the meadow, turning it over. A plan of sorts emerged naturally, so long as what they'd observed today was a regular routine. Should they observe another day, to make sure? Or strike as soon as possible, and if things diverged from the routine, just busk it? But actually, no matter how many times they observed the routine, the next time could always be different. And God knew what Mick was going through in there, but it surely wasn't much fun. So they would go for it. Tomorrow morning, first thing.

She felt better for that. She was almost back at Mick's. Hungry. Late for breakfast.

CHAPTER 32

I felt rested, as if my sleep had been more real than drug-induced. I sat on the edge of the bed while the internal gyroscope reset. Stretched. Felt properly hungry for the first time since they got me.

I breathed deep and slipped easily back into that meditative zone. The golden light was still there, pulsing. Perhaps it's always there and to see it you just have to look in the right way. Perhaps it only stops when you die – then you'd not be aware of it stopping, because you'd be dead. But subjectively, phenomenologically, if you were connected to this inner light, as your body slipped away, you'd never be aware of its end. So it would be your eternity. That was much more important than all this crap.

But the crap demanded attention. I felt better because they'd left me a good while without topping up the drugs. I could pretend to be dangerously ill, from the prolonged drug regime. Or feign illness by meditating myself into a kind of hibernation – slow down my heart and breathing, reduce my temperature. Perhaps then they'd not bother topping up the drugs. I'd heard of mystics, yogis, doing it. Worth a try. Authenticity was all.

***

The lights were on. There was someone in the room, holding my wrist. Taking my pulse? I focused on staying in the hibernation zone. I believed my pulse was very slow, my temperature low.

'Oh fuck,' the visitor said. Scots biker Cruickshank.

My face was slapped, hard: right cheek, left cheek, right, left. I let my head flop with the blows, concentrated on breathing and stilling my mind.

'Wake up, for fuck's sake,' Cruickshank was saying. 'If that fucking idiot's killed you we're fucked. Wake up!'

I held on to the deep trance. Cruickshank slapped me some more. Sighed. Left.

***

I woke in the dark feeling good again. I lay still, listening. Low-frequency vibrations leaked into the quietness of the room. Traffic. A truck downshifting for a corner or junction. I could be almost anywhere. But it was not the constant drone of a major trunk road like the A34 or the M40.

There was a splash of light as the hatch opened, followed by the familiar Glaswegian growl saying, 'Stay on the bed.' Bright lights, door opening. Cruickshank, carrying a tray. I lay still, on my back. Feeling weak. I didn't have to fake a feverish pallor. Cruickshank was sitting on the chair, doing something on the tray – putting stuff into the hypodermic, fumbling, not confident.

I didn't like the look of it and couldn't help coming out of my trance. 'Where's Eric?'

'Fucked off, hasn't he. Tosser. Left his van behind.'

'You don't have to keep drugging me,' I said, my voice low and trembling. 'I'm really not well. I couldn't get out if you left the door open. No strength. Can't balance.'

Cruickshank looked at me, seemed to be considering.

'I promise to stay on the bed. Please. Don't give me any more of that stuff. It'll kill me.'

Cruickshank laughed. 'Nice try,' he said, grabbing my nose with his left hand, tipping my head back, thumping me in the midriff with his right.

I should have expected it. I wasn't expecting the second one either.

'Right. Questions,' he said. I curled up, facing away from him. 'Don't even think about lying. Because some of them I already know the answers to. Understand?'

I grunted.

'Why did you install a bug in Sefton-Shaw's house?'

My answer came in bursts. 'Thought... some kind of... conspiracy... to do with Glebe Farm. Sefton-Shaw. Others. Didn't know who. Wanted to know more.'

'Any installed elsewhere?'

'No.'

Another punch to the diaphragm.

'No, fuck.' I was hurting, close to sobbing.

'What did you hear?'

'Not much. Three of them. A meeting. Just getting started. One suspicious. Did a bug sweep. Found it. That was all. Three people. Including Sefton-Shaw. Planning something. Don't know what.'

Another punch. I was yelping in pain on each in-breath.

'You suspected who the others were, didn't you?'

'Maybe Alleyn. Lawyer. And someone to do with uni admin. Don't know name.'

'That's it? Nothing else?'

His fist hovered over my abdomen. What could I give him that was true, that he wouldn't know already, that might muddy the waters and buy me a few seconds of recovery time?

'Their rubbish,' I said. 'Sefton-Shaws. Live on Hawaiian pizza. Whatever that is.' My eyes tracked his fist. I didn't like what I was doing. It felt dirty. But the fist was hovering. 'Found message written in lipstick. Saying, "How come we spent two million last

251

month and I didn't even get a bunch of flowers?" Something like that.'

Cruickshank laughed and thumped my midriff again. 'That's all? What do you know about that money?'

'Nothing,' I said when I could.

'Good.' He picked up the syringe, squeezed out the air. He grasped my arm and stuck the needle in, careless of where, then emptied it and pulled it out. It was quite painful.

I lay back, resigned. I watched Cruickshank pick up his tray, go out, close the door.

Lights out. Music on loud. Thrash metal.

In the dark, bright eyes glowed.

Just my imagination.

CHAPTER 33

NAOMI

Naomi lay with her head on one arm of Mick's sofa, her feet on the other, looking out the window at two birds on a branch. 'Two little turtle doves,' she said. She'd found an unopened bag of Kilimanjaro at the back of the fridge, an old Red Lion pack under a bedside cabinet, and now had a mug of coffee in her left hand and a smouldering cheroot in her right. It crackled when she puffed, sometimes sent out small sparks. She blew smoke at the ceiling.

'That smells good,' said Andrea, through the open bathroom door. 'They're collared doves, not turtle doves.' She was also drinking coffee, lying in a tepid bath and studying a crossword.

'Smells better than it tastes,' Naomi said. 'How do you know? You can't even see them.'

'Because turtle doves are practically extinct, thanks to Mr Monsanto and his mates. A cross one-eyed vicar lying on the floor. Nine letters. Something, something, M, six somethings.'

'They're pussycats, these guys,' Naomi said.

'The bikers? Really?'

'Cruel bullies. If you're a small mammal or bird, you can play dead. In which case they just wait.'

'And if you try to escape, they just bat you back down,' said Andrea. 'Yes. They love that game, cats.'

'But if you don't play the game... don't play dead or run...'

'What else can you do?' Andrea asked. 'Fight back?'

'Not so much fight back,' Naomi said, 'as fight *first*. Get your retaliation in first. Funny, I keep thinking that. Must find out where it comes from. But a cat would soon lose interest if the first thing a mouse did was leap up and bite its nose. Wouldn't it?'

She stood, stubbed the nub of the cheroot out in the sink, rinsed her mug. She crossed to the window. The doves had gone, replaced by two jackdaws. She came to a decision that she knew every other decision that someone would have to make – that she would have to make, probably – would flow from.

'You and me to go in and get him out. Okay?'

'Er...' said Andrea.

'The minder will be one of the pussycats. He'll try to stop us.'

'Well, yes,' said Andrea.

'We've only ever seen one at a time. We'll need some way to stop him stopping us. And while we're doing that, the others can distract or immobilise the fat cats. Sefton-Shaw, Alleyn, Donald Cruickshank. To stop them interfering.'

'Fat cats and pussycats,' said Andrea. 'It's a good plan, as far as it goes. But – dare I say? – it lacks detail.'

'True. So, let's start with subduing the minder. Are you ever going to get dressed?'

Andrea pulled the plug, climbed out of the bath and poddled into the living room wrapped in a large white towel.

Naomi made space for her on the sofa and said, 'Axminster.'

Andrea frowned, then said, 'Oh yes.' She reached for pen and newspaper. 'When are you thinking? Tomorrow?'

'Yes,' said Naomi. 'Early. Like today, but...'

'Not just watching. Okay. So we surprise him.'

'Yes,' said Naomi. 'Overpower him before he can respond.'

'Sounds easy.'

'Don't want to harm him. Too much,' said Naomi, thinking aloud. 'So guns are not a good idea.'

'And where would we get guns?'

'I do know a few people, you know? You do too. But what we really want is something to just put them out of action for a few minutes, while we tie them up or whatever. Like those things the police use. That don't kill people. Or not very often.'

'Tasers, yeah,' said Andrea. 'Electric shock things. Could Kanhai get hold of one?'

'He might, if he didn't care about ever working again. Too much to ask.'

'Even for his bosom buddy?' Andrea closed her eyes, stretched. 'I suppose it is. Hmm.'

She was thinking, so Naomi let her.

'Those things they use to stun animals,' Andrea said, 'Like if a lion escapes from the zoo. Or if they want to tag an elephant. Fires a dart. Tranquiliser gun.'

Naomi pulled out her phone, Googled.

'Tranquiliser gun. For sale. Not regulated in the US,' she read out. 'What about here?'

'I know where they'd have one,' Andrea said. 'Probably. The wildlife park. Burford.'

'You know someone there.'

'I do.'

'Vets will need them too.'

'I know a vet,' Andrea said. 'In Witney. I could ask her.'

'Good thinking,' said Naomi. 'Get two.'

'Two?'

'One each. And a few darts. You get on with that, I'll talk to the others.'

***

Naomi looked at her phone. 03:00 Saturday 8 July. 'Come on,' she said, nudging Andrea. 'Up. Leave in half an hour.'

She put the kettle on and made a strong brew. She drank hers while Andrea went through the bathroom.

At three twenty-five, there was a quiet tap on the door. Mick's mother Sandra came in. They hugged.

'Welcome to Mission Control,' Naomi said. She should have been nervous, but wasn't. She poured tea for Sandra, and for Denise from the office, who arrived looking wide-eyed and excited.

Andrea came out of the bedroom and stood beside Naomi. Naomi introduced her to the others. They were dressed identically, in camouflage combat pants and matching sweaters, with dark olive elbow and shoulder patches, like soldiers. *Or,* Naomi thought, *like an idea of what young women soldiers look like, in army recruitment ads.* They put on serious faces, faced Sandra and saluted.

Andrea picked up a bag, emptied it onto the coffee table and picked up items as she named them. 'Two tranquiliser guns. Two insulated cold-packs, six darts in each. A small phial. Syringe.' She took out a dart, showed it to Denise and Sandra. 'A stun dart,' she said, peering closely it. 'We have twelve. Loaded with carfentanyl, a powerful opioid. And xylazine. An alpha-2 agonist.'

'An alpha-2 what?' Sandra said.

'Agonist,' Andrea said, reading the label. 'No idea what it means. My vet says it'd stop anything up to 150 kilogrammes. In human males that's the ninety-ninth percentile. So enough for the biggest biker. Mustn't use too much or we'd be in OD territory, especially with smaller people. And in case we do overdo it, we've got this.' She held up the phial. 'Okay? Atipamezole. Just in case.'

Denise and Sandra nodded.

'We timed each other,' Andrea said, 'reloading. From firing a dart to being ready to fire the next. Three seconds or less.'

She's being kind, Naomi thought. She took the dart packs from Andrea and slipped them back into the bag. They were cold from being in the fridge overnight. Naomi was still smarting from her inability to match Andrea's reload time of two seconds dead. But her personal best of just over three seconds should be okay. She checked through her own bag, which held bolt cutters, wrecking bar, Stanley knife, gaffer tape, cable ties and a first aid kit.

'You cool with this?' she asked Denise and Sandra.

They were.

'Whatever's necessary,' Sandra said. 'He's my son. He might be an idiot, but...'

Naomi smiled and nodded. 'Any questions?' she asked. Shaken heads all round. 'Right then. With any luck you'll hear from us by six thirty. Until then, no news is good news. From us to you. And from you to us. Okay? Any disasters, we communicate. You should hear from Tom and Linda by six thirty too, and Gail and Kanhai. Text me if you haven't.'

She took a deep breath, turned to Andrea. 'You set?'

'Yesserooni.'

CHAPTER 34

DENISE IN THE OFFICE

Denise spent half an hour with Mick's mum Sandra, rehearsing the distinctive tone and intonation of the Murdoch Alleyn receptionist. At four thirty, she dialled Alleyn's home landline from her mobile, caller ID withheld.

She let it ring six times. No answer. She hung up, waited two minutes and dialled again. It rang five times and was answered on the sixth. She hung up immediately. She waited two minutes then dialled again. The call was answered after two rings. She put the phone on loudspeaker. The respondent grunted.

'Oh Mr Alleyn, is that you? I don't know what to do?' Denise said, in character.

'Unh.'

'The police have been on? The alarms went off at the office? About four o'clock? And they have my number as first contact?'

'Unh.'

'And they've got someone in custody? For trying to break in?'

'Unh.'

'Break in the office? And they picked me up? From my home in Yarnton, where I live? And took me to the police station? Anyway, this man they arrested? He told them he was looking for you? And they asked me to identify him? And do you know what?'

'Unh. No. What?'

'It's your friend Mr Cruickshank? From the university? Only he looks a bit odd? Like he's on drugs or something? And he's… well, he's got women's clothes on? And make-up? And…'

'Oh fuck.'

'Anyway, he wants to see you? And the police want to see you? They've taken him to Gablecross? A police station in Swindon?'

'What?'

'Swindon? Police station? Gablecross?'

'Why the fuck?'

'I don't know? Do you know it?'

'What?'

'Where it is? Swindon police station?'

'Why there, for fuck's sake?'

'It's off the A420? On the right before you get to Sainsbury's?'

'Yes, but why?'

'So can you get over there now? Is what they're asking?'

'Where are you?'

'Kidlington police station? I'm with one of them now? The police? I just made a statement?'

'Let me speak to him.'

Denise turned to Sandra, fighting to suppress a giggle. 'He wants to speak to you?' she said. 'What did you say your name was? And will you speak to him?'

'PC Smith,' Sandra said, also in character. 'And yes.'

'It's a her?' Denise said to Alleyn. 'PC Smith?'

'Put her on,' Alleyn said.

'Here she is?' Denise said, passing the phone to Sandra.

'PC Smith speaking. Mr Alleyn, how do you do. How can I help you?'

'Constable Smith,' said Alleyn. 'Can you please tell me what on earth is going on?'

'Certainly, sir,' said Sandra. 'We have this gentleman, sir, in custody. He says his name is Donald Cruickshank and he is a client of your firm. He hasn't been charged yet. Partly because he wants you there, sir, and refuses to speak to the duty solicitor. And partly because, frankly, sir, he's not in a fit state to answer questions. But he has asked for you specifically. Sir.'

'And why is he in bloody Swindon of all places?'

'You'd have to ask the officer in charge that question, sir. That's Sergeant Davies. Who is at this time also making his way to Swindon. But it could be something to do with the disturbances last night, sir. In the city centre. And the fact that most of our holding cells are out of action awaiting refurbishment. What time shall I say you'll be there, sir?'

'Oh for God's sake. All right. What time is it now? Four fucking forty-four. Christ.' He paused, Sandra waited. 'Swindon for the love of Christ. It'll take an hour. Say six o'clock.'

'Thank you very much for your co-operation, sir. Please ask for Sergeant Davies on arrival, sir. Have a good day now. Mind how you go.'

She ended the call, checked that it really was ended and handed the phone back to Denise.

'Phew,' she said, grinning like a frog.

'Nice one,' Denise said. 'Quarter to five. Time for another brew.'

CHAPTER 35

TOM

Tom stuck his left arm out and steered a decrepit old tractor off the A34 southbound at the South Hinksey interchange. He drove slowly up to and round the roundabout, and took the Boars Hill exit. The tractor, once red, was now a mix of faded pink, grey undercoat and rust. It had no lights, no registration plates. On its tow-hitch, also without lights or plates, was an old wagon loaded with clay. Over his shoulder Tom could see his wife's beige Nissan Sunny following, hazard lights flashing. The roads were empty.

They went up Hinksey Hill, forked right onto Foxcombe Road, then right again onto Berkeley Road. Opposite Foxcombe Hall, Tom took the tractor and trailer into Berkeley Close, while Linda reversed the Nissan into the entrance to the Close and waited, engine running, hazards on.

The glow of the eastern sky gave enough light for Tom to manoeuvre the tractor into position outside Springfield House, its rear wheel across the narrow pedestrian gate, the trailer snug against the electrically operated vehicle gates. Behind the gates a black Audi SUV was parked next to a lustrous Goodwood-green Bentley: neither would be able to leave until tractor and trailer were moved. Any pedestrian wanting to leave would have to negotiate the tractor's large rear wheel, or the trailer with its sticky clay, or the hedge and wire fence behind the house.

Tom killed the engine and pocketed the keys. He took an oily rag from his jacket pocket and wiped down the steering wheel, gear stick and handbrake handle. He climbed down from the seat, carrying a small bag. He laid the bag on top of the nearside rear wheel, opened it and took out a sharply pointed knife. He went round the five accessible wheels, gently tapping the handle of the knife with the heel of his hand. A cool, quiet jet of air hissed from each hole.

He took a spanner and screwdriver from the bag and disconnected a red and a black wire from each end of a black metal cylinder on the nearside of the tractor's engine. He removed the cylinder then put it and the tools in his bag. He gave the flaking paint of the tractor's hood a farewell thump with the heel of his right hand, walked back to the waiting car, opened the nearside door and climbed into the passenger seat. It was ten minutes before five. He sent a text to Denise: *parked ok*

Linda switched her hazards off and turned right, up the hill, down to Wootton, through Cumnor, Eynsham, Cassington, and back to Glebe Farm, avoiding main roads and cameras.

CHAPTER 36

KANHAI

It was dark except for a hint of dawn in the east. The only traffic Kanhai had seen was a National Express coach going to Birmingham. He parked near Gail's Volvo and looked up and down the crescent. He carried two bulky bags to her front door and rang the bell.

Gail opened the door. Kanhai smelled toast. Gail shut the door behind him. 'Coffee?' she asked.

'Later,' he said. 'Let's get on now.'

He handed her one of the bags.

'Change here,' she said. 'I'll pop upstairs.'

They left the house at four, wearing police costumes hired by Kanhai's wife, Bethan, from the party shop in Jericho. They got into Gail's Volvo, and a minute later drew up twenty yards from Donald Cruickshank's house on St Margarets Road.

They pulled the peaks of their caps down over their eyes. Each had a large LED torch, switched off. They took out their phones, both set to silent. Kanhai dialled Gail; she accepted the call. Neither spoke. They each put a bluetooth bud in an ear and their phone in a top pocket, leaving the line open. Kanhai slung a black rucksack over his right shoulder.

They walked to the gate, scanned the house. All windows were in darkness, a car in the drive. Gail went to the front door, waited. Kanhai went to the rear of the house, checked the windows at the back: also all dark. 'Good to go,' he said quietly.

He heard Gail respond, 'Bell now.' He heard the sound of the bell ringing that Gail's phone was picking up, and a similar sound of a slightly different texture coming from the rear windows of the house. Cool, he thought. She's holding it down.

He checked his watch. Ten past four. Not light yet. The bell rang on. A light showed.

'Light on upstairs,' he said.

'Nothing here,' Gail said.

He waited, ready to re-join Gail at the front if Cruickshank showed up there, but carefully watching the back of the house.

Two big curtained windows on the ground floor lightened very slightly. Then a quiet click, from the back door, ten feet from where he stood. He watched, still and silent. The door opened slowly outwards. A figure stepped out backwards, young, slight, pale, wearing only trainers and jockey shorts.

The boy turned, slowly scanning the garden until his eyes picked up Kanhai's dark motionless shape. A tiny squeak and he bolted for the street.

'One coming,' Kanhai whispered. 'A runner. Let him go.'

Through the open door he could hear floorboards creaking and shuffling steps. He waited. Another figure backed out, closed the door and turned.

Kanhai switched on his torch, shone it in the man's face, and said, 'Good morning, sir,' quite loudly.

Cruickshank jumped; he looked like he was about to bolt too.

'I wouldn't, Mr Cruickshank, sir,' said Kanhai, keeping his torch on Cruickshank's eyes. 'I'm Sergeant Davies,' he said, holding up an ID. 'There's no need to worry, sir. Just a few routine questions.'

He kept his light trained on Cruickshank's eyes. Gail arrived at his side and shone her light there too. 'This is PC Smith. If we could just go inside for a couple of minutes? A few routine questions. Then we'll be away and leave you to your morning.'

They shepherded Cruickshank back through the door.

'Now then,' said Kanhai, gesturing towards the second door on the left. 'This one, I think. Just sit here, sir,' he said, indicating one of six heavy wooden dining chairs around a table. 'Constable, get the lights please.'

Gail went out to the hall and switched off the only light that was on, above the stairway. The house was again in darkness. She came back and stood in front of Cruickshank. Kanhai gave her his torch. She shone both torches in Cruickshank's eyes.

'Is this really necessary?' Cruickshank said.

Kanhai moved behind him and sorted out some cable ties from his rucksack. He took Cruickshank's right wrist behind his back, fixed it to his left, then fixed his wrists to the back of the chair. He fixed his ankles to the chair-legs.

'Is this really necessary?' he said again.

'Oh yes, sir, I'm afraid so,' Kanhai said. 'Standard operating procedure.' He took out a roll of black gaffer tape and a small towel, created a gag and blindfold. Cruickshank squirmed and made a sort of sound, but soon stopped.

'Now sir,' said Kanhai. 'You have been secured for your own protection. Please be patient. A senior officer will be here to interview you shortly.'

Cruickshank made another noise, more determined, and strained at his bindings.

'What's that, sir?' asked Kanhai. 'You're asking something? What's this all about, is it?'

'Unh,' said Cruickshank.

'Well, we're not supposed to tell you really. But I'm sure you're not the type to be mixed up in this sort of stuff. So I'll just give you a clue.' He whispered, 'Boys. Under-age. And drugs.'

Cruickshank slumped in his chair.

Gail and Kanhai went silently out the back door. Kanhai locked it behind them and threw the keys onto the lawn. Not far. 'Somebody'll find them,' he said.

They walked back to Gail's car.

'Did he see our faces?' asked Gail.

'I really don't think so.'

Gail drove them back to her house.

Kanhai sent a text to Denise: *all done and dusted.*

CHAPTER 37

NAOMI

They approached the roundabout by the bikers' café well before sunrise. Naomi took the third exit for Dorchester, driving slowly and carefully, not wanting to attract the attention of lurking plods or anyone else. She reversed into a "Staff Only" bay behind the used car place. They got out their bags and walked through the area between the backs of the shops and the workshop units, keeping to the left, the more shadowed side. There were no people, cars, vans or bikes.

'Any CCTV?' she said.

Andrea shook her head.

They tried the rear entrance to the café. It was locked. They peered inside – nothing to see, checked the open area again – no-one around. They crossed and entered the alley where the jailer had taken a tray in through the side door. Naomi tried the door as they passed it: solid wood, an ordinary Yale, locked. All as expected. Not high security, though. A wrecking bar might get it open, if push came to shove. Tempting.

Andrea anticipated her thoughts. 'Come on. We've got a plan and we don't know what they've got inside. Don't start ad libbing now.'

At the back of the alley, there was a three-foot gap between the end of each unit and the chain-link fence that separated the business park from the lake. Naomi put her bag in the space to the left, behind the next-door unit. She turned to Andrea, feeling nervous and needing reassurance.

Andrea grinned, looking like she did this sort of thing every day. She knelt down and took the two dart guns from her bag, then gave one to Naomi, saying, 'Loaded. Safety on. Five more darts in your cool pack, which fits on your belt. Remember?' She demonstrated. 'Remember how to re-load?'

'Yes,' said Naomi. *Of course I do*, she thought, attaching the pack to her belt. *No need to rub it in.*

'Six each should be plenty. Even for a small herd of elephants.'

'Unless he shoots first, with real bullets. Or he's come mob-handed and can rush us. Or we miss. Or we can't get within effective range, which is ten metres. So we should be able to do that. Or we get him but he shoots back before the tranqs take effect. Or…'

'Naomi, darling,' Andrea said. 'Shut up.'

Naomi shrugged. She pointed to the gap between the chain-link fence and the back of the unit where Mick was being held – they hoped. 'You in there,' she said. 'Me over here. And we wait. Okay? Until he's going in with the tray. Get him then, if possible. Or follow, if he goes in and leaves the door unlocked. Or wait for him to come out for his spliff 'n' piss or whatever. Ideally we get him when he's going in. But whenever, we shoot first, ask questions later. Okay?'

'Okay, *bwana*,' said Andrea. 'Good luck.'

'And if anything goes wrong, we busk it. And we do whatever it takes, okay? Whatever it takes.'

'Yes indeedy,' Andrea said, settling in her hiding place.

Naomi hunkered down amongst weeds, Coke cans and coffee cartons, her back to the wall of the next-door workshop, feet against the fence. She took a small rectangular mirror from a jacket pocket, wiped it, wedged it into dry grass and garbage to her right. No-one would notice it if they weren't looking for it. She adjusted its angle so she could comfortably watch the entrance to the alley and the side door and settled down to wait.

Light spread from the east. A last star dimmed over the lake in the west. A wren pipped alarm notes, a blackbird practised a melody, a stormcock sang the blues. A line from Omar Khayyam came to her mind. She wondered how far she could get.

Awake for morning in the bowl of night. Has flung the stone that puts the stars to flight. And lo something something. Something something in a noose of light.

Could do better.

CHAPTER 38

I woke. It was dark, as usual. My midriff was tender, my arm sore. All was quiet. I sat up, stretched, yawned. I'd had enough of this. I had to do something.

In any trial of strength I'd come off worse. All I had going for me were my wits, and an element of surprise, because I'd established a pattern of predictable quiescence. There were limited hiding places from which to spring a surprise: either side of the door, where I was out of view from the hatch, or under the bed. That was it.

No chance of launching an attack from under the bed; I'd have lost before I got myself out. So the door. It opened inwards. The obvious place was to its right, behind it as it opened. But if they saw I wasn't on the bed and edged the door open a few inches, looking through the hatch, they'd see me there, and a forceful push of the door would trap me against the wall. No good.

There was more space to the left of the door. The last couple of visits, Scots biker Cruickshank had come alone. Was he right- or left-handed? I didn't know. Which hand did he carry the tray in? I conjured up a mental image. Both hands. So one or both would be encumbered. He'd have to come a little way into the room before he could see me, low down in the corner. I'd knock the tray up into his face, follow with a body-charge, create confusion, see what happened. It was unlikely to lead to anything but another beating and more knock-out drops, but what the hell.

I settled to wait on my haunches in my chosen corner. My eyes kept closing. I ran through all the U-Roy numbers I knew. My eyes were closing again. I switched to Radiohead. Jonquil. Heavenly Stems. Foals.

I woke again, wedged in the corner, tears tickling my cheeks. Something had disturbed me. I didn't know what, but I'd sensed a change. In air pressure? I straightened, stretched and scrunched down again. Someone was here. This was it. It was no use crying. It was time to take the fight to the enemy.

The hatch slid open and bright light flooded the cell.

'What? Where the fuck are you?' A Scottish voice, full of anger. Cruickshank, looking for me through the hatch. 'Get on that fucking bed now or you're in for a proper kicking.'

I pressed myself into the angle, out of sight from the hatch, concentrating on deep breathing and holding myself ready for instant violent action.

Cruickshank spoke again, quieter. 'Where the fuck is he? Never done this before.'

Speaking to a companion? I hoped not.

I heard the key turn in the lock, watched the handle move, the cell door begin to open. Then a different voice, more distant. 'Locked.' Coming from below. Not good. I'd been banking on only one jailer to deal with. Even against one it was a long shot.

'You sure? You checked?' Cruickshank. Loud, impatient, close. 'Either the little fucker's hiding somewhere or they've got him out somehow.' Then quieter again: 'And locked up nicely? And tidied up after themselves? Nah. He's in here, got to be.'

I kept still, quiet, trying to be ready for any opportunity. Cruickshank held the door a few millimetres ajar, but clearly wanted to see where I was before coming further in.

The other voice again, an Oxford native, subservient. 'Gray?'

'Fuck off now.'

'Er. Graham?'

'What the fuck is it?' Cruickshank. 'The fucker's hiding somewhere.'

'Gray? We got visitors.'

Footsteps, scuffling, a sharp ping, another.

'Oh Christ. That hurts. Jesus, it hurts.' The subservient voice.

'What the fuck?' Cruickshank, finally paying attention to his companion.

I steeled myself. My chance was coming.

'Ouch, ya bastard!' Cruickshank bellowed. 'Move, ya dozy cunt! Get the bastards!'

Now or never.

I was a lion.

Roar like one.

Thunder and mayhem.

Now.

I launched myself through the door.

'Geronimo!'

CHAPTER 39

NAOMI

She'd given up on the Rubaiyat. She had gone through all the nursery rhymes she liked, then those she didn't like but could remember, and was working on those she didn't like and couldn't remember. She was struggling with 'Georgie Porgie, Pudding And Pie' when she heard a door closing, some distance away.

She looked across. Andrea had heard it too.

A man's voice, sounding annoyed. 'Lock it. Keys.' Talking to himself, she hoped.

Scuffed footsteps. Coming this way? Yes. Across the open area, from the back door of the café.

She watched through the mirror hidden in the tangle of grass and garbage by the fence. A shadow crossed the ground at the far end of the alley. A waft of tobacco smoke. A man came round the corner, into the alley: a big man, in silhouette, back-lit by the rising sun, smoke wreathing his head. He was walking towards the side door of the unit, keys jingling in his right hand, followed by a smaller, rounder man.

Two of them. Hell. She fingered the dart pouch on her belt.

They came nearer. The first one was Cruickshank, the Scots biker. The second, shorter, tubby, carried a tray. He looked like an accountant on his day off. She didn't recognise him. He was saying, 'It's alright for you. He's best mates with your brother, so he'll see you right whatever. What about the rest of us?'

An Oxford local, she thought. *And a bit of a whinger.* She didn't know him. She glanced across. Andrea held up a hand: wait.

Cruickshank turned on tray-man, stabbed an index finger into his chest, with emphatic rhythm. 'You. Shut. The fuck. Up.' Tray-man was backing off a step with each stab. 'You're worried?' he said. 'You think I'm not? That's one fucking evil bastard, that one. And his fucking mates are worse. But there's fuck all any of us can do except do what the fuck we're told. And not in any way what-so-fucking-ever fuck it up. Not even fucking slightly. Okay?'

Tray-man shrugged.

Cruickshank turned, led the way to the side door, unlocked and opened it and went in.

Naomi nodded to Andrea. They got carefully to their feet, ready to follow. She peeped round the corner, watched as tray-man went in and closed the door behind him. She was first to the door, Andrea to her right and just behind. It would help if this wasn't locked. She tried the handle. It turned. She pulled on the door. Locked. Bugger. But never mind. They'd just have to get them when they came out for a smoke, or when they were leaving.

She put her ear to the door, heard footsteps. There was something hollow about the sound – on stairs? And a voice, distant. Cruickshank, saying, 'Did you lock the door?'

'Yes.' The Oxford voice, nearer.

'Wants a good slam, don't forget.'

'Oh. Well. I thought I… Shall I…?'

'Check it, yes. Because I didna hear no slam. And get on with it, for fuck's sake. The sooner I can fuck off home the better pleased I'll be. Giving me the fucking creeps, this place.'

Naomi pressed her ear to the door, straining to imagine what was going on inside. She pictured a banister rail, stairs. She heard more footsteps, then the Scots voice, Cruickshank, raised. 'Where the fuck are you? Get on the fucking bed now or you're in for a proper kicking.'

Talking to poor Mick?

The same voice continued, but lower, unintelligible.

She whispered to Andrea. 'If...' She nodded, convincing herself. 'When we get the chance. If they come out together. I'll take Braveheart. You take tray-man. If it's just one of them...'

'You shoot,' said Andrea. 'I'll be back-up.'

'Okay. Be ready.'

Andrea held up her gun and thumbed the safety off.

Naomi followed suit, waited, ear to the door. 'And if we can...' she began, but stopped. She felt the door moving in its frame, a millimetre forward, a millimetre back.

'Locked.' The Oxford voice, tray-man.

'You sure? You checked?' Cruickshank again. And more inaudible mutterings.

The door's edge moved an inch towards her. Two inches. *He's opening it so he can slam it shut,* she thought. *So now.* She grasped the edge of the door and pulled hard and sudden. It came wide open. Tray-man stood, eyes wide, looking at Andrea and her gun. One of his hands stopped in mid-air, reaching for where the door handle had been. One still held the tray. They stepped up to him, side by side, Naomi on the left, Andrea right, weapons an inch from his chest. Naomi looked him in the eye, raised a finger to her lips. Looked past him.

A cluttered workshop. Motorbikes in whole and in part. Shiny chrome exhausts, wheels, boxes, tools, grease guns. Puddled oil on the floor. Smells of petrol and Swarfega. Open wooden stairs to a balcony. On the balcony, Cruickshank stood at a yellow door. Brightly lit, his back to them, he was looking through a hatch, hand on the handle.

Naomi pushed tray-man gently on the chest with her gun, finger still to lips, an almost silent 'Shh' from her mouth. Tray-man backed up the steps, still holding the tray high, still staring open-mouthed. He was probably thinking he hadn't really needed to open the door to check it was locked. Too late now. She gestured to him to keep going, backing up the stairs. They followed him, side by side, two steps behind.

When tray-man was one step below the landing, she glanced at Andrea, raised a brow. Andrea grinned, nodded. They stopped. Raised their weapons, took aim.

Tray-man had one foot on the landing. He spoke over his shoulder. 'Gray?'

'Fuck off now.' Cruickshank said, still peering through the hatch.

'Er. Graham?'

'What the fuck is it?' Cruickshank said, sounding wound up. 'The fucker's hiding somewhere.'

'We got visitors.'

Cruickshank looked round. *Okay, this is it*, Naomi thought. *Never shot anyone before. But a first time for everything.* She squeezed the trigger and fired a dart, aiming for his leg.

Missed.

Started re-loading.

Cruickshank stared at them and moved back to the yellow door, reaching for the handle with his left hand, groping for a pocket with his right.

Andrea shot tray-man in the thigh and reloaded.

'Oh Christ,' tray-man said, wincing, pulling on the embedded dart. 'That hurts. Jesus, it hurts.'

Naomi shot again. Hit Cruickshank. Upper arm.

Reloaded again.

'Ouch! Ya bastard!' Cruickshank shouted. He turned back towards the door, pulled out the dart and looked at it, frowning. He looked up at Naomi and Andrea, then turned to tray-man, who was swaying across the landing, pushed him towards the stairs. 'Move, ya dozy cunt! Get the bastards!'

Naomi knew the tranquilisers took time to act. It was ten seconds for a detectable effect, thirty to down a big animal. All they had to do was wait. Play for time. Back off. Shift outside, quick-ish. But two angry men were coming at them from a height. It didn't feel good. And a strange blood-chilling noise started up.

Behind Cruickshank and tray-man the yellow door opened. A pale, skinny figure in bloodied white bounded out, screeching like a banshee.

What on earth is that? Backing off could wait. She aimed at Cruickshank, shot another dart. Missed him. Missed tray-man. Hit banshee amidships.

Tray-man sagged against the rail, dropped his tray over the edge. It looped down, landed with a clatter on the sky-blue teardrop tank of a Harley. A wrapped baguette splatted in a pool of oil. A syringe bounced off the bike and rolled, dribbling, under a wheel. Tray-man sank to the floor, half on the stairs, half on the balcony.

Cruickshank looked to be caught in two minds, eyes flickering between Naomi and Andrea on the stairs and the screeching banshee hopping from foot to foot in the doorway.

Cruickshank's eyes went blank. He dropped to his knees and fell slowly at banshee's feet, on top of tray-man. Banshee swayed erratically, unbalanced. Its eyes caught hers.

'Oh fuck,' she said, looking closely. 'I think I shot Mick.'

Mick sank slowly, coming to rest on top of Cruickshank and tray-man. His screech died to a gurgle, fell silent.

'Bugger me,' said Andrea.

***

Naomi looked at Andrea and scratched her head. 'I suppose,' she said, 'you could call that a qualified success?'

'I want to hear the fat lady sing before I call it anything.'

'Right enough.' Naomi tried to pull herself together. 'Let's just tidy up and go, shall we? First thing: get this pile of bodies organised.'

'And collect up the used darts. They have to be accounted for. And returned. Three we used, didn't we?'

'Four. You hit tray-man. I missed Braveheart, hit Braveheart, and hit Mick. Inadvertently.'

'Okay, four,' Andrea said. 'We need to take them all home with us.'

They took Mick by an arm and shoulder each, hauled him through the door and propped him up in the corner. Naomi checked his breathing. Andrea gently removed the dart from his midriff. Naomi pulled down his eyelids. There was no response from his eyes. She looked at his bruised face, the sores on his wrists. 'I hope he's going to be all right,' she said. 'You don't think we should give him a shot of that other stuff, that reverses it?'

'The darts are supposed to be relatively harmless,' Andrea said, hauling on unresponsive limbs. 'But not always, if you believe the chat rooms. All-American weirdos mostly, so a pinch of salt needed. These are the best, my mate says, and safest. And we mustn't give that antidote unless they're seriously ill. But he's breathing okay. And look at his arms.'

Naomi looked. They were covered in red dots, red lines, multi-coloured bruises. 'Yes,' she said. 'He's had enough needles.'

They hauled Cruickshank into the cell, onto the bed, face down. He was heavy and smelled stale.

'How long will it take to wear off, did you say?' Naomi asked.

'Depends. We're okay for fifteen minutes. After that…'

'After that we'll be gone,' Naomi said.

They manoeuvred tray-man into the cell, propped him by the bed, hoisted him on top of Cruickshank.

'Don't they look sweet?' said Andrea.

'Not very. Come on. You start getting these bastards tied up, nice and tight. I'll run and bring the car round.'

Ten minutes later Naomi pulled out onto the main road heading for Oxford. Mick was whickering gently on the back seat. 'What time is it?' she asked Andrea.

'Five to six.'

All the energy had drained from her body. She just wanted to stop the world.

'Call the flat,' she said. 'Kettle on. Strong tea.'

CHAPTER 40

A stomach-wrenching stench of wet dog and diesel. *Die Übelkeit über alles*, as my mum used to say. Nausea rules, okay. I covered ears and eyes and tried to stop breathing. The chance of regaining unconsciousness slipped away. Not good.

A voice, female, chirpy. 'He's coming round.'

Andrea. Unwelcome context flooded my mind. The ignominious end to my rebellion, almost before it had started. When Naomi shot me.

'Give him a poke, see if he stirs.' Speak of the devil. That was Naomi.

A touch on my leg, a gentle shake. Easy to ignore.

A sharp jab to my bruised abdomen, less easy. I turned away. What I wanted was more of Eric's cocktail. Cat, horse, roofie. Any or all.

'Mick?' Andrea again. 'Mick?'

Another jab in the stomach. I opened my eyes. A hideous green blur of trees flashed past the car's windows. My car, being thrown round bends too fast. I hunched down, stomach heaving. 'Leave me alone,' I tried to say. What came out sounded wrong. I tried again.

'Leave you alone?' said Andrea. 'Is that right? But you might like a heads-up.'

'What?'

'We're just going past the Trout. You're nearly home.'

I wasn't ready for this.

'And.' Naomi again. 'Another heads-up. Your mum's going to be there.'

I sat up straight, head between the front seats. 'What? Who? Where?'

'Your mum.'

'In my flat?'

'Yes.'

'What the fuck is she doing there?'

'And Denise,' Naomi said.

'Denise?'

'Denise from the office.'

'Denise from the office is in my flat?'

'Yes.'

'What the fuck is she doing there?'

'He keeps saying that,' Andrea said.

'Mission control,' Naomi said. 'That's what your flat was. Like NASA. And the mission was to rescue you. Which we've just done. No need to be so effusively grateful.'

'I don't want to go there.'

'Gail might turn up too,' Naomi said. 'Maybe Kanhai.'

'Am I throwing some kind of fucking party?'

'Linda and Tom won't come, although they've also been in action this morning. They're going back to Glebe Farm while they still can.'

'Don't take me home. Please. I can't bear it. Take me... somewhere else.' Ideally somewhere that would have supplies of Eric's cocktail, or an effective substitute. 'Hospital! Take me to the hospital.'

'Mick,' said Naomi. 'You're home, now. Here we are. Time to step up.'

CHAPTER 41

DENISE IN THE OFFICE

Denise nursed a cup of tea at the window of Mick's flat, looking down at the street. 'Amazing, isn't it?' she said to Mick's mum, Sandra. 'Stuff happened, all over the county, in glorious synchronicity.'

'Good planning,' Sandra said. 'Credit to Naomi. She's good. Knows how to collaborate. And delegate.'

'Surprising what you can do, though. Surprising to me, anyway,' Denise said, trying to puzzle out why she felt that. 'I mean, people do it in companies, all the time. Someone decides what needs doing, you do it, you get paid. But...'

'Ordinary people,' Sandra said, 'doing it for themselves, because they want to, without anyone paying them?'

'Exactly,' Denise said. 'I wonder what they're all doing now, the enemy. Mr Alleyn, driving back from Swindon, leaving puzzled policemen behind him. He'll be annoyed. Poor Mr Cruickshank, tied up in his kitchen, hoping someone finds him soon. Should we do something about that?'

'Later, maybe.'

'And the Sefton-Shaws. They've got kids, they'll be awake. I bet he's breathing fire down the phone about that old tractor and trailer. But soon they're going to realise they've all been had. Simultaneously. And that Mick got sprung while they were looking the other way.' Denise laughed, delighted to be part of this. It was such a change from credit control. 'They won't like it,' she said. 'Oh look. Here they are.'

'Who?'

'Well, definitely Naomi and Andrea. Is Mick in the back?'

She made space for Sandra at the window. They watched Naomi get out from the driver's side. It didn't look like the air was full of celebration. Naomi and Andrea had their feet on the ground and their heads in the back. 'Look at the body language,' Denise said. 'Something's up.'

She found herself clutching Sandra's arm as Mick emerged. He looked up at their window, an expressionless face coloured in bruises, wearing what might once have been lounging pyjamas, dark stains all over. She gripped Sandra's arm tighter as Mick tottered and crumpled onto the tarmac. Found herself pulling Sandra up by the armpit as Naomi and Andrea raised Mick to his feet. 'Sorry Sandra,' she said. 'Come on.'

They went to the door. The threesome were struggling towards Mick's landing.

Denise stayed by the flat door. Sandra went down a step, grasped Mick by the shoulders, studied his face. Naomi and Andrea supported him, looking less than happy with the situation.

'Look at the state of you,' Sandra said to Mick. 'Death warmed up. Come on. Inside.'

Sandra led the way into the flat, held the door as they all trooped in, said 'Kettle' to Denise, and 'Sit him here' to Naomi and Andrea, indicating the sofa. 'Or... no, on his bed.' She turned back to Denise. 'Come on,' she said. 'Shake a leg. Tea. Toast. Marmalade. Ibuprofen.'

Denise bustled, glad of something to do. The others settled Mick in the bedroom. She brought the required stuff on a tray, put it on the bedside table. Sandra moved a very feminine-looking sponge bag to make room for it and raised an eyebrow. Denise knew what Sandra was wondering, because she was wondering the same thing.

Sandra sat on the bed, on Mick's right; Naomi sat opposite, on his left. Andrea stood awkwardly at the foot of the bed. Denise realised there was a tug of war going on, and Sandra was winning. 'No. No hospitals,' she was saying. 'Peace and quiet. Look at his eyes. Dull. Tiny pupils. Obviously drugged. What've they been giving him?'

Denise caught a glance between Naomi and Andrea, which seemed to mediate a negotiation about how much should be said and who would say it.

Naomi spoke. 'Don't know. Something in a syringe. Why don't you ask him?'

'Yes,' said Sandra. 'Michael. Were you being drugged? Can you hear me?'

Mick's head twitched. He might have been nodding.

'Were they drugging you? What with?'

He tried to speak, coughed, tried again. 'Cat. Horse. Roofies.'

'Cat horse roofies?' Sandra asked. 'Can anyone translate?'

Denise had no idea. She realised that Naomi's eyes had settled on Andrea, who shrugged, cleared her throat, said, 'Well, ketamine. Heroin. And, erm… Rohypnol?'

Denise was shocked. Heroin, everyone knew about. Most people, she thought, were terrified of it. Rohypnol she'd heard of. The original date-rape drug. Pretty strong stuff on its own. 'Ketamine's what a farrier gives a nervy horse, to stop it kicking,' she said.

'Also known as horsey-horsey,' Andrea said. 'Used to come as big yellow tablets. Not sure now. Lots of kids still do it, I hear.'

A noise. The bedroom door swung open. Gail poked her head round it. 'Oh my,' she said. 'How are we all? God, is that Mick? Oh God, Mick, are you all right?'

He grunted, looked away.

Denise felt like she sometimes did in staff meetings in the office. Somebody needed to move the situation on a bit, and the somebody who needed to do it was her. 'Okay,' she said. 'It's been quite a day already, and it's still not eight o'clock. Too early to party. Let's leave Mick to his breakfast with his mum. The rest of us can have a cuppa and catch up. Out there.' She indicated the sitting room with a nod of her head, driving Gail and leading Naomi and Andrea.

'That,' Naomi said, as they settled on the sofa, chair and rugs, 'is all the thanks you get.' She giggled, somewhat inappropriately in Denise's opinion. 'You find him, organise his rescue...'

'Shoot him in the stomach,' said Andrea.

'What?' said Gail.

'Only a flesh wound,' said Naomi. 'With a dart, not a bullet. And anyway. You can't make an omelette...'

'Tell us what happened,' said Gail.

That sounded to Denise more like a command than a request. She seconded it. There were whole chunks of the morning's events that were opaque to all but the active participants. But before Naomi could start, Sandra joined them from the bedroom. Denise thought she looked slightly less anxious.

'He's nodded off,' Sandra said. 'Thought I'd leave him to it for a bit. He's had half a slice of toast and half a cup of tea and a couple of ibuprofen. From what I can make out, he's been drugged into almost permanent unconsciousness since they picked him up on Wednesday.'

'He probably needs some sort of managed withdrawal,' said Andrea. 'I'm sure we can organise that somehow. Perhaps if me and Naomi—'

'Yes he does,' Sandra said. 'In fact, the only time he seemed to come to life at all was when I told him I had a little stash of opium at home. Don't look at me like that, Denise!'

Denise took back control of her face, forced a smile.

'I'm not a dope fiend,' Sandra said, 'and I'm not going to turn him into one. It's left over from a trip on the Magic Bus in the

285

seventies. Not touched since. He's agreed to come home with me for a few days. As long as he gets the opium.'

'Do be careful,' Denise said. She hated drugs. 'Only give him a bit at a time.'

'I will. But he needs peace. Rest. Security. So what we'll do is, I'll stay here. When he wakes up I'll take him over to Finstock, to my place. They're not likely to come looking for him out there, and if they do we'll have Friday. And I'll borrow my neighbour's shotgun, for the look of it.'

'But...' Naomi said.

'I'll tell Mrs Swainston,' Sandra said. 'Lock up the flat. Everyone else can go home. Go about your normal business. Behave as if nothing has happened. Don't know anything about anything, if anyone asks. Denise, can you ring me every day or so? If there's any news I'll give it to you and you can pass it on. And vice versa?'

There were nods all round, some rather grudging, Denise thought. It clearly wasn't up for debate.

'And,' Sandra said, 'thank you all for what you've done. Splendid effort.'

'And you,' Naomi said. 'We'll come over.'

'Yes, that would be lovely. In a day or two. I'll let everyone know how he's getting on through Denise. As I said.'

CHAPTER 42

DETECTIVE INSPECTOR JONES

Jones's phone was buzzing and vibrating. The screen showed:

09.20 Saturday 8th July

Unknown Number

Olwen was out with her friend Jane, her side of the bed cold. The tea she'd brought him earlier had a beige skin of milk fat. It was his first day off for a couple of weeks. He accepted the call and sipped his tea, but soon wished he hadn't. The tea was awful and the caller was angry.

'I've already spoken to your front desk three times. They keep saying they'll organise something but nothing's happening. Sort it out, please, right now.'

Who was this guy? Obviously someone with a sense of entitlement. 'I didn't quite catch that, sir,' he said. 'Poor signal. DI Jones here. Not actually on duty but at your service, sir, I'm sure. Who's calling please?'

'Sefton-Shaw. Conrad. City council director.'

'Mr Sefton-Shaw, good morning,' Jones said, putting on his most respectful tone. The man might be up himself, but he was friendly with the Chief Constable. And with Alleyn. 'What's the nature of the problem?'

'There's a tractor and trailer parked across our gates.'

'Across your gates?'

'That's what I said, man. Ancient, they are. Tyres flat as pancakes. A load of putrid earth in the trailer. No key. No sign of who put it there.'

One hell of a prank, Jones thought, *if it's kids.* 'Not been upsetting any farmers, have you, sir? No idea who's responsible?'

'I don't give a fuck who's responsible. I want it gone.'

'Where are these gates, sir?'

'Do you mean what's our address?'

'That'd be a start.'

'Don't be facetious, officer. Springfield House, Berkeley Close, Boars Hill OX1 5HX.'

'Is Berkeley Close a public highway? Adopted by the Council?'

'No. It's a private road. What difference does that make?

'If it's a public highway, the council would be responsible for dealing with obstructions. If it's a private road…' But best not go there, he'd only be onto the Chief Constable. In fact, best tell him what he wants to hear, get him off the line and get the kettle on for a decent cup of tea. 'I'll send someone over immediately, Mr Sefton,' Jones said.

'Send a fucking tow truck, for Christ's sake.'

Jones's phone vibrated – another incoming call. 'The officer will assess the situation and take appropriate action, sir. He'll be with you very soon.'

Jones rang off and checked who was calling. Clappison. It was not even half past nine, on his day off. He took the call.

'Sir, sorry to bother you. Clappison, up at the hospital.'

'What are you doing there? Not one of ours, is it?'

'No. The one that was here wasn't one of ours. He's gone. Two that weren't here but are now, neither of them is ours.'

Give me strength, Jones prayed. 'Constable,' he said. 'Start at the beginning, please.'

'Yes sir. It may have passed you by, sir. Not yesterday, the day before, there was an anonymous emergency call, for an ambulance. Paramedics turned up, found this guy out cold with a head wound, propped up against a white van.'

'Where was this?'

'By an industrial unit, Dorchester way... Did you speak, sir?'

'No,' Jones said. At least not voluntarily. He knew Alleyn's muscle ran the bikers' café near Dorchester, and the workshops behind. And Alleyn had threatened he'd take care of Jarvis if Jones didn't do it for him. Could the casualty have been Jarvis? 'Carry on.'

'They took him into A&E. He was admitted, treated for concussion and a minor fracture, sedated. Clearly the victim of an assault so they called us. PC Dodds interviewed him yesterday afternoon, came back with a story about someone being held prisoner in this industrial unit, and tortured.'

Jones groaned. If this wasn't Alleyn upping the ante, he'd eat his hat. If he still had a hat to eat. The girls' school fees were already overdue, and if Alleyn decided he no longer needed Jones...

'You all right, sir? I'll carry on? I talked to Dodds this morning and we went over for a look-see at this industrial unit. We had to force entry, sir, as we could hear cries of distress and were in fear for the safety of whoever was inside. We found two gentlemen stacked up on a bed, cable-tied to it, apparently under the influence of drugs. They refused to answer questions. We got them in an ambulance and they're being checked out now at the hospital. We have them under guard. I came over to interview the guy with concussion, see if he could throw any light on these two, because of the coincident locus. But he'd discharged himself, six o'clock this morning. Gave a false ID too, so...'

Raging incompetence, Jones thought. And 'coincident locus' – Clappison's way of saying 'in the same place', while throwing up a verbal smokescreen to cover his ineptitude. 'This industrial unit,' he said. 'Not part of a small business park by the roundabout on the A465, is it? Behind a café where the Hell's Angel wannabes hang out?'

'It is indeed, sir. How did you know?'

'Christ, how do you think? I've been keeping an eye. Listen. Don't let those two walk as well. Keep a PC on each of them. Get them in the station as soon as they're fit to move. If they've been drugged I want to know what with and how it was administered. What time is it? I'll see you at the station at eleven. Meanwhile get over to Springfield House, OX1 5HX. Sort out Conrad Sefton-Shaw. Someone's parked across his drive.' His phone vibrated. 'Not a global emergency but he's a city council director and we don't want him throwing his weight in our direction, so look after him. Another call coming in, must go.'

Jones stood, shook his head, took his phone to the window. He looked out at the paved patio, the neatly mown lawn beyond it, his wife's wilding experiment beyond that, then the edge of Bernwood Forest, and the soft rolling fields away across to Brill Hill in the north. It would be a nice day for a walk. Thank God his wife wasn't here, listening to what his day off was turning into. She'd be telling him to get out now, full pension or not, before they carried him out. The incoming was from Alleyn. He should have been expecting it.

'Jones. What the fuck is going on?'

Alleyn sounded like he could explode at any moment. Jones could do without it. He was glad they were talking by phone rather than face to face. 'James, hi,' he said, deciding on assertive rather than knuckling under. 'Hope your morning's going well. Mine's a shitstorm so far…'

'Don't tell me. I just got back from Swindon. It was them, I know it. They're trying to run us ragged, the bastards. One of yours, a woman, PC Smith, sent me…'

'To Swindon? We don't have a PC Smith.'

'Well, whoever she was, she sent me to fucking Swindon. My secretary was with her, in your station. Said your cells are full so Donald's in custody in Swindon, ask for Sergeant Davies when I get there. So at six fucking a.m. I'm in Swindon and no-one knows what I'm talking about and they ring Kidlington and no-one knows anything there either.'

Couldn't have happened to a nicer guy, Jones thought, suppressing a grin. 'Hang on, James,' he said, 'I need to catch up here. Where are you now?'

'Back in Sotwell,' Alleyn said. 'At home.'

'Who's Donald?'

'Donald Cruickshank,' Alleyn said. 'Graham's brother. One of ours. Uni properties.'

'Okay,' Jones said, thinking, *One of yours, maybe, not one of mine.* But what a morning. Was any of this connected to Clappison's hospitalisations? 'I'll see what's going on and get straight back.'

'No you don't,' Alleyn said. 'I know what's going on and it's a wild goose cluster-fuck set up by these protest bastards, I know it. Conrad's blocked in, there's no answer at Donald's or 10cc or on Graham's mobile, and that idiot kid's on his own at the café. Where are you?'

'At home. Oakley. I just talked to Conrad.'

'Meet me at Donald's. Ten thirty. 73 St Margarets Road. I'll drop by the café on the way.'

No time for a cuppa, Jones thought. He couldn't go on like this. He showered and dressed and was parked outside Donald Cruickshank's house on the dot – a generous detached North Oxford villa, Victorian, worth millions. Donald Cruickshank was doing all right.

Alleyn hadn't arrived. Jones tried the front door. Locked. No-one answered the doorbell. He went down the side of the house, wondering whether Alleyn was setting him up. But why would that be in his interests?

The back door was locked too. He looked round the unkempt back garden. A derelict-looking shed. Footprints in long dewy grass. A pink plastic unicorn in the middle of the lawn. A bunch of keys attached. He picked it up.

He tried one in the back door. Then another, which fitted. He eased the door open and poked his head in, heard a moan. Someone in pain or despair. He followed the sound on tiptoe, into the second room on the left. A man lay on the floor by a dining table, tied to a fallen chair, swathed in black tape, very red in the face, choking. An emergency, there was no time to worry about ID or evidence. Jones took a sharp paring knife from a knife block and started to cut free the man's mouth and nose. He was panicking, struggling, not helping at all.

Alleyn ducked through the doorway. 'What the fuck?' he said. 'Is that Donald?'

'Hold him for a second, will you?' Jones said. 'So I don't cut the idiot's throat while I get this tape off his gob.'

'It is Donald,' Alleyn said. 'Donald? Tell me. Who did this? Jones, cut all these ties for fuck's sake.'

Donald was beyond conversation, beyond rationality. He fought Alleyn's restraining arms, and wailed.

Jones gave up hope of preserving a crime scene and got busy.

'There,' he said, cutting the last of the cable ties. 'Donald Cruickshank, is it? Get him up, let's have a look. Mr Cruickshank, if you can understand what I'm saying, we need you to calm down and co-operate. Tell us who did this to you.'

They hoisted him onto a chair. He was shaking with fear. Jones took his pulse: racing, close on 200 bpm. Looked at his eyes. Pinprick pupils, erratic gaze. 'Won't get much sense out of him until he's been sedated and sorted out a bit,' he said. 'I'll call an ambulance.'

'Leave him be, he'll come round,' Alleyn said, his face relaxing into its normal impatient frown. 'Listen. I'll tidy up here. I looked in on the café and 10cc on the way, your lot's all over it. Find out what's happening there. See if you've got this twat's brother Graham anywhere, he's gone AWOL. See if you can find Mick bloody Jarvis, he's been sprung. And for fuck's sake, get a lid on all this and keep it there.'

Jones was tempted to tell Alleyn where to get off, but this wasn't the time. 'I'll see what I can do,' he said, heading for the door. 'Don't expect miracles.'

CHAPTER 43

Light licked round blackout blinds. A hint of incense. On top of the wardrobe, a glum robot in black, white and red, made by my brother, when he was into Lego. Twenty-five years ago? The spare room, in my mum's house. Safe.

I drifted, then woke again slowly from a soft dream of coconuts and Dutch liqueurs, dark eyes and dimples. I was cocooned in a warm cyclone that spun out from my chest, filled my body, filled the space around it. A beautiful feeling, unfamiliar, that came from where? From my heart, it felt like. Was this the source of all the heart hype, all that hackneyed imagery? Were valentines of flesh and blood, really? Strange that I'd lived for thirty-four years and was only now knowing this feeling. Strange too that it should come when the only person on my mind was Kimberly. I'd heard nothing from her for weeks. What was happening in her life?

The door clicked. I opened an eye. My mother put a mug of tea on the bedside cabinet and sat on the side of the bed looking at me with a concerned frown that always drove me mad.

'Thank you,' I said, opening another eye. 'What day is it?'
'Saturday.'
'Saturday the what-th of what?'
'Eighth of July.'

'Is that all? How long was I in that place?'

'They snatched you Wednesday morning, on your way to a meeting that had been set up for the purpose of getting you to a known place at a known time. You got out this morning. So three days.' She stood, went to the door. 'I'm going to turn the main light on. I need to have a look at you.'

I flinched at the brightness.

She was looking at my arms. 'Would you look here,' she said. 'Covered in sores and bruises. Horrible.' She went out and came back with three tubes of ointment and a tub of Vaseline.

'Hydrocortisone,' she said, holding up one tube. 'Stops itching and soreness. Savlon. Antiseptic. Arnica, for bruises. Vaseline, to stop wounds drying out, help them heal faster. Slap it on. Everywhere there's broken skin. Back in a minute with another kind of tea.'

'Don't scratch!' my mum shouted, coming back into the room. I stopped scratching.

'Keep up the ointments for a few days,' she said. 'And drink this tea. It'll be bitter, but you'll acquire the taste. Rest for a bit. I'll be out for an hour, while Pete from next door runs me into Wolvercote to fetch your car.'

I lost track of time in the gentle dark narcosis. I surrendered control again, to a more benign jailer. I acquired a taste for opium tea instantly. It helped me recover the rhythm of meditation, and touch the strange inner light that had made imprisonment bearable. Could I ever reach it without drugs? I hoped so. I'd check. In a day or two.

***

I drew on the small pipe, took the smoke deep, blew out slowly.

'Tuesday morning,' my mum said, frowning at me over her cup of ordinary tea. 'You prefer the pipe to the brew. Bad for the lungs though. Don't go getting used to it.' She blew on her tea.

'There's not much left. And I'm not getting any more.'

'How much is there?'

She peered into an old 35mm film canister. 'Three fills of the pipe,' she said. 'One more this evening, leave two for tomorrow?'

'How about three this evening and bugger tomorrow?'

'No,' said Sandra.

'Two this evening, one in the morning.'

'You sure?'

I nodded.

'Up to you,' she said. 'Four o'clock now. So one at seven, one at ten. That okay?'

'Okay.'

'I was talking to Denise earlier, in the office,' she said. 'She's told them you had a riding accident. You on a horse! Imagine. They're asking can you come in on Friday to meet the Murdoch Alleyn project manager.'

'Oh.'

'And Denise said Naomi's desperate to come and see you. Desperate.' She sniffed. 'So I said you'd call Denise tomorrow morning about Friday's meeting. And that Naomi could come out tomorrow afternoon, all being well. She'll ring first to make sure, okay?'

'Okay.' Why did I feel dread? Surely I wanted to see her?

My grandad nudged my shoulder. *'Mick,'* he said. *'Follow the path with the heart in it.'*

Which one's that, then?

'You'll know it when you see it,' he said.

Gee thanks.

***

On Wednesday morning I was up early. I swallowed a tumbler of fresh orange and was pulling on trainers when my mum appeared with my final hit of black stuff.

'Don't want any more,' I said. 'Thanks, but you can put that in your pipe and smoke it.' I laughed, she didn't. *Should have had it*, I thought, my back twisting in sudden need. *Out*, I thought. *Get out of here.*

Friday was willing. I took her up the hill, over the main road and followed a trail into Wychwood. I stomped along, still fragile but beginning to feel human again. Thinking how lucky I was to be enjoying Friday's throw-me-this-stick dance and kicking through the rustle of early leaf-fall. Which made me think...

What do you call a man that's covered in dead leaves?

Russell.

With a seagull on his head?

Cliff.

With a spade in his head?

Doug.

Without a spade in his head?

And so on. Old, but they always made me smile, if no-one else. This release from imprisonment made me feel re-born, my mind beginning to play, work, ask questions, but in no hurry for answers. I needed to know how Naomi and Andrea managed to find my prison and turn up with stun guns, and what was happening with the land deal. But a restless energy made me want to move my feet and that seemed more important. Time would fill the gaps. And Naomi would be over later.

Nervous again, I kicked at a log that wasn't as sogged and rotted as it looked, getting a trainer full of leaf mould and a bruised toe. I decided to tell Denise I wasn't meeting anyone from Murdoch Alleyn on Friday; I'd be at the seaside, having a swim and an ice-cream and hiring a deckchair.

***

'Thank you.' Naomi accepted a cup of tea from Mum and took a seat across the fireplace. 'Well. Where to start.'

Mum smiled expectantly. I wasn't sure about this.

'Actually, Sandra,' Naomi said. 'Perhaps I could have a little time alone with Mick. Because, well… you know.'

Mum reddened. 'Of course. No problem,' she said, and bustled out.

She's furious, I thought. *Never mind.*

'I'd like to start, actually,' I said, when we were alone. 'With apologising for standing you up at the Standard last Wednesday. Couldn't do much about it, but still. Sorry.'

'It seemed pretty awful at the time,' she said. 'I didn't know what to think. But Gail convinced me that you'd never let anyone down like that, unless something like what happened, happened. Or worse. She helped me eat the takeaway too. It was good.'

She paused, gave me a long cool look.

What now? I waited, returning her gaze.

'It was only a week ago,' she said. 'A lot can happen in a week, can't it?'

Fair enough, a lot had happened. But did that account for the strange look in her eyes? 'It can,' I said. 'It did. But what is it? Something's on your mind, I can tell.'

'Oh, just how things pan out,' she said, eyes flicking to the window. Opting for evasion over directness, I thought. 'I was just thinking how things might have been, if you'd turned up at the Standard, and we'd had our takeaway. And so on.' A tender look strayed across her face, chased off by the return of cool. 'But you didn't. You couldn't. So.'

She told me how they tracked down my prison and got me out. 'And we have to thank you,' she said, 'for the use of your flat. I stayed there from Wednesday. Looked after your lovely dog, when I could get her away from Mrs Swainston. Can I open the curtains a bit? And the window? Getting hot.'

I felt cold, but didn't say.

She did the window, talking over her shoulder. 'Andrea was there too. Thursday and Friday. Nice, isn't it? Nice flat.'

'Yes. I'm very lucky,' I said, still puzzling about what wasn't being said.

'Thursday, after I'd brained that biker with a wheel brace, I was in pieces. Shaking. Needed company. So Andrea brought pizza. We raided your wine store, I'm afraid. And we launched the whole rescue mission from there, early Saturday morning. Your mum was great. And Denise from your office. God, she's a good mimic. She can do Alleyn's receptionist's voice perfectly.'

'I remember her. Not my finest hour.'

'No. But Denise has been at it again. Yesterday,' Naomi said.

'How so?'

'Well, they weren't holding you hostage and making demands or anything. So we thought their main reason for disappearing you was to keep you out of the way, and the rest of us busy worrying about you, while they got their bid in and their sweeteners lined up and their fixes in. We wanted to find out more about the bidding.'

'Good thinking.'

'The deadline for submissions was midday last Monday, 10th July. Denise rang them just after midday, using her Murdoch Alleyn receptionist voice. Asked for Donald Cruickshank. Not in. Got his secretary. Just checking that they'd received the final bid on time, and everything was in order, on behalf of Mr Alleyn and Ballator. They had, ten o'clock, two hours before the deadline. And could she just check that it was the right version that was sent, because Mr Alleyn made the submission himself, and he sometimes gets confused about version control.'

'Crumbs.'

'She got her to read out the first few lines of the executive summary. And the numbers bit. Just to check.'

'And she did? Crikey.'

'They're bidding six hundred and fifty in total. Two hundred up front.'

'Millions?'

'Yes. A million an acre. The second two hundred to be released when the council commits funding to infrastructure projects – roads, schools, all that. And the balance as detailed planning comes through. No other conditions.'

'Jesus. No wonder Sefton-Shaw is a key player, delivering on planning and infrastructure.'

'Denise asked how the Ballator bid stood in relation to the others. And this secretary, who must be very indiscreet, or naïve, or thick… anyway, she told her. In confidence. Three bids on the shortlist. Ballator's is the highest and the only one that's effectively unconditional. So even before the official decision on the eighteenth, they're negotiating detailed terms with Ballator. Like making the payment schedule time-limited, so as detailed planning comes through or after two years, whichever is earlier, kind of thing.'

'So they've done it, near as. Despite all our efforts.' It was a flat feeling, like losing in the final of a knock-out competition. All that for nothing. I stared out the window. A red kite was slipping through the wind over a row of Leylandii, up the hill behind the house. A solitary magpie was watching me from my mum's lilac tree, the first I'd seen that day. I gave it good morning and crossed fingers. I whistled Friday, who appeared and had her head scratched. I heard my grandad say, *Mick, this isn't football. This is real life. Players get carried off but the game never ends.*

'What about the others?' I asked.

'Well, Andrea's been on the phone to her dad for hours. She's furious. Gail, I don't know, not been in touch. Tom and Linda went quiet after they blocked Sefton-Shaw's drive with an old tractor and trailer.'

'Where did those come from?'

'Glebe Farm. Old ones of Tom's.'

'Traceable?'

'Tom said not. I did check, you know? No plates. No chassis number. Engine from a scrap-yard. They'd sat in a barn for twenty years, no use and no value in them. Dumping them on the Sefton-Shaws was cheaper than getting them taken away.'

'Okay.' I felt there was something I wasn't seeing, but couldn't work out how to make it visible. We'd both gone quiet. I shivered. Friday cocked an ear. I realised I was breaking into a sweat, and suddenly found Friday's doggy smell nauseating. 'Excuse me a mo.' I dashed to the loo. Ran cold water, splashed my face repeatedly. Then hot. Then cold again. Towelled off, I studied my eyes in the mirror. Bloodshot. Dull. Yellow where they should have been white. My hands were shaking.

This is no good, I thought. *This won't do at all. Get a grip.*

I rounded up bathroom bits and pieces into my sponge bag. In my room, I put my sponge bag and stuff in a rucksack. Back in the sitting room, I found Naomi and my mum talking quietly. They stopped as I entered, so were no doubt talking about me. I'd had enough of this.

'I'm off then,' I said. 'Thanks for everything, Ma. But gotta go now. Let you get back to normal.'

'I'm not sure you're ready yet.'

'I am. More than,' I said, shivering again.

'If you're sure,' she said. 'Keep your head down, though, won't you? Don't want any more rescues.'

'I will. And thanks for coming out,' I said to Naomi.

'My pleasure,' she said. 'I'm going too. I'll come out with you. Thanks for the tea,' she said to my Mum. 'Let's stay in touch.'

I opened the tailgate of the Golf. Friday jumped in. Naomi leaned in after her, scratched her head. Friday wagged and smiled.

I looked at Naomi, not sure what I was feeling, feeling nothing much. What's happened to me? I felt empty; I would actually be glad to see the back of her.

'You don't look well,' she said. 'Can I help? Get you anything?'

'Thanks, I'm fine.'

'Before I go,' she said. 'I did want to ask you. But we can talk about that another time…'

'What?'

'How it was, being a prisoner. What happened. You were sore and bruised and blasted on drugs, and you've not said a word about it.'

I looked away. The red kite was still riding the wind. Seven magpies tumbled through somebody's apple tree. *That story need never be told*, I thought. 'Another time,' I said.

'We should get the gang together,' she said, 'for a pow-wow. At the Globe, like before. We were supposed to be doing it last Monday, you know? But couldn't, because you were incommunicado.'

'I forgot,' I said. 'Sorry.' She stepped back as I pulled down the tailgate. 'I'm free any evening. Just let me know when to turn up.'

I couldn't wait to get moving. I got in, started up, drove off. I glanced in my mirror. She stood, arms folded, watching me go.

CHAPTER 44

Naomi had set up the meet for the following Monday in the Globe. They were all there when I arrived, busy catching up. I sat down, feeling strung out and nervy. Sefton-Shaw had left me alone since my escape. I didn't expect it to last, but thought they'd probably come at us from a different direction. I was hiding behind ten-day stubble, baseball cap pulled down over still-bruised eyes, attracting curious stares but concealing nothing. Naomi smiled as if she understood.

In my mind the purpose of the pow-wow was to see how people felt. Should we give up, or could we still do something worthwhile together? I didn't mind if others had other purposes. I was in two minds about carrying on myself, and hoped our discussion might make things clearer.

'Before we start,' I said. They all kept chatting. I did my stand up, clear throat, sit down routine. Silence. 'Now we know for certain what we're up against, what they're capable of, everyone should have the chance to bail out. For those that stay in, we need to be sure of each other. Like one for all and all for one.'

My hands had pretty much stopped shaking. I looked round. They were waiting for me to continue, so I did. 'If you don't want to make that commitment, fine, but please leave now. Because once you've heard stuff, you can't unhear it. If anyone gets done for this, we'll probably all get done. They'd see us as a conspiracy. And there are others involved, who we need to keep absolutely quiet about. Like my mum. A work colleague. An old mate.'

Everyone kept quiet.

'Is that understood? Absolutely quiet.' I was being a bit harsh, but what the hell. 'So, knowing we're under fire from the cops and the robbers, is everyone happy to stay in? Gail? Andrea? Tom? Linda? Naomi?'

Tom and Linda looked at each other, said nothing. The others nodded agreement. I looked round again, meeting eyes, checking. 'Everyone's staying in? Good.' I was turning into a blasted chairman. But I'd started so I'd finish. 'We could go round the table. Andrea, how about you tell us about Glebe Farm and reskilling and the muck drop? And anything else that comes to mind. Naomi, anything you've picked up from waitressing at Harry's. And you've been talking to Denise in my office. Then we'll talk about Murdoch Alleyn and Ballator, and what we got from Springfield House. Who they are and what they're up to. And the money, where it comes from, where it goes. Okay?'

'Can I just ask first,' Gail said, 'about what happened when you were disappeared? We all know bits, but...'

It'd take hours to pick through all that. I didn't want to spend a minute. 'I'll write it down,' I said. 'When it's not too raw. But at the moment, no. Andrea. Glebe Farm?'

Andrea began talking. I could hear the words she said, but couldn't take in their substance. The others seemed absorbed: I stopped trying. My attention was re-captured when she said something about 'tomorrow' and there was a collective 'wow'.

'Sorry, missed that, what's that about tomorrow again?'

'Pay attention, Mick,' Gail said.

'What we've been talking about for the last five minutes,' Naomi said.

'Wake up, love,' Andrea said. 'The muck drop. Tom's doing

the muck drop. Tomorrow night. We'd planned it for yesterday, but I couldn't get the press lined up. So it's midnight tomorrow, outside City Hall. The Oxford Times will be there. Maybe Radio Oxford.'

'Wow, well done.'

'You can come along too, if you like. As an innocent passer-by.'

'I will, thanks. Sorry, dimmed out there. Rude.'

Naomi reported mounting excitement amongst Conrad Sefton-Shaw and his lunching buddies. 'There's bits in the press too. They're calling it the new Silicon Valley,' she said. 'But it's more like the new Gold Rush, if you do the sums. Oxford to Cambridge is a hundred and ten miles. They're talking ten thousand new houses per mile. Whoever builds those houses will make at least two hundred and fifty billion pounds. Profit. And the same again from all the other stuff that will come with them.' She met my eye. 'Half a trillion. Profit. To say nothing of what the landowners will make.'

'An awful lot of money,' I said. Too much to imagine.

'Ballator are off to a flyer with Glebe Farm, so you can see why they're excited,' Naomi said. 'They're talking Oxford up as the UK tech hub, saying the OxCam Growth Arc is just one spoke of the wheel. And if you look at the map, it's true, all roads lead to Oxford. Routes from Southampton, Bristol, South Wales, Gloucester, the West Midlands, the East Midlands. Several from London. It's immense.'

'I don't get it,' Gail said. 'Who wants this? There's resistance everywhere, especially from their own voters. Perverse.'

'It's not for the voters, they take them for granted. It's for the people who fund the party. Pay the piper. Anyway,' Naomi said, 'the other thing. Ballator's bid. Up for decision tomorrow. The two hundred mill up front is now split to fifty on signing and one fifty when agreements are in place with various bits of the university. Funding chairs, that sort of thing.'

'Chairs?' Tom said.

'Professorships.' Naomi looked at her notes. 'Russian Science and Civilisation. Caihong Wu, Professor of Chinese Culture. Post-Capitalist Economics. And so on. They're into due diligence and money laundering and all that with the uni finance people. Because they're asking, as you would. How can they afford it?'

'It's a good question,' I said. 'They're a big builder, but it's an awful lot of money.'

'I heard there's a rights issue,' Andrea said. 'To shareholders. Underwritten by an investment fund.'

'Who's that then?' Gail said. 'The investment fund.'

'Don't know. But if the rights issue falls short, the fund will own a chunk of Ballator, and have a lot of influence in the uni.'

'Brilliant,' I said. 'Faceless financiers. Could be anybody. Hedge fund proprietors. Russian mafia. Triads.' Sounded like a joke, but wasn't. 'Or,' I said. And paused, trying to catch a thought that had flitted across my mind. Couldn't.

Time to move on.

I passed round pieces of paper. 'Some of you have seen these already. They're transcripts of recordings from the bug in Springfield House. We put it downstairs, in a smoke detector. Good job their dog likes me.'

'Does it still work?' Tom asked. 'As a smoke detector.'

'It still worked as a smoke detector when it had our bug in it, yes. Until they found it. Whether it still does...' Alleyn had found the bug and smashed it. Just the bug, or the detector as well? 'No way of knowing,' I said. 'Okay. We got a few snippets. I've not printed all of them but these'll give you the idea. The first is Conrad talking on the phone, probably to Donald Cruickshank, university admin boss.'

I waited while they read. 'Sefton-Shaw's in charge locally. He's controlled by someone pretty scary.' I passed round more papers. 'Then this, a few days later. The voices are Conrad. James Alleyn. Donald Cruickshank. Have a read.'

My own capture and incarceration by Alleyn's biker buddies were clearly foreshadowed. Stupidly, forewarned had not been forearmed. I still wondered what they had planned to do with me. Just hold me until they'd done what they needed? Or fake a fatal accident. Or just disappear me. They'd not concealed the identity of my jailers, so where did that leave them?

I was still surprised by the amounts of money they seemed ready to spend to smooth their path. Talking about forty thousand pounds to keep Linda and Tom quiet as if it were small change. And buying off Naomi by enabling her dream project on a site they weren't interested in themselves. This must be part of what 'Payroll etc' meant, in the intercepted email. Anyone around the table could already have been bought off or otherwise got at. Time to test the water.

'Can I just ask? Has anyone been approached? Andrea, has anyone approached you? Offered you money or something to go away and keep quiet? Or to stay involved but basically to spy on us? Or threatened you if you wouldn't?'

'No. Wish they would.'

'Anyone else? Tom?'

'Someone has,' said Tom.

All eyes on Tom.

'I told him to go fuck himself,' Tom said, making eye contact around the table.

'Who? What was the deal?' Gail said.

'That lawyer, Alleyn. Big bastard, isn't he? Offered us like it said on that sheet. Twenty thousand each, and jobs at an estate out past Witney, Ashton Hall. Big pheasant shoot. Gamekeeping for me. Housekeeping and cleaning for her. A house, tied to the jobs. And we had to forget Glebe Farm and have nothing to do with you lot, ever.'

It showed how deeply damaged Tom was. In his position I might have taken that offer.

'Linda,' I asked, 'what about you? Did they approach you too?'

'No,' she said. 'No. Only through Tom.' Her eyes were down, she seemed very tense. She and Tom might have disagreed about whether to accept it.

'I'll try to summarise,' Naomi said. 'Clearly a conspiracy. Sefton-Shaw and individuals in the uni and in Ballator, doing things for money that aren't exactly in their job descriptions. So that's corruption, you know? Sefton-Shaw's using some sort of coercion to keep them in line. Especially Cruickshank, the uni guy, who's the flakiest. They may have the ear of someone in the police. Like the one who tried to put pressure on that friend of Mick's.'

Great, I thought. And we're keeping Kanhai's name out of this.

'What I don't see,' Gail said, 'is what the big idea is. What are they really trying to do?'

'Depends on who you're talking about,' Andrea said. 'Ballator wants a square mile of greenfield site, with an inside track on planning. The college wants half a billion for the land. The council want growth and planning gain. That's the local context.' She looked round the table. 'But it's a strategic site, in the UK's answer to Silicon Valley. Commercialising world-leading research, from Oxford and Cambridge, and a whole bunch of other unis and hi-tech start-ups and R&D outfits too. Genetics, pharma, materials, IT, aerospace, auto, defence, robotics. So if the strings are ultimately being pulled from Russia, or China…'

'Crikey,' said Linda.

'Gosh,' said Tom.

'What are we going to do?' Gail said. 'Take it to the police?'

'What, our evidence? Don't see it,' Andrea said. 'Obtained illegally. So the police wouldn't use it, even if they weren't on the payroll. And we'd be in deep shit.'

'We've no reason to think it's anything to do with China or Russia,' I said. 'But I have been trying to set up a back door into the police, through a friend who knows people there.'

'Is that Kanhai?' Gail asked.

'I'm trying to keep names out of this, if you don't mind,' I said, trying to send a telepathic message, which might have got through, from the sudden look of introspection that crossed her face. Or was she just thinking how touchy I'd got lately? I knew I had. Blame drugs, or withdrawal from.

'My friend was setting a meeting up a few days ago,' I said. 'But something cropped up, as you know. I'm back on that now, so we can feed them what we've got, anonymously. Any other thoughts?'

A lot of shrugs, no suggestions. Silence fell.

Naomi broke it. 'I was right, wasn't I? First thing I said, way back, was, there's something fishy going on. Just had no idea how big and how fishy.'

Warmth for her flooded through me. She was still on side. And it wasn't just me, I realised: she'd had a difficult time, and come through, still engaged and positive, and the others too. I'd been so self-centred, preoccupied with my own battles. Did the air of negativity I was sensing come from me?

'No need to rush,' Gail said. 'How about, see if the Ballator bid wins tomorrow. See what that throws up. Let's give ourselves a week or so? Sure to have a better idea of the way forward then.'

Gail's suggestion was greeted by silence and no obvious enthusiasm. It was sensible, but also an admission that we couldn't stop the deal happening. Tom was going to spread muck; others might want to do more than just wait for a week. Or perhaps not: they were all looking down at their hands, beer mats, spilled drink puddling on the tabletop. I felt a sudden exasperation. *What's the good of this? Why are we doing it? What difference will it make? Can I go home now?*

***

Tuesday 18th July dawned: decision-making-meeting day at uni property services, ahead of muck-drop midnight at City Hall. I was up early, walking Friday by the river. The willows at the tail of Trout Island flamed as the sun rose behind us. I couldn't stop thinking about Kimberly, feeling impotent, feeling I should be doing something to help her but not knowing what. My eyes watered in the cold northerly wind. Beads of moisture rolled down my cheeks.

The flat smelled rank after the fresh air of the meadow. I ran a number five buzz cut over my hair and a five-millimetre trim over the scuzzy beard that had appeared since my capture, put on some office clothes, and saw a deranged stranger staring out of the bathroom mirror. My hair could have been more evenly trimmed; my eyes were red, my skin pasty grey, bruised. But what did it matter? No-one cared.

In the office, Denise's riding accident story had pre-empted any curiosity. No-one asked anything, which suited me fine, I wanted to sink into work and normality. A new project was waiting, a design study for an online payments company. Their idea was that people often want to buy a set of related things from different suppliers, but don't want any of them if they can't have all of them. Like arranging a holiday; you want all the trains, boats, accommodation, car hire and so on to be available for the right dates at reasonable prices before you say okay, book the lot. The software would build up the bookings but if any element failed it would unpick the lot and come back to you. I started to rough out a general approach to maintaining contextual information in such multi-server multi-part transactions. I was in the zone, in a comfortable world of intricate hypotheticals. I surfaced when my phone vibrated. It was well past noon.

Caller ID: Naomi. Did I want to speak to her? My mind was still scaffolding a quite different set of considerations and was reluctant to engage with doubt and despair. Voicemail kicked in while I hesitated. I stood, stretched, walked to the stairwell to listen to the message.

'Mick, hi. Just to let you know Ballator's bid won. As expected. Don't know where we go from here. Call me if you want to talk. Bye.'

An impersonal tone, almost bored. Or down and alienated. I didn't know where to go from here either. Except out to lunch.

I picked up the usual from the usual place, took it to a bench near the end of the canal, fed crumbs to a chaffinch and a chirpy crew of sparrows, tried to take stock. My brush with Kimberly seemed like a distant memory. Any small hope I'd had that something would come of it had faded. I'd no idea where I was going with Naomi. And I didn't know where we could go with the Sefton-Shaw thing, now that Ballator owned Glebe Farm. I only knew that if we were going on, it had just got a lot more difficult. I went back to the office, to the comfort of hypotheticals.

I worked late. Went home. Walked Friday. Went to bed.

***

My mobile was throbbing on the bedside table. 07:05. Another Wednesday morning, another call from Naomi. I found myself thinking, Now what? There was a time I'd have been delighted.

The phone gave up, thank Christ. I settled back and began thinking about the kettle. My phone throbbed: Naomi again. I wasn't ready for this, whatever it was, without tea inside me. I let it go to voicemail. I got out of bed, made a mug, took it back to bed. A thought struck: they were doing the muck drop last night. I'd said I'd go along and had completely forgotten.

Never mind.

Naomi left a voicemail.

I had one new message and three saved messages. I played the new one.

'Turn the radio on. Radio Oxford.' She seemed to be sobbing.

Some disaster at the muck drop? What could have gone so badly wrong that she was crying about it?

I found Radio Oxford. Caught the end of a song that must have been annoying in 1967 and was unbearable fifty years later. Then the local news.

First item. 'An Oxford City planner and his wife are believed to have died in a blaze last night at the family home on Boars Hill. Our correspondent Matt Arnold reports from the scene. Matt, can you tell us what you can see?'

'Well, Fiona,' the correspondent said. 'I can see fire crews hosing down the remains of the house and a lot of hazy smoke. Beyond, I can see Oxford, that sweet city with her dreaming spires, to coin a phrase. By the house and on Berkeley Road, blue flashing lights. Police cars, a Major Incident Support Unit, three fire engines, ambulances. A lot of people, looking busy, mostly. Fire-fighters, paramedics, police, crime scene people, around twenty in loose white cover-alls, picking through wreckage, raking the garden. And some men drinking coffee, not in uniform, standing round an old tractor and trailer parked at the end of the Close. Detectives, I think. Because one of them is…'

'Matt, thank you. Do we have any more on what happened?'

'Well, Fiona,' he said. 'Yes. In a way. Detective Inspector Jones gave us a statement earlier this morning. Very brief. Saying they believed that they had two fatalities, both adults. And we don't have this officially, but three survivors, all children. And a dog. I've been talking to a neighbour, Mrs Whitehead, who says that the fatalities are Conrad Sefton-Shaw, who worked at the city council, and his wife Kimberly.'

'Matt, thank you. Have we had verification of this from the authorities?'

'Well, Fiona. No. And the survivors are the couple's teenage son Alasdair, and their twin daughters, Bella and Charlotte, aged five. They're at the hospital, with social services staff. They escaped with the family's dog, a mastiff, and raised the alarm with the neighbours, Mr and Mrs Whitehead, who looked after them until social services arrived.'

'So Matt, the police haven't confirmed the identities of the victims.'

'Well, Fiona. No. Not as such. They all seem very busy actually. Except for the group drinking coffee, who look like they're waiting for something. And we're behind a crime scene tape in the car park of Foxcombe Hall, across the road from the small cul-de-sac where everything is happening. But Fiona. You remember? Two months ago. My first assignment for Radio Oxford.'

'Yes Matt. Is this…'

'Relevant? Well, Fiona. Possibly. There was a protest about developments at Glebe Farm. I interviewed the protestors but the council's representative, Conrad Sefton-Shaw, one of the fatalities here, wouldn't speak to me. The protestors were angry, talking about scheming liars in the dreaming spires. And it occurred to me that…'

'Thank you, Matt, we'll have to leave it there. In other news, a man is being questioned after a woman was allegedly raped on the towpath near Folly Bridge. The Oxford Hospitals Trust has signed a twenty-year management contract covering all the area's hospitals with an American firm, Colorado Facilities Management. And two people are being held at St Aldates Police Station after a muck-spreader coated the facade of city hall at midnight last night. Now the traffic reports from around Oxfordshire. Natasha.'

I reached out, switched off the radio.

I couldn't breathe. Couldn't believe.

I lay on the bed, thumped the mattress, shouted at the ceiling, 'No! No! No!'

It couldn't be. It was just not possible.

I took a deep breath and screamed it out.

I wanted to throw something. I wanted to throw my cup at the wall. I drank the last drops of tea, still warm. It doesn't take long for your world to break.

I decided not to throw the cup. I took it to the kitchen, rinsed it. At least the kids survived, I thought. And the preposterous Lovelump. Though what state they'd be in, what sort of future they had…

Kimberly burned to death? My hands shook. My breath was coming in gulps. I pulled out a handkerchief and mopped my face. She'd been tied to the awful Conrad by modern unreconstructed wifehood, but was breaking free. I'd not seen her since I planted the bug. I'd been missing her, without really being aware of it, these last weeks. I'd miss her forever now.

CHAPTER 45

Where did Conrad's death leave us? It didn't mean Glebe Farm had gone away. We were still in danger from Alleyn and from the police. It all felt meaningless, but doing something might be better than doing nothing. There'd be time for grief later. Tom and Linda were in trouble for the muck drop and might need help. Were the plods holding them?

I phoned St Aldates Police Station, who told me nothing; rang Kanhai, left a voicemail; rang Naomi. Her phone was answered by Andrea. Naomi was in the bathroom – would I like to leave a message?

'Just tell her thanks for the heads-up,' I said. 'It's awful, this business with the Sefton-Shaws. Don't know what to say. Awful.'

'Yes.'

'And tell her I'm trying to track down Tom and Linda. You don't know if they're still in St Aldates, do you? No. Okay. Speak later.'

I put toast on, made more tea. The ping of a text coming in – Kanhai: *t+l bailed by alleyn.*

I rang Glebe Farm, in case they were home already. No answer there, or on their mobiles. I'd try again in an hour.

I dropped Friday with Mrs Swainston and hurried down the steps two at a time, wanting not to be late for work, but unable to think, my head full of a desperate keening high B flat. Out the main entrance and I was hit hard from left and right by heavy shoulders and swinging elbows. Downed, my head bounced off something hard. The garden wall. I was lifted and thrown down. Hands were at my throat, shaking me, banging the back of my head on the concrete path.

They stopped. I played dead.

'Open your eyes.' A man's voice, deep, with a Welsh accent, from the Valleys. Stale coffee breath. Someone hoisted me to my feet, held my arms. I felt myself swaying.

'Open your eyes. Look. ID. Police officers.'

I kept my eyes shut, groaning.

'Give the cunt a caution.'

'You do not have to say anything,' a voice said, behind me. This one was higher pitched, sibilant. Home counties, a trace of trans-Atlantic. Probably the son of a stockbroker from Gerrards Cross. I'd heard the voice before. 'But it may harm your defence if you do not mention something when questioned which you later rely on in court. Anything you do say may be recorded and given in evidence.'

Flecks of Gerrards Cross spittle spattered the back of my neck. I went to wipe them off, but he was pinning my arms. I opened my eyes. *Whoa, better and better.* Valleys's eyes glared into mine across five inches of loathing. Swarthy was the word. Pock-marked. Lank hair, dark, greying. Nose three inches from mine. On its tip, a red zit with a yellow-white crown. I went cross-eyed trying to get it in focus. It looked sore. I fought to keep disgust from my face, probably unsuccessfully.

Gerrards Cross spoke from behind me. 'In the car, sir?'

'Yeah. Cuffs,' said Valleys, turning away.

I couldn't remember his name, but Gerrards Cross was the cop who'd interviewed me in the hospital, months ago. I could have given him some helpful advice. Like, don't be Mr In-Between. Get rid of the moustache, or grow a beard. Have your hair short, or long. Dress comfortable, or look sharp. But I didn't.

They pushed me into the back of a scruffy Skoda Superb. Gerrards Cross drove to the police HQ in Kidlington, swiped through two barriers into a half-empty car park, swiped through automatic doors. We went up two flights of stairs, Valleys breathing heavily, lagging. We swiped through more doors and went down a long corridor, through double doors marked Specialist Pro-Active Team into a large, empty, open-plan office and on to a small, windowless cubicle, one of three in the near right corner of the room. They went out and locked the door.

My new cell: solid pine door, splashed top to bottom with something dark and sticky; metal grill at head height, shutter behind it; wooden-topped table, scratched, graffitied, coffee rings, more sticky stains, metal legs bolted to the floor; two chairs, same style and condition.

I sat on one, my back to the door, my elbows on the table, my head in my hands. Why was I here? What was going on? My fingers probed bumps, blood, throbbing bits of scalp. I began "in two three four five, out two three four five" breathing and felt my heart slowing.

There was a sound behind me: the hatch in the door sliding open. I closed my eyes, heard the hatch close and the door open. Two people entered, not Valleys or Gerrards Cross. Neither spoke. They raised me to my feet, moved me away from the furniture, spun me round. I opened my eyes. A man and a woman, both in uniform. The man seemed to be happy in his work, the woman less so. They sat me down again, took away my phone, belt, shoes, watch, wallet, notebook. They made me sign a list and left.

A few minutes later the hatch slid open again, then closed – somebody checking, like suicide watch. I started counting seconds. At three hundred and twenty the hatch opened and closed again. Five minutes. Counted again. At three hundred and some it opened again. I started counting hatch openings. After twelve, about an hour gone. Another twelve. Two hours. Another. Three hours.

I had my mantra going. Despite everything I felt joy bubbling up from the deep well that meditation taps into, when it's working. I decided to get as deep as I could, ignore these oiks, say nothing, engage not at all.

The hatch opened for the ninety-fourth time and Valleys and Gerrards Cross came in. They were straight into quick-fire questions. 'Do you know Conrad Sefton-Shaw? Kimberly Sefton-Shaw? Have you ever visited Springfield House in Boars Hill? Have you ever visited the Murdoch Alleyn offices in Summertown? Do you know James Alleyn? What do you know about a company called 4G? What about Arrow Technologies? S4S? Who do you know in Berlin? Have you ever visited 10cc Bikes in Dorchester?'

Interesting. S4S was the make of that smoke detector. Arrow Technologies was where Kanhai sourced the bug. How did they know that? From Alleyn, who'd found it?

Disengagement would be easier if I didn't hear the questions. I sat up, straight-backed, eyes closed, smiling, mantra ticking away internally. I let loose externally with Om, an octave above bottom E, starting deep in my abdomen and booming out. Feeling how close the golden inner light was. Let the joyous noise swell, let my soul walk in beauty.

They asked and asked again. Shouted. Pushed me off the chair. Picked me up, held me horizontal, dropped me. I stayed limp. I kept the mantra going, Om booming, eyes clamped shut, beaming like a lighthouse.

The atmosphere slowly changed. Gerrards Cross was kicking me, repeatedly but half-heartedly.

'What time is it?' Valleys asked.

'Half five, just gone,' Gerrards Cross said.

Nine hours since they bounced me outside the flats. I'd had enough of this.

'I've had enough of this,' Valleys said. 'Get him out of here.'

Gerrards Cross hoisted me off the floor, held me upright.

I opened my eyes. Valleys had his face in mine again. It was unbearable. I shut my eyes.

'Listen, you. You're not going to get away with this crap. We'll pull you in. Any time. Midnight. Three in the morning. For the next five days. Or weeks. And we'll give you hell. Until you talk. We know you know stuff. And you're going to give it up.'

'We'll get your girlfriend in too,' Gerrards Cross said. 'The lovely Ms Goodman. Give her some of the same. Or something different.'

I opened my eyes, caught a bristly leer. I felt sick and closed them again, then raised the Om boom to maximum.

'Get him the fuck out of here,' said Valleys.

***

I limped out to the main road, past the Mayflower Chinese, along to the bus stop. I had some sore bits but nothing broken. There was not much damage to visible bits. They'd been careful. And it had taken my mind off Kimberly and her family for a while.

I caught a Number 2 to First Turn, walked the ten minutes to the flat. I collected Friday, evading questions from Mrs Swainston, and emailed Denise in the office to apologise for taking an inadvertent day off. I fed the dog and took her for a walk. I was pleased with how close I'd felt to the golden light. I'd begun to think that touching it had been more to do with Eric's narcotic cocktail than with meditation, but now I was sure I could get there without drugs.

I turned on Radio Oxford for the news, asking myself why the plods were interested in me – in us, what they knew about our connections with the Sefton-Shaws and how they knew it, what they suspected, whether anyone else had been 'questioned'.

My phone pinged – Kanhai: *intros aldermans 630 tomozz.*

His friendly ear in the force, thank God. Sent a confirmation. The fire was no longer the lead item on the news, pushed back by breaking news about Colorado FM's takeover of local hospitals: the company was better known for managing casinos. The fire story followed: 'Police have not yet named the victims, but neighbours report that they are Conrad Sefton-Shaw, fifty-two, director of sustainable development at the city council, and his wife Kimberly Sefton-Shaw, thirty-seven, actor, dancer and businesswoman. Their oldest child Alasdair, twelve, is in hospital under observation. The couple's twin girls, Bella and Charlotte, five, escaped unharmed and are in the care of social services. A police spokesperson described the circumstances leading up to the fire as unexplained. They are releasing no more information pending forensic results and further enquiries.'

Actor, dancer and businesswoman. Did I know anything about her?

And Alasdair, alive but poorly. Who would be going to see him?

I sent a text to Naomi, saying to look out. I thought about contacting the others, but I just couldn't. The fire, the deaths. Terrible in every way. And it was beginning to dawn on me that people might think I had something to do with it. I couldn't bear it.

I brewed up a couple of crushed green seed-heads from my pot of purple poppies and took a large mug to an early bed. I couldn't stop puzzling about what had actually happened in that house.

***

Thursday passed slow and sombre in the office. I kept fighting off hellish imaginings of the fire. I couldn't stop picking at a Kimberly-shaped hole in my soul. I felt numb and guilty and quite unsure of how I was supposed to be feeling.

I got to the Alderman's at half six for Kanhai's introductions. The phenomenological barmaid had left, replaced by a small man with big biceps. I took a pint over to join Kanhai and his friend by

320

the window. Kanhai introduced Detective Sergeant Angus Grant, then left us to it.

Grant looked to be in his fifties, medium tall with short grey hair, a deep tan and laughter lines radiating from steady grey eyes. I was nervous about meeting another policeman after yesterday's bruising experiences but Grant looked like a fish from a different kettle. Traces of the Highlands were evident from his first word and his opening gambit seemed candid enough. He'd known Kanhai's father since transferring from Inverness to Oxford in the 1980s. They'd been neighbours in Kidlington. He'd known Kanhai most of his life. 'I gave him a reference for the job at TVP,' Grant said. 'He tells me he trusts both of us, and we can trust each other, because we both know how to keep our mouths shut. I'm inclined to believe him.'

'Yes. I see,' I said, looking at him, trying to decide whether he was what he seemed, a nice guy who happened to be a policeman, or the good cop part of a "good cop, bad cop, even worse cop" trio involving yesterday's clowns.

'Och well, fair enough, you're giving little away there,' Grant said. 'But listen. He's done favours for both of us. Of a nature that there's an assurance of mutual destruction, if anything comes out. For me and for him. And for you, he says. So it won't. Okay?'

'Okay with me, yes,' I said, not sure what I was agreeing to.

Grant nodded. 'And before we start,' he said. 'I need to just check that you had nothing to do with that fire.'

'No. No I didn't.' I was aware of his scrutiny. 'Certainly not directly. I feel guilty because I think that if we – if I – hadn't started meddling, if I'd left the Glebe Farm stuff alone, then perhaps the fire wouldn't have happened. I don't know why I think that. No evidence at all. But no, I had nothing to do with it in any direct sense.' I didn't know what happened to the smoke detector after Alleyn found the bug in it, but didn't see how that could be my responsibility.

'Good.' He leaned back, stretching legs out under the table. 'One thing that Kanhai's doing for me, just so you know – he's keeping me in the game by adjusting my records on the HR system. So I haven't yet appeared on the list of who's due to retire in the next year, which comes out every April. Och, somebody will spot it eventually, but I can't see how it can be traced to me – I haven't touched anything. And Kanhai says he's left no fingerprints in the system, so it'll go down as admin error or software glitch.'

'Why do you want to stay in the game?' Surely most people at Grant's time of life would be longing for retirement.

'Partly I just love it. Some of it, anyway. And I've nothing much else to do, that I want to do. My wife left, took off with a fireman twenty years since, give or take. She turned the kids against me. Well, against both of us. Until she died, last year. I see a bit more of the kids now. I do a bit of gardening, and I go fishing now and then. But you can't go fishing every day, can you? You'd soon get fed up with it.'

I'd never considered going fishing every day. 'I'm still puzzled,' I said, 'why you're keen to carry on policing, and why Kanhai thought it appropriate to introduce us.'

Grant pulled out an empty pipe, which he sucked on intermittently and absent-mindedly. 'The answer to both those questions really comes down to the same thing, if you really want to know. And remember, this is just between us. It's not the sort of thing I'd want my name attached to publicly. Or even privately, beyond these walls. Okay?'

'Okay, yes.' I was still unsure about where we were going, but so far it seemed like one-way traffic, from Grant to me, and I could cope with that. And he seemed happy to be doing all the giving, for the moment.

'It's to do with priorities,' he said. 'In the force and the CPS and the courts. The way I think of it, there are four main types of offender. There's the nutters. Psychopaths, who can spring from anywhere in society, any class. They just really love hurting people. They're high-profile but low incidence. There's the low-lifes. Like an underclass, criminality part of their culture. They love

TV soaps and being unpleasant on Facebook. Trolling, though they wouldn't know that's what it's called. If they read at all, it's poisonous garbage like the Sun, Express, Mail. Hopeless really. They hate anybody that's not in their own little bubble. They'd hate themselves too if they could only see themselves. But do they engage in that sort of reflection?'

'I'm guessing not.'

'No, they do not. Awful people. Most of our time goes on them and their nonsense. If you took the costs – police time, CPS, courts, probation and so on – and gave it to them instead, in cash, and said look, stop the nonsense, here's your share, we'll pay you to just go home and stay home and stop it; if they did, you'd save a lot of trouble.'

'Wouldn't you need an army of social workers and educators, re-training schemes, investment in jobs and so on? Because aren't they just people who've been badly brought up, badly educated? There but for the grace of God, and all that.'

'Well, perhaps. A lot of it is values. What's right, what's wrong, what's important. You get it with your mother's milk, if you're lucky. It's much harder to shift later. You'd be needing a permanent Labour government for that. And of course, the great mass of ignorant pillocks that keep the toffs in power are just this sort of low life. It's a self-perpetuating sub-culture of ignorance.'

'Well,' I said, 'I never expected to hear a policeman talking like that. You'll be a Labour man then?'

'Through and through.' He grinned. 'Joined when Michael Foot became leader. I'm union rep at the station. But even Kanhai wouldn't know that I'm branch secretary for the party, for North Oxfordshire.'

'You mentioned four main types of criminal. What are the others?'

'There's the accidentals,' Grant said. 'Ordinary people who are almost inadvertent lawbreakers. Take a chance on bulking up an insurance claim until it becomes fraudulent, try-ons like that. To the average punter, if the victims are corporate, there's no victim. But to the company that's losing out, it's money straight on to the bottom line if they can cut it down a bit. And these corporates have the ear of government and local authorities. And can influence police priorities.'

'So those three types, nutters, low-lifes and accidentals, take up what? Seventy per cent of police time? Eighty?'

'I'd put it at ninety-nine point nine nine. Round here, anyway.'

'So the other nought point nought one per cent?'

'Professionals. White collar crime, serious fraud. Often people with political connections.'

'Do those connections somehow steer police time away from this type then?'

'Well, it does get attention in the Met; they have specialist units there. But it gets next to none here. Except what I put in off the clock, with a bit of technical help from you-know-who. We can't do much by way of prosecution, that takes resources. But a word in the ear, so they know we know what's going on, sometimes makes them tidy up their act a wee bit. It's clever, capable people. Wealthy already, but wanting more. With professional advisors and friends in high places. The first problem is to separate out the illegal from the legal-but-close-to-the-edge. The force won't put effort in when it's likely charges won't stick. Even if they're charged and found guilty, it'll be a fine that's small change to them, or community service and a warning. Meaning, be more careful in future.'

'Surely people get put away sometimes, don't they?'

'About once every two decades. But even then, all they have to do is pretend to go senile and they're out. Like that guy, you're probably too young to remember – CEO of a big multi-national. Guilty of fraud in the hundreds of millions. Sent down for five years. Out in a few months, because he had Alzheimer's. How did they know?'

'Dunno. Was he something to do with beer?'

'Dry stout. They knew he was going senile because he couldn't count backwards. He couldn't open a door. He didn't know who was president of the US. Couldn't possibly have been putting it on, could he? So he gets out and what do you know? Full recovery in no time. Well. He was one of the unlucky ones. Mostly they pull strings early enough to head off any trouble. But it's gentlemen of his ilk that you've got involved with, if Kanhai's telling me right. It's the chance to get after them that keeps me in the force. And it's because Kanhai knows that about me, and knows something about what you've been up to, that makes him think we can help each other. So what do you think? Are you going to fill me in?'

I looked at Grant looking back at me. I trusted Kanhai completely. Kanhai trusted this man, and vice-versa. 'A couple of things,' I said. 'First, how do you get on with those guys I was talking to yesterday? Or rather, wasn't talking to.'

'DI Jones, wasn't it? Daft Dafydd. Not your biggest fan, is he? Sort of my boss. Hard bastard. Known to cut the odd corner. Funny thing is,' Grant said, taking a sip, looking at the ceiling, 'he's quite the family man too. Lovely wife, an artist, quite other-worldly. And two kids he dotes on. So there is another side to him. Not that you see it in the job.'

'I had him down as from the Valleys. Has he been here long?'

'Not as long as me. No-one has.' He sighed. 'He transferred up from Cardiff ten years ago. I wish he'd go back. And take DC Clappison with him. That one's a bright spark. Post-grad fast-track. A right arse-licking little toad. Did you like his moustache?'

'Not much. From Gerrards Cross?'

'Stoke Poges. He drinks cappuccino, so there's often a rim of dried froth on it. Known as Shep, because he trots along at his master's heels and gazes soulfully at him in meetings. God, they're a pair.'

'So you don't exactly work hand-in-glove with them?'

'No I don't. And in case you're wondering, they don't know

I'm here, they won't hear anything about what we say here, and I wouldn't give them the skin off my porridge.'

Grant came across as a very genuine guy. I had one more worry to explore. I thought I knew what the answer was going to be, but had to ask: 'If I fill you in on what we've been up to, I might kind of incriminate myself. And some friends. What are the chances of keeping our names out of it?'

'I don't know,' Grant said. 'I can promise to do my best. I'd have a better idea if I knew what you've got.'

I felt not a trace of suspicion. It would have been easy for him to give a false promise, but he hadn't. He'd been open and honest. I realised that I trusted Grant and liked him. 'I'll send you our dossier,' I said. 'Have you got a secure email?'

***

It was a close, humid Friday morning. The flat smelled sour, in need of a good clean. Later. I took breakfast to bed and was reaching for a book when my phone pinged. A text from Kanhai, saying Linda and Tom had been picked up again and were at the police station on St Aldates. There was no point ringing to enquire. I'd drop in on the way to work, see what I could find out face to face.

I arrived at the front desk just before nine, a bit nervous after Wednesday's encounter with Valleys and Gerrards Cross, aka Jones and Clappison. But this was a different police station, one I'd never been to, and I'd not done anything all that wrong.

I was surprised at how busy it was and how deeply miserable everyone looked. It took half an hour and more good-natured patience than came naturally to learn that I couldn't see them. They were being processed, whatever that meant.

Could I leave them a message?

I could, and left one asking them to call me as soon as possible.

I went on to the office. I was late again, after missing Wednesday altogether. I had my head well down when Tom called at eleven, sounding very tired. They were out, all charges dropped. Could I meet them for a quick chat?

They were in a corner of MacDonald's on Cornmarket. It was surprisingly busy, like the police station, and everyone seemed just as miserable. But it was noisy and anonymous.

'We're not supposed to be talking to you. Or Andrea. Or any of you,' Linda said, looking like she'd much that.

'But we had to let you know,' Tom said. 'We're out of it. That lawyer, Alleyn, came to see us yesterday, at the farm. He said... what did he say?'

'He'd act for us pro bono,' Linda said.

'Yes. Meaning he'd be our lawyer, for free, basically. On condition.'

'On condition,' Linda said, 'that we have no contact with you lot. That we stop protesting. And that we take their offer. Money and jobs. Move to Witney and shut up. And if we do that we'll be out and free and all charges dropped. It's not justice, we know that. But it's better than losing everything and going to prison.'

'They fetched us early this morning – two police, a man and a woman,' Tom said. He looked completely defeated. 'Took us to St Aldates. Charged us with criminal damage. Obstruction. Resisting arrest. Something else... what was it?'

'Actions proscribed by the Terrorism Act 2006,' Linda said. 'Apparently we could get twenty years just for that.'

'That's right. They said we could phone someone and suggested him, Alleyn. He came straight away, said the deal was still on offer. We told him we'd take it. He talked to the detectives for us and they let us go, just before I called you. We have to clear our stuff out of Glebe Farm today, all of it. Move into this place near Witney, this afternoon. It's like a gatehouse on an estate. He's sending a removals van and some help. We can still do our farm sale, through an auctioneer mate of his. We've signed the papers and they'll take care of everything. We don't even have to go back there for it. In fact, we can't. We can't go back there at all, after today. And we can't talk to your lot about it. Or the papers. Or anybody else come to that. Never.'

Tom looked more puzzled than angry.

I was sceptical about how helpful Alleyn's help was likely to be. 'Thanks for letting me know,' I said. 'And good luck. You're taking a risk just meeting me, aren't you? So I won't hang around. I'll let the others know. You can always call us, don't forget. Because you never know.'

I stood and shook Linda's hand, then Tom's. I had to ask. 'Alleyn. Do you trust him?'

They both looked away.

***

I called Naomi on my way back to the office.

'I just had two bloody horrible detectives here,' she said. 'Inspector Jones and Constable Clap. I just kept saying I didn't have to answer their questions and I didn't know anything. They got a bit pushy. I said I hoped they didn't mind, I was recording our conversation on my mobile. They looked like they wanted to grab it and stomp it flat but I started to do a commentary and they left, looking furious.'

'I'd like to hear that. Can you send it to me on Signal? That'll back it up too, so if they try to wipe your phone it'll be safe.'

'Already done. Stop mansplaining.'

'Okay,' I said. 'Okay. Thank you. And well done. I saw them on Wednesday, did I tell you? Wish I'd thought of your phone trick. What were they asking?'

'How do we know each other, you know? You, me, Andrea, Tom, Linda, Gail. Is there anyone else? What brought us together, what we've been doing, what we're trying to achieve. Do I know the Sefton-Shaws? Ever been to their house? Ever been to Glebe Farm, Murdoch Alleyn, Ballator, uni property services? Who do I know in Berlin? And so on.'

'They asked me about Berlin. What's that got to do with anything?'

'That's your mum. You know they put trackers on our cars? Kanhai found them first and warned us. Your mum took one from Gail's car. Chatted up some Germans who were driving home that day in a posh new Merc. Slipped the tracker under a wheel arch.'

*****

I found an annoyed Denise waiting for me in the office. I apologised for spending more time out of it than in but that wasn't the problem. It was my visitors that had upset her: two policemen, big, angry, unpleasant. I was to call DC Clappison at my earliest convenience.

I did, and was immediately on my way back to St Aldates Police Station. On the way I called Gail to warn her of what might be coming her way. The others already knew.

The police station was still busy. I was told to take a seat and wait to be called.

I took a seat and waited.

It was noisy and dirty. Late morning sun came through the windows behind me, lighting sections of tiled floor. The pattern of light and shade moved round, shrinking until one o'clock, then slowly stretching further across the room. I was expecting a verbal and physical pummelling from Jones and Clappison. Every hour of waiting was softening me up for them.

At two o'clock I asked at the desk. Someone would see me shortly.

At quarter past three a woman approached. Stout, fifty-ish, reeking of tobacco and instant coffee. She was wearing a dark red jacket, black skirt, patches of dust on her elbows; her keys and glasses were strung round her neck with an ID card that I couldn't read.

'Michael Jarvis?' she asked.

'Yes.'

'Come with me, please.'

I followed her through double doors, down a long brick-lined corridor painted in pale mint-green gloss, up a flight of stairs, along another minty corridor then left through an archway. A printed sign said 'Fingerprinting Section', with a hand-written card, 'Biometric Research Centre', sellotaped on top.

She stopped at a door labelled 'Section Manager'. She unlocked it, ushered me in and directed me to a blue plastic chair in front of a cluttered desk. She sat behind the desk.

'What's going on?' I asked, still standing. 'I was asked to come here immediately. By DC Clappison. Four and a half hours ago.'

'Sit down, please,' she said. 'I don't know anything about that. I was asked to do your biometrics,' she glanced at her watch, 'ten minutes ago. So if you could just sign this form.'

She pushed a clipboard towards me, with a biro and a form headed Biometrics Consent BRC8c.

'What am I signing for?'

'Just to say that we can take your biometrics for use in research and investigations.'

'What are my biometrics, anyway?'

'Oh, just height, weight, some body and face measurements, cheek swabs, blood sample, fingerprints, retina scan, that sort of thing.'

She spoke fast, slurring the words as if she said them several times a day.

'For use in research? What sort of research?'

'Research and investigations,' she said. 'Mostly investigations. Criminal cases, usually.'

'Do I have to sign this?'

'No sir, of course not,' she said, sitting back with almost a smile. She'd been here before. 'Although in the context of an investigation... Let me just remind myself what the actual context is.'

She woke up her PC, clicked and typed.

'Ah yes, the fire up on Boars Hill. Two fatalities. Not a criminal investigation. Yet. They're just trying to find out what happened. But in general, sir, refusal to provide biometrics voluntarily may be interpreted, sir. To your detriment.'

'To my detriment? What does that mean?'

'Just that it might be considered suggestive of involvement, sir. Or guilt. Or just that you've something to hide. And you'll understand, sir, that lots and lots of prints and DNA traces and what-not have been collected from around that site. And so if you had nothing to do with it, your biometrics will serve to eliminate you from enquiries. And any data gathered will of course be destroyed at the end of the investigation. Provided you're not found guilty of something, of course.'

She laughed.

I echoed. 'Ha ha.'

'If you're worried, sir,' she said, 'I can call someone down to explain.'

'Oh no, that's not necessary.'

'I just need to check something, sir. Please stay where you are.'

She left the room. I leaned across and had a look at her display: a screensaver of swirling patterns. I hit a key. It was password protected. Blast.

Footsteps. I sat back in the blue chair, looking at the ceiling.

'So just to be clear, sir,' she said, resuming her seat. 'It would probably be best for you to sign the form and give us the samples and so on voluntarily. Because, well, I just checked with the colleague of Inspector Jones who put in the request. And he says that if you refuse, you could become a person of interest in relation to the fire and the deaths. In which case they would require you to assist with their enquiries. In which case we'd collect your biometrics anyway, and it could mean holding you. Only until they can eliminate you, of course.' She paused. 'If they can. And if they can't, well. Two suspicious deaths, they could probably hold you for up to thirty-six hours without charge. And then they'd have to let you go. Or charge you. Or get an extension. Unlikely to be a problem in a case like this.'

'Oh, all right. Give me the form.'

I signed with a flourish.

She took the clipboard back, removed the form and looked at it. She tore it up and threw it in the bin.

'Really, sir,' she said. 'Mickey Mouse? Pathetic.'

She pushed another form across the desk.

CHAPTER 46

That evening in the pub I sat side by side with my new friend from the constabulary at a table by the window, our backs to the bar, watching dusk fall over a line of moored narrowboats. Smoke drifted from their chimneys.

'I read your dodgy dossier,' Grant said. 'Interesting. No use in court, of course, your methods being a tad outwith the law. But it shows you were on to something. Fraud, at least. Conspiring to commit an unlawful act. I can use it to drip-feed a few suggestions to colleagues. Where to look, what to look for.'

'Good. But you won't say where the suggestions came from?'

I'd been thinking about my encounter with Grant's colleagues on Wednesday. I still didn't know how they'd connected me to Naomi and the others. But DI Jones would no doubt see us in a different light if he knew the extent and nature of our interest in Conrad and his cronies. And if he dug a bit he might see that we couldn't have set up the surveillance without help, and that our only associate with the relevant know-how was Kanhai. Kanhai with his wife and baby, his job and mortgage, his normal life that he trusted me not to jeopardise.

'Not likely,' Grant said. 'Anonymous source. We all have them.'

'Right. Thanks.' I wasn't sure whether to take the "not likely" to mean "no chance", or to take it literally, meaning possible but not probable. It was ambiguous. Perhaps that's what he intended. I was also unsure about becoming an anonymous source. Unpleasant phrases came to mind: "copper's nark", "stool pigeon". I'd read about sources being heroically protected against all threats, but also about them being given up under pressure, or inadvertently, through some slip. Either way, supposedly anonymous sources could end up being thrown to the wolves.

The more information I could get out of Grant, the more the threat of mutually assured destruction would come into play; and if I was going to get anything at all out of him, I'd have to accept all this ambiguity and uncertainty. I could only press on. 'You were saying you'd had sight of the report on the fire?'

'Yes. Well, I helped write it actually. The first draft, that is, of the police part. We're still working on it, obviously. Early days yet. But the fire people have done their bit. That made interesting reading.' He broke off, gestured with his empty glass, went to the bar to fetch two more pints. He could tell a story – he'd hardly started and left a cliff-hanger already. He came back, set down the drinks, sat, fiddled with his unlit pipe, took a swallow of beer.

'Thanks,' I said.

'*Bitte.*' He chuckled to himself. 'That's a sort of bilingual pun, isn't it?'

'The draft report?' Was I punning too? 'What did it say?'

'Right. Well, it seems the fire started in what you might call the sitting room, at the eastern end of the house, looking out over the back garden. Right under the parents' bedrooms. There was an open fireplace, wooden fire surround, log basket. Actually, have you been there?'

'Yes,' I said, quickly thinking which of my visits to admit to. 'Weird, actually. Me and Gail went to scout the place, to work out how to bug it. Pretending to be Jehovah's Witnesses. They'd sussed me though, in a way. Or Kimberly had.'

I'd been avoiding thinking about Kimberly.

'She sent Gail upstairs to see Conrad in his study, where some sort of hanky-panky got started, apparently, that Gail refuses to talk about. But Kimberly took me in the sitting room. There was this thing about how she'd fancied me for ages, from seeing me at the bus stop on the school run. She thought that was why I was there. So yes, I can picture it. Go on, please.'

'So it's not impossible that some of the unidentified prints in there might be yours?'

'Not impossible at all, no.' I was thinking, *Oh fuck*.

'Hmmm.' He gave me an old-fashioned look. 'Good to hear you say that. Because since you visited fingerprinting yesterday, they've managed to match some of the unidentified prints. To yours.'

'I see,' I said, feeling the ground shifting beneath me. 'Where were they, then? My prints. Any idea?'

'Several places. The front gate. On a bottle in that sitting room. A window catch. Other places.'

He was looking steadily at me, clearly expecting a response, perhaps more about when and why I'd been in these places. I just nodded, doing my best to maintain a neutral expression.

'Okay,' he said, after what seemed like a long silence. 'The sitting room. Internal stud walls, plasterboard on wood frames, insulation on the external walls that was billed as fire-retardant but produces toxic smoke then catches fire if it gets really hot. All up to building regulations when it was built, but not now. The log basket was full. They kept a pack of firelighters and a big box of matches in the basket. That was the source of the fire. It started in the corner of that room, but it was when it broke through into the hall and stairwell that it really took off. A lot of the ground floor wasn't much damaged. Upstairs was, though.'

'Hang on,' I said, thinking of going in there with a Bible in my hand, a Bible that I'd read from cover to cover in my teens, between *The Lord of the Rings* and *The Catcher in the Rye*. Thinking of a stylised sky-blue tree and embroidered mandalas. 'Lots of people have that sort of set-up with a log basket by the fire,' I said. 'My parents used to. They don't all burn down.' I wondered how much he knew and would be prepared to tell, how much I should be prepared to tell him.

'No. This one did though.' His eyes held mine. 'What I'm going to tell you is confidential. Must not be repeated. Not to anybody. Until the report is published – which it won't be until we have answered a few more questions. Okay?'

I nodded.

'Okay. Box of matches. Someone struck seven matches that didn't take, which dropped on the hearth. Then one took, which they put back in the box, so the rest of the matches caught too. Must have been like a small explosion. Put the box next to the firelighters, maybe dropped it. The firelighters caught, ignited the logs, and it was away.'

Grant paused again, sipped his beer, fiddled with his pipe.

I was struggling to see how it could have come about by accident. But speculation was useless without knowing more, and having finally got Grant going, trying to hurry him would be counter-productive. I took a swallow of beer and waited.

'We don't know who struck those matches,' Grant said. 'But there's little doubt it was arson. So manslaughter. Or murder.'

'Murder.' Jesus Christ. The sleeping house. Some malevolent spirit approaching, bringing death. I knew the Sefton-Shaws didn't set intruder alarms at night, so anyone able to pick a lock or spring a window catch could get in. 'Why do you say murder?'

Conrad Sefton-Shaw may have been the target. He had cocked up, abducting me then letting me escape. And just as all the guys who worked for him were ruled by fear of him, he was ruled by fear too, of someone else. Sefton-Shaw's role could be protecting his guys from this malevolent spirit, who had zero tolerance for cock-ups, and who, having seen Sefton-Shaw make one, took him out.

But if not... had one of my own gone beyond the pale? Not Naomi, surely. She'd alerted me to the news on the radio on Wednesday morning. Would she have done that? Something stopped that speculation in its tracks. It couldn't have been Naomi.

Gail could have decided to avenge her mother. She had an aristocratic sense of entitlement. Her mother had been her whole life, until Conrad's carelessness initiated her decline. But surely if she was out to get Conrad, she would have been sure to get just him. I couldn't see her as an indiscriminate killer.

What about the others? Linda wouldn't have struck the match. But keeping watch while Tom did it, that was possible. And Tom was used to having the power of life and death over his fellow creatures, and to using it. Though he surely wouldn't have faffed around using eight matches to start a fire. Unless he was working in the dark.

Timing was an issue too. I didn't have a handle on it, but it was the same night they'd done the muck drop in the city centre. They'd been arrested immediately afterwards. I couldn't see them organising themselves to burn a house down and then do the muck drop, one after the other.

But they'd been organised by Andrea. And Andrea was no stranger to extremes and no respecter of the law. She saw no reason for human beings to assume superiority over other beings. Could she have decided on an eye for an eye, a family of humans for a family of dormice? I tried to make myself believe it was impossible. It wasn't long since we almost dined together in my bathroom... Reflecting on what I'd learned about her since, I shuddered. Of all of them, Andrea stood out as the most likely candidate, with or without Tom and Linda's help.

'They're thinking murder because two people died in a fire that seems to have been started deliberately,' DS Grant said. 'And for some reason they have you in their sights. Possibly someone high up is leaning on Daffy for a quick result and you're his best bet. But there were two really odd circumstances. One, there was a

337

mount for a smoke detector in the room where it started, but the detector itself was missing. The daily thinks she might have seen it in a bin, a few weeks ago, but wasn't sure. Yes, what is it?'

My face must have betrayed something. Better be up front. 'That was where we had the bug,' I said. 'The smoke detector in that room. You saw the transcript? The last thing it picked up was…'

'Yes, Alleyn finding it. And disabling it, maybe just stomping on it. Okay. So Alleyn smashed it and Sefton-Shaw didn't get round to replacing it. Explaining the missing smoke detector and why the fire had such a hold before anyone woke up. Thanks.'

'Makes me feel responsible.'

'You're not responsible for maintaining their alarms. And two,' he said. 'The parents slept in a separate suite, almost half the top floor. Entered from the landing. Inside the suite, there are doors off into two bedrooms, each with en suite, plus dressing room for her. Both bodies were at the door to the landing, inside the suite. The door was locked. Looks like they were trying to get out, but couldn't. No sign of a key.'

'Oh Christ.' The horror of it filled me up. Trapped and unable to do anything about it. As a child, my mum had drilled it into me. Never go to sleep without knowing how to get out if there's a fire. 'I don't know anything about the layout,' I said. 'Never been up there.'

'Gail had been upstairs though?'

'Yes. Just to Conrad's study.'

'As far as you know,' Grant said.

I shook my head, tears pricking my eyes. I was conscious of Grant watching me, as if weighing up something. The implications of Gail having been upstairs? Whether to say more, ask more? I pulled myself back into dispassionate enquiry mode. The key, Grant had mentioned.

'Did they usually lock it, then?' I said.

'The daily says the key was always on a hook by the door. As far as she knew they never locked it. But there's no key. If they'd locked themselves in they'd have been able to get out.'

'Or it would still be there, in the lock.' I was trying to imagine what it would have been like, how it could have happened. 'So someone locked them in. Took the key away. And started the fire. And that's why it could be murder?'

'Yes,' Grant said. 'If they were killed by an arsonist who just meant to burn their house down, but who thought they weren't there or that they'd be able to get out, you might think manslaughter. But if someone locked them in their rooms and then started a fire underneath, that would point to...'

'... murder, yes.' I gulped some beer. *Stick to the facts, to the surface*, I told myself. *Don't cry.* 'So when was all this happening?'

'One thirty to three. Most likely between two and half past. It was well on its way when the neighbours called it in around three. We really need to find that damned key,' he said, then stopped. He seemed to have sunk into morose introspection.

I felt my tension go down a notch. At least that timing removed Tom and Linda from the equation; they had been in holding cells at St Aldates Police Station. It made it more difficult to put Andrea in the frame. She'd hung around with her journalist buddies after the midnight muck drop. Could she have gone up to Boars Hill, broken in, locked the parents up and started the fire by half past two? It didn't seem plausible. And surely it had to be someone who knew the layout of the house. In our crew, that was me and Gail. I hadn't done it. That left Gail. I could just about see her seeing off Conrad, but she'd never put the children's lives at risk, I was certain.

'What about the children?' I asked. 'They said the boy was kept in hospital, poor little sod. He wasn't locked in as well, was he?'

'I'll get to that,' Grant said. 'So you come up the stairs, the parents' suite is to the left. In the middle of the house, there's two rooms, front and back. Front was her studio. For photography. And tanning. And...'

'Tanning?'

'Yes. Sun-bed. Set up like an in-house beauty parlour. Plus costumes and... toys, you know... and, well, all sorts.' Grant frowned, coloured. 'And at the back, his office. Also quite a set-up. Desk and computer and that. Then more dressing-up stuff. Masks. Gimp masks, they call them, apparently. Always thought a gimp was an erratic sort of limp, but there you go. And lots of black leather. With studs. And black rubber clothing. For men. In various sizes.'

'You were there yourself then?' Despite the gravity of the events, I was amused by Grant's evident discomfort, perhaps due to deep-seated values surviving from his Scottish upbringing. 'Must be odd, that, picking through their leftovers.'

'I was, yes, and it is,' Grant said. 'But that's the police role, looking at the people, trying to get a sense of who they were, what happened to them, why.'

He picked up his pipe, put it down. 'Top of the stairs, to the right, beyond those two rooms, four more bedrooms: two guest rooms, the boy's room, the twins' room right at the end. Two bathrooms. Apparently the dog alerted the twins and they roused the boy from his bed. He was lucky; he already had high levels of carbon monoxide.'

I remembered the boy's awkwardness in his podgy teen body. His disastrous choice in clothes. The cruel treatment he received from his father, which he passed on to his playmates and sisters. He wasn't the pleasantest boy I'd ever met, but what could you expect with parenting like that? And I had a strong feeling he'd begun to rebel against his parents, and could grow into something quite different, as children do. 'What about the twins? Turned out to be heroes!'

'Got themselves and the boy and the dog out through their bedroom window, onto the garage roof. And their teddies. They raised the alarm, knocking on the neighbours' door. The neighbours still have the dog. '

'Who has the kids?'

'Social workers couldn't find any family or friends prepared to look after them, even temporarily. The boy's still in the hospital. The twins are in emergency foster care, in Coventry.'

'Coventry?'

'Yes. Nearest available, I suppose.'

I tried to imagine how they'd felt, being bustled away to hospital, then into the care of strangers in a strange town. 'How were they dressed? When they escaped.'

'I don't know.' Grant looked puzzled. 'Not in the report. Why do you ask?'

'Just curious,' I didn't know why I'd asked, was just trying to picture it. 'If you found the key, what would that tell you?'

'Depends where we find it. We're still looking. Riddling through the ashes, again. Searching across the heath, down drains, all that.'

***

I woke on Saturday morning convinced there was a dead rat under the floorboards. I sniffed from room to room. The hall was worst.

If your neighbours don't mind, 5.30 a.m. isn't a bad time for housework. My cleaning stuff is in a cupboard in the hall. When I opened the door a wave of stomach-churning stench hit me. Two black bin liners had settled in, dripping brown goo onto the vacuum.

How had I forgotten them? The not-yet-examined garbage from Springfield House, collected the night we planted the bug. I could dump them, but what if there was something important in there? Did I care enough? Sorting through them would be awful.

Ab honesto and all that. I opened all the windows, covered the table in newspaper, pulled on rubber gloves and wrapped a damp handkerchief round my nose and mouth. I put the sacks in the bath then cleaned the hall cupboard. Tipping the first sack onto the table was unpleasant but it felt better to be doing something. I didn't waste time. Just pizza boxes and decomposing grot in the first one, which I double-wrapped in new bags and put back in the bath.

A damp clump of stained paper, twenty or so A4 sheets, appeared halfway down the second sack, among takeaway cartons and vacuum cleaner emptyings. Smudgy chromatographs of browns, blues and yellows from inkjet printing.

I teased them apart, looking for anything legible. Three sheets had recognisable text. One had just standard clauses from a Will. The other two were stapled together. I flattened them out. Figures were printed in columns: a spreadsheet, headed Drascombe Golf and Tennis Club Income & Expenditure Account. Very boring pieces of paper. I turned them over. The back of the first was blank. On the back of the second, my name leapt out of four blocks of half-legible handwriting with much crossing out and some parts scribbled over. I read and re-read the legible bits.

Dear Mick,
~~You may be surprised to~~ I hope you don't mind me

Dear Michael,
If you are reading this you'll probably

Mick, hi. I need to ask you a favour. You don't have

Dear ~~Sandra~~ Ms Cleary
Please forgive my conta
out of the blue like th
to nothing, pray God B
to check, get a second o
asked me to express my t
happen to my childr
in the event of my

Could it be Kimberly, drafting a message to me? I'd never received it. And to my mum? What did she want with her? She'd mentioned doing some research, enabled by my business card. Was this it?

I found my evidence file, compared this writing to the 'Dear soon-to-be-ex' message on a bank statement. The 'e's were the same, and distinctive, formed like a Greek epsilon. I worked away at the fragment addressed to my mum. It looked like she'd been working on a will. That might be the context. I made some guesses, probably way off the mark, but possibly plausible, and came up with:

> *Please forgive my conta*cting you
> *out of the blue like th*is. It will most likely come
> *to nothing, pray God. B*ut I wanted
> *to check, get a second o*pinion. My solicitor has
> *asked me to express my t*houghts about what should
> *happen to my childr*en, Alasdair, Bella and Charlotte,
> *in the event of my* death

I closed my eyes and tried to stop shaking. I couldn't help thinking it had a ring of truth. But what on earth did it have to do with my mum?

***

I'd got rid of the source, but the flat was still stinking and I had to get out. I drove over to Cornbury and jogged with Friday through Wychwood, down over the Evenlode, up through Ascott and Chilson. I was broken into brittle pieces by the half-written unsent messages from Kimberly, wanting to drown in sweat and tears.

Eight miles in, endorphins flowing, the mantra of movement was helping. I was running ever more slowly up an ever-steeper slope into the woods above Chilson when my phone rang.

Andrea.

I stopped, glad of a breather.

'Mick, it's awful. Tom's dead.'

I couldn't respond.

'Mick, can you hear me? His new boss found him this morning, in the cottage. OD'd on morphine, apparently. Tom on morphine? Can you imagine? And Linda's disappeared. They can't find her.'

CHAPTER 47

DETECTIVE INSPECTOR JONES

Jones was called to the Commissioner's office "for a quick word". He was relieved to find the Chief Constable there too, leaning on the windowsill.

'Come in, Jones.' The Commissioner spoke from behind a clear desk, waved at a chair. 'Sit. Terrible thing. Terrible. That poor man. Driven to it by worry, I dare say.'

'We don't know it was suicide,' the Chief Constable said.

They'd be talking about the death of Tom Simpson, the recent Glebe Farm tenant. Clappison had taken the call earlier and phoned Jones at home when he realised who the deceased was. Jones was shocked and puzzled. Sudden death rarely made sense, but this came out of the blue; the poor guy had lost his home and his livelihood, but seemed to have found a way of coming out the other side. Clappison was at the scene now, with the SOCOs and uniformed officers. Jones had a funny feeling about it, and would have been there himself but for being called to the bigwigs.

'They could have dealt with it more sympathetically, couldn't they?' the Commissioner said. 'St Mark's. They gave him and his wife practically no notice and no support. Mrs Simpson wrote to me, you know, asking for help. Nothing I could do of course, but still.'

'St Mark's weren't doing anything illegal,' the Chief Constable said. 'And they found them somewhere to move to, didn't they? Or at least their lawyer did. And jobs. And arranged the farm sale, made them a few grand I dare say. Anyway, not our business. Jones, we're discussing arrangements for the inquest. The autopsy is in hand, with Professor Robinson.'

'Yes ma'am.' The farmer's death was sad and surprising, but he couldn't see why the Commissioner and the Chief Constable were involving themselves in it.

'Have you tracked down Mrs Simpson yet?'

'No ma'am. I've got people on it. She'll turn up soon, hopefully.' Though if she wanted to stay hidden, it wasn't going to be easy to find her. He just hoped she didn't turn up dead.

'We don't want it to drag on. When she surfaces, you'll need to get her up to speed straight away.'

'Yes ma'am,' Jones said, feeling put upon. 'I'm not sure that's really my department...'

'Your department, Jones,' the Chief said, 'does what I ask it to. Find the wife, get your hand-holders to hold her hand and get her on board with the inquest arrangements. And your department – in fact, let's say *you* – will be giving evidence. What verdicts would be available to the inquest?'

'You want me to run through them?' She was being uncharacteristically brisk, as if someone had handed her a firework with the fuse fizzing and she wanted to hand it on to someone else, pronto. To him, in fact.

'Yes. Please indicate their likelihood in this case, based on what you know so far.'

'Yes ma'am. The bare facts as we understand them, subject to ongoing investigations and lab reports et cetera: he drank hot chocolate containing a large quantity of morphine. We don't know who made the drink or whether he knew what was in it.'

'That's it?'

'Yes, at present.'

'It's not much,' the Chief said. 'But enough to consider possible inquest verdicts.'

'Very hypothetically,' Jones said. 'So. Natural causes is out.'

'Clearly.'

'Neglect is out. And industrial disease. The possibles are accident or misadventure, suicide, or unlawful killing.'

'So of those possibles,' the Commissioner, Martin Carter, said, 'which would give the best chance of getting this sorted out? Without protracted toing and froing, as it were.'

Jones could see what they wanted, but wasn't sure why they wanted it. 'Verdicts of suicide or unlawful killing have to be proved beyond reasonable doubt,' he said, 'which takes months, years sometimes.'

Protracted toing and froing, in other words. Though his gut was saying unlawful killing was clear favourite. By whom was a different question. They'd have to find Mrs Simpson to get anywhere on that – dead or alive.

'For accident or misadventure,' he continued, 'the test is within the balance of probabilities, much less stringent. And we have cases quite often, especially… well, with street people and so on. Accident or misadventure, alcohol- or drug-related. Coroners are used to it. You could say this case is drug-related.' He didn't like the way this was heading. The farmer just wasn't that kind of person, and if Jones was going to make that verdict stick, he'd have to misrepresent the poor man to the coroner. But that seemed to be what his superiors were asking for. 'Which would make it straightforward,' he said, 'as long as the coroner was satisfied and didn't want to dig further.'

'Thank you, Jones. Very clearly put,' the Commissioner said. 'The coroner will be Lord Tufton QC. My great-uncle Buffy, as it happens. Inquest on Monday. You'll give evidence. And you'll need to liaise with their solicitor about funeral arrangements. Cremation.'

He was being railroaded into things that went right against his professional instincts. And his sense of self-preservation, come to that. But he'd been told. He would make a detailed memorandum of this conversation as soon as he was back in his office. 'Yes, sir,' he said. 'The deceased's solicitor…?'

'James Alleyn,' the Chief Constable said. 'At Murdoch Alleyn in Summertown.'

Of course, Jones thought. *The bastard gets everywhere. But he might have told me.*

He walked slowly back to his office, sunk in thought. A message was on his desk: *Pls call Mr Alleyn asap.*

There was no end to it. Jones locked his door, turned everything off and sat for five minutes, head in hands, thinking how Alleyn had set the hook and reeled him in, all those years ago.

He'd joined the golf club and they'd met there by chance - or so he'd thought. He'd thanked Alleyn for sponsoring his membership, and Alleyn had invited Jones to visit his property in south Oxfordshire to advise on security systems. He'd been happy to take a look. He'd found an enormous new-build stately home set in wooded grounds of ten thousand square metres. He'd spent a couple of evenings working out a spec for the security, but had been surprised to receive a cheque in the post for 'consultancy services'. Only a few hundred pounds, very handy for a half-term holiday with Olwen and the girls, but hardly worth the fuss of filling in a Secondary Business Interests Form to notify the chief constable. So he banked it. And forgot about it.

He'd taken the blasted bait.

Months later, he'd been duty officer in St Aldates Police Station. A man was brought in from Oxford railway station, who looked like an ordinary businessman, a commuter. He'd dropped his briefcase on the platform, right under the nose of a transport police officer. The briefcase had sprung open and the officer knew a shrink-wrapped block of marijuana when he saw one. The man's solicitor was on his way. Jones had just told him it looked like an open and shut case, and was quite pleased with his wit, when Alleyn arrived and asked for a word in private. He walked Jones to the end of the corridor, an arm round his shoulder. Jones wasn't small, but Alleyn had towered over him.

Jones shrugged him off, said, 'Listen, Mr Alleyn...'

Alleyn said, 'No, DS Jones, you listen. You've done favours for me. I've done favours for you. That's how it works. This should be easy. It's not a lot of blow. You could let him go with a caution.'

Jones didn't like it and said so.

'I'm asking nicely,' Alleyn said, 'because we're friends. You don't want to find out how I deal with people who piss me off. Just let him go. Now.'

Jones bridled at that. 'What if I don't want to play that game?' he'd said.

'You're already playing that game. You need to realise which side you're on.'

'What if I blow the whistle?'

'You could try,' Alleyn said. 'Wouldn't recommend it though. You've nothing on me that would stick, but you'd lose your job. And pension. And never work again.'

Jones had seen the bleak reality of it. Alleyn hadn't let him go since.

***

Jones dug a bottle of Tamnavulin and a pack of Rothmans from the back of the filing cabinet. He opened a window and took off his shoes. He poured a stiff one, then put his feet up on his desk and lit up. He'd known this day was coming since he'd learned Alleyn had never been married and his 'wife in labour' story was pure moonshine. But the man had gone into overdrive since the fire and Sefton-Shaw's death. Alleyn and Sefton-Shaw had been close; perhaps Sefton-Shaw had been a restraining hand. Alleyn was becoming erratic and loading more on Jones every day.

He poured another stiff one – whisky from Alleyn, of course – and felt himself arriving at a reluctant but inevitable decision. He used to tell himself he was doing it for his family; now, for his family's sake, it had to stop. He had to put Alleyn in a position from which the lawyer couldn't threaten them. Not now, not ever.

If only he could also put himself in a position where he was safely retired and a long way away. That house on the Gower was still on the market – Olwen never stopped talking about it – but it was beyond their budget, even with Alleyn's contributions. Could he kill two birds with one stone? A couple of weeks ago he'd interviewed Robert Forster, one of the bikers Alleyn used as muscle. Forster was also a chartered accountant at Simms & Denby on Cornmarket. If he was entangled in Alleyn's unorthodox finances too, he'd take the hand off anybody who offered him a way out. And he'd seemed to Jones to be a flexible sort of thinker, prepared to do anything to avoid trouble with the law.

Jones put his shoes on, closed the window, restarted his office machinery, skimmed Forster's statement. The man could produce a lot of words that added up to very little by way of concrete information, a useful skill in what Jones had in mind. His mobile number was there. Jones called it.

'Hello,' someone said.

'Mr Forster?'

'Who's calling?'

Cagey, Jones thought. *Good*. 'DI Jones here, Thames Valley Police. We talked recently.'

'Detective Inspector, yes. How can I help?'

'I'd like an informal chat with you,' Jones said. 'Best not in your office…'

'Er…'

'…or mine. You're in Culham, is it?'

'Yes. Is there a problem?' Forster said.

'There's always problems,' Jones laughed, 'but nothing to worry about. Just background, really. Possibilities and probabilities. I'll explain when I see you. Next Monday? Seven-ish. The Plough, Clifton Hampden.'

'Okay.'

Jones rang off, took a breath. With the call to Forster he'd crossed a Rubicon, set something in motion. He could still call it off, but he felt better already and didn't think he would.

He called Alleyn. 'You were trying to get me earlier,' he said. 'About the dead farmer, is it?'

'Partly. Has his wife shown yet?'

'Not that I've heard. Can I just ask, have you been there, to their new place?'

'Yes,' Alleyn said, sounding cagey.

'When were you last there?'

'Yesterday.'

'Thought as much. You were probably the last to see them. You'll have to talk to Clappison.'

'You're kidding. What news on cause of death?'

'I'll be finding out in a meeting that starts in five. I'll call you later.'

'Make it before lunch. But first, Sefton-Shaw. The fire. You got Jarvis for that?'

'We're looking at him.'

'Do. Conrad hated him, and he was up to all sorts with Conrad and his wife. And speaking of his wife – you got a positive ID yet?'

'Not exactly. We've got DNA on him. The other body's badly burned. Adult female. They're struggling to get DNA, but who else could it be?'

'We're on Signal, aren't we. You with anyone?'

Jones heart sank. 'What is it?'

'Listen up. Conrad called me, one a.m. last Wednesday, right before the fire. He'd had a total blow-up with his wife – she thinks she's pregnant and she's leaving, right then.'

'Conrad not the father?'

'Brilliant, Sherlock.'

'Who was?'

'Who do you think?'

'Jarvis?'

'Odds on, I'd say. Anyway, she's packed bags for her and the kids and says she'll blow the gaff on him if he gets in the way. He obviously can't let that happen. He says okay, he'll call her a taxi. But he calls me. Says, send one of your boys round to collect her, in the Merc, with a sign on the roof. And...'

'Fuck's sake, James, why didn't you tell me this before?'

'And... he says send one of the babes too, to nanny their kids pro tem. One has decent English, Larisa, so I send her with Graham Cruickshank. He gets there, Kimberly's out for the count, Conrad's sloshed her one. Conrad quite takes to Larisa. Graham brings Kimberly and her luggage back...'

'Christ. The female remains...'

'Larisa, yes.'

'Sweet Jesus. Where's Kimberly?'

'In solitary. Doesn't know where she is, hasn't seen me or anyone she knows. Well looked after. Needs to stay put 'til things have settled down a bit.'

'You can't do that!'

'I can. Get used to it.'

'But everyone thinks she's dead. Her kids think she's dead! They need her, for Christ's sake. And we need to talk to her.'

'You're kidding. Call off the DNA tests. Make sure those female remains go down as Kimberly, positive ID. I'll decide what to do with her in due course.'

He sees people as disposable commodities, Jones thought. *If Kimberly is alive, people will ask who the woman who died was, shining an unwelcome light on Alleyn's trafficking operation. But the world thinks Kimberly's dead. And if its left to Alleyn, she soon will be.*

Jones couldn't let that happen.

CHAPTER 48

I was at the far end of the meadow, jogging with dog Friday. My phone rang. DS Grant. Six a.m. was too early to talk to policemen, even friendly ones. It went to voicemail. I listened back when I stopped for a breather on the rainbow bridge.

'Morning Mick, hope I'm not disturbing you. A couple of things you ought to be aware of. Don't want to do it on the phone. Could we meet for a chat? That coffee place in Summertown, across from the Co-Op? See you there at eight unless I hear different. Mine's an Americano, if you're there first.'

Grant arrived at 8.15. His Americano was still warm. I was on my second.

'Things are warming up,' he said. 'I've to be back at the station by half past so I'll be brief. First. Daffy Jones and his mates have finally got moving on some of the hints I've been dropping, from your dodgy dossier. They've turned up some big money transfers through Sefton-Shaw, funding stuff in St Mark's. That's the college that owns Glebe Farm. And in various uni departments. And money going into Ballator. Corporate bonds, beneficial ownership unknown. And the college and uni both making payments to Ballator for things that seem to have happened only on paper. Are you with this?'

I nodded, sort of with it, but puzzled. Why go to all that trouble?

'What I don't get,' Grant said, 'is why go to all that trouble? Daffy thinks it's about Ballator getting cosy with the uni, the uni making sure Ballator bid high, the college getting top dollar for the land. An arty type in our press office said it might be like a dead shark shuffle. Don't know what that means.'

It dingled a bell, something I'd read years ago. 'I think it was something to do with diamonds stuck on a skull.'

'A shark's skull?'

'No. The shark came earlier, but the same guy. He was so avant-garde no-one could see how good he was. Except one very rich person who bought lots, became a patron. The artist borrowed big from this patron on the quiet and engineered the very public sale of this skull for a ridiculous sum. But he bought it himself, in some hidden way. Like the sale was to a consortium of investors who didn't want to be named but were actually him and his mum. Then he could use the proceeds to repay the patron's loan.'

'But that's just a money-go-round. What's the point?'

'The point is, work he couldn't sell for hundreds suddenly goes for millions. He's not starving in a garret, he's super-rich. And of course, his patron's collection, which cost hundreds, is now worth millions too.'

Grant frowned, digesting the shape of this. 'You're kidding,' he said.

'Oh no I'm not.'

'Can't be legal, though, can it?'

'Oh yes it can. Apparently.'

'Well, I'll be…' Grant said. 'But I still don't see how it relates to this case.'

A tickle at the back of my brain said, *Think about this later.*

'Anyway,' Grant said, 'Clappison found the boy Alasdair's laptop, in a treehouse of all places, with heaps of blackmail stuff on it aimed at that university admin guy, Donald Cruickshank.'

'He's a right one, that Alasdair. What did he have on Cruickshank?'

'The boy had been lurking on a gay dating site, posing as an eighteen-year-old. Cruickshank was on there, tried to hook up with him. Unwitting, of course. But that got the boy started. He spied on him, caught him taking cocaine in the bathroom at Springfield House during a dinner party. Accused Cruickshank of touching his bottom, threatened to tell his father. Then threatened to tell his mother that he'd seen Uncle Donald playing with his father. Without any clothes on.'

'Lordy.' I began to laugh then caught myself. The boy was still in hospital, his father and mother dead.

'They'd already got Cruickshank taking pay-offs from Sefton-Shaw,' Grant said, 'so they got him in and gave him the third degree and he squealed like the proverbial. Gave up Alleyn, who'd been desperately trying to clean house since the fire, but there was too much there for him to disappear everything. On top of which, the Ballator board did a double-quick internal enquiry and decided they'd be happier without him. They'd already got Glebe Farm, so ditching Alleyn now wouldn't have been a bad move, even if he was still squeaky clean. The fact he wasn't just made it easier.'

'Couldn't have happened to a nicer bloke,' I said. 'So happy endings. In parts, anyway.'

'I suppose. Though Daffy seems reluctant to bring Alleyn in. Maybe because he's a lawyer.' Grant paused, shrugged. 'Speaking of Donald Cruickshank... a curious thing: he has a brother. Graham.'

'Oh?'

'Motorcycle enthusiast. Know him?'

'Don't think so.' I didn't want my incarceration and liberation coming anywhere near the public domain.

'Him and his mates were Alleyn's muscle. And distributors of various illegalities. Goons, really. One of his mates turned up at the hospital two or three weeks ago with concussion, and stories about a kidnapping and someone being held prisoner in a workshop out by Dorchester.'

'Really?'

'Shep took it on, DC Clappison. Went out, found the spot, and indeed there was some truth in it. But the prisoners he found were Graham Cruickshank himself, the motorcyclist – that is, Donald's brother – and a bloke called Forster, also a biker, with a day job as an accountant. Tied to each other and to a bed. On top of each other, as if they were... doing something rude. Anyway. They were in this very well-insulated loft. Soundproofed. Kitted out like a prison cell. Or torture chamber. Over a workshop unit, just off the A465. Forensics say others had been held there; they can tell from blood stains and hair and saliva traces. Some quite recent, some going back a year or two. But no-one's saying anything. And the guy who originally came in to report it has vanished. Would you credit it?'

'No, I wouldn't,' I said, trying to look bored.

'Doesn't seem to connect to this case. But good that Shep went digging when he did, or these blokes might still be there. Just not quite so alive.'

I swallowed and looked away. Bloody Naomi. And Andrea. They might have told me.

'One last thing,' said Grant. 'Before I dash. Still no definite ID on the female remains found with Conrad Sefton-Shaw. Too badly burned, apparently. Though there's no reason to doubt it's Kimberly. Anyway, some source of Daffy's told him she was pregnant, and it wasn't Conrad's. Daffy fancies the father as someone with a motive for offing Conrad.'

'Christ. How far gone was she?'

'Only four or five weeks. Very sad. Why do you ask?'

'Four or five?' I said, counting. I felt sick.

'Are you all right?' Grant said. 'You've gone green. What is it?'

He looked at me. I looked at the brown dregs in the bottom

of my tall thin mug. I felt like he could see right through my soul.

'What is it?' Grant repeated.

I tried to meet his scrutiny.

'Surely it couldn't... You didn't... Did you? It couldn't be...'

'Well,' I said. 'Strictly speaking. Yes. It could be. Oh God.'

His face went grey. 'What are you like?' he muttered. 'And what the fuck do I do with that?'

'Nothing. Please. Nothing at all.'

He shook his head. 'Jones already fancies you for their murder,' he said. 'If I tell him...'

'I had nothing to do with them dying. Telling him won't help anybody.'

Grant stood and made for the door, then stopped, came back and loomed over me, his knuckles on the edge of the table. 'You know,' he said, 'that I'm not usually one to give unsolicited advice, am I?'

'No, no,' I said. I could feel the shakes starting, my eyes pricking.

'But you,' he said, 'you could do worse, when you've an hour to spare, than going up to the women's centre at the hospital and sitting in the outpatients' waiting room. There's a café. Sometimes. Sit where you can see the entrance. Be discreet. But just get a feel for the comings and goings, for the other side of the story. How the other half lives... the female half. With the consequences of... well... Just do it sometime. Okay?'

'Okay.'

I would have agreed to anything.

***

Wednesday, a week since the fire, five days since Tom died. I'd woken to a cool grey morning, picked up my book, put it down. I found myself thinking about fatherhood. I didn't know for sure the child was mine, but I'd be surprised if it wasn't. And it hurt. I didn't know whether it was a boy or girl. I felt cold and angry. Angry with whoever had cut off a world of possibility, before anyone except Kimberly suspected it existed.

I put the kettle on, fed Friday, looked out across Godstow Road. Someone was sitting in a car on the approach to the zebra crossing. A white Prius. It was a poor place to park. Dangerous.

I put my boots and Friday's leash on and walked out. I gave the driver of the parked car a glare. It was DC Clappison. What was he doing there? He nodded back, looking smug.

I carried on and got a good stomp going for a five-mile round trip via Binsey and Godstow. Clappison was still there when I got back, still doing whatever he'd been doing, which looked very like watching my flat, which pissed me off. I went up to the car and knocked on the nearside window. Clappison pressed a button, wound it down.

'Sorry to bother you,' I said. 'You may not realise that you're illegally parked. Better move on or someone will call the police. They're like that round here.'

I walked on before he could respond and put it out of my mind. I wasn't looking forward to today. Work in the morning, Tom's funeral at 2 p.m. It had been organised surprisingly quickly.

I arrived at the crematorium at half one and parked by a bed of deep red roses. There were small heaps of ash between the bushes, and what looked like ice lolly sticks, with names and dates on them. I walked slowly to the buildings, feeling emptied out, and joined the crowd milling around outside. A board showed two services starting at the same time. The gathering mourners were unsorted. I scanned the crowd, caught DS Grant's eye. I wasn't sure he'd want to be seen with me in this context, but he beckoned so I went over.

'Rum do, this,' he said.

'No kidding.' I was deeply suspicious about Tom's death and Linda's disappearance. I'd been thinking how convenient both looked from Alleyn's perspective. 'What's on your mind?'

'Well for one thing,' he said, 'his wife's still missing, isn't she? You'd think they'd wait a wee while, give her a chance to show up.'

'They do seem to have rushed it, don't they? Not a week since he died. From an accidental overdose, they decided?'

'Aye, so they did,' he said. 'Fast-acting morphine in little duck-egg blue tabs. Could have been left over from treatment Linda had a couple of years ago, they say. But no-one to ask, with Linda vanishing too. And no sign of the packaging. They come in a blister pack, in twelves. Seems he took three packs, stirred into a mug of hot chocolate. Enough to kill a small family.' He gave me one of his stares. 'You've known him...?'

'By sight, all my life,' I said. 'He was part of the architecture round Wolvercote. I got to know him better these last few months.'

'Thought so. How does it sit with you, then? The accidental overdose theory.'

'Not well. Wish Linda would turn up.'

'Don't we all?' he said. 'Doubtless she could shed light on it.'

'If she's still alive.' I wasn't hopeful.

'When did you last see them?' Grant asked. He didn't look hopeful either.

'Friday morning. Alleyn had just sprung them from St Aldates. Before the fire he'd offered them money, jobs, a house, to leave Glebe Farm and drop the protest stuff. They turned him down. But after the fire, and your man Jones's little games, and a couple of nights in the slammer, they thought again. Alleyn got them out and made all the bad things go away. I think they wanted to trust him.'

'They did,' Grant said. 'They signed lots of paperwork, giving him power of attorney. They made new wills with him and his secretary as executors. Had them stitched up, didn't he?'

***

After the service Naomi and Andrea were out and away sharpish. I stood in line to pay my respects to Tom and Linda's son David

– we were on nodding terms from dog-walking on the common. I shook his hand said how sorry I was. He clung to me, looking dazed. Perhaps I was a familiar face.

'You all right?' I said. 'Anything I can do?'

'Not really, ta. It just hits you sometimes. I'm not used to being the one up front. Dad was always the big man and my mum was always there. Down to me now. Who are all these people? It's too much. And it's been such a rush I've had no time to think about it at all.'

'You got it organised very quickly.'

'That's Mr Alleyn, Dad's lawyer. He's not shown up today but he got everything sorted licketty spit.'

'Well, good luck with it all.' I gave his hand a squeeze. 'Let me know if I can do anything.'

I walked back down the main drive, full of dark reflections. I paused by the burgundy roses and stared without seeing, breathing their dusky perfume. If not for the fire, I'd have been on the way to becoming a father. Of sorts. And in a tectonic shift of barely conscious feelings, I suddenly knew how happy that would have made me. And how differently I'd come to feel about Kimberly.

I took a clean white handkerchief from my breast pocket, dabbed moisture from my eyes, followed the orange tails of bees navigating the roses.

Three people dead. Linda missing. Tom overdosing didn't add up, whether it was deliberate or accidental. Was he murdered? Probably. By Linda? Never. So who? Did Linda escape or was she rubbed out too, by the same person? Disposed of elsewhere, and lined up to take the blame?

I hadn't a great deal in common with them, except the village and a love of collies. But they were genuine, ordinary people, nice to be with when not out of their depth and terrified. I was partly responsible for getting them mixed up in something that may have led to their deaths. And to the deaths of the Sefton-Shaws. Of

Kimberly, and the beginnings of our baby. What kind of guilty did that make me feel?

If what we had been digging into meant enough to someone that it was worth killing for, several times over, couldn't it lead to more deaths? Naomi, Andrea, Gail and I all knew as much as Tom and Linda did, unless they knew something they'd not shared. I didn't know what to think. I smelled the roses and sank into dark red nothing.

***

I woke up groggy on Thursday morning, having spent half the night fretting. Things were piling up and I was just letting it happen. *'Not good enough,'* my grandad would have said.

Down in the street, the white Prius was parked by the crossing again. I wasn't being paranoid. They were watching me and wanted me to know it. They had my fingerprints at the scene. They thought I had a motive for killing Conrad. They had no other suspects. They thought I'd done it. I knew I hadn't. I also knew there was no way I could prove it.

I shivered, suddenly cold. I took the I Ching down from its shelf, threw yang yin yin, yang yin yin. Thunder on thunder, with moving lines in the second and fifth places.

Exciting power. Peril above and below.

Sometimes a storm is needed, to clear the air. Let it come.

Though you look out with apprehension, smile and talk cheerfully.

Though you are in fear, set your life in order and examine yourself.

Be willing to face fear.

The moving lines:

Danger. Many times you lose treasures. Don't pursue them: you'll get back those you need.

Danger. Amid the startling movements of the times, not all is lost, yet there are things to be done.

I took Friday out, avoiding Clappison in the car but aware

of eyes on my back. Some clarity emerged through the rhythm of running. No-one knew who'd started the fire, but with no evidence pointing anywhere else, Jones was only looking at me. I needed to persuade him to lay off me. And all of my friends were similarly light on alibi.

I texted Kanhai, the best hacker I knew. He arrived at 7.30 p.m. I cracked a couple of San Miguels and filled him in.

'So all you need is something that lets you put the squeeze on DI Jones, so he'll take you out of the frame for murder,' Kanhai said. 'Oh my. And what's our starting point? A general feeling he's bent. Which may be true, but it doesn't mean he's left any sort of trail.'

'One thing,' I said, 'is the questions he was asking, when he had me in Kidlington. What did I know about S4S? Arrow? In other words, the bugged smoke alarm. That was right after the fire, before I met Grant, before Jones had any contact with Alleyn at all, as far as we knew. But he could only have got that from Alleyn, he was the one that was aware, had a scanner, found the bug. And Grant told me how reluctant Jones was to bring Alleyn in.'

'So we could start with Jones and see what we can find,' he said. 'But no doubt most of what he does is innocuous. We'd have to look at everything to find the one place where things are hidden.'

'Not exactly a targeted strategy.'

'No. Or we could look closer at Sefton-Shaw's links to Alleyn, and see if anything there connects Alleyn to Jones. Back to square one if it doesn't exist, but...'

'...better than shooting in the dark.'

'Remind me what we know about anything going from Sefton-Shaw to Alleyn.'

'Two of the big payments from Sefton-Shaw's payroll account went to businesses owned by Alleyn. The bikers' café, and something called MA Compliance and Diligence.'

'I'll start there,' he said. 'Were you going to cook us something? Go on then. I'll shout if I need anything.'

In the kitchen, I cleaned and chopped a leek, an aubergine, two onions, three cloves of garlic and six mushrooms, put them in a wok with a splash of olive oil and stir-fried slowly. Four good handfuls of rigatoni went in boiling water. I dribbled cold milk onto two heaped teaspoons of cornflour and made a thin paste, then heated more milk in the microwave, poured it over the slightly browned veg in the wok, brought it to the boil then stirred in the cornflour paste. While it simmered I added paprika, black pepper, fresh chives from the pot on the windowsill, herbes de Provence, a tiny pinch of turmeric and half a pound of roughly chopped vintage cheddar. I stirred until the cheese slicked into the sauce then added the pasta, the hard side of al dente. I stirred it, tipped into a casserole dish and put it in the oven at one hundred and fifty degrees.

I opened two more beers and went back to check on progress.

Kanhai was reclining on the sofa looking smug. I handed him a beer. He handed me a printed A4 sheet.

I sat next to him and raised a bottle. I scanned the sheet, said, 'Oh my,' read it through carefully, said 'Oh my' again. I felt a weight of worry lifting. There were still things to do, but I knew I could do them.

'Thanks mate,' I said.

'*De nada*,' Kanhai said. 'That's the summary. The detail's all in a folder on your desktop. By the way, isn't there a Serie A game on tonight? Starting about now?'

I pointed him at the laptop and dished up the pasta.

Full time: Fiorentina 2, Milan 1.

I said goodnight to Kanhai then emailed what he'd found to DS Grant and Naomi, with a message saying: *I had nothing to do with the fire, but DI Jones thinks I did. If anything happens to me, have a look at the attachments. You'll know what to do.*

CHAPTER 49

Why was I waking before five every morning? I was out with Friday by half past. DC Clappison was already in place by the crossing. I gave him a nod. On the way home an hour later, I knocked on his window. He lowered it.

'I need a quick word with your boss,' I said. 'You can run me over to Kidlington in fifteen, okay?'

He didn't reply, but his expression said it wasn't okay at all.

I showered and changed. My phone rang as I left the flat. It was DS Grant.

'Mick,' he said. 'Thanks for your message. I think I know what you're planning. Just remember, he has a dangerous temper on him at the best of times and he's not going to like this. Is there any way I can smooth the path?'

'Are you at the station?'

'Yes. He's here too. Arrived ten minutes ago.'

'Great. Please just keep your phone handy. I might give you a shout to join us, if things get sticky. Or I might just use you as a prop.'

'Okay. Good luck.'

'Call you later whatever.'

In the Prius, Clappison looked even more glum than before.

He'd probably been on the phone to Jones and picked up an earful. I almost felt sorry for him.

'What's this all about, then?' he asked, doing a distracted seven-point turn in front of two buses and a surprising number of cars, vans, lorries, cyclists and people with pushchairs.

'Just need a word with Inspector Jones. In private.'

'About what, though?' He wouldn't leave it alone.

'Oh, the usual things,' I said. 'Lawyers, guns, money.' Whose song was that anyway? The plod looked sideways at me, bemused. I gave him my warmest smile.

He pulled up in the car park at police HQ in Kidlington, got out, adjusted his pullover and said 'Follow me.' I followed him up to where they'd tried to interview me last week. He ushered me into the same corner cubicle, went out and locked the door.

I poked the recorder in the middle of the table and ran my fingers over a surface gouged with swastikas, union jacks and obscenities. I was nervous, but it was like going on stage: if you weren't nervous, you were in the wrong head space. I knew my part and I loved to improvise. I breathed deep, got my mantra going and waited. I lost track of how long for. I didn't care.

The lock rattled. The door swung open. Jones and Clappison came in. Each put a mug on the table. The coffee smelled good.

Clappison closed the door, stood with his back to it and straightened his pullover.

I sat and leaned back.

Jones sat opposite me, elbows on the table, jowly chin on the heels of his hands. His head seemed disproportionately large. He was giving out a "We've got you, buddy" vibe, but saying nothing.

I smiled back and waited. I knew whose self-possession was going to crumble first.

'Well?' Jones said. 'You wanted to talk to me. Talk.'

'As I said to your colleague earlier, it's best if we talk in private.' I looked Jones in the eye and smiled again.

He sneered back. But I wondered whether there was a slight

tic in the corner of his eye, a tiny tremble in the hand supporting his chin. Perhaps he had an inkling that something out of the ordinary was coming his way, or was finding that the longer you keep a guilty secret, the more vulnerable you become.

He raised his head. 'Wait outside,' he said to Clappison, nodding at the door. 'Right there.'

Clappison reached for his coffee but I got there first. 'You can leave that,' I said. 'Thanks.'

Jones looked for a moment as though he might intervene on Clappison's behalf, but then shrugged, gave half a smile and let it go. Clappison snorted, shook his head and left.

'Right,' said Jones, settling his chin back on his palm, elbow on the table. 'Tell me.'

'First, tell me,' I said. 'Are we being recorded?'

Jones looked at the machine on the table. He shook his head. 'No. Off,' he said.

'So no other recording device?' I said. 'Hidden?'

Jones shrugged. 'What can I say? No.'

'It's just,' I said, 'that we might talk about things that you'd really not want anyone else to hear. At all. You see? So, okay.'

Jones bellowed. 'Clappison!'

Clappison appeared.

'Turn the tape off.'

Clappison glanced at the recorder in the middle of the table. 'It's off already, sir.'

'Not that one. I meant...' He glanced at the ceiling.

'It's not tape, sir,' he said, with the beginnings of a smile. 'It's all digital now.'

Jones straightened and looked away. 'Constable,' he said, 'turn it off.'

'Yes sir,' said Clappison, smile gone. He went into the outer office then came back. 'Off now.'

Jones signed for him to shut the door and waved a hand at me.

'Okay,' I said. 'You know of a company called Dewi Security?'

Jones might have been controlling a flinch. 'Don't think so,' he said. He glanced at something behind my left shoulder, frowning.

I followed his look. There was nothing there. That was a tell, that glance up and right. That was a lie.

'Really?' I said. 'Odd, that, since it pays you five grand a month. And the same for your wife. Sixty thousand a year each.'

Jones inhaled sharply, his lips compressed into a pale anticline.

'You and your wife are the only directors and are listed as the beneficial owners. Do you remember the company now?'

'Oh, Dewi Security, did you say?' said Jones. 'Sorry, must have misheard.'

'So you do know of it?'

'Yes, of course,' Jones said. 'I don't have much to do with it. Too busy here. My wife's business, really.'

'Really?' I said. 'I understood your wife was an artist. What does the company do?'

Jones drew himself up and looked down at me. 'Not sure what business that is of yours.'

'Humour me,' I said, leaning forward to meet him eye to eye, our noses a foot apart across the table. Thank God the zit had subsided.

He growled, shook his head and pushed down on the table, elbows out, like he was about to get violent. But then he seemed to take himself in hand and sagged back. 'Security, obviously,' he said. 'For art shows. Galleries. Exhibitions. That sort of thing.'

'Really?' I leaned back too, waiting.

Jones growled again. 'Get on with it.'

'With pleasure,' I said, nodding. 'Funds come into the company from various sources. Didn't notice any art galleries among them. For the last two years, just one source, paying that nice, regular ten thousand a month. Like a retainer?' I paused.

Jones cleared his throat. Twice. 'I wouldn't know the details,' he said. 'Probably we're sub-contracting. And those are from the prime contractor.'

'Really?' I said. 'In June, there was a bigger payment from the same source. Does that ring a bell?'

'Er…'

'One hundred thousand. And recently, two weeks ago, the same again. A good customer! Do you remember who it was?'

'No, oddly enough,' Jones said, shaking his head. 'My wife never mentioned it.'

'No? Strange,' I said. 'A lot of money.'

This was becoming rather unkind, but that wasn't going to stop me. *In fact*, I thought, *this guy is lying through his teeth*. And though he might be a small cog in a large machine, that machine has killed three people, one of them pregnant with my child; left three kids as orphans; and could end up sending me down for life. Perhaps a little unkindness was warranted. I sat up straight and found myself looking down on Jones.

'Your customer is MA Diligence and Compliance Services. Does that ring a bell?'

Jones stared at me and shook his head, face grey, coughing. He glanced over my left shoulder. 'No. As I said, it's really my wife's business.'

He's wondering how far this is going, I thought. I lifted the mug, took a sip. 'Mmm. Nice coffee,' I said. 'Actually, can I just make a quick call? It won't take a moment.'

I stood, pulled my phone out and dialled Grant's mobile. I moved to the corner and turned my back.

'Jarvis here,' I said, before Grant could speak. 'Yes, I'm with him now. He's saying that Dewi Security is his wife's business. He knows nothing about it.'

Grant caught on, helpfully filling in with a quiet "rhubarb rhubarb" when I paused.

'That's right,' I continued, into my phone. 'Never heard of MA Diligence and Compliance. Does that sound likely?'

I paused again. Grant rhubarbed.

'Good idea,' I said. 'Do you know where to find her?'

More rhubarb.

'Okay. Magdalen Road.' I spoke loudly, for Jones's benefit. 'Is that the art studios?'

Jones was tapping me on the shoulder.

'Just a minute,' I said. 'He wants to say something.'

'Don't ask her,' Jones said.

'He's saying don't ask her.' I turned to Jones. 'Why not?'

'Just,' Jones said, 'don't ask her. I'll explain.'

'Okay,' I said. I spoke into the phone again. 'Put that on hold. He's going to explain. Thanks, speak later.'

I offed the phone and turned back to Jones, who had a wild look in his eyes, like panic. Was he wondering whether this was some sort of sting?

'So, please explain,' I said. 'MA Diligence and Compliance Services.'

Jones was staring at the table, white-faced, shaking his head.

'No?' I said. 'Still can't explain? Shall I go on?'

Jones didn't raise his eyes.

'Registered address at Murdoch Alleyn in Summertown,' I said. 'Owned and directed by James Alleyn and Graham Cruickshank, brother of Donald Cruickshank of uni services, who you spoke to last week.'

Jones was still staring at the table and shaking his head.

'I think I'd better just sketch in the rest of the chain. In case you're not aware of it all. We're nearly there.' I tried for a reassuring smile. 'MA Diligence and Compliance use a private offshore bank called Coupe and Lombardy. All the payments of substance into the MADC account come from another account at the same bank, in the name of the late Conrad Sefton-Shaw. All the recent payments into Sefton-Shaw's account come from an investment trust registered in the Cayman Islands.'

'How do you know all this?'

'You're not denying it's true?'

He said nothing.

'Do you know where that trust gets its funds from?' I asked.

He raised his head and met my eye with a squinty frown. 'Alleyn said there was some connection with the uni,' he said. He gave the smallest nod, as if to say "carry on".

'Interesting,' I said. 'Perhaps he's telling it straight for once. We tried to find out but couldn't. Someone in your Media Relations said it was like – what was it? – a dead shark shuffle? You might ask her about that.'

He didn't look interested, just stared over my left shoulder.

'What we do know,' I said, 'is that what's been coming to you is the tiniest crumb from their table.'

Jones sniffed and shrank further into his chair.

'We wondered, actually, if there may be a Russian connection,' I said. 'Because there was a guy with that sort of accent, at that café near Dorchester.'

'The bikers' place?'

'He seemed to be calling the shots with this gang of heavies who also seem to be James Alleyn's buddies.'

'What was he like, this maybe-Russian?'

'Short grey hair. Grey suit. Good English, very precise, very slight accent. Smoked yellow cigarettes. His lighter was a completely convincing replica pistol.'

'So you're saying Russian money, through an offshore trust, behind Ballator's bid for Glebe Farm?'

'Possibly. Whoever's putting in the money is getting inside the deal on a rather special square mile of farmland, with outline planning. You've seen the brochure?... *key element in strategic Oxford-Cambridge development arc... first step towards Britain's Silicon Valley.* Pretty cute, to be at the heart of that and nobody knows who you are. With government support, infrastructure funding, county and city on board. And you guys making sure no-one asks difficult questions, when actually, you're the ones who should be asking the difficult questions, aren't you?'

I took a breath. Jones stared at the table.

'You might ask why I'm telling you this. Why I'm not shouting it from the rooftops.' I wondered the same thing myself, stirred by my own rhetoric. But if I was up on a multiple murder charge I could shout what I wanted and no-one would hear a word. So, stick to the mission.

Jones raised his head, alert to a sudden air of possibility. 'Well, there's probably some cash to spare, if you...'

'Thanks, but it's simpler than that,' I said. 'You've got me down as the prime suspect for the Sefton-Shaws' deaths. I can't prove I wasn't there when the fire started. So I'm just going to tell you, and you're going to accept, that it wasn't me. And it wasn't Naomi, Andrea, Gail, or poor old Tom. Or Linda, wherever she might be. Actually, you don't know where she is, do you?'

Jones screwed up his eyes, shook his head.

Not lying, I thought. 'So you call off the hounds and I'll keep quiet. Or you'll be reading the shabby story of how DI Jones pays his little darlings' school fees on the front page of the Oxford Times. And by the way, copies of what I've told you, and the evidence it's based on, are held by two independent people, with instructions to do the needful if anything happens to me.'

Jones's eyes were opaque.

'So,' I said, 'do we have a deal?'

Jones sighed. He looked up and sighed again. He shook his head as if to clear it, rolled his shoulders. 'Are you a man of your word?'

'I do my best,' I said.

Jones raised himself to his feet and held out a hand.

I stood, took it, shook it. There was nothing funny about the handshake.

'One question,' he said. 'Where did you get your information?'

I almost laughed. He was a real optimist if he expected a straight answer to that. 'Sorry,' I said. 'Must protect my sources, I'm sure you guys do the same. But you aren't the only ones that can put pressure on people. And people are only human, aren't they?'

He sniffed.

'One last thing,' I said. 'Was it your idea to push the inquest through so quickly? For Tom.'

'No,' Jones said. He looked at me with the crinkled frown that I was beginning to recognise as a sign of truthfulness. 'No. It was very unusual. It came from the Commissioner and the Chief Constable. Why they took an interest I don't know.'

'And the funeral?'

'That seemed to come more from Alleyn. As executor.' He frowned at the table. I gave him the raised eyebrow. 'Oh, I see,' he said. 'Alleyn. You think he might…'

'…have had something to do with Tom's death?' I said. 'Well, I do. And Linda's disappearance. *Cui bono*, isn't it? Who benefits. I'm guessing Tom had something on him and tried to use it. You can't ask Tom. You could ask Alleyn, but what's he going to say? What I think is, Alleyn's a total nutjob, and with Sefton-Shaw dead, no-one's in control. Actually, could Alleyn have benefitted from his death too?'

Jones nodded slowly, eyes focused on the far distance.

***

I stood by the Thames on Saturday morning, the air fresh after overnight rain. Beside me, Friday was trying to take over my mind, to make my body throw sticks. I was thinking about Gail and Grant. Would they find a way of moving on, she from losing her mother and Grant from a broken family and too many years of policing? I'd seen them together yesterday evening, at a corner table in the Jericho Café. I tried to catch an eye but they were engrossed. I could imagine them rambling the Ridgeway, hiking the Highlands, breathing clean, cool mountain air together. Wouldn't that be good?

My phone rang, caller ID withheld.

'Michael Jarvis?'

'Speaking.'

'DC Clappison here, TVP Kidlington.'

Sod. 'What can I do for you?' I said.

'You can come over to the station. A quick chat. Could you be here at... What?'

A voice in the background, female, said, 'Eleven.'

'At eleven?' Clappison said.

'Today? I suppose so. What's it about?'

'I'll explain when you get here. Just ask for me at the desk.'

Sod, I thought again, hanging up. I'd no other plans and plenty of time, but... Friday nudged my hand with a tasty stick. I threw it across and down the river, giving her a good chase and swim. I walked on a few paces. She was back. I threw it again. And again.

Clappison had set me thinking about my session with Jones yesterday. I hoped it wasn't to do with that. It had gone well, but Jones wouldn't have liked it. He might have wound Clappison up to get back at me. Or Clappison could be out to get me for his own reasons.

But a strange insight, almost a liberation, hit me. An hour of Kanhai's digging had given me enough power over Jones to shift the focus of a murder investigation. If I could face him down, albeit at the sacrifice of some integrity, could I, with the sacrifice of a bit more integrity, do a bit more for what was left of the gang? And the dormice? I knew stuff that St Mark's College, university administrators, the council and Ballator Developments wouldn't want made public. That would give me power if I chose to use it and was cool enough to pull it off. I'd need to identify the right person: someone who could make things happen and who had a lot to lose.

What was happening to my values? They were becoming unstable, by the feel of it. Was this what growing up meant? A transition from idealism to realpolitik? From youth to adult? A bit late, granted. I didn't see how we could stop the Glebe Farm project altogether, but keeping us all out of jail would be a small but important victory. And there might be more small victories that were worth having, were better than complete defeat. I'd have a chat with Grant and Gail. Make a plan.

My phone rang again. Naomi. I let it go to voicemail, not wanting to break my train of thought, but the train was broken anyway. I listened to the message.

'Hi, it's Naomi. I'm with Andrea, in Dunmore Copse. You want to join us for a drink this evening, to catch up? About seven. The Globe. Let me know if you can't. Ciao.'

**

Clappison collected me from reception at 11.15. He looked different. Short hair. No moustache. Jeans, sweatshirt, trainers. Had he found himself a girlfriend?

He led me through the station, up to the large open-plan SPAT office. It was deserted. He bypassed the awful cubicles in the corner, thank God, led me to a desk at the far end, pointed at a visitor's chair, adjusted his sweatshirt and sat down opposite. He opened a file, shuffled some papers, massaged his upper lip. 'The Sefton-Shaw family,' he said. 'How much do you know about them?'

'Nothing, really.'

'Really? Okay. I'll run through some stuff, please add anything that comes to mind, that we might not know about. Okay? So. You met the twins, Bella and Charlotte, and their brother Alasdair – now in emergency foster care in Coventry.'

'Yes, poor sods. What's going to happen to them?'

'Good question. It'd normally be social services sorting that. They look for relatives or close friends willing to take them on. Failing that, they put them up for adoption, though that's easier with younger children apparently. Anyway, they couldn't find any suitable friends or relations so asked us to help. Which is what I've been doing.'

374

He pulled out a pale yellow sheet with handwritten columns of green text. 'Right,' he said, pen poised. 'Conrad first. His first wife, Catherine. Re-married fifteen years ago, now Mrs Thyssen, lives in Cheltenham. Had two children with Conrad. She's brought them up with no help from him. Wants nothing to do with him or his subsequent children. Anything to add?'

'Nothing,' I said.

He made a mark on his list. 'Next. His mother. Eighty-two. In a care home in Devon. Alzheimer's. His father, also called Conrad, died ten years ago in South Africa. A brother, Barry, aged forty-four. In prison in South Africa. Armed robbery. Not due out any time soon. No living uncles or aunts. No first or second cousins. Anything?'

I shook my head. What a family. But what had this to do with me?

'We could trace two more distant cousins,' Clappison said. 'Robert Slater on Vancouver Island, Canada. He'd never heard of Conrad. And Christine,' he read carefully, 'Giannopoulou. Lives in Romania, met him once when they were children. Both asked about the estate. Neither interested in the children.'

'Can't say I'm surprised,' I said. 'Conrad was a nasty piece of work.'

'Yes. Now... Kimberly. Did you know she'd filed for divorce?'

'She said she was going to.'

'She did,' Clappison said. 'I'm still going through a stack of paperwork from her solicitor. But the strange thing. They were married sixteen years ago in an Oxford registry office. She's on the register as Kimberly Anastasia Trevithick. It says 'unknown' in the parent-related boxes. There's no trace of any birth or adoption or immigration record. All I found before her marriage is one reference to a nineteen-year-old debutante in London. She travelled abroad, must have used a passport, but there's no trace of one being issued in that name or her married name. She's a mystery. Best guess, she married on a forged birth certificate, travelled on a forged passport. We don't even know her real name, or why she was using forged documents. Anything to add to that?'

'No,' I said. 'Nothing. Anastasia Trevithick sounds like a Mills and Boon character.' Trevithick sounded Cornish. That rang a bell. But no-one knew who she was, where she came from. How was I ever going to find out? Not that it really mattered to me now. Or to anyone else, except her children. Weird, though. Everyone came from somewhere. 'So no relatives for either of them?'

'That's right. So we looked at close friends. Conrad's closest associates were Alleyn and the Cruickshank brothers, all currently under investigation. Not fit and proper persons. Conrad was at war with the Whiteheads next door, over boundary issues, noise, the dog, hedge trimming. They're not interested. And Kimberly seemed to have no friends of her own at all. Except you.'

'Me?' I was her only friend? God, what a bleak prospect. 'She told me he didn't like her having friends. Didn't allow it.'

'Is that right?'

'You couldn't really call me a friend,' I said. 'I only met her five or six times. We weren't close.'

'You were close enough to get her pregnant.'

Oh. I hadn't realised this was an established fact, let alone common knowledge. 'How do you know that?' I asked. Had they done DNA on the remains?

'Information received,' he said, smiling a thin smile, like he'd moved his queen two squares and turned a dull exchange of pawns into checkmate. 'So we seem to be a bit stuck. No family. No friends. Well, thank you for your time. I'll get that written up and you can come in and sign a statement, if you don't mind. Two o'clock Monday afternoon?'

CHAPTER 50

Saturday evening, I kicked a stone and slammed a gate and stalked down the meadow to Jericho, Friday at my heels. Life was a mess in too many ways.

Friday said hello to everyone and settled under the table, her chin on Andrea's feet. I got a round in. A pint for me, spritzers for Naomi and Andrea, Campari and soda for Gail, who looked lighter and younger with a new short hairdo. There were only four of us now. No Tom and Linda.

'One thing I should fill you in on,' I said, distributing drinks. 'I had a chat with DI Jones yesterday. I think I persuaded him that none of us had anything to do with the fire at the Sefton-Shaws.'

Andrea looked at me sharply.

'Actually, just checking. That is true, isn't it?' I said, my eyes on Andrea's. 'No offence, but I had to consider all possibilities when they had me in their sights for murder. And I concluded that if any one of us could have done it...'

'It wasn't me,' Andrea said.

'Good,' I said. What next? I had things to say, if no-one else stepped up. They didn't, so I did. 'I've been wondering what's behind it, this deal, why they did it the way they did. Because there could have just been like a gentlemen's agreement, so Ballator could include some magic ingredient in their bid, and St Mark's could say Ballator's was the preferred bid because of that ingredient, whatever it was. But they had Ballator making grants to St Mark's and the uni. Payments on spurious contracts in the other direction. Sefton-Shaw easing the way with his payroll fund. But was that all context-building and smokescreen and lubrication? Because the money financing it comes from an investment trust in the Caymans.'

'Angus was talking about that the other night,' said Gail.

'Angus?' Andrea asked.

'Grant,' Gail said, colouring. 'Detective Sergeant Grant. Mick's friend.'

'Yes?' I said. 'It was something he said that got me thinking about it. It's fuzzy and a bit complicated, so bear with me.' I took a sip of my pint. 'I think it might work like this. First, St Mark's owns lots of land, across the country but especially around Oxford, and Buckingham, Northampton, Bedford, Cambridge. Anybody spot a pattern?'

'The corridor,' Andrea said. 'The growth arc.'

'Yes. And most of that land is what?'

'Farms. Woodland,' Andrea said. 'A lot is green belt. Or was.'

'Yes. What's the value of farmland? Per acre. In that area. Roughly.'

'Between ten and twenty-five thousand, at a guess,' Andrea said.

'What's the value of that land if it's got outline planning? Like Glebe Farm.'

Naomi said, 'Depending on how much land, what state it's in, and what the consent is for... half a million an acre? But I've never come across a site this big – six hundred and fifty acres – being sold with outline planning. Anything over a hundred acres is unusual. I'm not sure there's a precedent.'

'Right,' I said. 'So St Mark's has set a precedent. For a big chunk of farmland with outline planning, a million an acre and unconditional bids.'

'Good spot,' Andrea said.

'Thanks,' I said. 'I looked up St Mark's assets. Around six hundred million at last count, half in this sort of land in the growth arc. If they got outline planning for their agricultural land, its value would go from three hundred million,' I checked my notes, 'to around twelve billion.'

'Crikey,' Gail said. 'So that's why all this financial stuff?'

'Partly,' I said. 'St Mark's College upped its asset values enormously. But all the old colleges have land holdings. The uni has some too. God knows what this will do for their combined asset values. That's point two.'

'There's a point three coming,' Andrea said.

'Well, this is even more speculative,' I said. 'Ballator financed the Glebe Farm purchase partly from its own resources, partly from corporate bonds, but mostly from a share issue, underwritten by an investment trust registered in the Cayman Islands.'

'I hear,' said Andrea, 'that the share offer's going to fall way short. So the underwriters are going to end up with a large slice of Ballator.'

'How come your finger's so firmly on the pulse?' I said.

'Oh, just talking to my dad,' Andrea said. 'He takes an interest.'

'I see.' I felt I was being out-played somehow. 'Anything else pertinent come up?'

'He says that St Mark's has been pushing through outline planning applications for a year or two, right across its agricultural holdings, but that it keeps a very low profile and has done nothing about detailed planning applications until Glebe Farm.'

'That kind of makes my point.'

'He also mentioned,' Andrea said, 'that before the share offer, the investment trust already held twenty-nine percent of Ballator. With the underwriting, they could end up with a majority holding. So they could take them private and buy out any shareholders they don't trust.'

379

She was a lot more on the financial ball than I was. 'So point three is really the question: who's behind this trust?'

'Well, that looks pretty obvious,' said Andrea.

'Does it?' I said, feeling a bit cheesed. I'd been thinking so hard about this. Russia or China had always looked good, until a strange suspicion took shape. 'Who is it then?'

'St Mark's College. Maybe the uni too, and other colleges. But St Mark's for sure.'

I was aware that my jaw was dropping, that I was staring at her, but could do nothing about it. Gail was staring at her, too. Naomi was thumbing her iPhone.

'It's *cui bono*, isn't it?' Andrea said. 'Who benefits? As you said, St Mark's has increased the value of its assets by billions, basically by selling Glebe Farm to itself. It's what they call a dead shark shuffle, in the art world.'

I scratched my head. 'You don't know someone in the press office at Thames Valley Police, do you?'

'No,' Andrea said.

I noticed Naomi give Andrea a look, saying something like, *Oh yes, you do.*

Andrea looked at the ceiling and ignored her. She said, 'And of course, as well as upping asset values, they'll be upping income too, from rents and leases and so on. Because they'll keep the freehold and sell long leases wherever possible. They'll have hundreds of high-tech business tenants rather than a handful of broke farmers. But the main thing, my dad thought, is how much they could borrow, with that sort of collateral. Tens of billions.'

Still trying to meet Andrea's eye, Naomi handed her phone to me. The Fellows page, St Mark's College website. On the left, a circular mugshot. A sallow, thin-faced man with short grey hair. Text to the right.

Professor Udvari Tamas. Professorial Fellow in Mathematics, St Mark's College, Oxford. Pioneer in the use of AI to understand and predict the behaviour of markets.

'It's him,' I said. 'Grey-suit. From the bikers' café. A professor. Christ.'

I tapped for more.

Professor Udvari's work has explored markets as diverse as stocks, bonds and financial derivatives; fine wines; fine art; land; cocaine and its derivatives; and commodities.

I slumped, physically and mentally. I was beginning to see that the people we'd been skirmishing with, like Sefton-Shaw, Alleyn, Cruickshank, were expendable foot-soldiers in this campaign. That the campaign had succeeded. That the commanders were untouched. And that grey-suit, Professor Udvari, was one of them.

Depressing. I closed my eyes, and thought, *Interesting too.* If Udvari was pulling all their strings, did the fact that he was so highly placed, in such an elite institution, make him slightly vulnerable? And did the fact that he was a completely cold-hearted and evil bastard make it okay to exploit that vulnerability? In a good cause, of course.

I opened my eyes.

Naomi was looking at me, smiling, holding out a hand for her phone. 'Are you with us now? Good. Well done. All really interesting,' she said. 'And you're right, a bit complicated. But on another subject: the Sefton-Shaw twins, Bella and Charlotte. Does anyone know what's happened to them? Or what's going to happen to them?'

'Funny you should mention that,' I said. 'I was in Kidlington police station today, for an odd session with Clappison. He says the children have been sent to Coventry.'

'What?' said Gail.

'Literally,' I said. 'To emergency foster carers. While they try to find relatives or family friends to take them on. Clappison's been working with social services, tracking down distant cousins. There's a limited supply, and none of them are interested. He got me in to see if I could add to what he already knew. I couldn't. I'm going back Monday to sign a statement.'

'Keep us informed,' Naomi said. 'Those poor little mites. Because we were wondering…' She stopped, exchanged a look with Andrea. 'Well, anyway. There's a couple of things that we wanted you both to know about.'

I caught Andrea's eye. She winked at me.

Gail smiled and nodded and said, 'Go on.'

'First,' Naomi said, 'My old boss in planning is now head of department. He asked if I was interested in coming back. I'm starting on Monday. So, Mick, good news. I'll be able to repay your loans. I bet you'd given up on them.'

'I had, but great. Very pleased for you.'

'Yes, perfect,' Gail said.

'And the other thing is…' she said, glancing at Andrea.

'We've rehearsed this,' Andrea said.

They stood, linked hands.

'We're coming out. We're getting together.'

They beamed at each other, slipped arms round each other's waist. There were whistles and scattered applause from dart players and bar stool squatters. Gail and I joined in.

My heart beat loud, my mind raced. How could I have been so wrong? Should I have seen this coming? Things that I'd only half noticed began to reconfigure themselves, make a different sense. When she was crying in Waterstones and said she didn't know who she was. When she'd said all men were tossers. Some of the questions in the twenty questions game. The bet that wasn't and Andrea's bath-time visit. But what sense did that make? And what about Andrea's long-term loser boyfriend?

'Wow,' I said. 'Congratulations, obviously.'

It should have registered at the time that they'd spent time in my flat together when I'd been incarcerated. And I'd phoned Naomi several times since and got Andrea.

Was I surprised? Yes.

Hurt? Disappointed? Relieved? Possibly.

Confused? Certainly.

My eyes met Gail's. Her glance gave me strength to smile broadly. We all stood and joined in a group hug, Friday joining on her hind legs.

'Congratulations are in order,' Gail said. 'Need to toast the happy couple.'

'Perhaps,' I said, staring at the ceiling, shying away from Naomi and Andrea's news, trying to anchor myself elsewhere. 'We should let Grant know about Professor Udvari. See if he's any idea what to do with it.'

'Mick, there's time to be thinking about that,' Gail said.

'True,' I said. 'Okay. Naomi. Andrea. We wish you every happiness.' I paused but couldn't help myself. 'And I've been wondering whether we have to regard Glebe Farm as a total loss. Or whether there's something short of completely stopping it, that might take a little bit of the pain away.'

'Mick, enough,' Gail said. 'Yours will be a very large malt. They've got Cardhu up there, I can tell by the shape of the bottle. That'll do. For the rest of us... champagne?'

'I'll help you,' I said, getting up. 'But have a think, please. You too, Gail. Don't worry about whether it's possible. Just ping me with an idea or two.'

I followed Gail to the bar.

***

'Rabbits,' I said for luck, thinking it was the first of August, which it wasn't. And because I could see some. I was walking through Burgess Field with dog Friday in the quiet Sunday dawn, thinking about what had changed, what had not; what had been gained, what lost. At least I'd started today with hope in my heart. The walk helped clarify what I hoped to do next.

At nine o'clock, I rang Naomi and talked to her and Andrea. At ten I rang DS Grant, who was at home, having coffee with Gail, and made a plan. At eleven I called the porters' lodge at St Mark's College and asked to speak to Professor Udvari.

'Who shall I say is calling?'

'Jarvis.'

'Jarvis?'

'Jarvis.'

'Please hold.'

I held. There was a crackle.

'Speak,' said a voice.

'Hello,' I said. 'Is this Professor Udvari?'

'It is. Please state your business.'

'You don't know me, really. But we met briefly. Two or three months ago. In a café near Dorchester.'

'We did.'

'Is that a question?'

'No. We did.'

'I want to talk to you. I'll meet you in the SCR. Say two this afternoon?'

'For what purpose?'

'I have a question to ask. And depending on the answer, a suggestion to make.'

'You are Jarvis. Michael.'

'Yes.'

'Good. Two thirty. Please come to my office in the teaching block. Ask at the lodge.'

He hung up.

It was like talking to a robot in an old movie. But, first step accomplished. I sent a text to Grant.

***

Udvari sat at a large desk, pale wood and black metal, looking at me dispassionately. Floor to ceiling windows behind him, floor to ceiling books on the side walls. Bound journals and more books either side of the door I'd just come through. I felt I'd nothing to lose, though that wasn't strictly true. But I had my mantra ringing

384

like a bell, slow breathing on automatic, a bubble of joy in my heart and a genuine smile on my face.

I sat in a low hard-backed chair across the desk from Udvari, looking up at him. The desk was clear apart from a pencil, a pad of squared paper, a soft pack of yellow Jin Ling cigarettes and the pistol-shaped lighter.

I laid a folder labelled *Briefing Notes: Glebe Farm* on the desk. Put my notebook and pencil on top of the folder and propped my phone against them. 'Professor Udvari, thank you for seeing me.' I tapped the folder. 'This contains a summary of how the Glebe Farm deal worked. And an appendix listing the evidence on which the summary is based. There are those among us who would be very happy for it to be published.'

Udvari gave a puzzled frown. 'That sounds like a blackmail threat, Mr Jarvis,' he said, shaking his head. 'That is surprising. Because the deal was not illegal.'

It was blackmail, of course. I could live with that. I liked this new strategy, of turning our enemies' weapons on themselves. Using bad things to make good things possible, or at least to mitigate the harm done by their bad things. Doing nothing wouldn't help the dormice, would it? Doing nothing would achieve nothing.

'The Financial Conduct Authority might disagree,' I said. 'And some things that you did to make it happen are definitely of interest to the police. Witness the charges against the Cruickshank brothers, for example. But do you really want the world to know how one of its most distinguished academic institutions goes about its business?'

'Hmm. These are not unreasonable points. But in the press it would be a nine-minute wonder, if anyone understood it at all. Why should we worry?'

'We were thinking the same. Then we had an idea. You know DC Clappison did doctoral and post-doc research on multivalued logic?'

'I know his work.'

'He's preparing an article for the Journal of Ethics in the Academy.' He wasn't really, though he might, if I pushed. 'Provisionally titled *The Dormouse, the Cop and the College*.'

'About us? Me? The Glebe Farm deal?'

'As a case study, using what happened here to explore the relationship between academia and society.'

'Will it name names?'

'An open question. But everyone will know exactly what was done. In detail.'

'What if they all do the same thing?'

'That's a test of ethics and sustainability, isn't it? What would happen if everyone did this?'

He shook his head. 'What do you want?' he said.

'Some land and some help.'

Udvari held up a hand: wait. 'Please excuse me. I will speak with someone,' he said. He picked up a phone, stood and went to the window, his back to me. He made a call and said, 'Yes. Now, please.' He hung up and sat down.

The door opened.

I looked over my shoulder to see Graham Cruickshank, Donald's biker brother, come in.

'Lock the door,' Udvari said.

Cruickshank saw me and said, 'Oh good.'

Udvari stepped forwards, gripped my left shoulder. Cruickshank took a simultaneous grip on the right. 'He has become a little awkward,' Udvari said. 'It would be convenient if he were to forget a few things. Perhaps we can help him.'

I tried to rise. Tried hard.

'Please be still,' Udvari said. They forced me back onto the chair.

'Please hold him,' Udvari said. Cruickshank bent my arms up behind my back, then pushed them higher.

'Stop! That hurts. Let me go,' I said. Loudly, and getting louder. 'Please stop.' Cruickshank was getting close to dislocating my shoulders.

'No point in shouting,' Udvari said. 'This block is empty on Sundays.' He rummaged in a desk drawer, took out scissors and a ball of string and cut off three lengths. He tied my arms to each other and to my legs, and all to the chair. He went to the bottom corner of the bookshelf to the left of the window. Put a thick hardback book on the desk. *Introduction to Mathematical Philosophy*, Bertrand Russell.

'Did you know he wrote that in prison?' I said. 'Bertrand Russell.'

'Why was he in prison?'

'Pacifism,' I said.

'Is that so?'

He opened the book. A rectangular section inside was cut away. In the recess were syringes, needles, small bottles of clear liquid and sachets of white powder.

Udvari fitted a needle to a syringe, drew ten millilitres of clear liquid from one of the bottles, and approached me.

'You must be kidding,' I said. 'What the fuck is that?'

Udvari smiled. 'Not one of your favourites, I'm afraid. Something new, rather special. Propranolol. A beta-blocker. It will help you relax and forget your worries.' He smiled, looked almost apologetic.

'No,' I said, shouting. 'No! You can't. You can't do that.' I struggled but couldn't throw off Cruickshank's weight. 'No. No. Help. They're drugging me. Stop. Help.'

Cruickshank locked one arm round my neck, clamped the other over my mouth. I wriggled and whimpered.

'Please be calm,' Udvari said, grasping my upper arm, pushing back the sleeve of my T-shirt. 'This will not hurt. It will cause no permanent damage. Except to your memories.'

The door crashed open.

Someone had kicked it in.

Grant stepped through, in full Highland dress, followed by Gail, holding a camera, a small red light showing on its front.

'That's enough, gentlemen, thank you. DS Grant, Thames Valley Police.' He held up a warrant card. Udvari and Cruickshank froze, perhaps shocked and awed by the spectacle, perhaps realising they'd been set up. 'And can I introduce Gail Mycroft, on camera duties.'

Grant drew a dirk from the top of his right sock and cut my restraints. 'Thanks Mick,' he said. 'You can stop the FaceTime now, we got the lot. Well done.'

Udvari's face collapsed.

I shook life back into my limbs, picked up my phone, ended the call and smiled at Udvari. It was very naive of him, not noticing it. 'DS Grant, thank you,' I said. 'Love the rig, by the way.'

'It's remarkable what you can get away with when you've a kilt on,' he said, grinning. 'The porter didn't bat a lid when I marched past the lodge with my camera-person.' He looked around. 'You'll be okay now? I'll leave you to it. Call if there are any problems. And call by five anyway, for a catch-up. Gail, see you later.'

Gail nodded, concentrating on videoing.

'You'll take this lovely lummock with you?' I said, indicating Cruickshank.

'Of course.' Grant took handcuffs, disposable gloves and a plastic pouch from his sporran and slipped the cuffs on Cruickshank. 'Mr Cruickshank, you can accompany me to the station, if you don't mind,' he said. 'I'll take this, too.' He pulled on the gloves, repacked the Introduction to Mathematical Philosophy with the drugs and works, sealed the lot in the pouch and wrote on the label. He scribbled a receipt and handed it to Udvari.

'Gail, can you send copies of the vid out?' I said. 'To the usual. You'll be staying while the Prof and I continue our chat? Thank you.'

Gail sent off a video file.

The crowd thinned out, leaving just Udvari, Gail and me.

'Recording again?' I asked.

Gail nodded.

'Thank you. Professor Udvari, perhaps we could sit down again? Now, where were we...'

'You told me that you wanted land and help,' said Udvari, furious but controlled.

'Yes,' I said. 'Land. It'll be about sixty-five acres. Dunmore Copse, which is twelve acres. The farm buildings. And a buffer zone, following and including existing field boundaries, and not less than a hundred and twenty metres deep. And some adjustments to landscaping and routing for the overall site, to incorporate best practice for wildlife and bio-diversity.'

I found an A4 sheet with a sketch map of the Glebe Farm land. 'You may not know,' I said, 'that Andrea Turner of the Wildlife Trust did a survey there, with help from Tom Simpson, now dead, and his wife Linda, now missing, who were the tenants. They found three rare plant species. Each worth SSSI status in its own right, without the dormice. The archaeologists are excited too. The copse boundary is coincident with an ancient lake bed from the Younger Dryas, with habitation sites from upper palaeolithic and mesolithic. So the chances of developing that lot as envisaged in the outline planning are slim, now you don't have the city's planning director in your pocket.'

'Perhaps,' Udvari said. 'Perhaps not.'

'The copse and buffer zone,' I said, 'will be gifted to the Wildlife Trust. The farmhouse itself, the outbuildings, and the two acres immediately around them, will be gifted to Oxford Community Land Trust.'

'A lot of land altogether,' Udvari said.

'Ten percent of the whole.'

'Also help?'

'Yes. We need Ballator to work with us on a new outline planning consent, reflecting these changes, with a network of wildlife sanctuaries and corridors using existing hedgerows and scrub land; and wildlife bridges and underpasses, across the site. Removing through routes for road traffic. BNG all on-site.'

'BNG?'

'Bio-diversity net gain. Not outsourced to the Chilterns. Or the Cheviots. Or China. Bio-abundance net gain too. Also, Ballator will help with detailed planning for the farm buildings, for a co-housing and co-working community, then do the construction work and grid connections and so on.'

'What puzzles me,' Udvari said, 'is why you think I can help. As an individual, or representing the college. You know that the college does not now own the land. Freehold passed to Ballator.'

'Who owns Ballator?'

'You would have to ask them,' said Udvari, shrugging.

'You don't know who the majority shareholder is?'

'I think an investment group.'

'Yes. Operating out of the Caribbean. Marx Global Generic Investment Trust,' I said. 'Registered in George Town, Grand Cayman. It's all in here.' I tapped the folder. 'And Marx Global has just the one institutional investor.' I looked round. 'St Mark's College. And a small number of private individuals. Including...'

I smiled at the professor, who was near the top of the list.

'Yes, I see.' Udvari exhaled slowly, looking at the backs of his hands. *Fuck my old red boots*, I thought, *this might actually work*. I could hardly keep a straight face.

'You are asking a lot,' Udvari said.

'I'm not, really,' I said. 'I've some rough figures here.' I took an A4 sheet from the Briefing Note folder and passed it across. 'You'll see that it won't take more than six or seven percent out of the project altogether. Not much really. Less, if you accept that you were going to lose some of it to SSSI anyway. And just think of the PR value.'

'Yes. And think of the precedent set.'

'A good one!'

'The shareholders might disagree.'

'They might not.'

Udvari frowned. 'Why do you not ask for more?' he said. 'You would prefer to bring the whole deal down, if you could, would you not?'

'Of course. But on the face of it, the deal is done and Ballator have done nothing wrong. All the evil stuff's been done by Alleyn and his buddies, behind the backs of the Ballator board, orchestrated by you. Ballator have sacked Alleyn. The college could sack you if you got embarrassing. And everything else is deniable.'

'That conforms with my view.'

'So I can't see how we could bring the deal down. Clappison's paper would sink you and your buddies' careers. We'd get the college some bad press. And we will, if you don't play ball. But what good would that do for the dormice?'

'The dormice?'

'In Dunmore Copse.'

'How many dormice are there?'

'Six or seven, they say. In two colonies.'

He made a note on his pad. 'You want to take sixty-five million out of the project for six or seven dormice? Ten million each?'

I couldn't help laughing. 'You can't put a price on a dormouse, can you?' I said. 'Any more than any other conscious being. And they're really quite rare, compared to people. If you bulldoze those dormice... I'm not threatening you. But some people say, an eye for an eye, a life for a life. That we could spare six people better than six dormice.'

'That would be Andrea Turner?'

I didn't respond. He was right, of course. *But me too*, I thought. I felt the same. It wasn't hard to think of six people whose removal would make the world a better place. In my dreams.

'Please explain how we can know, if we give you this,' Udvari said, 'that you will not come back for more?'

'I will put all the evidence, all the documentation, all electronic copies, in a safe deposit box. When it's all done and dusted, you'll get the key.'

'If I don't believe you?'

'Tough.'

'If I don't agree?'

'Clappison will publish his journal article. I'll send my dossier to the Oxford Times and the FCA. The nationals will be interested.'

Udvari spun round in his chair and looked out the window.

I waited. Despite his apparent resistance I had a strange feeling I was pushing on an open door.

He breathed out long and slow. 'I should consult,' he said.

'Go ahead.'

He turned back to face me, picked up his phone and pressed a button.

'Good afternoon. Have you been following this?... You have. Good. So you understand the position. And the proposition. What is your view?... My decision. I see. Thank you, Master. We'll speak later.'

He put the phone down, turned back to the window and stared at the sky for what seemed like a long time. Turned back to face me.

'We will do it,' he said. 'It must go through the Ballator board. I will steer it.'

'Are you on the board?'

'Currently a co-opted member.'

'Can you call an emergency meeting? Say for Tuesday?'

'Wednesday would be better.'

'Okay. Please set it up. Let me know the names and emails of who's coming. I'll send them a copy of these notes tomorrow morning,' I said, indicating the folder on the desk. 'Two more things.'

'Yes?'

'I want to be there. Just to make sure everything's squeaky clean. And I'll write the agenda.'

CHAPTER 51

DETECTIVE INSPECTOR JONES

The meeting with Forster had gone well. The accountant seemed competent and eager to please. Jones had a plan and had screwed himself to the sticking point. At 7.50 p.m. on Sunday evening, he announced himself over the gate intercom at the entrance to Sotwell Barns, Alleyn's place outside Wallingford.

'You're late,' Alleyn said.

'Yeah, sorry.' He'd said he'd arrive at 7.30. Usually he was punctiliously punctual, but tonight he wanted to put Alleyn off his stride from the outset. 'Buzz me through, will you?'

They went into Alleyn's study – his den, he called it: all wood panels and leather, like a Bing Crosby movie. Jones declined a drink. Alleyn was supping something tall and fizzy like a thirsty fish, and already had red eyes and a runny nose. Jones sat across the desk from him. 'You were trying to get me again, this morning,' he said. 'Sorry to be so elusive. Ten kinds of hell going down, as you may realise.'

'What about the fire?' Alleyn said.

'We're still working on the assumption that the second body was Kimberly. I've not told anyone otherwise, so only you and me know. And your assistants.'

'They'll not blab.'

'Good. How is she?' Jones said.

'Going ape.'

'As you would. What's your plan?'

'She recognised Graham, from the taxi. Knows where she is. So it's difficult.'

'I'll bet.' As Jones had expected, Alleyn couldn't let Kimberly live.

'You charged Jarvis yet?'

'He's no longer a person of interest.'

'What? Why not?'

Jones shook his head, took his time. He'd never seen why Alleyn was so keen to connect Jarvis with the fire, but that was water under the bridge. 'There's things closer to home we need to talk about,' he said.

'What?'

Alleyn's eyes were down, his frown dark. He liked things his own way, always, and was perhaps sensing a change in the weather.

'We need to face up to some realities and start talking turkey,' Jones said, hitting the cliché button. 'All cards on the table. Because the shit is going to hit the fan sooner rather than later. And when it does there'll be fuck-all I can do to stop it.'

'What do you mean? What shit?'

Jones made himself tall, looked him in the eye. 'Murder. Tom Simpson. I'm sitting on stuff as hard as I can and trying to keep the bottle spinning, but when it stops, guess who it's going to be pointing at?' He stood, leaned across and tapped Alleyn on the forehead, quite hard.

'Me?' Alleyn seemed unable to believe what was happening to him. He leaned back, straightened up. 'What the…'

'Don't give me that,' Jones said, stepping towards the door. 'You made some simple mistakes. People generally do.' He opened the door, looked out and listened. He closed and leaned his back on it. He counted off points of evidence on his fingers.

'One. Your car's a bit conspicuous. Two. Some taxi drivers have good memories. Three. Trace evidence. Your DNA, on two cocoa mugs. Your hairs all over the place, and no-one else's, apart from Tom's and Linda's. Fingerprints likewise. Including on the morphine blister packs, which you could have found a more intelligent place to put than their neighbour's bin. Enough for a conviction right there. Four, you trusted your own people, and they hate you. Surely you know that? Five. You really should have got rid of Linda's diary.'

'Diary?'

'What did you do with her, by the way?'

'Nothing!'

Jones watched Alleyn slowly deflate, like a balloon with a slow puncture.

'Nothing,' he said again. 'I just shut her in a room upstairs. When I went back, she'd buggered off out the window.'

'When you were giving Tom his hot chocolate?'

'I didn't say that!'

'What did they have on you?'

'Nothing.'

'Must have been something.'

'Hardly anything.'

Jones waited.

'Linda put something on Facebook,' Alleyn said. 'About the deal we did for them. The house, the jobs. And mentioned my name.'

'Yes?'

'And someone said, "if it's the same guy that acted for my dad when he sold his farm, look out".'

'Go on.'

'It was years ago. A farm near Didcot. I don't know why he was complaining. I got him a good price. For farmland.'

'Something tells me the buyer wasn't interested in farming,' Jones said.

'The buyer happened to know the MoD wanted it, for some top-secret weapons facility. It was right by Rutherford Labs.'

'So the buyer resold it for a slightly higher price?'

'You could put it like that,' Alleyn said.

'You were acting for the seller but doing a favour for the buyer. And all this was on social media?'

'Bits were.'

'Who was the buyer?'

'That wasn't on Facebook. Your boss now, as it happens.'

'What? Not the Chief Constable!'

'Don't be daft. The Commissioner. Martin Carter. He'd not long left the army and was getting his property business off the ground. Alongside selling tanks to the Saudis and all that.'

Things that had puzzled Jones fell into place, like his superiors' interest in the Glebe Farm protests. If Sir Martin was under pressure to do Alleyn's bidding, he might be quite pleased with what Jones was planning.

'James, this is a mess,' Jones said. 'Sir Martin can't help you now. Neither can I. You need to realise the game's up. If you don't want to face the music, it's time to cash your chips and head for the hills.' He handed a folder across the desk. 'And here's the wherewithal. Passport, in the name of John Allenby. A plane ticket, Heathrow to Sydney, in that name. Cards, cash, bank account details, driving licences, phone et cetera.'

Jones didn't remember seeing Alleyn surprised before. But this was the sudden end of everything that made him what he was.

'Put together by professionals,' Jones said. 'I've got mine too, for Patagonia. We won't be contacting each other.'

Alleyn opened the folder, rifled through. 'This flight's tonight, for Christ's sake. Check-in ten thirty. I'd have to leave by nine.'

'The sooner the better, before some busybody at the station puts you on the Border Agency watchlist. Leave your car in the short stay with the keys under the front nearside wheel arch. It'll be picked up and sold, and the proceeds added to your stash.'

'Who's doing that?'

'That accountant, Robert Forster,' Jones said.

'Graham Cruickshank's mate?'

'Yes, him.'

'When's your flight?'

'Ten tomorrow, Gatwick to San Carlos.' Jones dug some papers out, laid them on the desk. 'You need to sign a few forms,' he said. 'Forster's set up all the financials. These give him power of attorney.' He pointed at two sets of forms. 'And these shift everything into his client account, from which, in due course, it will be credited to your Allenby account down under.'

'Can I trust him?'

'He's one of your people.'

'True.'

'Why don't you phone him?'

'Can I trust you?'

'You've trusted me well enough for years. Have I ever let you down?'

'Are you really going to Patagonia? You got the tickets? Show me.'

Jones pulled some papers from his folder, put them on the desk.

Alleyn scanned them. 'You're taking Olwen?'

'Of course. And the girls.'

'I'll call her.'

Alleyn plied his mobile.

'There's only me, her and Forster know about this,' Jones said. 'And you, now. She won't say anything unless I okay it.'

Alleyn looked at him, gave a slow nod. 'Olwen, hello,' he said. 'James Alleyn. Can I ask you a couple of questions?'

'Mr Alleyn, hello,' Olwen said. 'What do you want to know?'

'Where are you going tomorrow?'

'Is Daff there? Put him on.'

'He's on.'

'Daff, is it okay? Can I?'

'It's fine,' Jones said. 'He knows. Go ahead.'

'Patagonia,' she said. 'We land in San Carlos de Bariloche midday Tuesday UK time. That's 3pm local time.'

'And what will you do when you get there?' Alleyn said.

'We're going to our ranch in the mountains, on the Rio Villegas. It's so exciting! And it's just amazing what you can afford there, for what we got for our house here.'

'You've sold already?'

'Completed yesterday. New people moving in tomorrow. The ranch purchase completes tomorrow too. Mr Forster's looking after it all, he's a genius.'

'Okay, thanks.' Alleyn hung up, turned to Jones. 'What if I say no?'

'Your only other option,' Jones said, his hand moving under his jacket to rest on a shoulder holster containing a Smith & Wesson M&P, 'is to accompany DC Clappison to the station, under arrest for murder. In which case, consider yourself cautioned.'

Alleyn shook his head.

'Two options,' Jones said. 'Sign up and get out, or go up to the beak for murder. Sounds like a no-brainer to me.'

'If I go down for murder, you'll go down too. And Sir Martin.'

'I won't be here and Sir Martin can look after himself. Clappison's duty officer tonight. That's why you'd be going with him,' Jones said, watching the pieces fall into place in Alleyn's head. 'Me and Ols are off tonight anyway, whatever you do.'

'Tonight?'

'Yeah. Dump the car at Heathrow, transfer to Gatwick in the coach, using our new names. The girls are going straight to the airport hotel from their outward-bound centre in Poole. They think it's a surprise holiday. Olwen's buzzing.'

'What happens to all this?' Alleyn waved his hands, seeming to indicate his property, his affairs.

'Not your concern,' Jones said. 'Not mine either. Forster will tidy up and forward the proceeds.'

Alleyn shook himself, thumped the desk with both fists. 'Give me a pen,' he said.

Jones pushed one towards him.

'Where do I sign?'

'Ten places. Each marked with a little green post-it. Sign them all.'

Jones counted them off as Alleyn scribbled his signature through the documents. Alleyn looked nervous, but possibly relieved too. He certainly wasn't reading the documents he was signing. When he was done, Jones scooped them up and slotted them in his folder.

'Thanks,' he said, 'and good luck. I'll drop these with Forster on my way home. Just walk down to the car with me, will you? Where's the Porsche? In the garage? Bring your keys. I've got a little farewell gift for you.'

***

Jones tidied up and left Alleyn in the Porsche. He drove home slowly, wanting to arrive after Olwen's bedtime; he was feeling drained, and in no state to deal with her ever-insightful questions. At 11 p.m. he was sitting on a bench in the car park of Bernwood Forest, listening to the sounds of the woodland and the distant drone of the M40, and expecting a phone call at any moment.

It soon came, from Clappison at Thames Valley Police Kidlington. 'Alleyn's died at home,' he said.

'Alleyn? Dead?'

'Unexplained circumstances,' Clappison said. 'That's all I know so far. Thought I'd clue you in. Normal procedure?'

'Yes, why not?' Jones said. 'And by the way, I saw him earlier this evening, so I'll be standing back. You work to Grant on this. You'll need to assemble a team and get out there.'

'You'll make a statement?' Clappison said.

'Of course. In the morning. The bones of it will be: I was there about ten minutes, left by eight. He was guzzling fizz like there was no tomorrow. And on the coke, by the look of his nose. In an odd mood. Agitated. Talking twenty to the dozen about a trip he might take.'

'Thank you, sir. Will you call Grant?'

'No, you do it. Tell him we'll need a full search of the house and grounds, from first light. Call me if anything goes awry. Call me by seven whatever.'

***

Jones slept in the spare room, as he often did when a disturbed night was in prospect. Or rather, he didn't sleep, but lay there, thinking it all through. Being an acquaintance of the dead man, and a possible witness, he had to stay outside the investigation. But there was one thing not directly related to Alleyn's death that he would do: find Kimberly, if she really was being held alive somewhere, as Alleyn had told him. He'd be on that first thing.

Clappison called at 7 a.m. with an update. The butler and staff had seen and heard nothing unusual. It looked like a drug-related death. He'd been found in his car, with something that could be a suicide note. And travel documents in a false name had been found on Alleyn's desk.

Jones stared at his porridge. It matched his mood: cold and grey. Olwen refused to buy Lyle's Golden Syrup. She said he ladled it on, it wasn't good for him, and she wanted them both to have a long and active retirement, not to be shackled to a fat invalid for the duration. But she was upstairs in the bathroom. Listening carefully, moving quietly and feeling more guilty about this than he did about last night's business, he found the sugar jar in the pantry, tipped a generous dollop onto the porridge, stirred it in and took another spoonful.

It was still awful. His phone pinged: *Meet in Commissioner's office, 9am. Vanessa.*

A message from the Chief Constable, signing herself Vanessa? Was he in her good books, or was she softening him up for the chop? He scraped the porridge into the compost caddy, found the shoe-cleaning kit, did some spit-and-polishing, showered, put on a decent shirt, suit and tie. He went to shout goodbye up the stairs, but Olwen was coming down in her dressing gown. She handed him a cold hot-water bottle.

'So what happened?' she said. 'With James Alleyn. I heard your call, about him being dead.'

'He seems to have taken an overdose,' Jones said, emptying the bottle in the kitchen sink and hanging it on the back of the pantry door, feeling nauseous. One instinct said the less she knew, the better. Another said he owed her more than that. And that it mattered.

'Is it anything to do with that charade we went through last night?'

'Could be,' he said. 'I'm not sure how much you need to know about that. You did well though, thanks. Just right.'

'Daffy, I had a hand in it, I need to know what I did. And I need you to be honest with me.'

He looked at her. She was right, of course, moral compass pointing true as usual. But it was a long story. An embarrassing one. Would she still respect him by the end? 'Be honest, is it?' It was like diving off the highest board, not knowing whether the pool was full or empty. But slower. 'Right. Do you want a coffee?'

She sat at the kitchen table.

He put the kettle on and spooned Kilimanjaro into the cafetière. Nothing was more important than clearing the air between them. 'He'd been paying me for doing favours for him for years,' he said. 'That's how we could afford the girls' school fees, amongst other things.'

She nodded, as if she'd known all along, or this answered questions she'd asked herself. She normally left money management to him, but anyone who looked would see something was going on. And every year she had to sign off her tax return and Dewi Security's accounts. She always protested her innumeracy and he'd assumed she never looked at the detail. Perhaps he'd been wrong.

'Whenever I had a doubt,' he said, 'he'd threaten to tell all. Blackmail, basically. When I tried to back out, to draw a line, call it quits, he started threatening you and the girls. He'd had someone watching, had photos of the girls playing hockey and stuff at school. In the end I had no choice. If I blew the whistle on him, it would be the end of everything for us. And you can imagine what life would be like for a bent cop in clink. Or for the ex-wife of a bent cop, and his daughters, anywhere.'

He poured two coffees and joined her at the table. Having started, he had to tell her the lot. And as he told, a great weight lifted. If he was late for the nine o'clock meeting, so be it.

'He was into some heavy stuff. Drugs, fakes, weapons, people trafficking, prostitution. He ran sweat shop and internet scamming operations in his back garden, using east Asians who were effectively forced labour. It was bad enough having to keep him in the clear on all that.'

'Hence the big pay-offs,' Olwen said. 'I see. But he wasn't actually killing people.'

'Not to my knowledge. Not until Tom Simpson, the farmer. Unless he did the Sefton-Shaws too, but I can't see why he would. The Simpsons had something on him, from his past, that Linda found. That protestor guy, Jarvis, fingered him. We checked the forensics and it all stacked up. He'd have done Linda too, but she escaped out a window. So he said. He didn't seem to care that I knew. Then we convinced him we were making a run for it, to Patagonia, and his protection in the force was vanishing.'

Olwen was looking at him steadily, apparently not fazed by what she'd heard so far. 'So why did you have to kill him? Why not let him disappear to Australia?'

It was a good question. It needed a good answer. 'For one thing, I didn't trust him. He'd have a hell of a lot of money, but he wasn't the sort to economise, or to stick to his word. I didn't want to spend the rest of my life wondering when he was going to come back for more. So call that self-preservation.'

'And?'

'I'm a cop, he's a murderer. I had all the evidence I needed, but I couldn't bring him in.'

'So your sense of natural justice said he had to die?'

'Yes.'

'Doesn't that make you as guilty as him?'

'No. I don't feel guilty at all. He was bad enough before, but once he'd started killing... and I realised he was going to kill again soon. He had to be stopped.'

'He wasn't married, was he? No family. What's going to happen to all that money?'

'Well...' Jones hesitated. He wanted that money. It would make for a very comfortable retirement.

'Daffy, I can read your mind. No.'

'No?'

'There's those people, C.O.P.S. is it? They support the families of officers who die on duty. And I came across something the other day, a charity that helps pregnant women in prison. Fifty fifty.'

Jones swallowed. 'Yes dear,' he said. 'Good idea.' He was relieved; she was concerned with the fairness of outcomes, but seemed to have accepted that Alleyn had to die.

'How did you do it?' she said. 'Kill him.'

'When he'd signed all the forms, I said come down to the car, I've got something for you. It was a syringe loaded with fentanyl.'

'Surely he didn't just stand there and let you inject him?'

'No. I said, I'll just get it, sit in your car. As I got in his passenger seat I gave him a squirt of PAVA.'

'What's that?'

'Incapacitant spray. Gets in your eyes, hurts a bit, stops you doing whatever you're doing for a good fifteen minutes. Leaves no trace afterwards. He thrashed around a bit but stopped when I said, 'Hold still'. Long enough for me to slip the syringe in his arm. Which was covered in tracks, by the way, so he was a user. He was out in two seconds. Fentanyl's tricky, people often OD. I used enough to see him off. Cleaned up for prints on the syringe and so on, left it in his arm. Left a note in the foot well, as if he'd dropped it.'

'Christ.'

'I didn't enjoy it, Ols. It was horrible. But now and again you get these things that've just got to be done. This was one of them.'

***

The Chief Constable and the Commissioner were by the window, deep in conversation. The Chief looked round. 'Jones, good,' she said. 'Sit down. With you in a moment.'

Jones sat, checked his watch. He was only two minutes late. His head was spinning. Things had been moving fast. He wouldn't be surprised if the shit hit the proverbial very soon. He was surprised by how calm he felt. But Alleyn had been an utterly ruthless bastard, the world was better without him. And knowing that Olwen knew the truth and was still behind him made his heart glow. Moral compasses are all very well, but when it came to her daughters, she had all the morals of a tiger defending cubs.

The Commissioner sat behind his desk, picked up a pencil, sharpened it. The Chief Constable remained standing, near the window, upright, hands clasped behind her. She cleared her throat. 'Inspector Jones. We'd like to review some of the events of the last few months, with respect to possible connections between them, and to the actions and achievements of your department.'

'Yes ma'am.' It sounded rather menacing. Jones took a breath, straightened up, looked her in the eye. He realised he didn't really care. And it dawned on him that if it came down to it, they really could go to Patagonia. Olwen had been intrigued. He had to suppress a smile.

'The fire that killed Conrad Sefton-Shaw and his wife, in mysterious circumstances.'

'Yes ma'am.'

'The death of Thomas Simpson and the disappearance of his wife, Linda. Also in mysterious circumstances.'

'Yes ma'am.'

'Yes, Inspector. Sefton-Shaw, the city's Director for Sustainable Development. Responsible for planning and an active proponent of developments like Glebe Farm. At one time you had a suspect, for manslaughter or murder. Nothing came of it.'

'Nothing, ma'am.' Jones was addressing the Chief Constable, but was uncomfortably aware of the Commissioner watching him carefully from behind his desk. Jones turned to him, gave a solemn nod. The Commissioner solemnly nodded back. Jones couldn't make the guy out.

'No, Inspector. So the circumstances of their deaths remain mysterious.'

'Yes ma'am,' he said, turning back to her.

'Thomas and Linda Simpson,' the Chief said, 'were the tenants of Glebe Farm, and had recently moved to accommodation and employment near Witney. As you probably realise, the Commissioner and I were under pressure from highly placed persons to hurry everything along, the autopsy and inquest and so on. I... we, in fact?' She raised an eyebrow in the direction of the Commissioner, who looked away, studied the tip of his pencil. 'We were not privy to the reasons for this, and despite the inquest's findings on Tom's death, we still find that episode rather odd.'

'Yes ma'am.'

'We went for misadventure, drug-related, in order to expedite the process. What would your instinct have been, if there'd been no hurry?'

'Well, ma'am,' Jones said, thinking carefully. Best to be as honest as he could. 'As I see it, he wasn't the sort to experiment with drugs. And he struck me as a vigorous outdoors type, not given to introspection. And a family man. So I'd say suicide was unlikely. Which leaves unlawful killing. Manslaughter or murder.'

'Do you have any thoughts on who would benefit from his death? And his wife's disappearance?'

'Nothing concrete, ma'am,' he said. Nothing beyond the obvious, anyway. He hoped they'd get there without him handing it to them on a plate. 'We rather stopped looking, with the way the inquest was handled, and being busy on other fronts. But I did notice that the accommodation and employment that had been set up for them were rather short-term. As if those who organised it didn't expect them to be there for long, though they'd been led to believe it was permanent.'

'Couldn't have been a way of buying them off, could it?' the Commissioner asked, looking up, breaking his silence.

'Buying them off?'

'Promising them the earth, if they stopped protesting and vacated the farm. Then once that'd been achieved and the land deal had gone through…'

'… they became a burden. Or a liability,' Jones said, thinking that perhaps there were a few little grey cells under the Commissioner's well-groomed pate after all. 'Yes sir, I see what you mean. Could have been.'

'So,' the Chief Constable said, 'who could it have been that wanted them out of the protests and out of Glebe Farm?'

'Possibly the purchasers of the land, Ballator. Or St Mark's, the sellers. Or their agent.'

'And who was their agent?'

'James Alleyn,' Jones said. He could have written the script, and took care not to look too pleased with the direction they were taking. 'He was actually a golfing buddy of mine. I've known him since I came up here, ten years back. We played a round up at Hinksey not long ago. And I actually popped in to his place yesterday evening, to drop some papers in to do with the golf club accounts. I used to be on the committee. He still is. Was.'

'What sort of mood was he in?'

Jones tried to look thoughtful. 'A bit skittish,' he said, 'if I'm honest. Talking about a trip he was planning. Didn't say where.'

'So, Inspector. Last night, another death in mysterious circumstances. James Alleyn. Your golfing buddy. You were one of the last people to see him alive.'

'Indeed, ma'am.'

'He was a close friend and associate of Conrad Sefton-Shaw. He was the lawyer for Thomas and Linda Simpson, he arranged their accommodation and employment in West Oxfordshire. We've learned that he also acted for St Mark's College, on various briefs, and was senior non-exec at Ballator's, the property company, active in their successful bid for Glebe Farm.'

'Yes ma'am. A man of many parts.'

'Would you call that a conflict of interest? Acting for the buyer, the seller, and the evicted tenant?'

'I'm sure you could look at it that way, ma'am.' Odd that none of the parties had raised this when it could have made a difference.

'Tell us what you know about his death.'

'It's too soon to be drawing conclusions, ma'am. We're still all over the site.'

'Understood. But tell us what you know.'

'Yes ma'am. As I said, I saw him briefly early evening. He seemed very preoccupied, but then he often did. I'd left by eight, didn't stay to chat. His butler found him a few minutes before eleven. The butler would normally check with Alleyn around ten thirty, before retiring. When he couldn't find him, he looked to see if his car was around. It was in the garage, and he was in the driving seat. The butler went to speak to him and saw he was out of it. He opened the door, found a syringe in his arm. Checked his vitals, which were absent. Administered CPR, called emergency services. They rushed him into A&E but he was DOA.'

'So, looking like suicide? Or another indeterminate one?'

'Too soon to say. Suicide or misadventure, drug-related. I'm back out there as soon as we finish here. But I heard from the team that they've found what might be a note – no details yet. And a package of travel documents, passport, bank cards and so on, in a different name, but Alleyn's photo, suggesting he might have been about to do a runner.'

'Thank you, Jones. One other thing then, before we let you get back on the case.'

'Yes ma'am. A quick question first, if I may? Before we move on. You mentioned some highly placed persons who wanted you to hurry along the inquest on Thomas Simpson. Who were they?'

The Chief Constable turned to the Commissioner. He nodded.

'It was actually the Master of one of the Colleges,' she said.

Not all colleges use the term, Master. 'Was it St Mark's?'

'Possibly, Inspector,' the Chief said.

'Look,' the Commissioner said, 'it was the Master of St Mark's. Which happens to be my alma mater. The Master is also a personal friend.'

'I see, sir. Right.' Jones guessed that St Mark's was using him, but the Commissioner wasn't in on what was going on.

'Jones,' the Chief Constable said. 'That person you had lined up for the fire. Who was it? What happened to him?'

'Michael Jarvis, ma'am. Computer consultant. Insufficient evidence to hold further. Seems to have been in an emotional entanglement with Sefton-Shaw's wife, hence the forensic evidence of his presence in the house. Released without charge.'

'I see. Thank you. So these three situations. The Sefton-Shaws. Tom and Linda Simpson. Alleyn. Are they connected? Are they the tip of an iceberg? Is there a wider picture that they're part of? Is anything else likely to surface at some point?'

Jones sensed that this was a crunch moment, that a lot was hanging on how he answered, not least his pension and his family's future. He wasn't sure how to play it. Telling the truth, the whole truth, etc, was impossible. Only he and Olwen knew everything. Mick Jarvis knew quite a bit. But Jarvis had given his word and Jones trusted him – he couldn't put his finger on why. The fire at the Sefton-Shaws remained a mystery, once Jarvis was discounted, unless Alleyn had done it for reasons unknown. Alleyn had done for the farmers, and Jones himself had done for Alleyn, though he was going to make misadventure or suicide stick. He decided to opt for what felt like the line of least resistance. 'In my view, ma'am,' he said, 'there's no wider picture, no submerged iceberg. It's just three things that happened to happen. The fact that they all had some remote connection with the Glebe Farm sale is just coincidence.'

'Good!' the Commissioner said, leaping to his feet. He marched to the window, executed a parade ground about-turn and saluted Jones.

Jones reflexively rose to his feet and returned the salute. *The man's barking*, he thought, *if he thinks all that is coincidence. But he could just be pleased to have Alleyn off his back.*

Jones glanced at the Chief Constable, who had also risen and saluted. Her eyes met his. *She agrees*, he thought. *But doesn't want me rocking the boat.*

'Steady as she goes, Jones,' she said.

He nodded his understanding.

The Commissioner looked blankly from one to the other.

They all sat down again.

'One last thing before we let you get back to work,' the Chief Constable said. 'I see that you're due to retire at the end of March next year.'

'Yes ma'am. Seven months left. And a bit.'

'Any plans?'

'Hoping to go back to South Wales, ma'am. My wife's keen on

a place on the Gower. We have to consider affordability, cash flow. It's marginal, even with the lump sum from my pension.'

'It's just that we'd really value a safe pair of hands on the wheel here, for the next year or so,' the Chief said, 'at DCI level, while things get back on an even keel. If it turns out there is a wider picture and bits of iceberg start surfacing, we'd need someone in place with your grip on the detail, to steer a course through that sort of thing, should it happen.'

'Me, ma'am?' Not only was he not being fired, he was being offered a promotion to DCI. And pension was based on final salary. What was not to like?

'If it's of any interest, Jones,' the Commissioner said. 'Alongside the promotion, there might be something we could do by way of a little help with affordability, cash flow, that sort of thing. Think about it.'

'Yes sir. Ma'am. Thank you. I'll talk to my wife. Let you know.'

He left, trying for nonchalance.

CHAPTER 52

Monday morning, early, I walked Friday over the common with a mind like a swarm of bees, trying to think of anything but Kimberly. There was no point going to work when I felt like this, and I had to take the afternoon off to see Clappison anyway. I texted Denise to say I was taking a day's leave. There were other things I had to do.

I brewed coffee and noticed a text from the vets in Kidlington reminding me to book Friday's six-monthly check. I called: they could do today, one thirty. I'd take her on the way to the police station, kill two birds.

An email came in from Udvari, with details of the Ballator board members. So far so good. I sent them all the briefing notes, and an agenda:

Ballator Developments
Emergency Board Meeting (convened by Prof. Udvari)
10 a.m. Wednesday 2nd August, Board Room, Botley
Subject: Glebe Farm Project
Agenda
Introduction: M Jarvis
Aspects of the Acquisition (see Briefing Notes)

Proposed Partnerships with Wildlife Trust and Community Land Trust
Ballator's Role in Making it Happen
AOB
Documents attached: Glebe Farm Briefing Notes (M Jarvis)

I breathed out. Anything else, while I was doing things?

Linda. If she was still alive, she must have done a runner, and would still be hiding somewhere. Where would she have run to? I'd bet on local; she hadn't seemed like a traveller. I found the Oxford Mail website, small ads section. Kept it simple.

LINDA SIMPSON. Safe to come home. Call Mick.

I Googled *Kimberly Anastasia Trevithick*, the name Clappison had mentioned. I found an archive photo from Tatler: a debutante in a black ballgown, looking nervous and unsure, surrounded by oily oiks in bursting DJs. She was such a mystery. Where had she come from?

I headed off with Friday, jogged up the muddy river, skirting Wytham Wood. I cooled down at Swinford Lock, sitting in dappled sun, watching boats come and go, staring at the dark water and the busy network of spiders' webs spanning the lock-gates in strange collaboration, thinking about Kimberly. What a life she'd had.

My life was changed, whether I liked it or not. And she had changed it.

***

I took Friday to the vets for her check-up. She was in good shape but I should brush her teeth more. What fun. I went on to Thames Valley Police. Friday had never been in a cop shop before so I took her in.

We arrived at the duty desk a few minutes before two, feeling edgy. It was not my favourite place. I sat loose, back straight, arms at my sides, hands still. I closed my eyes and focused on the most distant sound. Clappison arrived at ten past. He gave Friday a look, but made no comment, and led us across the car park towards the operations building. DI Jones emerged from the door we were heading for. It was too late to avoid him, and he seemed to be greeting me and Friday with a smile.

'Who's this then?' he said, reaching down to ruffle her head. 'We had one just like this when I was a boy.'

'This is Friday,' I said. 'She came from the dog pound in Merthyr Tydfil, via a friendly vet.'

'The land of my fathers,' he said. 'Not force but fellowship.'

'Eh?'

'Catch you later,' Jones said. He smiled and strode off. I looked after him, puzzled. He seemed like a different man.

Clappison anticipated my question. 'He's been like that all day,' he said. 'Since a nine o'clock with the Chief. Rita says...'

'Rita?'

'His secretary. Says he's staying on for another year. He was due to retire next March and seemed desperate to get out, but...'

'There's some wish he would,' I said.

'You'd think he'd be upset,' Clappison said. 'About having to stay on, and about his buddy's death.'

'Whose death?'

'His golf buddy, James Alleyn. A lawyer. What is it?'

My face must have betrayed my shock. 'Alleyn's dead? How? When?'

'Last night,' Clappison said, opening the door into Operations. 'They're still doing the forensics, but it's OD or suicide.'

I looked back across the car park. Jones was unlocking a car. He must have sensed my gaze: he turned and raised a hand before getting in and shutting the door. I followed Clappison up the stairs. Alleyn dead? Suicide would surprise me, Alleyn wasn't the type at all.

Then I thought, *cui bono*? Who benefits from his death? Jones, of course. Apart from me and Kanhai, who else knew about Alleyn's hold over Jones? Grant could put two and two together, but he knew how to keep his mouth shut. Nobody else would have a clue.

'He's got his dream home now,' Clappison said, trotting up the stairs. 'Rita said he had an offer accepted this morning, a place on the coast near Swansea.'

We followed Clappison through the big open-plan SPAT office. No sign of Grant, but a hum of activity I hadn't heard before. Half of the twenty-odd desks were occupied by hard-faced men and women, on phones or typing into screens. The hum died as our arrival registered. All eyes followed us across the room. Friday walked to heel, ears pricked, sniffing.

Two women sat by Clappison's desk at the far end, one in uniform. The other rose as we approached. 'Emma, this is Michael Jarvis,' Clappison said. 'Mick, this is Emma Hardwick, from social services.'

I shook her hand. She was soft and round, with smiley dimples and short brown hair. Friday wagged her tail and put her nose up Emma's skirt.

'And this,' Clappison said, indicating the dark, straight-backed woman in uniform, 'is PC Dodds.' I leaned across and shook her hand too. Friday put a paw on her knee.

'Coffee?' Clappison asked.

I took the remaining chair. Friday tucked herself beneath it. No-one wanted coffee.

'Have a look at this,' Clappison said, handing me a document. 'And sign it, if it's in line with our discussion on Saturday.'

I scanned the statement. It seemed innocuous. I initialled the first page, signed and dated at the foot of the second and handed it back to Clappison.

'Thank you,' Clappison said. 'Would you like a copy?'

'Could you email it?' I said. 'Thanks.' I stood, nodding to the two women. I was hardly concentrating, my mind still buzzing with thoughts of Jones and Alleyn. 'I'll be off then. Good to meet you.'

'But…' said Emma from social services, looking from me to Clappison.

'Yes, bear with us a minute, please,' Clappison said. 'Something we need to run past you. Emma?'

I sat down again.

'Thank you,' Emma said. 'Mick, you're aware of the research that DC Clappison and I have been doing, looking for family or friends of the Sefton-Shaws who are willing, able, fit and proper to take on caring for Alasdair, Bella and Charlotte.'

'Yes,' I said. 'That's in what I just signed.'

'You know our search didn't produce many possibilities and that all three children are currently with emergency foster carers in Coventry.'

'Yes,' I said. I felt one of those tingles in the back of the neck.

'You're aware that Kimberly had initiated divorce proceedings against Conrad.'

'Yes.'

'And that Kimberly was pregnant when she died.'

'Yes, someone said.'

'With your child.'

'Why do you think that?' The tingle in my neck turned to a juddering shiver up and down my spine.

'She was in touch with someone in your family, with whom we've also been in touch,' Emma said. 'On that evening, before the fire, Kimberly couldn't get hold of you so she told them she'd just tested positive and that it must be yours.'

'My mum?' I said. Why didn't she tell me? Or was that obvious?

'She didn't pass it on?' Emma said. 'No. Because by the time she could, the fire had happened. But you'll understand why you are what we call a connected person. In fact, the nearest thing we've got to family.'

'What?'

Friday came out from under the chair and stood between us, looking from one to the other.

'It looks to us,' Emma said, 'that if it hadn't been for that terrible fire, you were well on course to becoming these children's stepfather. And the father of their sister…'

'Oh crikey,' I said, feeling like my plane was falling out of the sky. 'Was it a girl? I didn't know.'

'…or brother, I was going to say. We don't know either. You're also the nearest thing we have to a close friend of the family,' Emma said. 'At least, of one of them.'

'What? Me?'

'Of course. Of their mother. And the twins say they know you, and like you, trust you. You gave Bella a moustache, she says. I don't think anyone had ever done that before. Or anything like it. So with DC Clappison's help, we've done the initial vetting, checking they'd be safe with you.'

'What? The twins? With me?'

'And the boy. Usually takes a couple of months, but we took the liberty of having you temporarily approved as a carer under Regulation 24. So we contacted your GP, in confidence. And three referees.'

'Referees?'

'Yes. Detective Sergeant Grant. He seemed pleased to be asked. Kanhai Jamal, who's known you forever, he says. And your mother. Lovely woman! Said she'd given you a glowing reference to someone else, not long ago. Wouldn't say who. I could guess. But she was delighted you were, as she put it, taking life seriously at last.'

'But surely someone like me can't just… adopt, is it? Become responsible for children like these?'

'Special guardianship, not adoption. But why not?' Emma said. 'Are you a paedophile? Or on the sex offenders register?'

'No.'

'Criminal convictions? Or cautions? Particularly for violence.'

'No. Once got a speeding ticket.'

'Anger management issues? Pathological hatred of children?'

'No.'

'Do you have family or friends who could support you as a new parent?'

'Don't know. Could ask, I suppose.'

'We did. You do. And you'll be pleased to know that you came out of the initial assessment rated A*.'

I stood, tried to stop my arms flapping around. I didn't know what to say. I looked from the social worker, Emma, who was wearing a wide smile, to PC Dodds, also smiling, to Friday, who wagged and said *Yaroo*, and to Clappison, who was grinning. He'd fished out a sheaf of papers joined with green treasury tags, and had something to add. 'This lot came in last week,' he said. 'But I didn't finish going through it 'til this morning. From Sara Bhatti, Kimberly's solicitor, at Bowman's.'

He leafed through, looking for something.

'Lots of stuff. Where they'd got to in the divorce. Conrad wasn't contesting it. Decree nisi granted, 12th June.'

'12th June?' I couldn't believe it. That was the day I'd planted the bug. And...

'Yes. They'd have had their decree absolute by now. She was going to have custody of the children. The solicitor had drafted a new will, and sent a copy to Kimberly with various questions. Kimberly had sent her answers back. That's where they were before the fire.' He found the sheet he was looking for, folded the sheaf open, passed it to me. 'It hadn't been signed and sealed, but it will be pretty clear to the court what her wishes were. Question nine.'

9. In the event of your death before they reach adulthood, who would you want to take care of your children?
Definitely not Conrad. Not anyone in his family.
I'll check with him first but I'd like it to be my friend Michael Jarvis.
Flat 3 Wytham Court, Godstow Road, Wolvercote.

'Did she ever check with you?' Clappison said.

I shook my head, tried to hold back the moisture that wanted to burst from my face. Was that what the crossed-out stuff from the smelly bin bag was about? I could see it would be a delicate thing to ask. And she'd checked me out with my mother too, not just as a potential partner but as a potential carer for her children in the event of her death. That would be the other reference my mum had given.

'Oh lordy,' I said, beginning to realise how much I hadn't realised, like how isolated she'd been, and how much, for some reason, she'd really cared for me.

'That makes things even more simple,' Emma said. 'They have to be somewhere. They're quite old for adoption, people usually want to start with a baby. A teenager and twins, very difficult. We'd do our absolute best to keep them together, but it'd be next to impossible.'

I passed the papers back to Clappison, then sat down, elbows on knees, head in hands. Closed my eyes, tried to think. I remembered my grandad's voice saying, 'Follow the path with the heart in it.' I saw Kimberly's face, her eyes open, looking into mine. Her soft smile. That feeling of being inside a warm cocoon.

'What would happen,' I said, looking up, 'if I said I'd give it a go?'

'We'd formalise what we've done so far. Your temporary carer approval will last for sixteen weeks, while we do the full assessment for special guardianship. Alongside that you'd get some training. Assuming that's all okay, which it will be, a special guardianship order, in family court. They can be with you as soon as you like, in that process. With lots of guidance and support. We'd suggest seeing them with us for the first few weeks, while you get set up at your end.'

'How long altogether? Until the court thing.'

'Not long. Around three months. Definitely less than six.'

'I don't know about this at all,' I said. 'I hardly know them. And I'm not sure I'm ready for fatherhood. Single parenthood. Because that's what this is, isn't it?'

'How old are you again, Mick?' PC Dodds said.

'Thirty-four,' I said.

No-one spoke.

Dodds coughed.

How many times had I said 'I' just then? Was this all about me?

'Ay, ay, ay,' Emma said, stretching her shoulders. 'Can we just try something?'

'Whatever,' I said, my head a tangle of self-doubt, fear, embarrassment.

PC Dodds rose, crossed to the entrance, went out.

I caught a look in Clappison's eye. Like a magician about to saw someone in half.

The door opened.

All the detectives at their desks looked up, watched the door. Friday sat up, pricked her ears and yodelled *ya-ya-yoo*.

PC Dodds came through, ushered in two small children. The twins.

Who looked nervously round the room, until they saw me.

Charlotte's eyes lit up.

Bella shrieked, 'It's the new Daddy!'

They ran towards me.

I ran to them, I couldn't help myself. I fell to my knees and caught them in open arms.

'Oh my God,' I said, finding it hard to breathe. 'Yes of course. Of course I'll take them on. Please.'

Alasdair shuffled across the room. I met his eye.

'Battlegrounds?' he said.

'Your game's saved,' I said, 'on my laptop.'

'Okay,' he said. Acknowledging saving the game? Accepting my guardianship? Both?

Clappison's phone rang. He picked up, listened. He stood, turned away, his face grey. 'You're kidding,' he said. 'Go on then.' He put the phone down, shook his head, stood, turned back to us. 'Hold your horses, boys and girls,' he said, looking at the door. Everyone followed his gaze.

DI Jones came through backwards, arms out as if holding back a crowd. 'You can't do it like this!' He was shouting. 'That's an order. This is insubordination.'

'Sorry, sir,' Grant said, still half outside the room, supporting someone. 'There's things more important than orders.'

The room was silent.

'Look who turned up in Mr Alleyn's basement,' Grant said, pushing past Jones with a woman on his arm. Kimberly, alive. Thinner but okay. No burns. Tears were rolling down her cheeks. Her eyes were glowing. And... a small bump?

She half crossed the room, knelt, put her arms out.

The twins walked towards her, uncertain.

'Momma,' Bella said, very quiet. 'They said you'd gone away.' She sobbed and Charlotte shrieked and they hurled themselves into a hug.

Friday followed them, and Alasdair followed Friday, diffident and slow, fighting a smile.

I don't believe in ghosts. It really was her. I shuffled towards her too, still on my knees, then stopped, unsure. She raised an arm from the melee and beckoned. I joined the hug.

CHAPTER 53

Friday and I walked over to Glebe Farm on the morning of Saturday 12th August, nearly two weeks after Kimberly's dramatic return. I could smell the toast fifty yards from the farmhouse. Friday gave me a look: she'd caught the scent too, and wouldn't mind some. We followed a badger path through tussocks. Lovelump lumbered out to meet us.

I unlatched the outer door, sat on the bench in the hall, traded boots for slippers, added my coat to a row of hooks, went through the inner door to the farmhouse kitchen.

'Morning, Mick,' Linda said. 'Will you have an egg too?'

'Just tea, thanks, if there's a brew.'

Linda pointed to the pot. She'd responded to my ad and moved straight back into Glebe Farm. Kimberly and the children had moved in too, pro tem. I was still in the flat, visiting the farm every day. The twins were at the table, dipping toast soldiers into boiled eggs in blue and white striped eggcups. I flopped in an armchair. 'Where's Kimberly and Alasdair?'

'She's dropping him over with Kanhai,' Linda said. 'Alasdair wants to work at GCHQ when he leaves school. Kanhai's teaching him about phishing and worms.'

Linda looked more at home than ever, enjoying the twins and

a busy household. I poured some tea, broke a crust off a slice of toast, tossed half to Friday in her basket, half to Lovelump. I said, 'Good morning, Charlotte. Good morning, Bella.'

'Good morning, Mick.'

I took the tea back to my chair.

Linda spoke to me quietly as she headed for the hall. 'They've got something on their mind,' she said, glancing towards the table. 'Bella was asking about the old daddy. Somebody might have been talking. You could see?'

There was something serious in her voice. 'Okay.' I was coming to trust her intuitions. 'Where are you off?'

'Just into Summertown. Meeting Gail.'

'Give her my love.'

'What about you?'

'Natural History Museum,' I whispered. 'Or picnic on a punt. But don't say…'

'We heard,' Bella said. 'Dinosaurs. And pretty rocks.'

'And shrunken heads,' Charlotte whispered. 'Ugh.'

'That's Pitt Rivers, silly,' Bella said.

'She's right. But they are joined together,' I said. 'Bye then.'

'Bye,' Linda said from the doorway. 'Have a good day, all of you.'

I took my tea to the table. 'Charlotte,' I said. 'What's your best thing, in the Nat Hist?'

'The bees.'

'Ugh. Creepy crawlies,' Bella said.

'Bella,' I said, 'don't be awful. The bees are brilliant. As bees go. What's your best?'

'The sun model with the earth and the moon in the café. And hot chocolate.'

'Yes, all brilliant too. So. Nat Hist or punt picnic?'

'Both,' they both said.

'Ha. We'll see what the weather's doing. Why don't you brush teeth, wash chins, find shoes and get ready? We'll go in half an

hour. I'll wash up. If you're ready and I'm not, read a book. Okay?'
I reached for the last piece of toast, put a pat of butter and a dollop of marmalade on my plate and squeezed brown dregs from the teapot.

The girls hadn't moved. A glance passed between them, a get-on-with-it look on Charlotte's face. I munched and waited.

'Mick,' Bella said. 'You've got to promise.'

'Promise what?'

'Not to tell.'

'Not to tell what?'

'Not to tell at all.'

'Okay,' I said. Was this another of their games? 'I promise. I won't tell.'

'Because we might get in trouble,' Bella said.

I buttered the second half slice, sensing their nervousness. They were trusting me with it, whatever it was. That was good. 'Go on then,' I said. 'I've promised. I'll keep my promise. What is it?'

'It was our fault,' Bella said.

'What was?'

'What happened to the Daddy.'

'What? Steady on.'

Charlotte sat still and pale, staring at the table-top. Bella returned my gaze, all hunched shoulders and scarlet cheeks. How could it be their fault? They were just five years old. There was an expression, 'survivor guilt'. Was this it?

'We didn't mean it,' Bella said. 'They'd been shouting and we'd already got up for a midnight feast and gone back to bed and got up again and I just wanted to see what would happen.'

'What would happen with what?' She was passing highly charged pieces of emotional jigsaw to me, one by one. What was the picture?

'Because a match goes whoosh, doesn't it. When it strikes. I wanted to make a bigger whoosh. So I lighted a match and put it in the box with the others, to see if it would.'

'Make a bigger whoosh?' Jesus Christ, I thought, forcing down the horror that was forming in my mind. 'Did it?'

I tried to compose my face, hide my reaction. Whatever they said, I had to be calm and steady, for their sake. I must not frighten them or judge them.

'Yes. And I was scared and I dropped it and ran away. And Charlotte, you tell yours.' Bella's shoulders had unhunched, her blush faded.

'You tell it,' Charlotte said, still small and pale and staring at the table.

'You,' said Bella.

'You.'

Bella rolled her eyes.

Charlotte scraped together a small heap of crumbs.

'Oh, all right,' Bella said. 'I'll start it for you. Charlotte was cross with the Daddy for shouting at Momma. Weren't you?'

'Yes,' Charlotte said, looking up, looking like she was re-living the crossness. 'And when they're cross with us, they shut us in our room and say you can't come out until you are truly sorry.'

'They lock the door,' Bella said.

'Oh my,' I said, glad they were talking, needing them to keep talking, wherever it led. 'Grown-ups can be mean sometimes.'

'So she did it to them,' Bella said.

'Who, Charlotte?'

'Yes.'

'Shut them in?'

'Yes.'

'While you were playing with matches, downstairs.'

'Yes,' Bella said.

'Locked them in?'

'Yes,' Charlotte said.

'You were just doing to your dad what he did to you,' I said, 'when he thought you'd been naughty.'

'Yes,' Charlotte said. 'I finded a key and put it in the hole and made it turn. It was hard but I did it. And then I shouted through the door that they could come out if they were truly sorry. But they didn't hear. Because the Daddy was shouting and Momma was crying.'

'You said it didn't sound like Momma,' Bella said.

'Well, it didn't. But…'

'But your momma escaped, didn't she?'

'Yes,' Charlotte said.

I looked at them, looked through them, saw two small girls doing two small things in different parts of the house, in unwitting collaboration. I forced myself to breathe deep and put on an encouraging smile.

'Charlotte gave me the key,' Bella said.

'What did you do with it?'

'Gived it to my teddy. She keeps it in her pocket. And we were scared so we hided in bed.'

'I'm not surprised you were scared,' I said, my mind conjuring the gathering storm: hungry fire, fighting adults, roiling smoke.

'Then Lovelump came and climbed on the bed. And we fetched Alasdair. He was all chokey. We shut the door because of the smoke. Nobody came to tell us what to do. So I got my teddy and Charlotte got her rabbit and Alasdair opened the window and we jumped down on the garage. And the lawn. Two big jumps. I got scratched. On my arm.'

'And I hurt my knee,' Charlotte said.

Bella rubbed her arm where the scratches had been. Charlotte stood, balancing on one leg. Both looked like a weight was lifting with the telling, but they needed my response. I remembered things I'd done at their age that were just as naïve and stupid, just not so devastating in their effects. And more recently, come to that. If I could do this right, it might take the weight away for the rest of their lives.

'When I was five,' I said, 'I woke up one morning and I wanted to make a waterfall down the stairs. I got a pointy rail from my train set and made a hole in my hot water bottle, which was a grey rabbit.'

The twins were intent. They loved stories.

'But,' I said, 'there wasn't enough water. So I made a hole in my brother's hot water bottle too. His was a red dog. But there still wasn't enough water to make a waterfall. Just a puddle on the stairs. I was disappointed. Then my mum came and shouted and said that I might have caused an accident and she'd never get the mark out of the carpet and how stupid I was. I was only trying to make a beautiful waterfall and didn't mean to do a bad thing. I never forgot that.'

'She should have helped you,' Charlotte said.

'Helped me?'

'Yes,' Bella said. 'Make a waterfall. But in the garden, not on the stairs, silly.'

'Yes,' Charlotte said. 'That's what our Momma would do.'

I walked to the window, looked across the field. 'I know,' I said, turning back, 'that you didn't mean it to happen like it did. The fire and all that. Thank you for telling me. You've been brave. You weren't to know that what you were each doing would add together in the way it did. It was an accident. It wasn't your fault. No-one is to blame. Okay? But some people might not understand that.' Which was something of an understatement. This information could blight their whole lives if it fell into the wrong hands. 'So let's not tell anyone about it. Except perhaps your mum, do you think?'

They both nodded.

'Okay. Your mum. No-one else. And if ever you want to find out about something, like how to make the biggest whoosh with matches, or if ever you aren't happy with how we do things, like what happens if you're naughty – just say and we'll sort it out. Okay? All promise?'

They nodded again.

'Say it.'

'We promise.'

'I promise too. Go on then. Teeth, chins, shoes.'

They ran upstairs.

The back door opened. Kimberly came in.

It still felt strange, hugging her. But I managed it. 'How's your bump?' I said.

She put my hand on it.

'The twins have something to tell you,' I said. 'It might need some thinking about.'

'Good,' she said. 'I've something to tell you that might need thinking about too.'

'Go on.'

'The poor woman who died in the fire, Larisa. One of Alleyn's smuggled people. The police thought she was Kimberly. I wanted to let them carry on thinking that, so that Kimberly would be dead and I could be someone new, but Grant wouldn't have it, nor Jones. They had to inform Larisa's family. But at least I can stop being Kimberly, and go back to Helena. Like I was before I left Tulloch.'

'Tulloch?'

'Near Loch Garten. Strathspey. I never met my dad. A man called Uncle Bill lived with my mum. He wasn't nice. I ran away when I was fourteen. He's dead now. They're all dead. And I'm free to be who I want.'

'So who's that?'

'Helena Jarvis,' she said, 'if you don't mind.'

ENDNOTES

Dear Reader,

I hope you enjoyed reading *The Price of Dormice* as much as I enjoyed writing it. I would love to know what you think of it.

A collection of short fiction is due out in late 2024, containing stories about characters you have met here, amongst others. And work is in progress on more novels featuring Mick and friends.

You can keep up to date with these and more at

stevelunn.net

where you can also find news about bookish events, organise an author talk/reading, in person or online, for your book group, bookshop, library, sitting room or whatever, download the occasional free story, send me a message or ask a question about almost anything…

Please do!

With thanks and best wishes,

Steve

ACKNOWLEDGEMENTS

I would like to thank the many people whose help and support have been essential to the evolution of this story.

My writing teachers – Elizabeth Garner, in Oxford; Cathy Galvin of The Word Factory, and Alison Woodhouse; Elizabeth Reeder, Bea Hitchman and Mahsuda Snaith at Moniack Mhor; Harry Bingham, Morwenna Loughman (now at bks) and everyone at Jericho Writers.

Mentors, editorial advisors and writing friends, especially Patricia Murphy, Linda Proud and Pen Rendall.

My fellow learners and workshop partners, especially Gillian, Heather, Jane, Pete, Ruth and Siobhan.

My first, second and third readers.

Marjory Marshall of the Bookmark, Grantown-on-Spey, her Wee Crime Festival stalwarts, and our buddies in the Highlands.

Harcourt Open Arms, the Rotifers, Ahimsa.

The Durham lot and the Kylebhan crew.

The technical specialists who advised on surveillance, computer security, hacking and financial jiggery-pokery.

The brilliant people at the wildlife trusts, bird and mammal societies, Greenpeace, SAS, STARC and WASP, and others who share a passion for the under-dog, the under-appreciated, and other small creatures.

And most of all, my wife Imogen Rigden, and our family and friends.

Thank you all so much!

NOTE ON DEDICATION

In the opening pages, this book is dedicated to Catherine Robinson and Richard Gordon, who lead the volunteer friends of the Trap Grounds and Burgess Field in Oxford, and whom I'm privileged to count as friends. If there are no dormice on these reserves, it's not for want of trying.

NOTE ON THE TRAP GROUNDS

In 1999, the area known as the Trap Grounds was the last remaining wild open space between the city centre and Oxford's northern suburbs. It lies between the canal and the railway line near the Frenchay Road canal bridge. Oxford resident Catherine Robinson, collector of the graffiti on the opening pages of this book, was instrumental in securing the designation of the Trap Grounds as a Town Green in 2006.

The area consists of three acres of reedbeds and four acres of scrub. It is an invaluable resource for small creatures. It was 'waste land', owned by St John's College, Oxford, and used as a rubbish dump. It is now owned by Oxford City Council and is managed for conservation, recreation and education by the Friends of the Trap Grounds (trap-grounds.org.uk) in partnership with the Council's Parks & Open Spaces team.

The 'Legoland' graffiti appeared when the city wanted to build forty-five houses on the site, in addition to 2,000 other dwellings already built or under construction nearby. The Friends of the Trap Grounds had to take their fight for Town Green status all the way to the House of Lords. These forty-five houses would not have been affordable, coming in at some £1.2 million each in 2024 prices.

The Friends manage the area as a nature reserve, working hard to create a rich mosaic of wildlife habitats. Many creatures owe their existence to their work, including common lizards, slow worms, water voles, pipistrelle and noctule bats, glow-worms, banded demoiselle damselfly, reed bunting, bullfinch, turtle dove, song thrush, spotted flycatcher, and buttoned snout moth.

Community groups hoping to protect wildlife and green spaces in their area by gaining Town Green status should note that the methods used by Mick and friends in this story may be illegal, and that, like many other processes, gaining Town Green status has become much harder since the UK general election of 2010. Expert advice is available from the Open Spaces Society (www.oss.org.uk).

NOTE ON BURGESS FIELD

Burgess Field is a reclaimed landfill site, now home to a nature reserve. It is located alongside the eastern edge of Port Meadow, just north of the new railway bridge at the end of Aristotle Lane, covering an area of approximately thirty hectares (seventy-five acres). It is a mix of rough open grassland, scrub and small copses, with a belt of more mature trees along its northern end. The Friends of Burgess Field work with the City Council to preserve and enhance the reserve as a resource for wildlife, recreation, education and quiet contemplation.